THE MINITONAS DIARIES

———— BOOK THREE ————

SANDRA V. KONECHNY

WINDING TRAILS: THE MINITONAS DIARIES (BOOK THREE)
Copyright © 2024 by Sandra V. Konechny

This is a work of fiction. Names, characters, places and incidents either are the product of the author's imagination or are used fictitiously, and any resemblance to actual persons, living or dead, businesses, companies, events, or locales is entirely coincidental.

ISBN: 978-1-4866-2433-1
eBook ISBN: 978-1-4866-2434-8

Word Alive Press
119 De Baets Street Winnipeg, MB R2J 3R9
www.wordalivepress.ca

WORD ALIVE
—P R E S S—

Cataloguing in Publication information can be obtained from Library and Archives Canada.

Dedicated to my siblings,
who are among my best friends.

Foreword

"ARE WE EVER going to find out what's in the trunk?" ask those readers who seek me out. And here's another frequent question: "What's the big secret on the Fischers' farm?"

I can finally assure you that this volume of The Minitonas Diaries will satisfy those curiosities.

Here's the thing: Minitonas is a small Manitoba community. Even so, the people living there have interesting matters going on in their lives and I pick up on some of it. More is going on than there appears to be at first glance. But it's worth paying attention to these details, getting involved (as only readers can), and coming away with something worthwhile in our hearts and minds.

From here on, the spotlight will shift. Crisis points in the lives of other Minitonans will come into focus. This small town will soon have new developments to work their way through the rumour mills.

Acknowledgements

SPECIAL GRATITUDE IS extended to my beta readers, who consist of a few family members and friends. Your feedback *always* asked for more to the story and that has inspired me to keep writing. Your encouraging words mean a great deal to me.

I must also thank my good husband, Michael, who when asked if I should pursue publishing, without batting an eyelash, said, "Go for it!"

I want to thank my parents, Ed and Ruth Tiede, who instilled in me a love for Jesus and the Bible from the time I was born. (Dad lives with Jesus now, but he still deserves credit where it is due.)

I would like to express my deepest gratitude to the editor and staff at Word Alive Press for their commitment and expertise in refining the manuscript, and for ensuring the messages may clearly reach the heart of the reader.

My deepest gratitude, however, is reserved for Jesus. In my view, we wrote the story together. Every time I got "stuck," I'd pray, *What happens next?* Soon insight would come. If the reader comes away with a blessing, wise thought, or word of help—thank Jesus, the Saviour. Such as it is, I cast this meagre crown at Jesus's feet (Revelation 4:10). To Him be the glory forever and ever.

Prologue

ON HIS SIXTEENTH birthday, Hugh Richard Fischer ran away from home to escape an often drunk and abusive father. He had the good fortune to fall in with a family in Winnipeg who offered him a place to live, helped him complete his formal education, and afterwards encouraged him to enter a trade. However, his unresolved past presented recurring social issues that eventually led him to return home with a plan to start over on the now vacant farm of his youth.

Ella Rose Bauman left her country home on the earliest day possible to take up nurses training in Winnipeg, but also to live a life with her friends, free from the moral restraints applied by her conservative Christian parents. While she enjoyed the pleasures of loose living, eventually she got pregnant, which resulted in an abortion that sent her into the depths of depression. Her anguish was compounded by the sudden loss of her mother due to stroke. Unable to function normally, Ellie also returned to the home of her youth—to rediscover the values in which she was raised, and to heal.

Historically, the Baumans and Fischers were near neighbours, their farms being across from one another. In the same week, Hugh and Ellie became reacquainted and cautiously began a friendship as they both sought to begin new chapters of their lives with a clean slate.

Eventually their friendship became close and they divulged their deepest pain and secrets, helping each other to face their demons and survive. This led them to discover their mutual love and desire to face the future together as a married couple.

Over the next three months, they got their new home ready, re-entered the workforce, established family ties, and put on the wedding of Ellie's dreams. The day following their wedding, the story resumes…

One

January 2, 1981

THEIR FIRST MORNING together as a married couple was a leisure-ly affair. Hugh and Ellie, clad in the new velour housecoats they'd received at Christmas, ate their decadent and delicious breakfast slowly, reviewing the highlights of their wedding the previous day.

"I can laugh about it now, but yesterday I felt sick when you didn't show after your music started up," said Hugh drily. "Mind you, when you finally did make your appearance, it's an understatement to say you were a sight for sore eyes."

Ellie smiled over her mug of coffee. "Thank you. I did hope you would be wowed by all my bridal preparations." She tucked a blond tress behind her ear. "I'm sure it's every girl's dream to be her most beautiful on her wedding day, for the sake of the man she fell in love with and with whom she's entrusting her life. That's what it was for me."

She reached over to place her hand in Hugh's. He gave it a mean-ingful squeeze and looked directly into Ellie's blue eyes.

"I know we're supposed to meet at the hall this morning, to help with taking down the decorations and clean up, but is there any hurry, do you think?" asked Hugh searchingly.

"I really doubt it. I'm sure the others will want to sleep in—that is, if the kiddos let them. I think we have lots of time…"

About an hour later, they dressed and prepared to leave their tiny nest. Just as they were heading out the door, the phone rang. Hugh picked up the receiver.

"I thought you might like to know that the bottom has fallen out entirely around here," said Margo with a slight slur.

"What do you mean? What are you saying?" asked Hugh, both puzzled and vexed.

That his sister's high drama was beginning to annoy him was an understatement. He was trying to enjoy a few honeymoon days with his new wife, for crying out loud. Yet Margo seemed determined to dominate his time by making it all about her.

"I mean... I lost my job this morning," said Margo before breaking into a weird cackle.

Hugh refocused on her call. "Are you serious?"

Ellie watched his face change from annoyed to surprised and then concerned.

"Oh yeah," continued Margo in a strange tone of voice. "The boss and his wife met me at the door of the shop and fifteen minutes later escorted me out of the store." She offered up another of those weird giggles.

"I... I don't know what to say," he stammered.

"There's nothing to say," she returned in the same fuzzy voice. "If I play my cards right, I may get lucky and it'll all be over by tonight."

There was a quick click and then all Hugh heard was the dial tone.

"Margo again?" asked Ellie, hoping it wasn't.

Hugh nodded, frowning. "She told me that she got fired this morning and her bosses escorted her out of the store."

"Oh dear. On top of last night's bombshell, with Larry leaving her for another woman, she must be reeling," said Ellie, suddenly uneasy.

"Yeah... but what's worrying me more is what she said next." Hugh stared off into the distance somewhere beyond his new wife.

"What did she say?" Ellie waved a hand in front of Hugh's face.

Hugh blinked. "She said if she was lucky it would all be over by tonight. Then she hung up."

Ellie and Hugh looked at each other. The same possibilities crossed both their minds.

"I don't want to," began Hugh, somehow slumping within his tall frame. "But I think we should make a run for Dauphin and check on her. I have a bad feeling about this."

"Me too. Though we should go to the hall first and explain our worries to Rob and Sarah. At the very least, we'll have to pick up the wedding gifts and bring them back here before we hit the road."

Hugh opened the door. "Right. Let's not waste time then."

To their surprise, all three of Ellie's brothers and their families were at the hall. Most of the decorations were already dismantled, somewhat organized to be packed away and stowed for another occasion. Gus's family was getting ready to head back to their home in Edmonton.

"You're late! What's your excuse?" teased Sarah in mock sternness.

Ellie answered her sister-in-law with a bold truth she hoped would deflect this attempt to produce a blush. "I was getting to know my husband in a brand-new way."

"Touché!" Sara laughed and raised her hand for a high-five.

Together Hugh and Ellie explained the upsetting new developments with Margo over the past twelve hours. Immediately the brothers and their wives expressed sympathy and understanding. Everyone agreed they were wise to attend to the situation and helped load Hugh's half-ton with the large pile of wedding gifts still displayed on a side table.

As much as Ellie appreciated the gifts, she realized most would have to be stored until they built their permanent home. The present cottage, although new, was much too small to accommodate everything.

After the hugs, goodbyes, well wishes, and expressions of gratitude, Sarah quickly made up a turkey shepherd's pie in a tinfoil pan and added some other leftovers from the banquet to send along with the couple. Given that the day ahead portended little time for cooking, the newlyweds were grateful for Sarah's thoughtfulness.

Back at their place, Ellie ruled that the gifts should be immediately stored in the shed next to the house, the same one that had earlier served as Hugh's summer cabin, affectionately nicknamed the Ritz. She resolved to go through everything on a mild winter day soon. At present, she had enough utensils and linens to get by, to Hugh's immense relief.

The longer Hugh thought about Margo, the more his gut told him that his sister was in a bad way and they should get to her as soon as possible.

They were back on the road in less than a half-hour. The driving conditions were reasonably good, at least until they passed through Cowan. Thereafter the sunny skies became overcast and snow fell thickly.

"Slow down," urged Ellie. "Getting there five minutes later isn't going to make a difference."

"Are you sure of that?" snapped Hugh.

"Perhaps not absolutely. But if we end up in the ditch or in an accident because of your driving, I'm certain it will profoundly and adversely affect whatever help we can provide to Margo. Please slow down. At least to the posted speed limits."

"Ellie," he barked. "I know how to drive."

"Listen here, husband. You may not talk to me that way under any circumstances... Freddie!"

Hugh screeched to a halt and pulled over onto the shoulder. When the truck had stopped, he turned to Ellie in the centre of the bench beside him.

"You of all people should know *never* to call me by that name," he said in a calculated tone.

"I do. And I never will... unless you start treating me like your dad treated your mother. You need to know right from the get-go, I will not stand for it. Being married does not mean the courtship is suddenly over and you can get away with being disrespectful or mean regardless of the pressures you're under."

There was no mistaking she meant every word.

Hugh opened his mouth to speak and then clamped it shut. He slumped over the steering wheel.

"I'm sorry, babe," he said. "I mean it. You're right. I lapsed into a Pa-like moment and I'm so ashamed."

"I forgive you." Ellie put her arm around his broad shoulders. "I have an idea, something we should have done right after you took Margo's call this morning. Let's pray."

"Right. We should have done that first thing."

With the truck idling, they clasped hands and together lifted Margo to the Lord in prayer, asking for Him to preserve her during this devastating time, for wisdom to know how to help her, and for safe travels getting to Dauphin.

After that, Hugh pulled back onto the highway and drove along at the posted limits at peace with Ellie and his own heart.

The snowy conditions worsened as the wind picked up. Drifts formed on the highway, causing a thumping sound as Hugh drove through them. To distract themselves from their rising anxiety and useless speculations over Margo's troubles, they turned up the volume on the country radio station and crooned along.

By the time they reach the intersection of Highways 10 and 5, the snowstorm had abated significantly, much to Ellie's relief.

Hugh chuckled. "When did you get to be such a worrywart? Braving the elements begs an adventure and I figured you were an adventurous spirit."

"I like to think I have an adventurous spirit, too. But I'm not foolhardy. Adventure is fine, provided the adventure zone is safe. If adventure means flirting with death... well, that's just plain stupidity."

Wisely, Hugh didn't respond.

A few minutes later, they were driving through Dauphin.

~

"Why won't she answer the door?" Ellie shivered as she stood in front of the entrance to Margo's house. "Obviously she's home. Her car is here."

"Let's try the side entrance of the garage."

Luckily it was unlocked, as was the interior door that led to the kitchen. They quietly let themselves in and soon after saw Margo sitting at her grand dining table. Her blond-highlighted head was lowered on her outstretched arm. She appeared to be sleeping, but on the table was a bottle of whiskey three-quarters empty. A small bottle of aspirin lay on its side, also empty.

"Oh my gosh!" shrieked Ellie. She began to shake Margo.

Hugh immediately caught onto the gravity of the situation. "Should we call an ambulance? Get her stomach pumped?"

"Help me get her to the bathroom," said Ellie, taking control of the situation. "I want to try and induce vomiting."

With one on each side of her, they raised Margo to her feet. Moans escaped her lips. Her eyes fluttered open and then closed again.

"Wake up, Margo!" shouted Hugh as they half-carried and half-dragged her into the ensuite that adjoined the master bedroom.

Ellie set her up on her knees so her head was poised over the toilet bowl. Pulling back Margo's head, her mouth fell open and Ellie quickly thrust her finger down the woman's throat. Straightaway, she gagged and began to heave the contents of her stomach. The stench of vomit together with alcohol was overpowering and Hugh couldn't take it. He left the room while Ellie remained to ensure Margo threw up safely.

Afterward she flushed the toilet repeatedly to diminish the foul odour. When Margo was through retching, Ellie calmly moistened a facecloth with warm water and gently wiped her sister-in-law's face.

"Can you stand, do you think?" asked Ellie.

Margo trembled and looked about uncomprehendingly.

Together, Ellie and Hugh escorted the zombie-like Margo into the sitting area next to the kitchen and sat her on the black leather couch. Immediately she tried to lay down, but Ellie refused to let her.

"No. Sit up and stay awake."

"What should I do?" asked Hugh, flummoxed and fearful. "Make some coffee or something?"

"Sure. That will help make her alert."

Hugh headed for the kitchen while Ellie was kept occupied preventing Margo from lying supine on the sofa. A few minutes later, he returned with a mug of steaming coffee.

"Here you go," urged Ellie. "You'll feel lots better when you get this inside you."

But Margo pushed it away. "Don't want it," she mumbled, lolling her head onto the back of the sofa.

"Listen to me. You need to do this." Ellie brought the mug to her lips.

Margo turned her head away. "Leave me alone. Just let me die…"

"Margo. Smarten up and open your mouth!"

Something in Ellie's tone caused both Margo and nearby Hugh to snap to attention. Despite her inebriation, Margo took the mug of coffee and sipped some.

"Good girl," encouraged Ellie in a gentler tone.

"Now what?" asked Hugh when Margo had finished the coffee.

"If it's not storming outside, let's take her for a walk around the block. The exercise and fresh air should help wear off some of the effects of the alcohol. Hopefully then she'll be able to think and speak coherently."

Still in bad shape, it took both Hugh and Ellie to dress Margo in winter wear. It was as if she were a child. Flanking her on each side, they walked up and down the street until Margo could walk on her own. Only when the three of them began to shiver from the cold did Ellie consent to going back inside.

"I've got a splitting headache," complained Margo after they'd removed their winter gear.

"I'm sure you do," said Ellie evenly. "But I won't give you anything for it now. You're still way too drugged."

"We can talk to distract you from the pain," said Hugh. "Tell us what happened this morning. Why did your boss fire you?"

Margo sniffed and rubbed her temples. "I've been accused of theft."

Somewhat shocked, Ellie blurted, "Theft? Are you falsely accused?"

Margo rubbed her temples some more. "I don't want to talk about it."

The newlyweds exchanged glances.

Ellie tried another topic. "Was the whiskey bottle full when you started drinking today?"

"I don't remember," mumbled Margo wearily. "I don't think so."

"What about the aspirin? Did you swallow a full bottle of tablets?"

"I swallowed whatever was left. I didn't count but there weren't very many." With that, Margo began to cry. "Why did you stop me? I'm losing the house. I lost my job. Plus I'm on my own now. It's over for me."

Hugh crossed the room, sat next to his sister, and put his arm around her. "No way is life over for you, Margie. You can always get another job. Once the dust has settled between you and Larry, you can get yourself another place. You can start over. That's what I did six months ago, and now I'm doing well. So can you."

"You haven't called me Margie since I was little," said Margo with a smirk. "Anyway, I don't care what you say; the future doesn't look bright. And I don't want to talk anymore. I want to lie down and don't try to stop me."

She threw Ellie a dark look, then pulled herself up to standing position. Reasonably steady, she walked to her bedroom and shut the door behind her.

As soon as they were alone, Ellie scooted across the room to sit with Hugh on the sofa.

"What are we going to do about Margo?" she said in a voice just above a whisper. "We can't leave her like this."

Hugh reached for the remote, turned on the TV, and increased the volume. Ellie furrowed her brow and looked at him askance.

"If we're going to talk about Margo, I'd rather she didn't hear," he explained. "You're right. She can't be left alone. Clearly she's a danger to herself. But even if we spent the night, it would be too soon to leave her tomorrow too."

"I agree. She's already slid into a deep depression." She paused, sighed, and then said the obvious. "We'll have to bring her back to Minitonas with us. I don't see any other way."

"And then what? We don't have room to put her up. Do you think Rob would let us keep her at the farmhouse?"

"Maybe... but I don't like the idea of her being on her own. As of Monday, you and I will be back at work. What about your Aunt Gertie? I bet she would be willing to care for Margo. She'd do it for the memory of your mother, if nothing else."

"That's actually a good idea and I think you're right. She *would* do it for my ma's sake... and out of the goodness of her heart."

"In which case, we should pack up her personal belongings ourselves. Let's look around for luggage."

"If we take her away from here, you realize she won't be coming back," Hugh pointed out.

Ellie processed his words for a few seconds. "She won't be back to work or live here, but I have no idea what she would want as keepsakes. For now, I think we bring only her clothing and toiletries. We'll make another trip, if necessary, after she and Larry work out their settlement."

After looking around, the only item Hugh found that looked like luggage was a large zippered bag with handles. Ellie said it would do. She quietly stole into Margo's room and began going through the dresser drawers, selecting a temporary wardrobe that ought to suffice for a few weeks until a more permanent residence could be established for her.

Margo's soft snores assured Ellie that she slept soundly; her breathing was regular. Ellie noted that she lay atop the bed and had covered herself with the small quilt she had been given by Aunt Gertie for Christmas, made from clothing associated with her deceased parents. Somehow it surprised her, since Margo had objected to the source of fabrics. Perhaps she had reconsidered the value of the memento. Or perhaps it had merely been the handiest coverlet available.

Meanwhile, Hugh drove downtown to see about finding some empty boxes. The grocery store had small ones that he doubted would be of much use, but he took a few on the principle that something was better than nothing.

As he cruised along the main shopping district, he noticed the clothing store where he was pretty sure Margo had been employed. A flash of inspiration caused him to pull over.

"Is your boss or manager in?" asked Hugh politely of the salesgirl behind the checkout counter.

The girl offered a professional smile. "Yes. Can I say who's asking for him?"

"Tell him it's Hugh Fischer, and that it's important."

The girl disappeared somewhere in the back of the store but momentarily returned with a gentleman in tow. Hugh judged him to be in his sixties based on his head of silver hair. He wore a suit and tie. Upon drawing near, he held out his hand which Hugh grasped for a polite handshake.

"Pleased to meet you, Mr. Fischer," said the man. "I'm Claude Livingston. How can I help you?"

"I have a question to ask, but I think it would be better to ask it in private." He glanced at the salesgirl.

"All right, we can discuss it in my office," said Mr. Livingston, turning on his heel.

Hugh followed him to the rear of the store. Mr. Livingston indicated a seat for Hugh to occupy while he closed the door and sat in his chair behind the bureau. He looked at Hugh expectantly.

"I drove from Minitonas to check on my sister," Hugh said. "She called me last night to say her husband had left her, and then again this morning to tell me she'd been fired. When my wife and I got to her, she was almost dead from a suicide attempt. She's okay for now, I think. My question is, what happened here? Why did you find it necessary to fire Margo?"

As Hugh spoke, he watched Livingston's facial expressions change from friendly to bland to angry—and finally to resolute.

"I'm sorry you found your sister in such a state, but I take no responsibility for it other than that I might have exercised my other right to have her arrested," the man said testily.

"I didn't come to defend her. I came only to learn the truth because she won't talk about it with us."

"I'm not surprised. My salesgirls have witnessed her being dishonest with the staff room coffee money, and removing notes from the till. Not a lot at any one time, but no amount of theft can be tolerated, as I'm sure you can understand. She's also suspected of pinching items, though I don't have solid proof about that. It's just that the inventory doesn't jive with sales. The discrepancy is very concerning."

Mr. Livingston sat back in his chair and crossed his arms. The dark look on his face held a warning, as though daring Hugh to challenge him.

"Understood." Hugh exhaled deeply. "I'm getting the picture. We intend to bring Margo to Minitonas with us. That leads me to my last question. Do you have empty boxes we could use to pack her clothing and personal effects?"

With a sigh of relief, Claude Livingston led Hugh to the rearmost part of the shop where they received their shipments. He gave him all the empty boxes they had.

Continuing further up the street, Hugh noted an insurance sign on an office building that he believed was the company where his brother-in-law worked. Another fit of curiosity led him to park in front of the building and go in.

He asked the receptionist to see Larry Owens. After the woman alerted him, she led Hugh down a short hallway to said agent's door.

The practiced smile quickly left Larry's face upon recognizing Hugh.

"I was expecting to hear from you sometime, but I didn't think it would be this soon," said Larry grimly.

Hugh pulled up a chair to sit across from Larry. "I ought to be honeymooning. Instead I find myself in Dauphin trying to keep my sister from falling apart."

"It's been over between Margo and me for a long time. If you couldn't see it coming, you're blind in one eye and can't see out of the other," stated Larry straightforward. "The girl I'm with now actually loves me and wants me around. In fact, she's carrying my baby. I'm going to be a daddy. At last."

Larry leaned back in his chair and cradled his head in entwined hands. His mouth resumed a faint smile.

Hugh coughed and leaned forward, making eye contact. "Back to Margo. She was fired from work this morning and has since tried to take her life. Ellie and I got here just in time to rescue her."

The colour drained from Larry's face. "Whatever our differences are, I'm not responsible for that."

"Maybe not, but I thought you should know," said Hugh tightly.

"On the other hand, your news suggests I won't get a lot of hassle from Margo to sell the house. I'm already working on it, and I think I have a good possibility in the works. It depends on the cooperation of at least three parties. Anyway, thanks for stopping by."

"Wow. What a piece of work you are! I tell you that your partner just tried to off herself and all you can think of is how it benefits you." Angry, Hugh stared intently at Larry, who stared right back. Who would blink first?

After a minute, Hugh broke the tension.

"Here's what. We're taking Margo back to Minitonas with us to help her get back on her feet somehow. In the meantime, whenever you have need to communicate with her over the sale of the house or terms of divorce, you'll have to go through me." Hugh rose. "Now that I know you're just as selfish as she is, you won't find me an easy mediator."

He reached for the door handle to let himself out.

"I have no intention of being greedy or unreasonable," said Larry, rising also. "I just want out."

~

"What took you so long?" Ellie felt relieved to finally be seeing her groom again. "I couldn't figure out how you could get lost in Dauphin. It's not a big city."

Hugh told her about his stops to talk first with Margo's former boss and then with Larry. After summarizing those meetings, Ellie applauded his good thinking.

Over the next while, the two filled boxes with Margo's clothing, footwear, and sundry accessories. Many of the garments still had tags on them and certain tops were repeated in different colours. This led Hugh to remark on the missing inventory at the shop, and for Ellie to observe that there were enough articles of clothing on hand to open a whole new shop in size medium.

Eventually the closet and drawers were empty and the half-ton loaded.

The last thing to do was wake Margo. Much to their relief, she didn't put up much of a fight when they told her she was coming home with them. Still groggy, she consented to putting on her winter coat and boots and trudged out the door behind Hugh. Ellie locked the door behind her, then urged Margo to take the centre seat.

"No," said Hugh irritably. "I want you to sit next to me, not my sister!"

"Given that Margo might use that arrangement to suddenly leap from the truck as we're cruising down the highway, I think we should forgo our preferences."

Hugh reluctantly complied. "I hope this isn't symbolic of the future, that Margo is always going to be coming between us..."

Two

AT BREAKFAST THE following morning, Ellie reminded Hugh that they were expecting his cousin David to have lunch with them. Still in her pjs, Margo was pushing bites of pancake around on her plate, but she looked up sharply upon hearing the news about David.

"I don't want to be here when he comes," she insisted. "I don't want to see him."

Hugh and Ellie looked at her in surprise.

"What's the problem?" asked Hugh, not so gently.

"I don't want to see anyone… or pretend to be cheerful… or listen to a bunch of chatter. I just want to be alone… be a hermit somewhere. Can you make that happen for me?" She sounded plaintive.

Ellie exchanged knowing glances with Hugh. "Margo, I'm pretty sure I know how you feel in light of your unexpected, back-to-back losses. It will take time to adjust to your new reality. But to check out completely by yourself doesn't sound healthy to us right now. After the weekend, I think you should see a doctor. It may be appropriate to give you some medication for a season until you get your bearings again."

A hot tear slipped down Margo's cheek. "Well, I'm pretty sure neither of you knows anything at all about how I feel," she said bitterly.

She set down her fork with a clatter, got up abruptly, and went into the washroom, shutting the door with a bang.

"I knew this wasn't going to be easy," said Hugh under his breath.

In low voices, he and Ellie discussed a few options on how to accommodate Margo's request and finally settled on depositing her at the café in Minitonas. They would arrange for her to be given a light lunch. She could people-watch or read a book until they picked her up again. That way, she would be alone… yet not alone. Hopefully that would keep her from another attempt at harming herself.

Late in the morning, Hugh transported a sullen Margo into Minitonas. He escorted her to the corner booth near the front window of the café, where she would be able to watch the traffic and people come and go while she sipped on a beverage. He promised to come for her as soon as their cousin had left.

Margo heard everything Hugh said but remained silent and glum. She noticed that he spoke with the waitress before he left and supposed she had been asked to babysit. The thought made her angry. It had never occurred to her that life could change forever on the turn of a dime. She found it astonishing that in the space of a few hours she had gone from being an independent woman to a moneyless victim, subject to the plans and decisions of her brother and his wife. She acknowledged they had shown her kindness, yet they also stood in the way of everything she wanted. Regardless of what had led to the breakdown of her marriage, and losing her job, she believed her life was her own to direct. The failure, embarrassment, and shame of recent developments were too difficult to live with. She couldn't bear the thought that people would stare and whisper behind her back. Better to dissolve into oblivion.

But no. Ellie had to go all heroic and bring her back from the brink.

Margo decided that she hated Ellie. On the one hand, she was nice; on the other, she was a bossy know-it-all. Worse, her brother went along with everything she said. Right now they weren't giving her the one thing she wanted: complete solitude. What she wouldn't give to crawl into a hole somewhere and close it off so she couldn't be found or bossed around, couldn't be…

The waitress stopped by and asked if she would like more coffee. Without speaking, Margo held out her mug and watched the brown liquid pour and swirl to the top. Despite feeling deeply low, she enjoyed the steaming aroma. Instead of returning to her anti-Ellie thoughts, she stared out of the window without thinking about anything and watched the traffic come and go.

⁓

After Hugh had left for Minitonas, Ellie bustled around the cottage tidying things up so everything appeared impeccably clean and orderly—magazine picture perfect. David Johnson, the only son of Aunt Gertie and Uncle Ed, had made the surprise trip to be at their wedding. Before he returned to his life in Toronto, he had asked to have a visit with them for the sake of making further acquaintance. Having heartily agreed, she was now making final preparations to receive their first real guest—two days after the wedding. Given the unexpected problems they'd dealt with since then, it felt more like two weeks ago.

A crustless quiche baked in the oven, filling the air with tantalizing, mouth-watering aromas. A tossed salad and platter of raw veggies waited in the refrigerator.

Ellie was in the process of setting the table for three when David pulled up to the house in his rented car. She watched him exit wearing the same camel-coloured trench coat and dark grey fedora in which he'd shown up at the wedding. He took a moment to scan the prairie vista, white as a sheet of paper, interspersed with clumps of bush, before walking up to the house.

Ellie opened the door before he had a chance to knock. They greeted each other with delighted smiles.

"Welcome here. You hold the honour of being our first official guest," said Ellie, taking his coat and hanging it on their new coat tree. David removed his hat and hung it on top of his coat.

Ellie noted that he was a smart dresser. Today he was clad in dark espresso slacks and a beige V-necked knit sweater over a peach-coloured shirt. His brown hair was professionally styled in a short preppy fashion that suited him to a T. Facially, he resembled his mother.

"Then the honour is all mine," responded David cheerily. "It smells awfully good in here. You must be one of those increasingly rare girls who's learned to cook from scratch."

"Guilty as charged!"

"Nice little place you got here." He looked around the room, taking in the border of quotes painted around the top of the walls. He turned on his heel, reading the words. "Those appear to be quotes from the Bible. Am I right?"

"Yes, you are. At least most of them," said Ellie, impressed. "You're familiar with the Bible?"

"A good education includes being conversant with the classics. The Bible stands among the greatest of masterworks."

She offered a friendly smile. "Hmmm. You're right as far as that goes, but the Bible is more than classic literature to me."

"I take it you're religious then."

"By the common definition, that's how you would peg me. For my part, God isn't a matter of religion. He's simply a fact of our reality in the same way flowers, people, and wind are facts of our reality."

"I see." David quickly changed the subject. "Where's Hugh?"

"He should be here any minute. He ran into town to do an errand."

She had barely concluded her sentence when Hugh turned into their driveway and parked alongside David's car. He bounded up the steps and entered the house, all smiles.

After more greetings, they offered David a seat in the armchair while the newlyweds sat close together on their new custom uphol-stered tartan sofa.

Ellie opened the conversation. "Have you enjoyed being with your parents over the last couple of days?"

"In a way. I've learned that both can be hilarious without even real-izing it. It usually shows up when they try to tell the same story. For instance, they were trying to jog my memory regarding the first time I faced an audience and recited a poem in the Speech Arts and Music Festival. Mother said I wore a smart navy sailor suit, but Dad said no, it was a suit, white shirt, and tie affair. Mother was so sure she wanted to go and fetch it because she saved it along with other baby clothes I once wore. Dad said she'll find the little suit in the same box and thus it won't prove her point at all."

Ellie chuckled. "I can totally picture your mother doing this."

"Then Mother asked if I still remembered the poem I recited," continued David. "I said I didn't even remember participating in the festival. She said it was 'Someone' by Walter de la Mare. But Dad said no, it was 'The Pirate Don Durk of Dowdee' by Mildred Plew Meigs. Mother adamantly disagreed; it was the whole first-grade class that recited *that* poem as a speech choir. They went at it for several minutes. Myself, I have no recollection of any of it. But it was entertaining to listen to their conflicting memories."

"I believe it. No doubt you were adorable in both your little sailor and Sunday suits," said Ellie with a smile.

David rolled his eyes upward. "If you show the merest bit of interest, I'm sure my mother will tie up hours of your time browsing through photo albums and regaling the boring stories of my infancy and youth."

"I know you practice law," interjected Hugh. "But do you have a specialty?"

David looked pleased to be asked about his work. "I mostly handle common-fare cases like divorces, real estate sales, last will and testaments, that sort of thing. My mother tells me you're a mechanic and that your lovely wife is a registered nurse."

"She told you right," replied Hugh, nodding.

"So what do you folks like to do when you're not mechanic-ing or nursing?" David settled back into the armchair and crossed his legs.

Hugh turned to Ellie and indicated she should answer first.

"I like just about anything that calls for creativity or making things attractive," said Ellie. "That includes refinishing furniture, interior decorating, sewing and crafts. I also like to cook. Pretty soon I'll be starting another project; designing a permanent home for us to build in anticipation of raising a family."

"Good for you." David seemed impressed as he turned his attention to his cousin.

"The last six months have been all about tearing down the worn-out buildings on this farm and preparing to put up new ones," began Hugh. "I have in mind to put up a double workshop plus an autobody bay, a Quonset to shelter my vehicles and equipment, and of course the main house Ellie mentioned. We'll begin those projects this spring. When that work's finished, I hope to launch a hobby of restoring some antique vehicles we found in our back bush."

"Seriously?" asked David, brightening. "I have an interest in antique vehicles myself. Every summer I like to walk through the antique car shows that come around. Some of the work and expense people put into these collector items is nothing short of incredible. Are your pieces handy? I'd like to see them."

"Yeah. They're at the other end of the yard. I tarped the Studebaker and the old Plymouth half-ton, as I didn't want the winter weather to take a further toll on their condition. But we can look. Let's go."

As Hugh got up, his face shone with excitement. David rose as well. They quickly put on their winterwear.

Ellie stepped out of their way but couldn't resist commenting. "I swear the only difference between men and boys is the size of their toys."

"That may very well be an astute observation," replied David with a wry smile as he pulled on his gloves.

"Lunch will be served in twenty minutes," reminded Ellie, "so please don't be longer than that."

Neither of the men passed comment as they hurriedly left the cottage. She wasn't sure they even heard her.

In their absence, Ellie quickly fixed a dressing for her salad and removed the quiche from the oven so it would settle before cutting it into wedges. Her dessert, a thrown-together apple crisp, had baked before the quiche and was still warm. She filled their glasses with ice and water and added the platter of raw veggies to the table.

Twenty minutes passed, yet through the window she saw the men still lingering next to the Plymouth. The hood was up and their heads were down as they looked over the vehicle's innards.

Another five minutes later, Ellie made a decision. Grabbing a Dutch oven from the cupboard and a large metal spoon, she stood on the porch and began to clang them together. Both heads turned in her direction. Apparently they got the message because the hood came down and they re-covered the body of the old-timer with the tarp.

"Sorry, honey," said Hugh as he removed his parka when they'd come inside. "I didn't think twenty minutes passed so fast."

"You were out there for longer than half an hour."

"My apologies," said David. "My enthusiasm got a little out of hand. And you know what they say: time flies when you're having fun."

They dug into lunch with gusto.

"Whatever you call this pie, it's every bit as good as anything I've eaten in a restaurant," David remarked.

"Thank you, David. We're planning a honeymoon in your area come May. What other sites apart from Niagara Falls would you recommend we take in?" asked Ellie between bites.

"The Casa Loma castle and CN Tower are popular tourist spots…"

But then David returned to the subject of vintage vehicles. Ellie tried to keep up with the talk of horsepower and V6 versus V8 motors, and after that about sparkplugs and radiators, fan belts and heaven knew what all… it got to be like another language—and all Greek to her.

When she could get a word in edgewise, she asked, "So tell us about your girlfriend, David."

He looked at her blankly, as if he had to recall what a girlfriend was. "I'm dating one of the secretaries in the office." For clarification he added, "But not my own."

"Will wedding bells soon be ringing?"

"Ahhh, no. I don't think so."

That was that. He returned to discussing cars and trucks with Hugh, this time about the various brands on the market, discussing preferences and pros and cons.

"I drive a Cutlass Supreme convertible," admitted David proudly.

Hugh whistled in admiration. "That's a cool car, no doubt about it."

When David noticed boredom reflecting off Ellie's face, he made more of an effort to include her by asking for her opinion on the merit of collecting vintage vehicles.

Ellie smiled appreciatively. "I get it. I really do. Even though it's generally an expensive hobby to restore the old-timers, they reflect the charm and personality of their era. I like antiques in a house, so it's fair to enjoy antiques in other categories too."

Hugh beamed and gave Ellie's hand a squeeze.

The time was going on 2:00 p.m.

"It's time I hit the road, Jack," said David, getting up. "I'm meeting an old colleague from my university days in Winnipeg this evening."

Ellie was surprised. "You're not going back to Swan River?"

"Mother and Dad have released me to fit in as much as I can before I fly back to Toronto Sunday afternoon," said David quickly before Ellie could make a complaint against him.

He didn't realize that his departure from his parents' place was, in fact, sweet news to the ears of his cousins.

They said hearty goodbyes, promising to keep in touch, and then David drove off. As soon as he was gone, Hugh called Aunt Gertie to discuss the matter of Margo while Ellie tidied up the kitchen.

"Of course I'll take the girl in," responded Gertie with sincerity. "It's the least I can do for one of Alice's children."

Greatly relieved, Ellie retrieved Margo's luggage and joined Hugh as he got back in the truck to head back to Minitonas to pick up Margo.

~

The waitress came over to Margo's booth bearing a tray of food. She set down a bowl of steaming chicken vegetable soup with a side plate of bun and butter and glass of water.

"I didn't order anything," objected Margo.

"It was preordered, and prepaid, by the fellow who brought you here," said the waitress.

"I'm not hungry." Her annoyance was starting to show.

"Even if you're not starving, you'll enjoy the soup and bun. Our cook, Mrs. Illichman, bakes fresh buns and makes homemade soup every morning, Monday to Friday. She should be world famous. That's how good her soups are."

Margo didn't argue. But she did sigh in such a way as to convey that she was doing the waitress a favour by not sending the food back to the kitchen. She watched the girl return to the rear of the café and disappear behind the double swinging doors before surreptitiously bringing a spoonful of soup to her lips. As much as she hoped to, she couldn't deny the broth was delicious. In fact, it was quite possibly the best chicken soup she had ever tasted. Certainly a far cry from the canned variety.

No longer caring whether she was observed, she buttered the soft, still-warm bun and slowly consumed her meal.

The lunch crowd began to stream in while she ate. A couple of old granny types took a booth adjacent to hers. She overheard them order the daily soup special. A troop of four men Margo supposed to be local farmers took a booth closer to the rear. A tall man sporting a cowboy hat over long black hair tied back in a ponytail at the base of his neck took a seat on a stool at the counter. Moments later, a couple of scruffy-looking dudes in faded parkas and toques entered and sat next to him. Then a reddish-blond-haired guy came in wearing nothing atop his head but a scarf wrapped tightly around his neck inside his winter jacket. Looking around, he caught Margo's eye, nodded politely, and picked up a copy of the newspaper lying on the counter.

She followed his movements to the rearmost booth of the café, then heard the waitress greet him by the name of Rory. She also heard him order a deluxe burger platter before losing interest in him altogether, other than to note that while he was obviously a man, he had the face of a cute boy. This struck her as an oxymoron: was he a boy in a man's body, or a man passing himself off as a boy?

Others walked in, but Margo had lost interest in people-watching. She glanced at her wristwatch and wondered how much longer she'd have to wait for her brother to come get her. The noisy chatter enveloping the café was getting on her nerves. She longed for a place to lie down and submit to the oblivion of sleep.

Keeping her eyes trained on the moving traffic outside, she allowed herself to think about her extreme fatigue and what had produced it. Larry. Their marriage of eight years had been fun at first, but eventually the novelty had worn off. Neither one had possessed the money to go to university, nor had the ambition to put time into more schooling. Larry had gone into the field of insurance and done fairly well.

Meanwhile, Margo had been attracted to the world of fashion and beauty. They'd begun to grow apart when Margo decided she wanted a career instead of building a family. They coped with their differences tolerably, at least until she'd received her inheritance windfall. Then Margo had suddenly gotten interested in property investment, having heard plenty of stories of people making big money in the real estate market. She had a powerful ambition to become a wealthy woman — to rise so high above her poor, humble beginnings that she would never need to recall the shame and embarrassment associated with those years.

She now allowed that she had bitten off more than she could chew. She should have taken time to study the art of investing instead of rushing headlong into something in which she lacked experience. Larry had tried to warn her, but she hadn't listened. Now he would be selling the big fancy house of her dreams. When that happened, she would insist on getting her inheritance back. Then she would seek the advice of financial experts to develop a better plan.

That Larry wanted out of the picture and take up with another woman meant nothing to her. They were done. She couldn't remember what she had seen in him in the first place. She was tired of fighting with him, tired of fighting, tired of him... so tired.

The waitress stopped by to pick up the empty dishes. Margo avoided meeting her eyes, having eaten the whole meal despite insisting she wasn't hungry.

Without more talking, the girl topped up her cup with hot coffee and went away.

Margo resumed staring out the window. A woman walked by wearing a smart new winter coat which Margo recognized as a style she had sold. It triggered thoughts about the years she had spent working at the fashion store. She recalled the joy she'd felt at first working someplace where she could watch the latest styles come in and buy them at a staff discount. Looking dowdy was absolutely a thing of the past after that. The boss looked after the accounting side of things while his wife managed the store and staff. Mrs. Livingston had taken Margo under her wing to tutor her in the arts of fashion as well as sales.

Then, the previous spring, Mrs. Livingston had wanted to retire, to spend a few years pursuing other interests while she still had the energy. The couple chose Margo to take over her duties.

Margo clearly remembered how honoured she had felt. She'd poured herself into the role, wanting to make the Livingstons proud.

Only after she and Larry bought the new house and she switched her passion to developing her dream home did things begin to go south. It wasn't long before they were house poor. It also put a kybosh on their habit of frequently eating out.

Thus Margo began to look for ways to pinch a little cash to keep up appearances. She'd thought no one noticed her indiscretions, but she was wrong.

Had it really been only yesterday morning when she'd arrived at the shop to find Claude and Stella waiting for her? She'd greeted them with exuberant wishes for a happy new year. But their smiles had been weak as they asked her to come into their office to discuss something.

There, Claude had presented written testimony by other staff regarding occasions when she'd been observed making dishonest transactions and pocketing the difference. She had also been spotted removing coins and dollar bills from the coffee fund can, and palming paper money from out of the till when she thought no one was looking.

Then there was the matter of inventory. Under Margo's watch, numerous items seemed to have gone missing for which there was no corresponding compensation in the till. The Livingstons had suggested that perhaps they'd been stolen by some of the teenage girls who liked to browse the store after school was let out. Was that plausible, they asked? Could Margo come up with a different explanation?

She hadn't been able to and hung her head, her face burning with feverishly hot guilt and embarrassment.

Mr. Livingston had then coolly stated that rather than have her prosecuted for theft, she would be fired. They escorted her out of the store. The staff made no eye contact as she went, seemingly too engrossed in the task of tidying the racks of clothing.

That had been only yesterday. It felt like years ago.

Margo sincerely hoped she would never again run into Stella Livingston. It would just be too awkward. On the other hand, she realized with great clarity that she was glad not to have to go to work there anymore. Now that she was out of fashion, she knew she was done with it. Whatever she did going forward, it wouldn't be any kind of retail. Maybe she'd consider hairdressing or bank-telling or secretarial work. But not sales. She was sick and tired of fashion stores, sick and tired of trying to please people, sick and tired of life, sick and tired of everything being so hard, just so sick and tired…

Having drunk three cups of coffee in addition to the bowl of soup, Margo now needed to use the facilities. She glanced at her watch and saw that it was nearly two in the afternoon.

Another round of anger flashed across her face. *Where the hell is Hugh? Does he mean to leave me here all day?*

Looking around, she noticed the door to the ladies' room behind the rearmost booth, the one with the baby-faced guy still reading his newspaper. Leaving her coat behind, she made a beeline for the restroom.

Upon emerging, she saw Hugh standing near the entrance. He smiled when he saw her, but she didn't smile back.

After gathering her winter gear, she followed him out the door to his truck.

"You missed a nice visit with your cousin," said Ellie cheerfully as Margo jumped into the cab. "But guess what? David's on his way to Winnipeg as we speak. We called Aunt Gertie and she's happy to have you stay with her. You can rest from your shock and take the time to figure out what you'll do next. Isn't that great? She has a guest room you'll have all to yourself."

Margo gave her a dark, withering look.

"Why can't you just put me up across the street in the Minitonas hotel?" Margo pleaded, turning to Hugh. "I wouldn't have to talk to anybody and I'd have all the peace and quiet I'm starving for. I could sleep around the clock if I wanted."

Hugh answered with an edge of impatience. "Because none of us thinks you're emotionally healthy enough to be completely alone right now. Since I'm taking responsibility for you, I've arranged for your care with Aunt Gertie. Hopefully it's only temporary. Hopefully you'll soon be back on your own two feet."

Margo said no more as he backed out of the parking stall and drove through the streets. Thinking about it further, she was at least glad to get away from the newlyweds. She was increasingly aware of their chemistry and it made her uncomfortable. Glancing across the bench, she realized they were holding hands. Hugh seemed to be massaging Ellie's fingers and it made her feel sick and tired again… just so sick and tired.

A few moments later, Swan River loomed large. Gertie, who had been watching for them, ran out of her house when they pulled up in front.

"Oh, Margo, I'm so sorry for your breakup with Larry." Gertie embraced her niece. "What a scoundrel he's turned out to be!"

"Truth be told, I don't actually care that he's left me," said Margo unemotionally. "But if you don't mind, I don't want to talk about it."

"Of course, dear," said Gertie, saddened.

The four of them entered the house in single file, Hugh carrying Margo's travel bag.

"I've boiled the water for tea." Gertie reached for her teapot.

Margo sat wearily at the kitchen table. "Not for me, Aunty. What I'd really like is to lie down. The last few days have been exhausting."

"Yes, I'm sure they were."

Gertie led Margo to the guest room. She set the woman's bag on the floor near the bed. "If you need anything—"

"I'll be fine," interrupted Margo. "I just desperately need to sleep."

"Of course, dear." Gertie gently backed out of the room and closed the door. But her face brightened as she returned to the kitchen. "Well, I guess it will be just the three of us."

"Ahh, the last couple of days have put us behind schedule, too," said Hugh with an eye on Ellie. "Can we take a raincheck on afternoon tea? We'd like to get back home and look after a few unfinished post-wedding matters."

Gertie was clearly disappointed. "Oh. Well, sure, if they can't wait."

"They can't. Thanks a lot for what you're doing for Margo."

As soon as the couple was on the highway and had cleared Swan River town limits, Ellie turned to Hugh. "What unfinished post-wedding matters were you thinking of?"

"I was thinking we've hardly been alone together since before Christmas, which seems like eons ago. I've hardly had you to myself as my wife since the wedding... and that seems like it happened a lifetime ago, too." He glanced at her seductively. "And that's what I want—to be alone with you."

"Well then, I can assure you we're on the same page, husband," said Ellie, matching his sultry tone. "I had some ideas of things I wanted to do to you."

"Really? Like what?"

"I thought I would start with a kiss behind your ear." She leaned over to kiss him there. "And then on your cheek..."

"That's so like you, Ell-phabet. You always begin at the beginning," said Hugh huskily. He looked her way with a smile meant to encourage her.

"After that, I was thinking of petting my God-given, personal teddy bear." Ellie unzipped his parka and undid a couple of buttons in the middle of his shirt. She slipped her hand inside and began to gently massage his chest. Tilting her head a little, she nibbled on his earlobe.

Hugh moaned appreciatively. "What's next?"

"Well... we could go here..." She removed her hand from inside Hugh's shirt and laid it on his thigh. In slow, practiced movements, she kneaded the muscles while moving gradually towards his hips.

Arching his back slightly, Hugh in turn laid his hand on Ellie's thigh. "You're going to have to hold your thought right there, babe," he said, beginning to pant. "I think that's all I can handle while we're driving."

Ellie giggled but didn't stop. They'd reached the corner of Road 150W. After completing the turn, Hugh pressed the pedal to the metal and they reached home in record time. No sooner had he shut down the truck than he turned to Ellie and kissed her with deep intensity. Both fully aroused, they bounded up the steps to their house and quickly shut the door behind them, ignoring the welcoming yelps of their puppies in the nearby pen.

Three

THE FIRST FEW days of married life passed blissfully. It felt good to get back into the routine of meaningful work. It also felt good to come home to an environment of love and acceptance.

With the holidays over, people were returning to mundane matters. Thus, the garage at the dealership where Hugh served as head mechanic was suddenly busy with oil changes and tune-ups as well as a few warranty repairs. This suited Hugh well because it made the day pass quickly.

On Ellie's days off, his drive home never failed to fill him with anticipation of a tasty homecooked meal and pleasant evening of enjoying her loving and satisfying company.

As for Ellie, she returned to her ward at the hospital to face a few changes. The head nurse had announced her decision to retire and one of Ellie's co-workers had been offered the vacant position. When Ellie was offered full-time work, she said she needed to discuss the opportunity with her husband. She did, however, request daytime shifts. Now that she was married, she wanted to have the same at-home hours as Hugh, whenever possible.

She did her best to resume her habit of soul work, daily reading a portion of scripture, journaling her thoughts, and praying while imagining Jesus sitting nearby, ready to listen to whatever was on her mind and heart.

But this required a bigger adjustment than she would have guessed. Their new living room sofa set wasn't as comfy as the one in the Bauman farmhouse. She found it hard to concentrate in her new surroundings.

As a couple, they spent part of each evening playing and working with their loveable mongrel puppies, Ruby and Ruff, in an effort to effect obedience training. Besides that, they frequently talked about what they wanted for the future, including a permanent family home and the other outbuildings Hugh was keen to construct. They also discussed ideas for their honeymoon, to be taken later in May. Separately and together, they saw the future as bright and promising, and generally uncomplicated.

Occasionally they brought up the topic of Margo, curious as to how she was doing under the care of their aunt. Yet Hugh stopped short of calling Gertie to ask for details. Some sixth sense advised him to avoid getting ensnared in long, detailed, and unhappy conversations above his paygrade. He determined to wait for trouble to come to him.

Ellie, too, felt reluctant to get involved. Margo was barely friendly toward her as it was. It wouldn't do to be accused of interfering.

Therefore, when Gertie showed up at the dealership midmorning on a Friday, asking to speak with Hugh, he immediately surmised that all was not well.

"I'm sorry to disturb you," said Gertie without preamble, "but is there somewhere we can talk?"

Hugh attempted some light-heartedness. "This must be serious. I didn't even get a 'hello.'"

"It is rather." Gertie cast her eyes to the floor.

Hugh checked out the staff room. No one was in there, so he took Gertie inside and pulled out a chair for her to sit.

"I'm afraid I can't help Margo." Gertie looked at him directly, her eyes welling up with tears. "She's… she's more than I know what to do with."

Hugh nodded gravely. "I can't say I know this version of Margo either."

"It's just that she won't listen to me. Getting her to eat something is like fighting with a rebellious teenager. She won't talk, not even in a light, superficial way. All she wants to do is sleep. It's not normal, Hugh. I understand she's depressed, but... the last couple of days, she's pretty much slept all day, or at least kept to her room with the door closed. But after we've gone to bed, she sits up most of the night in the living room, usually in the dark. I once got up to go to the bathroom and saw her silhouette in the corner easy chair. I called her name but she didn't answer. So I turned on the light, thinking I might be seeing things and going off the deep end myself. But it was her in the flesh. I saw a bottle of wine on the coffee table. I wasn't pleased about that, and my look must have indicated as much. She reminded me that I had said she could help herself to anything she needed. I replied that the invitation hadn't extended to our supply of alcohol. On that note, she swallowed what remained in her glass and walked past me to her room, shutting the door without another word. I had to clean up after her myself."

"Ellie has suggested you take her to see a doctor," said Hugh, shifting his weight on the chair.

"About that, I called my doctor on Monday to explain the situation and make an appointment," said Gertie. "But Margo refused to go. She said she's fine and just needs more time to herself. So I called the doctor back on Tuesday and begged him to make a house visit. Bless his dear heart, he came by after office hours. She did open up a little and he left a prescription, adding that she should feel the dark cloud start to lift in a few days. I filled that prescription and have been dispensing the capsules. I believe she's taken them, but so far we're not noticing any difference in the way she feels."

Gertie ended on a teary note and wiped her eyes and nose with some tissues.

"I don't know what to do, Hugh. I'd like to help, but it really doesn't seem to be working out with us. I think you should try and find other accommodations for her. I'm out of my element here."

"I understand, Aunty," said Hugh with a sigh. "Can you give me a day or two to try and come with something else? Maybe Ellie will have some ideas."

"I sure hope so. I believe Margo needs help, but I'm not the one to give it."

~

Hugh spilled the story of Gertie's fruitless week to Ellie over their supper. They both confessed to not being overly surprised. Nonetheless, it was discouraging.

As if thinking out loud, Ellie commented, "One of the roles of a pastor is counselling the members of his flock. I realize this doesn't include Margo, but he might know of some resources for this kind of situation."

A little while later, Muriel Wirt, wife of Pastor Leland, was ushering them into the manse's living room for a meeting.

"Before we begin, let's invite the Lord Jesus to be part of this." The pastor subsequently launched into prayer asking for right understanding and wisdom.

Following the amen, Hugh began to explain his worries and frustration over his sister. Occasionally Leland or Muriel asked for clarification, and sometimes Ellie added her perspective. At the end of the hour the Wirts had a pretty good idea what was going on.

"I feel responsible for her," said Hugh, anguished. "I'd have her stay with us, because she's family, but there's no extra room at our house. Do you have any suggestions for where she could live until she gets back on her feet? I'd pay the room and board. It needs to be someplace where she can't easily harm herself again."

"I understand," agreed Pastor Leland, "but I really can't think of..."

"We have an extra bedroom," broke in Muriel. "She could stay with us."

Leland turned to his wife with a shocked look on his face, "Are you sure, dear? You're already involved in so many ministries. I don't see how you can take on this woman and keep up..."

"That's just it. Many of my involvements aren't particularly important. The roles I fill at the church can be handled by anyone. They're just expected of a pastor's wife. I don't want to serve according to presumptions like that. I want to serve out of a calling on my life, just like you, Leland. As they told us about Margo, I felt the Lord nudge me. I believe He wants me to minister to this troubled woman."

Muriel turned to Ellie and Hugh and continued with conviction.

"I've been a pastor's wife for nearly twenty-eight years. I've had to wear many hats during that time, even while we raised our three daughters, who I'm happy to say are well married and building families of their own. I know a thing or two about coming alongside people who feel their lives are hopeless, who have damaged emotions and broken hearts."

"I'd be most grateful if you could help," said Hugh. "As I said, I'll gladly pay for room and board."

"I'll accept a small amount to cover her portion of food and utilities, but it's not my heart to profit from this arrangement," said Muriel quickly. She flashed a look at Leland to make sure he agreed.

"Whatever you think is fair," said Leland. "This will be mainly your undertaking. My plate is full without this additional responsibility."

There was more discussion regarding when and how Margo would be transferred to the manse. Given that Gertie felt overwhelmed, the Wirts proposed to bring Margo to their home the next day with only Hugh along to help with the transition, since he was familiar and trusted. Ellie was asked to stay out of the picture for the time being.

"Choose not to be offended," urged Muriel. "Most likely Margo sees you as the successful woman she wants to be and isn't. No doubt she's feeling great embarrassment over her losses." She turned to include Hugh in her sights. "And I can tell you that people don't like to hear hard truths from members of their family, even when they're right. They're better heard and accepted from outside the circle of kin."

Ellie agreed at once. "I totally get that. I can't accept criticism from just anyone either."

Muriel hesitated to carry on. Hugh noticed.

"You have permission to speak freely, Mrs. Wirt."

"I know you care deeply for your sister… but I'm going to ask you not to visit with her for a bit. I'd like some time to get to know the girl and establish some basic routines without disruptions, be they physical or emotional."

Hugh chewed on his lower lip, yet he nodded.

"Instead I'll try to keep you informed about her progress now and again. Based on what you've told me, she's likely to need some counselling, but perhaps some good, old-fashioned mothering will serve as well."

~

As Margo remained in her room later that evening, she overheard Gertie on the phone with someone. The bits of conversation she caught seemed to indicate that she would be leaving the next day.

Shortly after that, her aunt had come into the bedroom to find her lying in bed.

"Your brother has made arrangements for you to stay with his friends in Minitonas. They'll come for you after lunch tomorrow."

The relief in Gertie's voice could not be missed. She must have felt bad about it, because she proceeded to explain herself in apologetic tones.

"Look, things aren't working out between us. I want you to have a better chance at healing and happiness than what I can offer you."

Margo saw through the kindly spoken words; she was no longer wanted. That was fine with her. She didn't want to stay with Gertie either. Her aunt was right; things weren't working out between them. Aunt Gertie was nice, but smotheringly so.

When Saturday morning arrived, Gertie nervously suggested, "Margo dear, I think you should have a bath and wash your hair. You haven't done that since you've come, and your B.O. is becoming pretty noticeable."

It came as a bit of a shock to Margo. Suddenly, the idea of a bath sounded heavenly. She soaked in the tub for more than an hour, relishing the small comfort of a prolonged bubble bath.

After drying off, she realized that she didn't have the energy to blow-dry her hair. Instead she dressed in the same clothes in which she had come, combed her wet hair smooth, and tucked the longer locks behind her ears. Her makeup bag held no interest at all. She then stowed her few things in her travel bag, zipped it up, and carried it to the front door.

What followed was a stilted conversation between herself and her aunt while they waited for her ride.

"How are you feeling, dear?"

"Fine."

"Can I fix you something to eat?"

"No. Thanks."

"Would you like a cup of coffee?"

"No."

"We could turn on the television while we wait."

Margo didn't comment. Instead she rose abruptly, conveying anger and impatience, and stood before the living room window to watch the traffic go by. Gertie sagged unhappily into the armchair and stopped trying to initiate conversation.

It seemed an eternity before Hugh showed up, but at last he did. Margo hadn't been expecting the strangers he came with, however, and the sight of them caused another furore to well up within her. She hated everybody for controlling her, and making decisions for her, forcing her to do things she didn't want to do. Where did people get off on thinking they knew what was best, treating her like an imbecile? Or a baby? Or dangerous?

Margo managed to rein in her rage and quietly climbed into the back seat of the Wirts' car along with Hugh. At least they didn't expect her to participate in the conversation. The other three had a lively chat as they all returned to Minitonas.

Hugh didn't stay long after they arrived at the manse, citing all the work he needed to catch up on at home. He hugged her goodbye, then left her with the Wirts—complete strangers.

Curiously, though, she felt at ease with them. Muriel showed her their guest room and encouraged her to stow the clothing in her travel bag in the dresser drawers. After a while, Muriel said, she would look in on her. Then they would "talk."

The simple task of putting her things away alleviated the boredom Margo felt. Besides, she was curious to learn what the woman wanted from her.

An hour later, Muriel invited Margo to the living room where she found a tray awaiting her on the coffee table. It held a pot of tea, a pair of cups and saucers, sugar, cream and a small plate of banana loaf slices.

Leland had been called away, leaving the two women on their own.

"I would like for us to get to know each other," began Muriel. "I've heard about your story through your brother and sister-in-law, but I should like to hear it directly from you. Do you like your tea with cream and sugar?"

"Just sugar, thanks," said Margo, surprising herself. Up to this point, she had steadfastly refused any attempt at being made to eat.

Muriel poured the tea and stirred in an ample teaspoon of sugar before handing over the cup and saucer.

Right off the hop, Muriel commanded the situation, yet in such a way that it didn't rouse Margo's anger.

Margo took a sip as she looked around the room, as if debating what to say to her hostess—er, landlady... or whatever she was.

"It's okay if you don't want to spill all your beans at one time," Muriel said, noticing Margo's hesitation. "However, being truthful about what you do tell me is of paramount importance. Will you agree to that?"

Margo thought for a second and then met Muriel's gaze. "Yes." She broke eye contact to look out the living room window. "My husband and I haven't been getting along for some time, and he chose to leave me to live with another woman. It happened just after we got home from Hugh and Ellie's wedding. Then, the next morning, my boss and his wife fired me from my manager position at their clothing store in Dauphin. The unexpected double whammy sent me over the edge and I tried to end my life… which scared the H out of my relatives. But here I am—a little worse for wear, but still breathing. That's all I want to say."

She looked back at Muriel as if daring her to pressure her for more information.

"I can certainly appreciate how terrible that must have felt. Like being run over by a bulldozer," said Muriel compassionately. "I've been told that after you were revived from your brush with death, all you wanted to do was sleep, and that you've pretty much slept through the last eight days. Is that true?"

Margo nodded and then braced herself for criticism.

"That's totally understandable," continued Muriel. "After great shocks, we need time to process. That's one of the ways people do it."

Margo exhaled with relief.

"I'm thinking, though, that you've had enough time to get used to the new state of things, sad as it is. There's no need to wallow. Now it's time to pick up the pieces and begin to rebuild your life. I'd like to help you with that. We'll do it by taking baby steps. A good routine is a healthy way to begin restoring personal discipline and self-worth. Tomorrow I'd like you to be up, properly dressed in day clothes, with your hair brushed and your bed made, ready to join us for breakfast by 8:00 a.m. You can come earlier, but not later. Is that clear?"

Margo stared at her, surprised by the strict instruction. After a moment's thought, she nodded.

"Excellent, and thank you for your cooperation," Muriel said. "After breakfast, we'll do some household chores together and see how long your energy holds up. By the way, where are you in matters of faith?"

Margo furrowed her brows. "I don't even know what that means."

"Never mind. We can talk about that another day. For now you should know that you're in a household that honours God. It will show up in our reading materials, our choices in music, and in the conversations we have with others. We ask the Lord's blessing with every meal. I want to make you aware of this so you don't have to guess why things may be different here from other people and places you know."

Margo matched Muriel's matter-of-fact tone. "Whatever."

The week passed quickly and well. Muriel had Margo assist with dusting and cleaning floors, folding laundry, and preparing meals, not to mention some baking ventures. Margo appreciated that they worked together on all those tasks. She didn't feel like she'd been brought in as a slave to do the lady's housework. And by gaining a few new experiences in the kitchen, she even discovered that she liked working with food, much to her surprise.

On the nicer days, Muriel asked her to come along for outdoor walks, to enjoy the fresh air and exercise. Muriel's walking routine included stops to greet a few seniors who were shut inside due to the January cold. Margo didn't personally participate in the greetings, but through Muriel's example she started to take notice of the well-being of others. This, too, was largely a new experience.

Reviewing the activities they'd engaged in together gave Margo a sense of accomplishment and a measure of self-worth. Somehow, under Muriel's leadership and ministrations, the dark clouds of depression were pushed aside. Not by a long shot did she feel "normal," ready to participate in general society, but neither did she feel like life was so terrible that she should end it all.

Muriel never treated her like an invalid but as a capable adult. And she appreciated that she wasn't pressured to talk about her past or future, or even about how she felt in the present moment. She also didn't press Margo for her opinions on politics, religion, the feminist movement, or the price of eggs in China. Their conversations were light, centring mostly around the tasks they did around the house.

So far, all Muriel seemed to expect of her was a disciplined routine of being up at a reasonable hour and largely keeping active throughout the day. She didn't abide wholesale laziness. For that matter, neither did Margo. She had ambitions and was prepared to work towards her goals. It was just that at the moment she didn't know what they were and besides that, they seemed far beyond her reach. As yet, she didn't possess the energy to care.

Part of each afternoon was given to what Muriel called "quiet time." She would put on an LP recording to fill the background with sweet, soothing orchestral music while she read from a well-worn book. Margo later noted that it was the Bible. After that, Muriel seemed to take a nap, or so Margo thought. When she noticed Muriel's lips moving slightly, as if she were talking to herself, Margo realized something else was going on—and thought it rather weird.

Muriel encouraged Margo to do a little reading as well and set out a stack of four possibilities. Margo looked through the titles, which included *Pilgrims Progress*, *The Good News Bible*, *The Screwtape Letters*, and *Tom Sawyer*.

But reading didn't appeal to her, at least not yet.

Instead she sat in the rocker near the living room picture window and watched the sparse activities on the street while opening her soul to the consoling music.

Muriel seemed to understand and didn't push. She had a way about her that was both patient and kind, yet no-nonsense, knowledgeable and wise without lording it over her.

Margo found herself drawn to her hostess more with each passing day—not that she didn't like Leland, but he was seldom around.

One afternoon, Leland and Muriel announced that they would be heading into Swan River for a few hours to do hospital visitation. It would mean leaving Margo alone for the first time since she had come to live with them.

The thought was exhilarating, but Margo was very much aware that she was being both trusted and tested at the same time.

She watched them pull out of their driveway and slowly drive away, reflecting again on how quickly life could change in such a short time. She'd been with them a full week, having entered their simple, modest home angry and with a heart of stone. Since January 2, she felt like she'd been dragged through hell yet survived to see brighter days thanks to the kindly guidance of Muriel Wirt.

There was a bit of coffee left in the pot. Margo took her mug from breakfast out of the sink, filled it with the last of the brew, and went into the living room to her favourite rocking chair, where she could bask comfortably in the sunlight.

She must have dozed off while rocking, because the next thing she heard was Leland and Muriel entering the house and taking off their winter coats.

Until that moment, Margo had thought that being completely alone represented ultimate peace. But now she realized how much safer and more secure she felt that they had returned. It was like being under the care and protection of loving parents.

Oh my gosh, she thought to herself. *Where on earth did that thought come from?*

Four

ON SUNDAY MORNING, Hugh and Ellie hoped they would see Margo at the First Baptist Church. When they approached Muriel, that hope was met with disappointment.

"Of course she was invited." Muriel leaned against a pew while speaking with the couple. "She says she's afraid of running into people who knew her from times past. She feels unready to interact with anyone. Also, she insists she's not religious and therefore isn't interested anyway."

"That's not surprising." Hugh pursed his lips. "Are you finding her difficult to deal with?"

"Not at all," rejoined Muriel. "She does everything I ask of her and I haven't sensed any resentment. In my view I'd say she's made good progress this past week and that it shouldn't be too long until she's herself again."

Privately, Hugh and Ellie wondered what self that would be, but they didn't raise this question with Muriel.

"Well, I can't tell you how much we appreciate what you're doing for her," said Ellie sincerely. She linked her arm with Hugh's, preparing to leave.

"Me too," added Hugh. "I'm thinking you're a lifesaver."

Someone else approached hoping to catch a word with Muriel, so Hugh and Ellie departed.

After that, Ellie's nieces Charlotte and Beanie cornered them and begged to come to their place to play with the puppies they had been given for Christmas. The tricoloured mongrels had grown substantially in the past three weeks but were still small enough to be considered adorable. This was happily agreed to, and the girls spent a delightful afternoon together with their aunt and new uncle.

At length, Hugh determined that it was time for Ruby and Ruff to be returned to their fenced-in doghouse outdoors. Eight-year-old Beanie dressed to go outside with him.

As soon as they had left the house, fourteen-year-old Charlotte walked up to her aunt. "So how do you like being married?"

"I like it just fine," answered Ellie. "I love having a home of my own and being the queen of my castle."

"That's not quite what I meant," said Charlotte demurely.

Remembering her own curiosity over marital mysteries as a teenager, Ellie perceived that she was searching for some commentary on the intimate aspects of married life.

"If you're asking me about the birds and the bees, I'm not sure your parents would appreciate me having that discussion with you."

Charlotte grew defensive. "I know about the birds and the bees. We saw a film about it in health class at school. I was just wondering…"

"Charlotte, I'll tell you this," interrupted Ellie with a sly smile. "I love Hugh and being with him at all points of the day from breakfast to the next breakfast. And that's all I'm going to say about that."

A few days later, Ellie was slated for a twelve-hour shift from 7:00 a.m. to 7:00 p.m. She rose at 5:45 to shower, dress in fresh scrubs, and hurriedly eat a bowl of cream-of-wheat before kissing Hugh goodbye and driving off into the yet dark-as-night-morning.

On the drive into Swan River, she heard the weatherman forecast snow later in the day and a high of minus-twenty degrees Celsius. It was typical winter weather for their part of the Canadian prairies and therefore nothing to feel alarmed about. Besides, she was prepared for a roadside incident should she have one. In the trunk of her car was a rolled-up sleeping bag and emergency kit. On top of that, she was confident in her driving skills. She'd even taken a defensive driving course which included what to do in winter conditions.

Although breezy, the visibility was good and she arrived at the hospital in good time.

After plugging in the block heater of her car, she went inside to her ward and carried out a busy day looking after a full slate of patients recovering from their elective surgeries. At the end of her shift, Ellie was tired and looked forward to returning home to her husband.

It was snowing wildly. Gusty winds sent the white flakes swirling and accumulating into drifts throughout the parking lot. Feeling uneasy, Ellie nevertheless started up her car. While it was warming up, she brushed the snow off the windows and hood. She could still see across the street despite the churning snow and determined that she could make it home all right even if the drive took a little longer.

A few minutes later, she was on her way. The poor visibility was manageable—that is, until she reached the open prairie after passing the edge of town. Then she found herself surrounded by a complete whiteout.

"Do not panic!" Ellie commanded herself. "Just because you can't see the road doesn't mean you're in trouble."

But she wasn't very persuasive. Her worries grew.

She slowed to a crawl and kept watching for the yellow stripes in the centre of the highway. Only occasionally did she see one and found they were usually farther to her left than she expected, indicating that she hadn't been driving in the middle of her lane.

On second thought, it occurred to her that driving with her right wheels on the gravel shoulder would be a good way to know she was moving along the road and not aiming for the ditch or oncoming traffic.

Up ahead, she would have to navigate a big ess-curve. Not only was she afraid of hitting someone, she was concerned that someone from behind wouldn't see her in time to avoid a collision. She thought about turning off somewhere, going back to Swan River and sitting out the blizzard at Gertie's place. But the storm was now so opaque that she couldn't discern the entrance to a driveway or country road in which to make the turn.

Thus, white-knuckled, she carried on, slowly. At one point, a semitruck passed, kicking up the snow such that for a few instants she seemed to be encased in a solid wall of the stuff. Panicky, Ellie stopped the car until the dust-up dissipated.

Crawling along, she whimpered little arrow prayers to come through the ordeal safely.

After a while, she realized she was way past the ess curve and beginning the descent down the embankment to the bridge that crossed the Roaring River. On a suspicion, she braked and immediately began to fishtail. Great! Not only did she have a blizzard to deal with but icy roads, too.

With the car under control again, she crossed the bridge safely. The sedan seemed to need a little help crawling up the other side of the bank. Ellie applied the gas pedal for the boost.

Just as she got to the top of the other side, the blizzard intensified into a whiteout again.

Without forewarning, she suddenly saw the hazy red taillights of a vehicle in front of her—only inches from her own car. Ellie screamed and slammed hard on the brakes. The car spun around while back-sliding towards the bridge she had just crossed. She felt the car skid backwards into the ditch, completely falling off the highway with a snow-muffled *whoomph*.

Seconds later, another vehicle passed, creeping along at a snail's pace.

Shaken yet relieved, Ellie prayed. "Thank You, Lord for sparing me an accident both in front of and behind me."

But now what? She attempted to drive out of the ditch but only succeeded in spinning her wheels and sinking deeper into the snow.

Ellie looked at her gas gauge and saw that it showed only a quarter tank of fuel.

"This isn't good," she said aloud.

She was in trouble but had no way of communicating with Hugh or anyone to help. A glance at her watch informed her that it was already 7:45. Normally she would have been home before 7:30, so Hugh must realize by now that something was amiss. After a few phone calls to learn that she wasn't safely with Gertie or anyone else, he'd probably begin his quest to look for her. The thought both comforted and alarmed her. Absolutely she needed and wanted rescuing, but neither did she want Hugh to get caught up in the dangerous blizzard.

The real possibility of spending the night out in the storm began to register with Ellie. With gas in short supply, she thought it prudent to shut off the engine. She was warm enough in her parka and knee-high snow boots but noticed the air inside the car cooling off quickly. Pretty soon, her thighs felt chilly.

The sleeping bag in the trunk came to mind. The question was, could she get at it? She tried opening her car door but found it wouldn't move more than an inch; the packed snow was banked halfway up the side of the door.

Worry rose in Ellie's heart. "I need help, Lord. Please don't let me freeze to death. Please bring me a rescuer."

She blinked away tears.

A few minutes later, she heard the whine of a snowmobile. It stopped in front of the car. Through the swirling storm, Ellie saw a guy in full snowsuit gear disembark and wade through the deep snow until he reached the window on the driver's side of her sedan. He shone a flashlight into the car and Ellie rolled down the window to speak with him.

"Are you okay in there?" asked the fellow, loudly enough to be heard above the howling winds. "How long have you been ditched?"

"I'm okay. I've been sitting here around twenty minutes."

"You're stuck pretty good, and you're not dressed well enough to give you a ride in this weather," said the man. "It's safer for you to remain with your car. Can you hold on until morning light? The storm will be blown out and then it'll be possible to pull you out of the ditch safely."

"I could manage if I could get my sleeping bag and emergency kit out of the trunk," replied Ellie.

After asking Ellie to pop the trunk, the stranger waded through the snow alongside and around the rear of the car. Moments later, he returned with the emergency kit, the sleeping bag, and an odd colourful toss cushion. He handed them to Ellie through the window.

"I saw the pillow in there," he said. "Thought it would be useful to you."

"Thanks. I forgot I had it." Then another thought struck her. "Are you heading for Minitonas? Would you call my husband and tell him where I am and that I'm okay till the storm subsides? By the way, what's your name? Thank you so much for stopping to check on me."

"I'm not going into Minitonas, and my name isn't important. You're going to be all right until your husband finds you, and you're welcome."

He offered an encouraging smile.

Ellie watched him return to the snowmobile, start it up, and disappear almost immediately into the stormy night. He was no one she recognized from the district, although she had caught very few of his facial features within the helmet. She couldn't help but wonder whom her answer to prayer was.

Since she seemed fated to spend the next several hours waiting out the blizzard, she crawled into the back seat where she would have the most room in which to make herself comfortable. The first thing she did was take out the flashlight and use it to locate the emergency candles and matches. Then she noticed a protein bar next to the first aid package. Frowning, Ellie withdrew that as well.

She set the emergency case on the console and two candles atop it. Once lit, the interior of her car took on a friendly glow which helped to reduce her anxiety. Then she picked up the protein bar. Suddenly in touch with her hunger, she ripped open the wrapper and took a bite. While she chewed, she pondered the mystery of how it had gotten there. She knew for certain she hadn't stocked it. It had been at least a year since she had last checked the contents of that kit.

The only other explanation was that the stranger had one in his pocket and took the opportunity to add it to the other emergency items. Ellie supposed this was possible, but it sure didn't seem like he had taken the time to do it.

The oddity of the mystery stayed with her as she ate, yet she was thankful to have something to assuage her hunger.

She opened a rear window just a crack for air to keep the candle-light going. It also created a whistling noise. In time, she noticed that the two small flames kept the interior warmer than she would have guessed.

Wrapping herself in the sleeping bag, Ellie made herself com-fortable, with two things consuming her thoughts: prayers for Hugh, whom she knew would be worried sick, and the identity of the strang-er who had stopped to help and encourage her in a timely manner.

At 7:45, Hugh was officially worried but decided to give Ellie until 8:00 before taking action. He reasoned that if she had realized the severity of the storm and opted to stay in Swan River, she would have called to say so. The fact that she hadn't strongly suggested she was attempt-ing to return home. And since she wasn't back, she must either be creeping along very slowly or else had gotten sidelined enroute.

Hugh turned on the radio to listen for weather-related updates. While he fixed a thermos of hot cocoa, the announcer repeated the obvious: a major blizzard was underway and expected to last all night. All nonessential travel was strongly advised against.

He found storms fascinating to watch from within the warm and safe confines of home; not so much when a loved one wasn't also safely inside. That his bride and love of his life was out in the raging elements created knots in his stomach. It was time to go looking for her.

He made sure to dress well for winter conditions in case he should end up in trouble himself. While the truck warmed up, he pulled up as close as he could to the one remaining original shed to search for a shovel, chains, rope, and a flashlight. He looked around before leaving his yard and noticed drifts starting to form. A particularly big one covered the mouth of his driveway. Not wanting to lose more time clearing it away with his tractor, he revved the motor and blasted his way through, stopping just short of hitting the ditch on the opposite side of the road.

Whistling with relief, he straightened out and drove carefully towards Highway 10.

He found he could see through the storm better with his headlights off, and when he reached the main intersection he saw a large dark spot just ahead. With the headlights back on, he drew near and noticed a car hung up in the huge drift that had accumulated there. An older woman rolled down her window to speak with Hugh after he got out and approached the vehicle.

"Thank you for stopping," she said anxiously. "I guess I was driving too slowly to get through. I didn't even see the drift until I was almost on top of it."

"I totally understand," said Hugh. "Can you back up?"

"I'll try." The woman shifted the car to reverse but only spun the tires.

Hugh waded through the snow to the front of her car and directed the woman to try again. As he pushed, she was able to free herself. The shallowest end of the drift covered the opposite lane, so Hugh took a few shovelfuls of snow, tossed them aside, and motioned for the woman to pass while he watched for oncoming traffic. She did as he directed but stopped beside him to speak before motoring on.

"I'm so very grateful to you," she said loudly, to be heard above the winds.

"You're welcome," hollered Hugh in return. "I hope you get home safely."

He hurried back to his own vehicle and set himself on a course towards Swan River. The wide-open prairie produced such strong winds that he had trouble keeping the truck moving steadily along in his lane. He used the edge of the pavement as his guide to keep from veering off. The problem was that if Ellie was hung up somewhere, it would be in the other lane, heading east. He was necessarily driving west, from which point it was impossible to see anything on the other side of the highway. The yellow lines down the centre could barely be made out. He couldn't remember ever venturing out in a blizzard this severe and hoped against hope she was safely creeping towards home.

Eventually Hugh came to the slope that led to the Roaring River bridge. That's where he noticed larger-than-average snowdrifts forming in the semi-sheltered area than the shorter ones his truck thumped through as he crept along. Later approaching the ess-curve, he was forced to stop. There had been an accident here and the police were on hand to mark the event and assist the tow truck with traffic control as necessary.

An officer approached Hugh's truck, bearing a strong beamed flashlight while keeping his face away from the onslaught of the icy winds. Hugh let down his window.

"On your way to Swan River, are you?" asked the officer, his words muffled by the gale.

"I'm actually out looking for my wife," began Hugh. "She would have left the hospital shortly after seven. Normally she's home within the half-hour. I think she might be in trouble somewhere along the highway."

The officer nodded with understanding.

"It's certainly the night for it," agreed the officer. "You can probably begin your search turning around here. There've been no vehicles heading east along the highway in the last while." He looked away for a few seconds before turning back to Hugh. "I understand your concerns, yet it's a wicked night to be out doing anything, including a rescue mission. Take extra special care. Follow me. I'll help you turn around."

"Thanks, officer. I will." Hugh closed his window.

The police officer walked in front of Hugh's truck and led him across the highway until he was turned towards the east and could follow Highway 10 from the edge of the shoulder. Then the officer waved Hugh on and returned to the scene of the accident.

The knots in Hugh's stomach tightened as the gale blew in from the northwest. Now facing east, he could feel the push. Visibility was close to nil, but Ellie was out here somewhere; he could feel it. He was very afraid he would miss the clues.

"God, I need Your help," cried Hugh from the depths of his heart. "Show me where she is. Keep her safe. Keep us both safe…"

He drove slowly enough to frequently take his eyes off the road ahead to watch for vehicles that may have gone off the road to the right. Thus far, his flashlight revealed nothing amiss.

At length, he recognized that he was descending the slope to the Roaring River bridge. Conditions in the ravine seemed a little less intense, being somewhat sheltered from the elements compared to the bald prairie. He sped up a tad to climb the eastward slope and discovered a patch of black ice that caused him to fishtail a bit.

Halfway up, he suddenly slowed as he noticed an extra-large snowdrift accumulating across the lane. He found this curious; it probably meant the snow was banking against an obstacle. He came to a full stop just before the drift and saw to his right an unusually high mound of snow. More curious still, a soft glow seemed to be coming from within.

His heart quickening, Hugh got out of his truck to investigate. Running his hand along the top of the snow quickly revealed a dark vehicle underneath. With his arm, he brushed away snow from the driver's side of the windshield and saw the emergency candles burning, but no person until he aimed his flashlight at the back seat. He was pretty sure it was Ellie's green parka he saw partially under a blanket.

Overjoyed, he yelled her name and knocked on the windshield.

Ellie, who had been dozing, jerked awake. She saw the intense beam of the flashlight, but its brightness prevented her from seeing who held it. She had to shield her eyes to protect them from the harsh glare.

"Ellie!" shouted Hugh again.

"Hugh?" Ellie threw off the sleeping bag, swung her legs around, and peered through the window to see who had noticed her predicament.

Hugh put his face up to the window and they recognized each other at once.

Seeing Ellie in the back seat, Hugh ploughed through the snow against the car until he was able to free the rear door. Understanding what he was doing, Ellie waited until he had cleared a bit and then pushed the door open.

Hugh slid inside. The great winds put out the candles at once, but his flashlight provided welcoming light.

"Oh you silly, dear, foolish, wonderful man," cried Ellie, real tears filling her eyes. "You shouldn't be out in an evil storm like this for any reason. But I'm so glad you're here, not gonna lie."

It was a cumbersome effort, but she managed an awkward hug across Hugh's chest.

"Aww, babe, I was so afraid I wouldn't find you," he said. "But God helped me, I'm sure of it. You're off the road far enough to easily miss. You can tell me what happened later. Right now, are you all right? I have a thermos of hot cocoa with me to help warm you up. You must be cold."

"I'm all right. Really I am. Hot cocoa sounds wonderful, but it can wait. How about we see if it's possible to get me out of this ditch and home?"

"You're in pretty deep, and the large drift hemming you in wouldn't be easy to remove while it's storming," said Hugh, quickly assessing the situation. "I'll just take you home and we'll come back for the car when the blizzard is over."

"Makes sense to me."

They left her vehicle with Hugh leading the way through the thigh-deep snow that had reaccumulated in the last few minutes.

When safely back in Hugh's truck, he retreated far enough to bypass the huge snowdrift and then inched his way towards home. It took twice the usual amount of time, but at last they reached the driveway to their own home. Hugh revved the motor to blast through the drift that had once again filled the mouth of the lane, but it wasn't enough. He managed to get just off the main road, but then he was hung up entirely.

Hugh looked over at his wife. "I guess we walk from here."

"At least we're home." Ellie patted his arm. "I'm so thankful I'll be spending the night in my own bed, not in the back seat of my car."

Together they trudged through the growing drifts. When they finally made it to their cottage, they had to kick away the snow that had piled up in front of the entrance. Once inside, they each savoured the warmth and shelter of their tiny house with relief and not a little gratitude.

Ellie removed her winter things and then wrapped her arms around Hugh. "Honey, I'm so thankful to be back home safely with you. Mind you, I don't think I was ever in grave danger, even after I ended up in the ditch. The strange guy who stopped to help made sure I was okay and safe, and assured me I would be fine until my husband found me."

"What strange guy?" asked Hugh, tipping her chin.

Ellie told him the full story of her encounter with the man on the snowmobile. "I realize I don't know everyone in the valley," she concluded, "but I can't help wondering if I haven't had an angel experience."

Hugh frowned. "I'm not following you."

Ellie pulled away from him and retrieved her Bible. She flipped through the pages for several minutes until she found what she was after. "Here it is in Hebrews 13:2: *'Remember to welcome strangers in your homes. There were some who did that and welcomed angels without knowing it.'*[1] It just goes to show that angels may very well move among us and help us in answer to our prayers as God directs and assigns them."

"It's an interesting theory, but how would you ever know for sure?"

"I doubt we ever would…" Ellie retreated to their bedroom, slipped into some nightclothes and her pink velour robe, and returned to the kitchen to pour herself a mug of hot cocoa from the thermos Hugh had prepared.

Shortly afterward, Hugh also donned his pjs and robe and joined her.

Outside, the winds continued to howl and whistle, but both young people felt safe and secure in their little nest. Their previous adventures in the wild storm were nearly forgotten as a new perspective began to dawn on them. Without stating her intention, Ellie suddenly got up and switched off the overhead lights, plunging them into the dark of night.

"I just wanted to watch the effects of the storm," said Ellie softly.

She gently shoved the small dining table away from the window to create enough space to stand in front of it. Intrigued, Hugh stood beside her. The darkness clarified into deep shadowy shapes. Outdoors, a bit of moon cast light on the flying snow that rose and sank as the winds carried it along. Intermittently, the scene cleared between bouts of whiteout.

"Watching the storm from a place of safety kind of frees one to appreciate its power and beauty, don't you think?" said Ellie after a couple of minutes. "Look at the drifts mounting in the yard. They remind me of shifting dunes in a desert storm, or even ocean waves. Look. Already a drift has formed in front of the truck, and it's as high as the hood. It might even cover it if the storm goes on all night. Still, there's a beauty in its peaked shape. At least I think so. Even the different sounds the wind makes has a kind of melody. Can you hear it?"

"Sorry, babe, it just sounds like an unfriendly squall to me," said Hugh. "But I admit the force of it is impressive. Kind of gives me an

---

[1] Hebrews 13:2, GNT.

inkling of the power of God. I didn't realize you waxed on all poetic, like your brother Rob does sometimes. Must be a Bauman thing."

He put his arm around Ellie's shoulders for a sideways hug. She reciprocated by wrapping her arms around his waist.

Moments later, Ellie yawned. They left the scene of the storm, got comfortable under the covers, and fit their bodies together like nesting spoons. Soon they fell asleep to the music of the winds.

Five

ONE OF MURIEL'S church ministries involved preparing and giving out ready-to-heat-and-serve meals to people when they were recovering from surgery or perhaps following the birth of a baby. Every couple of weeks she prepared approximately half a dozen tinfoil pans of lasagne, shepherd's pie, or a wholesome stew, and froze them so they'd be available at a moment's notice.

The time had come to prepare more of these frozen meals.

The grocery store had a special on chuck beef roasts, so Muriel picked up a couple. Margo watched how she sliced up the roast and then cut the raw meat into cubes. Following Muriel's example, she sliced and diced the second chunk of beef.

"The meat needs to be coated in flour, seasoned, and browned in a fry pan before we put it in a large pot with vegetables so they all stew together," said Muriel. "Do you want to sear the meat, or peel and dice potatoes and carrots?"

"I'll sear the meat," replied Margo easily. She had gotten used to Muriel's instructive manner and wasn't offended by her direct approach.

Muriel quickly demonstrated her method for gently searing the raw pieces of beef and then turned to the sink to pare both a two-pound bag of carrots and small bag of potatoes.

"You can use the bacon grease from breakfast to fry the meat." Muriel pointed to a small dish to the left of the stove. "It will contribute some additional tasty flavour."

"Yum. Bacon improves the flavour of lots of meals."

They settled into an easy camaraderie as each took on different tasks. Margo had now lived with the Wirts for about four weeks and they had become comfortable with each other. At no time did Muriel press Margo for personal information. That went a long way in building trust in their budding friendship. Muriel followed the principle attributed to St. Frances of Assisi: "Preach the Gospel every day and only when necessary… use words." And another: "Practise what you preach."

Never having had a friend who claimed to be Christian, or been to a church of any denomination, except for a couple of weddings, Margo found Muriel fascinating. She was a mixed bag of conventional and worldly wisdom, no-nonsense yet kind and generous, diligent yet determined to take time to smell the roses. She gave of her time to those who called upon her, whether by telephone or by showing up at her door.

When this happened, Margo retreated to her room, partly to give the visitor some personal time with Muriel and partly to avoid having to explain her own presence or participate in the conversation. She would keep the door ajar, however, to overhear the problem and Muriel's counsel, often hearing something thought-provoking that helped her think through her own issues. She had also noticed that Muriel usually prayed by appealing to the God of the universe in very personal terms, like Father—as if He were like someone's dear daddy.

Margo's only idea of God, until now, had been vague, possibly a Force somewhere in the beyond not to be taken too seriously. *God* was most often invoked as a curse. Her own father, Freddie Fischer, had taken that approach without compunction. While growing up in their home, religion in general had been ridiculed, insulted, and wholesale disregarded.

When she and Muriel worked together, particularly in the kitchen, Muriel often recounted stories of her own memories as a young wife and mother bringing up three rambunctious daughters. While Margo couldn't relate, she enjoyed catching these glimpses of family life that bore such little resemblance to her own.

Spending time with Muriel produced in Margo a profound respect for the woman, even if she didn't completely understand her.

"You're so good at cooking and baking, I think you should have made a professional career out of it, you know like Betty Crocker or Julia Child," said Margo brightly as she stirred the cubes of beef around the frying pan so they wouldn't blacken.

"If I'm not mistaken, Betty Crocker is fictional," returned Muriel. "Be that as it may, my career has been multi-hatted and full-time. I've been wife, mother, and supporter to the church wherever we served… in that order. In fact, I prefer the word *calling* over *career*. I believe that God called me to these roles and that my part is to obey and invest myself in them wholly. Of course, I never receive a paycheque, like women who enter the workforce, but it's still my career and it's never failed to fulfil me. I daresay that's more than many women can say."

"But didn't you ever wish to become something more than just a housewife and mother or helper?" insisted Margo. "Besides, the extra money would have made it possible to have some especially nice things, or maybe to have the opportunity to travel abroad. Wouldn't you have liked that?"

"Before I share my thoughts on that, my dear girl, let me ask you a question." Muriel paused to look at Margo. "Why did you say *just* a housewife, mother, and helper? Do you think these roles aren't worthwhile or important? And if so, why?"

"Well… I do think there's more to life than waiting on a man, having his babies, and doing housework to fill your time. Besides, I've never found those roles, as you call them, interesting or attractive. My own mum was stuck at home all her married life. And from the moment I first noticed this to the day I left home for good, her life as a stay-at-home wife and mother was drudgery. She never had any nice things, nor did the rest of us kids. I swore that when I finally grew up and could be on my own, I wouldn't live a life like my mother's."

All the beef cubes were browned. Margo tossed them into the big pot with more energy than necessary. Muriel noticed.

"Hmmm. Would you have liked it if your mother hadn't been home to care for you?" Muriel asked. "You know… would it have been better if she'd been away 'fulfilling herself' somewhere while you and your sibs were left to cope alone? Perhaps you could look at it another way: she sacrificed her own desires to invest her time and talents into her family. To me that speaks of high priorities."

Now that the vegetables were peeled, Muriel began to cut them up into bite-sized pieces.

"My mum didn't have many choices married to my father," Margo said. "Truth is, he was pretty heavy-handed. You did as he said or risked being seriously hurt. My mother and brother took most of his heat. I made a vow to myself to never marry anyone who was remotely like my pa. No way was I gonna let any man control me like Pa did my mother. Ever."

"I'm sorry your early years were difficult for you and your family," said Muriel kindly. "Knowing it was like that helps me understand you better. Having said that, I can tell you truthfully that being Leland's wife, and the mother of our three girls, has been amongst my greatest joys. I'm not saying life was always easy. There have been plenty of challenges. Yet I don't regret the hard times, because I learned many valuable lessons through them—like what really mattered, and what was truly worth my time and energy. I learned that being in good relationships with people matters very much more than accumulating things. And another thing: I have the good fortune of having a kind and loving husband. I realize that's not true for everyone."

Muriel added the chopped vegetables to the pot, along with several cups of water.

"I'll admit that when I was younger, I was a little envious of those couples who could afford nicer furniture, wear name brand clothing, and live in fancier houses. But eventually I realized that stuff is just stuff. If you pay more for some than others, it's still just stuff. It has no power to keep me happy or content in the long term."

"Yeah, well, I never had anything nice until I left home and made my own money." Margo tidied up the kitchen counter. "It's still a wonderful feeling to have new things, not hand-me-downs or thrift store items. But you're right about one thing: the thrill of a new purchase doesn't last long. As soon as you get what you think you want, you turn around and want something else. But you were talking about happiness and fulfilment. I don't think I've ever felt fulfilled in anything, and my happiness has always faded away eventually."

Muriel didn't pass comment on Margo's disclosure, but she glanced her way with a smile as if to encourage her to keep talking.

"I thought marrying Larry would make me happy. Back when I first met him, I thought he was so good-looking and cool. And he had a nice car. At first everything was so exciting. The sex was good, too."

Margo glanced up to see if she had shocked and embarrassed Muriel, but the pastor's wife didn't bat an eyelash.

A little surprised, Margo continued. "His savings were enough for the deposit on our first little house in Dauphin. Soon after, I got a job at the clothing store. It was fun to buy nice things for our place and wear the latest fashions. But after a while, I found myself getting bored with Larry. The novelty of being together had worn off. He was just a guy, after all, with a few habits that drove me crazy!"

Muriel chuckled. "You mean like squeezing the toothpaste tube from the middle or leaving his soiled clothes on the floor instead of putting them in the laundry basket?"

"Yeah, there were a few dumb things like that, but mostly it became clear that we didn't want the same things in life. He wanted to settle down and have a traditional family. Not me. I didn't want to be stuck at home with a bunch of whining, snotty-nosed kids. Anything but that…" Margo sighed.

"I see the problem clearly," said Muriel with a half-smile. She added some beef broth powder to the mixture in the big pot along with salt, pepper, a bay leaf, and powdered garlic. She set the heat to medium. "While that's simmering, we can bake up a few banana bread loaves."

Muriel reached for a brown paper bag lying on the counter. Opening it, she withdrew a bunch of overripe, mostly black-skinned bananas. "We ought to get at least four loaves out of this, I should think. Will you please mash and measure the pulp?"

While Margo peeled and broke the bananas into a large bowl, Muriel searched for the instructions amongst the items in her box of recipe cards. A few minutes later, four loaf pans were thrust into the oven and the timer set.

Unless the day presented a break from their normal practice, Muriel's pattern was to fix herself—and now also Margo—a cup of tea around two in the afternoon and sit a spell. During this quiet time, she softly played instrumental music, read her Bible, and journaled her thoughts and prayers.

Margo joined in this routine insofar as she also drank a cup of sweet tea along with a snack, sat in the rocker next to the living room picture window, and read from a book. Right now she was a few chapters into a thick volume by Leon Uris titled *Exodus*, borrowed from the town's library. She found it quite compelling, but she wasn't only reading. Surreptitiously, she also studied Muriel. It never ceased to amaze Margo to watch the woman handle the worn Bible with such love and respect. It looked like most pages had words underlined, and there were snippets of notes between the leaves. Occasionally Muriel wrote something on a scrap of paper and tucked it into her Bible along with all the other notes.

Today, however, Muriel did something Margo hadn't seen before. After reading her Bible, she set it aside and closed her eyes. Margo was pretty sure she was praying. This time, though, a tear escaped Muriel's closed eyes and trickled down her cheek. Muriel wiped it away with her fingers, but another tear followed soon after.

This troubled Margo. Recalling their latest conversation, she presumed Muriel might be crying on account of her. Perhaps she'd said too much... that her disclosures regarding her family and marriage had been too shocking and different from Muriel's sweet, idealistic existence.

Margo didn't have the courage to ask Muriel about it. She didn't want to disturb the woman's private moments of soul.

Not many minutes later, the timer on the stove dinged and Muriel's eyes flew open. She cast a warm smile at Margo, who weakly returned one of her own. Muriel stood and returned to her kitchen. The small house was awash with the tantalizing scents of the simmering stew on the stove, as well as the banana loaves removed from the oven.

Margo breathed in the comforting aromas. "Would you like some help?" she called from the front room.

"Not yet," called back Muriel.

Margo returned to her book and tried to concentrate on reading a few more paragraphs.

About twenty minutes later, Muriel came into the living room and stood in front of Margo.

"This afternoon I want to make a quick call on someone who came home from the hospital this morning," Muriel said. "I'd like you to come with me this once. I think you'll find it interesting."

"Sure," agreed Margo, surprised. "But I can't imagine how I could be useful."

"We'll just have to see about that."

A few minutes later, Muriel carefully set a tinfoil container of hot stew and still-warm loaf of banana bread in a tote bag. Both women, clad in their parkas and boots, departed the house into the crisp but sunny afternoon. Margo wanted to, but didn't, ask whom they were calling on. She felt curious and uneasy at the same time, feeling Muriel was surely up to something. But she trusted her friend, too, and followed along for the four blocks it took to reach their destination.

A young man answered the door shortly after Muriel pressed the carillon button.

"Nice to see you, Mrs. Wirt," he said with a wide smile. "Come on in."

He stood aside as the ladies entered.

"I thought neither you nor Marlene would feel like putting a supper together on her first day back home, so my friend and I brought some beef stew and a fresh banana loaf." Muriel handed over her tote bag and began to remove her winter wear. "Both are still warm. How's the new mom doing, by the way?"

"Very well," replied their host. "She should be finished feeding the little peanut and can come and visit for a bit."

Not knowing why she had been brought along, Margo felt a bit awkward but followed Muriel's example in removing her outdoor clothing.

"By the way, Roger, this is my friend Margo. Margo, this is Roger, and you'll soon meet his wife Marlene," said Muriel by way of introduction.

Roger and Margo shyly shook hands.

He led them into the living room, cozily decorated in dusty pink and blue accents, as was the current trend in home décor. A bowl of mixed pink and blue silk flowers, prettily arranged, sat in the centre of the coffee table.

No sooner were they seated than Marlene made her appearance, carrying a tiny wrapped bundle. Radiant, she greeted the pastor's wife warmly and immediately passed the baby into her arms.

"I assume you came to meet Miss Amy," said Marlene.

"I did, of course, but I was inquiring about the new mom, too. How are you, my dear? Was it an easy delivery?" Muriel beamed into the wrappings. "By the way, let me introduce you to my friend Margo. I brought her along so she could meet your little one."

"Pleased to meet you, Margo."

Margo forced a wide smile and congratulated both Roger and Marlene. So that was it! Muriel had brought her to see a newborn firsthand, following their discussion on careers and personal fulfilment. Great! She was in no position to object unless she was willing to appear completely cold-hearted and uninterested, which she wasn't. But if Muriel thought that meeting a new baby would cause her to change her mind about wanting children, she was sorely mistaken.

Margo looked on politely as Muriel, encouraged by Marlene, unwrapped the receiving blanket to reveal more of the tiny perfection of brand-new humanity. Amy was awake; she kicked and flailed a bit as Muriel lovingly grasped the tiny feet and wee fingers in her warm hand. She gently stroked the baby's downy cheeks and hair, which was as light and short as peach fuzz.

"Well, aren't you just the most precious thing there is," cooed Muriel while Marlene and Roger looked on with glowing pride.

Shortly after, Muriel swaddled the baby snugly in the receiving banket again.

"I don't mind if Margo holds her," said Marlene generously.

Margo responded quickly. "Oh no, I couldn't... really... I don't think so..."

"It's all right," agreed Muriel. "Babies don't easily break and new life is a joy. Just try it, dear." She turned to Margo and laid the baby gingerly in Margo's arms.

Immediately Margo realized she had never held a newborn. She had been two years old when her younger sister Diane was born and there hadn't been any other babies in their lives after that. She hadn't been to see her sister after she'd birthed her own two kids, and none had been born into Larry's side of the family in all that time, either.

After Muriel let go, she adjusted the baby's lay in her arms and was somehow surprised how naturally she fit. Margo didn't unwrap the receiving blanket as Muriel had, but she did place her finger under the baby's exposed hand, and little Amy grasped it instinctively. This triggered a new feeling in Margo... and it wasn't unpleasant.

"Touch her cheek and tell me what it reminds you of," said Muriel, looking on.

Margo removed her finger from the baby's grasp and stroked the little cheek. "Velvet," she announced seconds later.

"I agree." Muriel offered a loving smile. "I've always felt a sadness that we lose that gorgeous skin quality as we mature. You have a beautiful daughter, Roger and Marlene. I'm sure she'll bring you many years of joy."

"Yes, ma'am. We're very thankful for our little girl," said Marlene with Roger nodding.

There was a bit more small talk, and then Muriel and Margo departed.

"Why did you ask me to come with if you didn't need my help?" asked Margo a moment or two later as they walked along.

"If you recall, I didn't say I needed your help, just that you might find the visit interesting," corrected Muriel. "I had the impression that you'd never met an infant, and that if you did, you might not automatically think they were all snotty-nosed inconveniences. I believe children are a gift from God. And if we view them in that light, family life can be quite wonderful."

"I'll only admit to one thing, which is that you're right to conclude I hadn't held a baby before today," said Margo. "As for changing my mind about having children, it would take more than one experience. Besides, I'll soon be single again. I'm sure you wouldn't want me to bring a child into the world without a traditional mate."

"That would be best, yes. But changing the subject, I'm aware of an opportunity you might be interested in."

"Is it something else to do with children?" asked Margo warily.

"No. The café's chief cook, Mrs. Illichman, is getting on in years, and by that I mean that she's slowing down. She doesn't want to quit and the owners don't want to let her go. They'd like to hire someone part-time to help. Mostly it would mean prep work—peeling, dicing, slicing, shredding—that sort of thing. I thought you might enjoy helping them out."

"Actually, I might," said Margo, surprised at herself. "I do believe I'm ready to participate in public life again, and a part-time kitchen job sounds like the perfect way to ease into it."

"Then let's introduce you to the powers that be."

Muriel veered down the back alley behind Second Street. They soon entered the kitchen of the café via the back door, where Muriel greeted Mrs. Illichman and the waitress who was preparing for the supper rush.

After a few minutes of casual interview, Mrs. Illichman agreed to have the café owner give them a call. Muriel's vouching for Margo was very helpful.

The women returned to the manse happy with their day's accomplishments. Margo found herself excited about the prospects of working with the locally famous Mrs. Illichman.

When Pastor Leland came home for supper, he too was in an especially good mood. It was the first day in a long time no one had called on him to ask for counsel regarding a personal problem or heartache.

After their dinner, the Wirts invited Margo to play a table game, which resulted in a chorus of light-hearted groans and laughter. Muriel was pleased to see Margo come further out of her shell as she moved quickly towards better mental and emotional health.

About ten o'clock, bedtime was declared. Margo paused outside the door to her bedroom and turned her attention to Muriel, who was on her way to her own bedroom further down the hall.

"Muriel, can I ask you something?" asked Margo tentatively.

"Of course. What is it?" Muriel stopped at the entrance of her room to look back.

"This afternoon… you were crying. Was that on account of me?"

Muriel didn't answer immediately.

Margo continued to stare, waiting for a reply.

"Yes," said Muriel at last. "I won't lie. I was praying for you, and it included a bit of crying. I'm sorry you found it distressing."

"Was it because of what I told you about my marriage? My family?"

"I saw with the eyes of my heart how deeply hurt you've been and how that has coloured your outlook on people and life. I asked God to do a great work of healing in you. And I believe He will, all the more so if you invite Him into your life. He loves you and wants to be your father and friend. And He wouldn't be like the natural father you once knew."

"I know that you and Leland totally believe in God and everything about the Bible and stuff, but it still seems illogical and far-fetched to me. Maybe someday I'll 'see the light,' as the pastor once put it. But…

well, I'm not there yet." Margo paused. "I'll say this, though. You're the kindest, wisest woman I've ever met. Thank you for caring about me."

"Oh! Well, that's easy to do. You're like a daughter to me," said Muriel. "I recommend you ask your brother about how he came to having faith in God. He was pretty resistant at first, too."

"Hugh? I know he's a lot mellower than he used to be, but I chalk it up to the Ellie effect. She has him wrapped around her little finger," said Margo with a touch of annoyance.

"If that's true, then it's mutual. Those two genuinely love one another. And faith, a personal relationship with God, is a top priority for both. I'm serious. Ask them about it."

Margo sighed. "Perhaps, but it won't be tonight. Good night, Muriel."

"Good night. Sleep well."

Six

THE PHONE CALL Hugh had been expecting came on the evening of Friday, February 13. His brother-in-law was ready to discuss the sale of his and Margo's house and the impending divorce.

"I want to come over tomorrow for the purpose of having Margo sign two different sets of papers," said Larry, sounding business-like. "I assume she's with you, or that at least you know where she is."

"Yeah, I know where she is," replied Hugh in a matching detached tone. "What are the details? I'd like to field them first."

There was a pause. Hugh waited.

"What exactly do you want to know?" asked Larry warily.

"What are your terms of divorce? How are you wanting to settle matters?"

"I'm advocating for a no-fault divorce, citing incompatibility. There are no kids in the picture to wrangle over." Then he added softly, "Thank God."

"I heard that," said Hugh. "But I agree that it makes parting ways a lot less complicated. Are you going to haggle over possessions?"

"Nope. I don't want anything that reminds me of that period of my life. I expect Margo will feel the same. I'm walking away with just my personal effects and my car. All I want is to start over, no outstanding ties."

"Can I presume you're selling the house for what you paid for it? That Margo will get back her inheritance?"

Larry sighed loud and long. "No, I wasn't able to make a deal as good as that. One of my co-workers is ready to upgrade from his starter home. I proposed to buy his house if he would buy mine. But it's still too rich for his budget. He has an older brother, though, who makes considerably more money. We twisted his arm to upgrade to my house, my co-worker will buy his brother's place, and I'll buy the starter house."

"How can you buy another house if you don't have two pennies to rub together?" asked Hugh.

Larry was silent long enough for Hugh to wonder if he was still on the line. "My girlfriend has enough savings for the necessary down payment."

"Sheesh! A two-timer then."

"Like the saying goes, don't judge me until you've walked a mile in my shoes. Besides, it's none of your business." Larry was plainly irked. "You asked me about the sale of our house. Well, the buyer drove a hard bargain. He's getting the house furnished with all the new appliances and furniture Margo outfitted it with, but for less than what we bought it for. Even so, the money we get has to go to paying out the utility bills we fell behind on, not to mention the credit card debt that was used to buy the furniture. And her clothes. And the lawyer's fees. There should be some loose change remaining and I promise to give her every leftover dime."

Hugh let out a breathy whistle and muttered an unintelligible word under his breath. "You know Margo isn't going to go for it," he said frankly.

"That she'll have a full-blown hissy fit, I have no doubt," agreed Larry in a tired voice. "But it's probably the best deal we're going to get. So far we've missed two mortgage payments. If I continue to wait, the bank may foreclose and then we'll get absolutely nothing. Not to mention, we'd still be saddled with maxed-out credit cards that would probably have to be written off through bankruptcy. This way, even if there's precious little money left, we can pay our out-standing debts and walk away from each other with a clean slate. I figure that's still a good deal. Probably as good as can be realistical-ly hoped for."

"I suppose… if you put it that way," replied Hugh glumly. "I get your logic, and she should, too, but it's still going to feel like being kicked below the belt."

"If you have a better solution, I'm listening. I've been doing all the work back here. She hasn't tried to get a hold of me or helped liqui-date our assets or *anything*. For someone who's invested so much, you'd think she'd be actively trying to protect her assets."

"She hasn't been very strong lately, mentally or emotionally, as you well know. The people who took her in have helped a lot in get-ting her back on her feet, but she's not yet her old self. Not a lot of confidence there."

"Whatever. We've got to get this done asap to salvage as much as we can." He suddenly sounded dispassionate again. "Are you going to help me with this or not?"

"Yeah. You're right. The sooner you deal with this stuff the better. Meet me at my place. I'll work out a meeting time for tomorrow after-noon."

Muriel Wirt was near the telephone that lay at the end of the kitchen counter when it rang.

"Good evening yourself, Hugh," she returned with a chuckle after he greeted her warmly. There was a moment of quiet. "I'll call Margo and you can make these arrangements with her yourself." She held the receiver to her chest while she called, "Margo. Telephone for you."

Margo came into the kitchen with her face screwed up as though to ask a question.

"Your brother wants to talk to you," said Muriel as she handed over the receiver. She left the kitchen after that.

Margo took a deep breath. "Hi Hugh," she chimed in a moment later, making an effort to sound cheerful. "How are things going?"

They exchanged typical small talk for a couple of minutes. It helped Margo brace herself for the unpleasant news she felt sure was coming.

"I got a call from Larry a short while ago," said Hugh carefully.

"Uh-huh. I figured it was only a matter of time. What did he say? What does he want?"

"He wants to meet you tomorrow to sign two different sets of papers."

"Two different sets of papers…"

"One is about the divorce he's filing for."

"Right," she said, snapping to attention. "Of course. Did he give you any details? You know, how things are to be settled and all?"

"I know the gist of it. He's going for a no-fault divorce, citing incompatibility. Since there are no children, he wants to settle the debts and walk away from each other free to pursue a new life, like a clean sheet of paper."

"I suppose I can agree to that," said Margo after a few seconds. "What else? What's the second set of papers about?"

"He's found a buyer for your house in Dauphin."

"I expected that…" She trailed off warily. "I feel like there's a 'but' coming."

"Well, kinda." Hugh hesitated. "It's a bit of a good news, bad news situation."

"Tell me the good news first."

"There's a buyer willing to buy your place, furniture included, and take possession a month from the signed deal."

Margo began to tremble with stress. "Okay, fine. What's the bad news?"

"The buyer is adamant on his offer to purchase. I don't know what the numbers are, but it's less than what you and Larry purchased the house for."

She closed her eyes and swore softly under her breath. "How much less?" she asked when she felt she could speak again.

"Sis, he didn't say. He did say it would be enough to settle the outstanding bills and credit card debt, and he'll give you whatever's left over. It would be possible for you to part without further obligations."

"But I would also come away penniless. Isn't that what you're saying?" said Margo, panic creeping into her voice.

"Again, I don't know. I get that there's no easy way out of this mess. I'm sorry, truly sorry, that things have unravelled for you."

He could hear Margo breathing heavily on the other end of the phone.

"What should I do?" she asked plaintively, about to break down.

"I think you should meet with him as requested and hear everything he proposes. One thing's for sure: the sooner you settle matters, the better. If you drag things out indefinitely, you'll both lose everything." After a moment, he added: "Remember this. I'm pulling for you. You pulled for me when I was between a rock and a hard place and now it's my turn to do it for you."

"Thanks, bro," whimpered Margo into the phone. "Fine. I'll see you both tomorrow. Where's the meeting supposed to take place?"

"My place. How about I pick you up in time to have lunch with us? Ellie hasn't seen you since the top of January. She cares about you and prays for you… like, all the time."

"Are you sure she doesn't think I'm the biggest loser ever? What would she know about the bottom falling out from under her?"

"She would know quite a lot about that, actually," said Hugh with an irritated undertone. "There's an awful lot about Ellie you don't know… and that's your loss. She's a great gal. I'd like you to give her a chance."

"All right, all right." Margo felt somewhat chastened. "Seems I've been wrong about just about everything. I don't know why I even try… see you tomorrow."

She hung up the phone and hurried to her room, closing the door firmly behind her.

Muriel allowed about five minutes to lapse before venturing to the guest room and knocking on the door.

"What?" called Margo, stifling tears.

Muriel opened the door and entered, closing the door behind her. "I presume you received bad news." She stood next to the bed where Margo lay curled in a fetal position.

"Depends how you look at it," wailed Margo, her face to the wall.

"Why don't you tell me about it for the sake of talking it out? Often solutions present themselves when we give voice to our troubles."

"I'd rather be alone. Maybe I'll know what to do about tomorrow after a good night's sleep."

"No," said Muriel with emphasis. "I'm not going to allow you to undo all the progress you've made. You're a grown woman, Margo. You can face your trials. Bad news comes around to everyone eventually and the right thing to do is face it squarely, not run and hide from it."

"You're right. I'm a grown woman, but I don't know who I am anymore. I don't know how to pick up the pieces of the life that's been pulled out from under me."

Margo turned around to finally face Muriel, who sat on the bed's edge.

"Talking it out will help you avoid going round and round in never-ending circles," said Muriel. "Like pet gerbils running on their wheels but never get anywhere."

Margo sat up, pulled her knees to her chest, and wrapped her arms around them. Twice she opened her mouth to speak and then closed it without saying a word. In an unexpected motion, she opened her arms, leaned forward, and fell across Muriel's bosom, giving way to fresh tears.

"My worst fears are coming true," she sobbed. "I'm about to lose everything I ever worked for, and I don't know how to stop it from happening."

Muriel rocked her in her arms for a couple of minutes. "I have a suggestion," she began. "Leland is away at an elder board meeting so we have the house to ourselves. Let's move to the living room where we can both sit comfortably and you can tell me what's so terrible about your terrible situation. I have a new tea we can try. It's bound to help."

Margo smiled weakly. "You always think a cup of tea will soothe one's problems."

"And it helps, doesn't it?" maintained Muriel with a lopsided smile. "Brings clarity somehow. It's uncanny, I know."

While Muriel boiled water for tea, Margo changed into lounging pyjamas and her long plush robe. She then moved into the living room and curled up in the Wirts' well-worn armchair.

Muriel soon entered bearing two large mugs steaming with apple cinnamon tea generously sweetened with honey. She set one down on the side table next to Margo and then settled into her own favourite spot on one end of the sofa.

She nodded to Margo, prompting her to begin.

"Hugh called to tell me that my husband is coming tomorrow afternoon to have me sign two sets of documents," Margo said in a neutral tone uncharacteristic of her. "One set are the divorce papers. The other is to close the sale of my... I mean *our* house in Dauphin. The divorce I readily agree to. Apparently he's filing for no-fault, citing incompatibility. I'm fine with that. There are no kids to haggle over and it would be a relief to just walk away from each other and start over. No baggage. Know what I mean?"

Muriel responded with a thoughtful nod.

"The other set of papers..." She faltered. Fresh tears slipped from her eyes. "Apparently the house has a buyer, but he's not willing to pay what it's worth. So we wouldn't get all our money out of it."

She paused to wipe away the tears with the palm of her hand. Muriel looked on sympathetically and waited for her to continue.

"I stand to lose every dime I put into it—my whole inheritance and the equity we built up. I'd come away broke and humiliated." Margo dissolved into tears.

"I don't really understand," said Muriel compassionately. "Why is your husband willing to undersell the house? Is he being vengeful, do you think? Perhaps if you told me how things came to be as they are..."

Margo looked through the living room window and for a moment chewed on her knuckles. Her face registered a torn spirit. More tears slipped from her eyes.

"Oh, what the heck," she said in resignation. "If I can't trust you with the details of my sorry life, then I can't trust anyone."

For over an hour, Margo expanded her description of the embarrassingly poor and difficult circumstances in which she had been raised, about how meeting and marrying Larry Owens had provided the first means of escape, promising that she could have a normal life like other people.

Then she spoke of the surprise inheritance she'd received from her maternal grandmother, someone she had no memory of ever meeting. The amount had been large, at least by her reckoning. It felt like she'd won the lottery.

Her immediate desire to invest it in real estate had been strong. She had been motivated to rise above her circumstances and become a respected woman of means and reputation, and it was now magically within reach.

But the fun of having and outfitting a fancy new house hadn't lasted long. When it became challenging to make ends meet, the relationship between her and Larry had gone from friendly tolerance to bitter estrangement.

Muriel listened without interrupting, except for the occasional question for clarification.

"If I understand you correctly, you and Larry weren't exactly in agreement when you bought the house," said Muriel.

"That's partially true. But it was more like he was divided on the subject. Half of him argued that the budget would be too tight, since he was paid strictly by commission and his income was inconsistent from month to month. But the temptation to get ahead captivated him, too. So I talked him into it. And when his worst fears became our reality, he blamed me for the bad decision. It's been nasty between us ever since."

"As I see it, this situation requires prayer and a lot of wisdom," said Muriel gently. "I'll pray that when you go to your meeting tomorrow, you have clear insight and understanding regarding the difficulties to be resolved."

"How about you come with me?" implored Margo. "You're the wisest person I know."

"No, my dear." Muriel spoke kindly but firmly. "I appreciate the invitation and your confidence in me, but this is your test, not mine. You'll do fine. You're a smart girl. I'm sure you've learned from your mistakes, including the realization that they can be costly. There's no help for it now except to accept the results graciously and begin anew, being all the wiser for it. Experience is a great teacher, it is said, and I heartily agree."

Leland returned just then and their discussion about Margo's troubles was set aside in favour of hearing about the more intriguing topics raised at the board meeting. Margo wasn't interested in these matters and therefore excused herself. She retired to her room where she simply put out the lights and went to bed.

But instead of falling asleep, she mulled over Muriel's final statement, basking in the fact that Muriel found her smart, that she could accept her mistakes graciously and carry on as a much wiser woman. She couldn't recall anyone ever pronouncing such positive words over her and they warmed her heart. As sleep overcame her, she almost believed she could face what the morrow would bring with dignity.

When Hugh pulled up to the manse at 11:45 a.m., Margo was ready. She came out to meet him well-dressed yet casual, her hair stylishly coiffed and makeup impeccably applied. Muriel was pleased to see she had taken pains to go into what was anticipated to be a difficult appointment physically and emotionally prepared.

Although not religious, Margo allowed Muriel to pray for her before Hugh arrived, reasoning that it couldn't hurt. And who knew? It might bring about as much luck as carrying around a rabbit's foot.

"Hey, you're looking pretty snazzy," Hugh remarked as they drove off, leaving Minitonas behind.

"Thanks." Margo had been nervous about seeing Hugh, since it had been several weeks, but he showed no signs of viewing her critically. His warm and friendly attitude helped her to breathe easily and relax.

"I hope you're hungry. Ellie fixed up a pot of chili with fresh home-made buns," Hugh continued, attempting to make light conversation. "My mouth has been watering for the past hour."

"Sounds wonderful. I've been learning to cook meals like that and make bread and buns from scratch, too."

"That's great! Do you like it? Cooking, I mean."

"Surprisingly yes," said Margo cheerfully. "It's more fun than I ever thought it would be. Muriel is a good teacher who doesn't mind showing me how to go about it. I've learned a lot."

"Good for you. I think cookery is a valuable life skill. You can bless people a lot with good cooking."

The short trip and light conversation were soon concluded as Hugh pulled into the driveway of their farm.

Ellie had been watching for them and threw open the front door to greet Margo with enthusiasm. For an instant, Margo felt uncertain and shy. She looked to her brother for reassurance.

"She's really been looking forward to seeing you," he said before getting out of his truck.

Margo took a deep breath and smiled as she opened her side of the cab.

"I'm so glad you've come." Ellie smiled broadly and opened her arms to greet Margo with a hug. "You look awesome."

Although a little stiff, Margo hugged her back and then removed her coat.

"It smells amazing in here," she said, looking around the small room. She remembered when Ellie had first shown it to her before the wedding. At the time, she'd privately thought it was decorated rather old-fashioned. Now it conveyed cozy comfort and respite. She could easily see why her brother and his new wife found this cottage to be a special retreat from a busy and demanding world.

Although she, too, had grown up on this yard, it bore almost no reminders of the unhappy life she had once lived there. That came as a relief.

Margo's heart suddenly ached with desire for a lovely retreat of her own. Staying with the Wirts had turned out to be good place to transition from the fiasco that had been her life, but she couldn't stay forever. It wasn't exciting to think about beginning fresh in her old stomping grounds, but one had to start somewhere.

This was the first day since leaving Dauphin that she truly felt she could be proactive about her future, largely as a result of Muriel and Leland's ministrations and encouragement. And now Hugh and Ellie were generously throwing in their support. Maybe, just maybe, something good could come out of the disaster she'd created.

Lunch was as delicious as it smelled. Margo unabashedly ate two helpings, much to Ellie's relief. She hadn't been sure what to expect from Hugh's sister since their rough dealings with each other at the top of the year. Without being obvious about it, she noted that Margo seemed to be of a healthy weight and mentally and emotionally even-keeled. She dared to hope the meeting with Larry might take place without high drama.

They kept the conversation light and newsy, avoiding questions that were too personal. The hour passed pleasantly and everyone seemed relaxed… until Larry pulled into the yard.

The mood changed at once. All three braced themselves for an awkward and unpleasant confrontation.

"Just remember, we're here for you," said Ellie as she squeezed Margo's hand. Margo returned a weak smile and squeezed back.

Although it was a Saturday, Larry entered the house carrying a briefcase and wearing a suit and tie, as if he was visiting a client. He greeted Hugh and Ellie with a business-friendly demeanour. Then he acknowledged Margo.

Hugh pulled out a chair for Larry at the kitchen table and placed Margo across from him; he took a seat for himself between them. Ellie offered each a cup of coffee. All declined. She then sat apart from them on the sofa to listen and observe while nursing the coffee she poured for herself.

Larry removed several files from his briefcase and looked directly at Margo. "What do you want to discuss first?"

"Doesn't matter." She cooly returned his gaze. "Start with what's on top."

The first file contained the application for divorce. Larry calmly expressed an overview of the no-fault approach. They would each walk away with their personal belongings, following the sale of the house. Any monies leftover after the debts were paid would be given over to her.

She had to sign in a couple of places to get the process officially underway. Larry handed her a pen and showed her where to place her signature.

Margo received the documents but laid down the pen. She then proceeded to read through every word on every page. It took several minutes, during which Larry drummed the table with his fingers nervously. Hugh, likewise, squirmed; his self-appointed role as mediator seemed unnecessary, at least for the moment.

Finally Hugh got up and poured himself a mug of coffee. He offered one to Larry, who accepted it gladly this time.

At last, Margo set down the papers and picked up the pen.

"Don't you want me to check it over first?" interjected Hugh.

"No. I understand everything and agree." She signed her name in all the required places, then handed back the papers. "Next."

He set aside the divorce file and opened the next one, which contained the offer to purchase for their house in Dauphin. This time he launched into a full financial breakdown of the deal, revealing the sale price as well as the cash that would come back to them after the mortgage and lawyer's fees had been cleared up.

From another file, Larry produced the invoices of all their outstanding utility bills and credit card debts. A summary sheet showed the figures totalled up. Subtracting this from the proceeds of the sale would leave a balance of less than a thousand dollars.

Larry repeated that he would give her every nickel and dime of this remainder. Then they'd each be free to pursue the life of their choice.

Margo listened gravely as she followed along with every explanation and the documents that supported them. She did her best to maintain a poker face.

But when the bottom line revealed that her worst fears had come true, she blinked back unbidden tears.

Larry noticed. "Look, I'm sorry it turned out this way… for both of us," he said tiredly. "It took a lot of effort to get a deal even as good as this. It's hard to sell a high-end house in the middle of winter. There are few buyers in this price range."

Margo waved him to be quiet. "I don't want to hear about it. I understand your many points, but something's missing."

"What do you mean, missing?"

"My car. What about my car? It's not quite paid for, but it's close. Am I going to lose that, too?" Margo indicated the bills and documents covering the table. "Where is it anyway?"

"Parked in the driveway where you left it," answered Larry stiffly. "Can't you look after that yourself? Or is my name on that loan, too?"

"Probably." Margo turned to Hugh. "Can you see any better way to deal with this… this situation?"

Hugh shook his head slowly. "Your best option is to deal with these debts as soon as possible. Otherwise they keep growing. If it came to bankruptcy, you would be left with even less, including a badly damaged credit rating."

Margo picked up the pen again. "Fine. I get it. Where do I sign this time?" she asked, her words staccato and her tone impatient.

After she had signed the papers, Larry quickly refiled the documents and returned them to his briefcase. Having got what he came for, he wanted to return to Dauphin as soon as possible.

Although ready to leave, he paused at the door and turned again to Margo, who stood alone in the area of the kitchen.

"I'm sorry, Margo, for my part in the mess we're in. I wish…"

But the words got stuck in his throat. He departed from the house without saying more.

~

"I just feel like such a failure!" cried Margo to Muriel after she'd been returned to Minitonas. The story of her meeting with Larry tumbled out even before she'd removed her winter coat. "The unavoidable reality is that I'll come away from this mess pretty much penniless. How am I supposed to make a new beginning? It's all very humiliating."

"It seems to me it could have turned out so much worse, though," said Muriel sympathetically. "Choose to be grateful for that."

"That's what Hugh and Ellie say, too. But it's not easy. What would you do if you were in my shoes?"

"Well, since you asked, the first thing I'd do is present the whole muddle to my heavenly Father and ask Him to show me what steps I should take. I got a greeting card once that read 'God is ready to assume full responsibility for the life wholly yielded to Him.' I believe that absolutely."

For once, Margo didn't challenge the idea or make any objection.

Surprised but heartened, Muriel continued. "Then, after I committed myself and my trials to the Lord, I would get a pen and paper and take stock of my interests, talents, and skills for the sake of pursuing the work, or perhaps a career, I was truly suited for."

"You're right. I need to actively work out a plan for myself. I've never made lists like the ones you're talking about, though. What do you think I'm good at?"

Muriel paused and sighed with disappointment. Yet again Margo was sidestepping the spiritual aspect of the matter. What would it take for the lost woman in front of her to see her need for God in her life?

"Speaking practically, you have good organizational skills," Muriel replied frankly. "You can clean and cook well. Beyond that, I don't know you well enough to suggest becoming a nurse or teacher or any of the many options available to women today."

"I might not mind having a job in a restaurant." Margo mulled the idea. "I think I'd like to try it out to see if I like it."

Muriel smiled. "Well, your wish has come true. While you were away, I took a call from the Minitonas café and you're being offered a part-time job as food prepper, from 8:00 a.m. till noon, Mondays through Saturday."

"Fantastic!" cried Margo happily.

Seven

SARAH HANDED THE telephone receiver to Rob, smiling excitedly. "It's the dealership. I'll bet your new pickup arrived."

That's exactly what the call was about. Within half an hour, Sarah and Rob Bauman were in Swan River examining their new vehicle. Their previous half-ton had been written off following an accident in the latter part of November. Their son Trevor and a few friends had T-boned Rob's truck. The young people had mostly gotten away unscathed, but Rob had gotten severely banged up, including a break in his left leg. He was fully healed now and back on his feet, serving in his various roles in the community, including at the First Baptist Church.

He sorely missed his truck, though, and juggling the use of their station wagon with Sarah's commitments had proven to be a head-ache. Had he been satisfied with the options on the lot, Rob could have procured another truck weeks earlier, but he had taken a notion to order one in the colour scheme he liked best, with all the bells and whistles.

The new truck was a beauty. Two-toned in burgundy red and white, the three-quarter-ton vehicle sported an automatic transmission with 350/V8 motor. The audio system included a radio and cassette player. Rob sat behind the steering wheel testing out the various functions, enjoying his new toy.

"Since I'm in town, I'll stop by the grocery store," said Sarah as she eased out of the passenger's side. "I'll meet you back at the house."

"I'll probably take the scenic route home," said Rob. "A new engine should be driven a bit slow at first, to break it in."

Sarah smiled knowingly. "Or maybe to show it off to a few of your buddies?"

"There's only one guy I'd like to have a little fun with on that score," admitted Rob. "I'll be home for supper, though. You can count on that.

About fifteen minutes later, Rob pulled up to the competing dealership in town and asked to speak with their head mechanic. A few minutes later, Hugh came into the front reception area, rubbing black grease off his hands with a rag. He noticed Rob straightaway and cracked his face into a broad smile.

"Did you ask for me, or are you waitin' for a sales rep?" asked Hugh slyly.

"I got no need for a sales rep," returned Rob. "But I thought I'd stop by to show you what a real man's truck looks like."

"You don't say." Hugh chuckled as he looked for a place to toss his rag. "Does that mean you bought one of those engines lined up out front?"

Rob smiled crookedly. "Instead of wasting words, come with me and I'll show ya."

In a gesture of exaggerated politeness, Rob opened the door and waved Hugh on ahead of him.

"Now here's what I call a truck," said Rob in an authoritative tone when they crossed the lot to where his new truck was parked. "Check this, and then eat your heart out."

"Pretty fancy, I admit." Hugh walked around the vehicle. "Nice red colour, too… the kind old men seem to like. You know, nothing too bright."

Rob rolled his eyes and then opened the cab for Hugh to see the matching interior. He went on to list its impressive specs, emphasizing its four-wheel drive.

Hugh listened patiently, his lips turned up in a smirk. "Yeah, it looks pretty good in here. But it's all about performance. You know that, right? Pretty won't go the distance. You should have gone for one of those horses on display over there." He indicated the row of new pickups on his right.

"Nah, I don't think so."

Hugh tipped his head back and laughed. "Well, you haven't made a believer out of me yet. In fact, I'm thinking seriously about trading up my truck for one of these beauties on the lot. Then we can compare notes and see whose vehicle outperforms whose."

"You can't say I didn't try to warn you," Rob teased. "But you know what they say: there are none so blind as those who will not see."

Hugh continued to snicker as Rob drove away.

Back at home, the kids clambered into the new pickup, exclaiming their approval.

Trevor sat behind the steering wheel. "I like how the driver's dash comes around, kind of like an airplane cockpit."

Rob raised his eyebrows. "If that's a hint that you want to take this thing flying down the road, I may reconsider ever giving you the keys."

Trevor chuckled but didn't say anything more.

"How come it smells funny?" asked Beanie, screwing up her face.

"That's just the smell of brand spanking new," her father replied.

The table talk over supper continued the same gushing excitement. Would their dad please give them a ride in it, implored the daughters? But the parents assured the family that this new truck was going to be around for a long while; there would be plenty of opportunities to take rides in it.

Trevor, however, was singled out for a different message.

"Tomorrow you can come home for lunch and take the afternoon off from school," said Rob.

"Me too?" asked Charlotte eagerly.

"Nope. Just Trev."

Trevor looked wary. "Sounds interesting… but why? Got a job planned for me or something?"

"Actually, I mean to fulfil a promise I made before the accident set back my plans. I want the two of us to go to Winnipeg and take in a Jets game. We'll leave right after lunch and spend the night at your Uncle Harold's place. Saturday night, the Jets are playing the Edmonton Oilers. We'll come back home Sunday."

"Yahoo!" Trevor leaped from his chair and flung his arms above him. "I'll get to see Gretzky play in person!"

"You mean the new star they're calling the 'Great One'?" asked Rob. Trevor nodded his affirmation. "Yeah, should be an exciting game."

"Can't we come, too?" begged Charlotte on behalf of herself and her little sister. "Just for the ride and to see our cousins?"

"Not this time, honey. This trip is just for me and your brother."

Rob and Trevor left Minitonas by 1:00 p.m. Although the temperature was bitterly cold, as one might expect for February, it wasn't windy and the sun shone brightly, lending an air of cheer and optimism to the afternoon. The clean white snow in the fields dazzled like a carpet of diamonds.

Father and son drove along in relaxed, quiet companionship until they reached Cowan. After that, the scenery changed from largely wide-open fields to scrubby bush. There wasn't a lot of evidence for human dwellings along this lonesome stretch of highway.

Rob hummed the refrain of a hymn. Trevor recognized it as one they had sung in church the previous Sunday morning. It brought him a measure of comfort. There was a consistency and steadiness to their existence. The physical, emotional, psychological, and spiritual aspects of their lives played out largely in harmony with each other. Their family life was characterized by strong, fair, loving parental leadership.

Rob stopped humming. "So which of all the pretty girls in your school have you got your eye on?"

Trevor was completely at ease engaging with his dad on the personal topic. "No one in particular. I mean, most of the girls are pretty in their own way, but I haven't got a favourite or anything. We're all just friends."

"Seriously?" asked Rob, glancing over at him. "You're a smart, handsome young man. I'd think quite a few girls would hope to get your attention."

"I think a lot of the girls maybe think I'm a little geeky. Sometimes I get razzed for skipping out on a get-together 'cuz I have homework to finish, or a paper to write."

Rob grunted. "Hmmm. Just so you know, that's one of the things that makes me proud of you, son. You've got a good sense of priorities and you abide by them. And sometimes, without prodding, you go the extra mile. Do you remember when I asked you to sweep out the garage last fall?"

Trevor nodded.

"I appreciated that you not only swept it out but also went through all the stuff that had been thrown in there or shelved. You threw out the useless garbage that had accumulated. With all the meetings I had to attend, I hadn't gotten around to it myself. And when you did it *unasked*, I was so relieved and blessed that I made a promise to bless you back. It was your mother who suggested taking you to a hockey game, and here we are… on our way."

"Thanks, Dad." Trevor practically glowed. "I'm pretty pumped about the game, especially since it's the Jets and Oilers. I told a couple of the guys where I was going this weekend. They're totally green with envy."

"They don't have to miss it. It'll be aired on TV."

"But it's not the same as being there."

They drove on, but their conversation subsided into a comfortable silence. They were each taken up with their own thoughts, with only a country music station creating soundwaves.

Suddenly Trevor piped up. "How did you know Mom was the girl you wanted to marry?"

"I thought you knew that story."

"I know you two met at Bible school, but not how you knew she was the one."

"Fair enough," said Rob. "I was in my second year of Bible school and she was in her first. We had both passed the auditions to sing in the college choir, so I saw her at every practice, which was a couple of times a week. Like you said, all the girls are pretty in their own way, but something about Sarah Reimer kept catching my eye. I found myself looking for her not only at choir practice but in the hallways, in the cafeteria, and at events going on around the campus."

Trevor adjusted his position on the bench, keenly interested. "You didn't talk to her?"

"Not at first. I took my time because I wanted to see what she was like, and because I felt shy."

"You're not shy," objected Trevor.

"I was twenty years ago, especially around girls!"

"So when did you finally get together?"

"Well, she still won't admit it, but I think she was sizing me up as well. One day she came into the cafeteria late for lunch. The table of girlfriends she usually sat with was full, but there was an empty seat right next to me. She asked if she could join us, and all us guys said with one voice, 'Sure!' Then she chimed right in. I think we were talking about cars and she contributed to the conversation like she knew what she was talking about. Pretty soon, the other guys got up to leave to get back to their classes, but I stayed behind until it was just her and me."

"Did you ask her on a date?"

"Not immediately. I asked where she was from and about her family and why she had chosen to come to Bible school. I liked her answers. *Then* I asked her to go for a walk with me that evening, so we could get to know each other better. After that we became a pair and the rest is history." Rob glanced over at his son with a smile.

"So it wasn't a love-at-first-sight kind of thing…"

"Not exactly," said Rob slowly. "But of all the girls I could choose from, my heart did single one out. And it was right."

"So why did you ask if I was interested in any one girl? Don't you think I'm too young for that?"

"I think you're too young to take a wife and support her, but not too young to find them attractive and exciting to be around. Girls can easily arouse powerful feelings in a guy. I was trying to fish out how you're managing those feelings."

"I think I'm doing okay, Dad. Don't worry about me," said Trevor with a trace of embarrassment.

"Hey, how are you liking the way this new truck runs?" He wanted to shift the discussion away from himself.

Rob got the message. "So far so good."

It wasn't much later that they reached the Trans-Canada Highway and turned east for Winnipeg. Dusk fell as they cruised the two-lane highway through the vast open prairie, covered in white all the way to the horizon. On the radio, the announcer played a few tunes, broadcasted the latest news, and detailed the weather forecast until they had safely reached the home of Rob's brother Harold and family where they spent a delightful evening in each other's company.

⌒

The hockey game was scheduled to start at 7:00 p.m. Since the arena was next door to the large Polo Park Mall, Rob and Trevor decided to spend a little time shopping, city-style. The two-tiered indoor plaza with its many shops and department stores almost overwhelmed the senses. They had thought about bringing home something interesting for the woman and girls, but in the end they couldn't decide. They agreed that women were usually happiest doing their own shopping.

As for themselves, they figured they had no need of anything. Trevor commented that he found himself confused by the large selection. His dad concurred, preferring for Sarah to shop on his behalf.

When he made his own choices, they were often met with disapproval anyhow.

All they walked away with was assorted candies to take back to the family they had left behind.

After a satisfying supper of Asian cuisine from the food court, Rob and Trevor reparked the new truck near the arena. A steady line of people, young and old, were already entering. Many fans were wearing white Jets jerseys as they took their seats.

"Do you want to a jersey?" asked Rob, noting a booth of team-branded mementos as they looked for the section indicated on their tickets.

Trevor hesitated.

Rob raised his eyebrows in surprise. "I thought you'd jump at the chance."

"It's just that the Jets are only my second favourite team," hedged Trevor. "Tonight I'll be cheering for the Oilers."

"Is that because of #99?"

"Yeah. The Great Gretzky is truly amazing."

"I see how it is…" Rob smiled and shook his head.

They found their seats in the middle of a row in the second bank of bleachers from the ice. They were great seats, offering a clear view of all the action from end to end. Flanked on both sides, though, it felt like a tight squeeze until they removed their parkas and settled in.

The crowd's excitement was catching as it rippled through the stands. Trevor even pinched himself once to assure himself he was really at a live NHL game.

Once the preliminaries were done, the teams were introduced and skated onto the ice with fanfare. The fans cheered wildly as the organ belted out the familiar notes heard so often on the game broadcasts.

At last the referee dropped the puck, getting the first period underway.

"Sheesh, those guys skate fast," said Trevor breathlessly.

"Don't they."

Boom! The Jets scored the first goal. Not long after, the Oilers answered with one of their own.

The first period ended with a one-all tie.

During the break, they bought colas and stretched their legs before returning to their places.

The second period brought the Oilers two more goals. One was scored by Gretzky, and he assisted with the second. Trevor was so excited that he rose to his feet as he cheered.

"Man, it's too bad Aunt Ellie isn't here to watch this," bubbled Trevor, almost shouting to be heard above the din. "The Oilers are her favourite team, too. She'd be going nuts right now."

The fellow sitting next to Trevor cut in unexpectedly. "I once knew an Ellie whose favourite team was the Oilers. What are the odds we know the same Ellie?"

The surprising question came from Trevor's left. Although he'd always been aware of the person sitting next to him, it came as an awkward shock to be personally addressed. He looked in the direction of the voice to see a handsome, preppy man smiling at him with practised friendliness.

"We're not from around here," said Trevor guardedly. "I doubt it could be the same person."

"The Ellie I know doesn't live here anymore either," continued the stranger. "She moved back up north this past spring."

Rob caught that. "Tell us who your friend is, and we'll tell you if she matches our Ellie."

"Her name's Ellie Bauman. I used to tease her about being disloyal to her home team." The man shifted in his seat so that he leaned far enough forward to speak with Rob directly.

"You don't say," said Rob, plainly surprised. "It's rare to find a needle in a haystack."

Trevor was intrigued. "How do you know my Aunt Ellie?"

"Your aunt, huh? We worked together at the St. Boniface Hospital. How's she doing?"

"Are you like… a nurse, too, or something?" enquired Trevor.

"Something. I'm actually finishing up my training as a doctor. I'm a surgical intern." The fellow spoke with evident pride. "What's she doing now? Is she nursing up at Swan River or thereabouts?"

"Rob Bauman here." Rob extended his hand across Trevor. "Ellie's brother. And you are?"

"Paul. Paul Richter." He accepted the handshake.

"Ellie is doing very well, and yes, she's back working as a nurse at the Swan River Hospital," said Rob sociably.

"She got married on New Year's Day," Trevor added.

The astonished look on Paul's face brought forth a chuckle from the blond female companion sitting next to him.

"You're talking about the Ellie who was your ex, right?" the woman next to him piped up.

Paul sent her a deprecating look. She returned the insult with a flash of her eyes. Trevor noticed the brief, sour expressions on their faces but didn't know what to make of it.

"Do you, like, want us to say hi to her or something?" Trevor asked.

"Sure, if you think of it," said Paul brightly as the former smile returned. "And you can add my sincere congratulations. On her wedding, I mean."

The boy nodded and their conversation ended abruptly because the Oilers had scored yet another goal. Shortly after that, the second period concluded and they all left their seats to stretch their legs.

Rob bought two mugs with the Jets logo embossed on them—to remind them of this father-son outing, he said.

The third period played out with even greater excitement than the first two. Motivated to win, the Jets doubled their efforts and the puck flew across the ice in every direction. However, after a valiant effort, the Oilers prevailed.

Rob and Trevor left the arena satisfied with their entertainment. Paul and his date also departed, filing out in the opposite direction, the unexpected exchange already forgotten as they hurried out of the arena to avoid the inevitable traffic jam.

"That was great, Dad, thanks a lot," said Trevor happily through chattering teeth.

"You're welcome, and I had fun, too," admitted Rob as they waited for the truck to warm up.

It seemed to take a long time to clear the parking lot with so many vehicles trying to exit at the same time. This wasn't a problem encountered at their local arenas, they noted wryly.

~

The trip home was almost uneventful, save for one thing. Sometime after they cleared Dauphin and turned up Highway 10, they came across a car that had somehow slid off the road and was hopelessly stuck in the ditch.

Rob pulled off onto the shoulder and both father and son got out to investigate. What they found was a young girl crying.

"Are you hurt?" asked Rob, looking her over and scanning the interior of her little green economy car.

"No, just scared," faltered the teenager.

"What happened?"

"I was driving along and a deer jumped out in front of me. I slammed on the brakes and started to skid out of control," said the girl through fresh tears. "This is where I ended up."

"It happens. You're not the first and you won't be the last," said Rob encouragingly. "Don't worry. We'll get you out."

"What's your name?" asked Trevor while his dad retreated to the truck.

The girl composed herself. "Tory. It's short for Victoria."

Rob backed up his truck so it was lined up to pull the car back onto the highway. While he set the chain to both truck and car, Trevor took the shovel and cleared away some snow from the front end of the car. Rob got back into his cab and began to drive slowly, pulling the chain taut.

"I'm no good at this," said Tory to Trevor sheepishly. "Do you mind driving till I get back on the highway?"

"Sure," agreed Trevor. He got in behind the steering wheel while Tory scooted over to the passenger side.

In short order, the car was out. Rob removed the chain and then checked the vehicle over for damage. When everything was deemed to be in good order, he went back to the truck, expecting Trevor to join him momentarily.

But the boy didn't come. Through the rear-view mirror, he saw the young people talking like there would be no tomorrow.

After ten minutes, Rob lost all patience and beeped his horn. Even then it took another minute for Trevor to finally leave the car and join him in the truck.

"What took you so long?" asked Rob, irritated.

"Calm down, Dad. Sheesh! I was just trying to build up her confidence so she could drive home. She turned sixteen last month and just got her driver's license a few days ago. This was her first solo trip out on the highway. She's a little scared." He hesitated a moment. "I gave her my number so she can call and tell me she got back home safe."

Rob looked at him in disbelief. "You exchanged phone numbers?"

"Yeah. What's wrong with that?" asked Trevor boldly. "As a matter of fact, while we were talking, I think maybe my heart singled her out."

He cast a knowing eye towards his father.

"Oh brother. Are you serious?" Rob wagged his head. "Boy rescues damsel in distress and then... well, I guess that's another way guys and gals find each other."

Eight

FEBRUARY WAS NEARLY over. The cold month had waxed and now waned to the doorstep of March, the month that tended to generate a sigh of relief since it signified the arrival of spring—that is, given just a little more patience. The winter often felt long and tedious, putting many people in crabby moods.

Hugh was home alone and in just such a temper. The workday was over and he'd finished his supper of leftovers. Normally Ellie would have been home with him, but his Aunt Gertie was hosting a Tupperware party and had invited his wife to attend. Ellie had felt that the kind and neighbourly thing to do was to participate.

Sometimes having time to oneself was a gift of solitude that restored the equipoise of the soul; other times it amounted to loneliness.

Nothing on television interested Hugh. Since he didn't yet have a heated shop in which to do his tinkering, he drummed his fingers on his knees and looked about the room, searching for an interesting way to pass the time. His eyes fell on the steamer trunk in front of him. It was a handsome old piece made of hard lumber, strapped and reinforced with brass corners. Hugh had always insisted it meant nothing to him; it was merely an uninteresting relic from the household of his youth.

Given its substantial weight, it clearly wasn't empty. And it was locked. Ellie had imagined it contained treasure. Hugh greatly doubted that, since he was sure his nuclear family hadn't owned any valuables.

The appearance of the keyhole suggested a slim skeleton key was needed, but neither had come across one in all their sorting and cleaning efforts.

Hugh's thoughts returned to a day the previous summer when Ellie had discovered a metal suitcase in the attic of the old house. That had been just before he smashed it down and burnt it. This suitcase, too, had been locked without a key to open it.

Their mutual curiosity had led them to seek out slim tools and knives. They'd eventually released the lock, since those old-fashioned locks weren't so cleverly made that they couldn't be picked open with a little diligence.

With a sigh, Hugh rose and went to the flatware drawer. He pulled out a thin-bladed steak knife. Before setting to work on the lock, he put on some music to offset the lonesome atmosphere. The music also helped build up his patience as he crooned along.

Breaking into the trunk proved to be a complex and tricky task. It crossed his mind more than once to simply break off the lock. But he was sure this would upset Ellie; she wouldn't appreciate having the grand old antique defaced. He could easily imagine her making him stop and then ask around the community to borrow skeleton keys with which to open it properly.

At a moment when he felt very close to success, his efforts failed again.

"Lord, I need help with this," he pleaded rather grumpily.

Once more Hugh tried to feel, as well as listen to, the knife tip as he inserted it into the keyhole, much like someone trying to crack open a safe. He held his breath as he gave it a little twist…

Ping! The mechanism popped out with an almost noiseless release. Astonished yet joyful, Hugh smiled broadly.

The exercise had taken the better part of an hour. Had anyone been with him, they would have expected Hugh to open the lid at once. Instead he slowly sank into diffidence.

Unbidden, a story he had read in some school literature class rose to mind. *Pandora's Box*, it had been called, a tale from Greek mythology. Given his difficult youth, he now wondered if opening the trunk wouldn't reveal something associated with bad recollections. Maybe it would tell him something about the past he'd rather not know.

"Don't be ridiculous," Hugh scolded himself. "Grow a spine. There's nothing inside this thing I can't handle. Probably all junk anyway."

Still wary, however, Hugh opted to tidy up after himself. He returned the steak knife and other assorted tools to their drawers.

Then he stood in front of the trunk and raised the lid.

The first thing he saw was a white satin and lace garment, somewhat yellowed. He immediately perceived that it must be his mother's wedding dress. It lay folded up in a blue paper-lined tray that made up the top layer of the trunk.

His eyes were quickly drawn to a thin sheaf of foolscap laid in the centre of the tray. The papers were slightly browned and had begun to curl at the edges. The topmost sheet wasn't exactly smooth and had puckered spots as if it had come in contact with drops of water. Hugh thought that was odd since the trunk was sound. No way could water have gotten inside; it had always been sheltered, even while the old house stood uninhabited.

Then it struck him: the papers might have been laid there wet... perhaps wet from tears.

His heart beat wildly. With trembling hands, Hugh picked up the small stack of papers. Without yet reading the words, he recognized his mother's handwriting.

Quickly returning the papers to where they had lain, he shut the lid. A great many powerful feelings flooded him—feelings he hadn't felt for a long time, not since he had bared his soul to Ellie the summer before. He thought he'd healed from those bitter memories, and to some extent he had. But seeing his mother's handwriting, touching paper that his mother had handled, had once more dispatched sorrow, anger, distress, and insecurity.

He would face it. But he would do it with Ellie at his side. She would be the filter through which he met whatever was written on those sheets of paper. She would help him make sense of them, and only then would they examine the rest of the trunk's contents.

Hugh glanced up at the clock. It read 8:35. It wasn't likely that Ellie would return for some time yet. He thought of his young dogs, Ruby and Ruff. Putting them through some obedience training and playing with them would provide some needed diversion.

～

Ten o'clock rolled around and Hugh got ready for bed. Still meaning to talk with Ellie before calling it a night, he returned to the kitchen to fix himself a cup of chamomile tea.

While waiting for the kettle to come to a boil, Ellie returned at last. Hugh met her at the door as she bounded up the steps.

"Brrrr," said Ellie, entering with a shiver. "It's nasty cold out there. Spring can't come soon enough."

She hung her parka on the coat tree and tried to put her icy hands on Hugh's bare chest by slipping them into his housecoat. He grabbed both her wrists before they met their goal, but then pulled her close and planted a long, sweet kiss on her mouth.

"Umm, what a nice way to be welcomed home," she murmured, lingering in his embrace.

"I'm making myself a cup of chamomile tea. Do you want some, too?"

"I'm afraid I'm tea'd out. Aunt Gertie laid out lots of refreshments. If I drink any more, I'll be needing the bathroom every hour through the night."

"Then come sit with me while I drink mine." Hugh took a seat in the middle of the couch. "I missed you tonight," he added as she snuggled up against him. "Sometimes I like having a few hours to myself, but tonight… I actually felt lonely without you here."

"Aww, honey, that's so sweet." She pecked his cheek.

Only then did her eyes fall on the lowered lock of the steamer trunk. She squinted, puzzled.

"How did that happen?" she asked in amazement. "Did you...?"

Ellie searched Hugh's face for the answer.

"Yeah, I did. I was bored. There was nothing worth watching on TV and I figured I should answer one of your prayers, so I picked it open. Took almost an hour, but it's unlocked."

"So... what's in it?" Ellie left the crook of Hugh's arm and sat upright in front of the great chest.

He tried to sound indifferent. "Dunno. Didn't look through it."

"Are you kidding me? You didn't look inside?"

"I lifted the lid, and then I shut it," confessed Hugh with forced patience. "I felt it was something we should do together."

Ellie studied her husband for a minute while he steadily returned her gaze.

"Did you see something... upsetting?" she asked softly.

"Not sure." Hugh looked away.

Ellie put her hand over his. "My sense is that you're afraid of what we might find. Am I right?"

Hugh simply shrugged.

"Do you mind if I take a look?"

"Go ahead. Knock yourself out. I gave you the trunk, remember?"

Taking a deep breath, Ellie slowly lifted the lid. She stared at the same folded, yellowing satin wedding dress with the thin sheaf of handwritten papers lying on it. For what felt like several minutes, but couldn't have been more than seconds, she gaped without speaking.

Finally, she turned to Hugh. "What's all that writing about?"

"I didn't read it," he replied honestly. "But I do recognize my mother's handwriting. I suppose I might be afraid of what she's written. I hoped you would read them first and then tell me what to be prepared for..."

Hugh swallowed hard.

"Of course I will, honey." Ellie felt the distress coming over her husband. "How about we leave them for tomorrow, or even some other day? But we can lift this top tray out and see what's underneath. Curiosity may kill this cat, but I'd like to risk it."

On that note, she lifted out the top tray holding the dress and papers and set it aside on the adjacent armchair.

The first thing they saw were lumps of linens. Tablecloths, napkins, and old newspapers had been used to wrap an assortment of dishes and glassware. They also uncovered a handsome mantel clock packed in an embroidered pillowcase edged with crocheted lace.

As soon as Hugh saw it, he recognized it as something that used to sit on the sideboard in the living room of the old house.

"I guess some people would consider it a keepsake, but I don't think it worked right when I was at home," he remarked.

"A jeweller would be able to tell if it's fixable. It deserves at least that much assessment." Ellie returned the few pieces she had disturbed to the trunk and laid the top tray back into place.

She closed the lid.

"It's getting pretty late," said Ellie, noting Hugh's melancholy expression. "I agree that your mom's handwritten papers could be a hot potato, given your family history. We'll look at them tomorrow… or whenever we feel up to it. Let's get some rest."

The night passed fitfully for Ellie. Partly, it was because her bladder needed emptying more than once. Partly, it was because the sheaf of papers still resting on top of everything else in the trunk seemed so foreboding. Hugh lay beside her, sleeping peacefully as any contented, well-loved child. Those papers had everything to do with him and nothing with her, but she was the one losing sleep over them. There was nothing logical or fair in that, she reasoned, but that didn't stop her from tossing and turning and imagining any number of shocking revelations the pages might contain.

About seven in the morning, while it was still dark, Ellie stole out of bed, wrapped herself in her hot pink housecoat and tiptoed into the kitchen. She took the time to fix an extra-large mug of café mocha. While the coffee brewed, she retrieved the thin sheaf of papers from the trunk and laid them on top. She stirred hot chocolate mix into the coffee and quickly scarfed down a granola bar.

She was ready to face whatever Hugh's mother, Alice Hunt-Fischer, had left behind as her final communiqués.

Ellie settled herself in the armchair—and as she read the first page, the expression on her face became quizzical. She fingered through the pages, scanning the contents. It seemed that Alice's writings ended with the most recent on top.

She carefully reversed the order of the papers so they could be read in the chronological sequence in which they seemed to have been written. Between sips from her mug, she solemnly read. Here and there her eyes glistened and she wiped the tears away with the back of her hand.

After she had read each page, Ellie laid them on the trunk, sat back in the chair, and continued to sip her mocha while reflecting deeply.

Just before eight, as the dawn lit up the morning, Hugh exited their bedroom clad in his robe. He appeared to be only half-awake.

"Morning, babe," he croaked and turned to pour himself a mug of strong black coffee. Seeing that Ellie occupied the armchair, he sat heavily on the sofa and drew a long sip of the joe.

Upon noticing the sheaf of handwritten foolscap lying atop the trunk, Hugh turned to her with a questioning look on his face.

Ellie's eyes glistened once more and she sent him her sweetest, most sympathetic yet half-hearted smile.

"What your mother did was something like writing out her last will and testament," she began. "There are three separate statements… or confessions… or letters. It's hard to know exactly what to call them. She acknowledges her great emotional and psychological pain. She also cries out to each of her children. I doubt they were all written on the same day. They are very sad… super apologetic… but ultimately, she wishes each one a good future that's much better than the poor, unhappy life they experienced at home. I would say the one that focuses on you was probably written first and is the most gut-wrenching. She was glad, for your sake, that you left when you did, but it also tore her up something awful and she never got over it. There's a line in there that's likely to produce a lot of guilt…"

Hugh pursed his lips and looked directly at Ellie. "I guess I should man up and read it for myself."

"It will both hurt and bless you, I think," said Ellie sadly. "Remember I'm here for you, sweetheart. But first let me tell you about the other notes."

Hugh nodded grimly.

"There's another sheet explaining about the contents she placed in the trunk. They're a collection of unused gifts from her wedding and the nicer things left behind from your grandparents. She hoped the three of you kids would divvy them up amongst yourselves in remembrance of her. She anticipated that the trunk might fall into a stranger's hand and asked the would-be owner to locate you guys and turn over the contents instead of keeping them. I thought that was interesting."

Ellie took a deep breath before continuing.

"The topmost letter, if you can call it that, is the strangest. I would say it's like listening to the ramblings of a deranged person. Maybe that's too harsh. Perhaps 'distraught' is closer. She doesn't come right out and say it, but if I didn't know better I'd say she wrote it to say goodbye and that she was somehow planning to end her life and that of your pa."

Hugh suddenly stood, drained his coffee, and took four steps across the room to drop the mug into the sink. When he turned to look at Ellie, his face was hard to read.

"I shouldn't be surprised," he said finally. "I can well imagine life became hopeless for my mother, especially after we were all done with school and gone."

"I'm sorry, love."

"I know," said Hugh just above a whisper. Then he drew himself up and spoke with determination. "Thanks, Ellalujah. I'm braced, thanks to you—my best friend. Let's have breakfast and then I'll deal with it like the adult I'm supposed to be."

Ellie exchanged her sober expression for one lit with a bright smile. "That's my man!" she said, then rose up to squeeze him in a grand hug.

After they had cleared away the breakfast dishes and dressed in day clothes, Hugh returned to his former place on the sofa and picked up the sheaf of papers. None of the items began with "Dear" or noted the date on which they were written. They might have been pages out of her diary, if she had kept one. He began to read.

Not a day goes by that I don't think of my one and only son. He was right to leave and I don't blame him. In a way, it was easier to live with Fred after that because he stayed away from us a lot more. Maybe Fred was afraid of what he'd done to the boy and that the cops would come after him.

But while things were a bit easier in some ways, I cried for missing my Hughie every night. The girls missed him too and for the longest time our house was as quiet as could be. Didn't seem much point in talking. There was nothing to talk about.

It was a happy day for the three of us when Margo got a letter from Hugh. He wrote that he was staying with a good family in Winnipeg, and that he would be finishing his schooling. That was good news and I was mighty relieved. We all were except for Fred. We didn't let on that we heard from Hugh.

After a while we got used to him being gone, but I still imagined him growing tall and handsome and finishing school with good grades that would make me proud. I hoped he would keep writing to us, but I guess he got used to being without us too.

Then Margo graduated and lit out as soon as she could. I couldn't blame her either. There was nothing here for her in these parts and I saw she had ambitions to make something out of herself somewhere far away from here. I hope she will have a good life doing something that makes her happy.

After that, Diane was almost all I ever had for company (I don't count Fred as being company) and after she graduated and left I thought my heart would just wither up and die. No one to talk to. I even thought about going over to visit with Lizzie Bauman but didn't risk it. You never know when Fred will show up and I dare not be away when he does.

How did I become a prisoner in my own house? But I did. I don't have a reason to live anymore, but I'm too afraid to hurt myself. Round and round my thinking goes. I get such painful headaches sometimes.

Oh Hugh, my boy, you must be working at a good job by now. Won't you think of me and come and take me away from here? Your pa doesn't hit me much anymore. But when he does, well, it just gets worse and worse. He's making liquor now and is drunk most of the time. It's like living with Jekyll and Hyde.

Remember that story, Hugh boy? I hope you don't drink, Hughie. It's the ruination of a life, you should know that.

You were such a handsome lad. I so wish I could lay eyes on you now. Fact is, I was a poor mama to you. I didn't have the courage to stand up for you against your pa. Can you find it in your heart to forgive me, son? I am terribly sorry.

Fact is I'm still a coward. Do you ever think of me? Do you ever wonder how it is back here? I think of you every day. I wonder if you found a good, pretty woman to marry and if you have little ones. Will I ever see my grandchildren? Are you still in Winnipeg? I expect so. People seem to like the city more than the country and little places. In my dreams, I run away to Winnipeg to find you. And when I do, you don't recognize me and say you have no mama. But you do.

Don't forget you have a mama, Hughie. Help me run away too.

"You were right. It hurts to read this," admitted Hugh, faltering, his eyes swimming with tears. "And she's right. I got used to being away from them all and it became an out of sight, out of mind kind of thing. It's a terrible son who forgets his mother. I am that terrible, selfish son."

"You weren't emotionally healthy yourself, don't forget," countered Ellie. "And don't fail to remember that you were trying to stay out from under your father's radar for their sake as well as yours. With no communication going on, how could you have known?"

"That's just it. I should have communicated. Like I told you, Margo became the go-between to make sure Pa never got wind of my whereabouts."

"I believe your mother knew that. But since she had no faith or hope in God, she fantasized hope in you."

"I suppose that makes sense, but it doesn't help me to feel better," maintained Hugh.

He turned back to the sheaf of his mother's writings. He scanned the items that focused on his sisters. They held a certain similarity to the first piece he'd read, but they were shorter and centred on imagining her daughters' independent lives away from home. Hugh wasn't mentioned.

As Ellie had explained, another note explained the contents of the trunk. It was packed with all the items in the house that Alice had felt were of some value to be shared between the three siblings. Hugh read that one dispassionately.

"I can maybe see Diane having an interest in some of the dishes, but not Margo," he remarked when he was through. "She's not one for old things."

"Agreed. But then again, we hardly know what's all in there. We... er... you get to choose some things as well."

"True, but... well, never mind. We can discuss that another time." Hugh set down the foolscap, keeping only the last, water-puckered note in his hands.

"That one won't be easy to take," warned Ellie quietly.

"I may as well face all the music at once," he muttered. "No sense in dragging things out."

As Hugh began to read, his face settled into a continual frown.

> I have to end this. It's impossible to go on. My bruises have so many colours they're kind of pretty. Some of them still hurt. No one remembers me. I might as well be dead. Dead sounds good. To sleep and never wake up sounds like heaven. Ha. That's funny. So many people think heaven is somewhere up in the clouds but they're wrong. It's to sleep and never dream or wake up. He's come back. I have to hide this.
>
> He's gone again. Gonna meet up with his buddies at the hotel bar, I expect. Anyway Fred said he

would take me to the big store in Swan tomorrow to get some groceries. There's no more oatmeal and the flour is low. Almost all the salt is gone too.

I have a plan. I will get dressed up nice to go to town. But if there is a God (I don't actually believe there is) and if he will help me to be brave just this once, neither Fred or me will come back. It will be all over and I can sleep in peace forever. And if there is a hell (I hope there is one) then Fred can roast in it forever. The flames will keep him distracted and he won't come after me no more. Ha, I'll have the last laugh, Fred.

Hugh has forgotten me. Margo is ashamed of me. I suppose Diane thinks I'm managing like I always have. I should have listened to the folks and Gertie all those years ago. They were right about the likes of Fred. I was stubborn and blind and foolish. Well, Gertie, I slept in the bed I made for myself like you said and now I've done my time. Paid the price. Gonna do one brave thing before I sleep and fade away. Lord help me not to fail.

When Hugh had finished reading that final note, he set it down on top of the others on the trunk and leaned back into the couch. He closed his eyes and entwined his fingers across his chest.

Ellie, worried that he was in great emotional pain, left the armchair to sit next to him. She put her head on his shoulder and covered his arms with her own. He accepted her loving embrace, taking encouragement and strength from it, but he remained quiet for several minutes.

Finally Ellie broke the silence.

"Talk to me, please," she begged. "Tell me what you're thinking."

"I've got a rotation of thoughts circling around in my head." Hugh blew out a sigh. "One is what my mother so clearly pointed out: I did absolutely nothing to rescue her or my sisters from the abusive life they were living with Pa. I spent the fourteen years away from them nursing my wounds and selfishly seeing myself as the only hard-done-by victim in this sickly predicament. Another thought is that my mom got it wrong. I didn't exactly forget all about her. It was closer to what she supposed about Diane… I assumed she was managing to eke out some kind of bearable life for herself, even after we were all grown and gone." He paused, then continued thoughtfully. "I've also been musing about the way they died. The report cited a single vehicle accident, cause unknown. This note strongly suggests that Ma did something to trigger it."

"That's how I read it, too."

They sat quietly, each occupied with their own thoughts.

"You know, something is hugely different," said Hugh after a while. "If I had read these letters just last summer, I'd have gotten mad enough to explode or hit something. Maybe even hurt someone. But all I feel is sadness. Some guilt, too, but the Lord will help me sort that out. A miracle has happened. The Lord has truly delivered me from my deep, perpetual anger. I'm experiencing the proof of it and it's awesome. God has indeed changed my life, made me a new creation, and it's all thanks to you, Ella Rose Bauman."

"Fischer," added Ellie with a smile.

"Seriously. I like how Michael W. Smith sings about it in the words of his song, *Amazing Grace*."

"Me too."

"My only regret now is that I didn't know this a long time ago. Then I could have done a right job of rescuing my mother—not just from a miserable life with Pa, but to tell her about deliverance from the chains of sin and unbelief as well."

"I understand, but I hope you won't dwell there," Ellie said. "There's nothing left to do now but trust Jesus to deal fittingly with the past.

He's our saviour, our healer, and also our *righteous* judge. He'll handle everything right." She took a deep breath. "I suppose you'll want to call your sisters to come over and go through the rest of the trunk?"

"Eventually. But it won't be today. Those things have been set aside for a long while. A time longer won't make any difference."

Nine

TWO WEEKS HAD passed since Margo began her new part-time job at the café in Minitonas, assisting Mrs. Illichman as the new prep girl. It didn't take long before the owners, Bev and Alan Benson, deemed her a valuable employee. She came to work on time, followed instructions, and worked with efficiency, doing a good job in the process. Although not sullen, Margo wasn't overly chatty, which contributed to her good work ethic. Her job description included washing dishes as well as pots and pans. It seemed a good fit for both employer and employee.

Payday came on Mondays following the two-week period just before. Margo received her first paycheque with mixed feelings. On the one hand, it felt so good to have money she had validly earned once more. On the other hand, it was a paltry sum, reflecting part-time hours at minimum wage.

Nevertheless, after she was done for the day, instead of going directly back to the Wirts' house, she first stopped in at the local bank and opened an account.

A bit later, she found Muriel preparing a shepherd's pie for their supper. As usual, the kitchen smelled wonderful.

"Bev kept you longer today, did she?" asked Muriel while spreading a mix of chopped vegetables over the gravy-laden hamburger already lining the bottom of a casserole dish.

Margo slumped into the nearest kitchen chair. "No, I opened an account at the bank before coming home. I got my first paycheck."

"Good for you!" Muriel looked up and saw Margo's dejected expression. "Not so good...?"

"Here's the thing," began Margo gloomily. "I like working at the café, but it doesn't pay well enough for me to hope to support myself, especially at part-time hours. I'll have to quit and find something that's full-time and pays better or else find another part-time job in the afternoons. Seeing as I'm stuck in Minitonas, I can't imagine the prospects are good. If only I had my car... I might be able to land a better job in Swan River."

"I see your difficulty. Have you talked with the Bensons? They may take you on full-time if you explained your situation. I happen to know Bev is very pleased with you thus far. Good help is hard to find, so I believe she'll try to accommodate your needs."

Margo raised her eyebrows. "And how do you know this?"

"I'm well-acquainted with Mrs. Illichman, and Bev too. They've both expressed what a good worker you are."

"Really?" said Margo with a note of pleasure. "I do try to be a good help."

"And it's been noticed. Keep up the good work. A good reputation is worth a lot."

That last comment stung Margo privately, but she didn't let on about the sudden wash of shame she felt. Instead she moved to another line of discussion.

"It's time I thought about living on my own again," said Margo. "I need to be self-supporting. I can't be taking advantage of your good graces forever."

"Be assured, neither Leland or I are pushing you out." Muriel then paused. "I know of a situation... but I'm not sure it would be of interest to you."

"Let's hear it."

With the shepherd's pie now assembled, Muriel popped it into the oven, wiped her hands on her apron, and sat at the kitchen table across from Margo.

"Last week, I believe it was Thursday morning, I was paid a visit by Lydia Harms' two daughters. Do you remember Lydia Harms?" asked Muriel.

Margo shook her head.

"She's one of the seniors I pop in to check on when I go for my walks, just to make sure everything is well with her."

"Right," said Margo with a nod. "I remember you doing that."

"Both daughters are married and have children, and even a couple of grandchildren as I recall. Katie, the elder one, lives out at Kenora, Ontario and Lorraine, the younger sister, lives in Alberta at Red Deer. They came in to visit with each other and their mother last week. Lydia isn't able to keep up with living on her own like she used to. Her eyes are poor and arthritis has claimed some of her fingers and lower back. Keeping the house clean as it should be and preparing proper meals for herself have become an issue. However, Lydia won't hear of moving into a seniors care facility. She's absolutely adamant, which is why they came to me.

"Of course, it never does to force people to do things against their will. They wondered if I knew of anyone suitable who might live with their mother as a paying boarder at reasonable rates, and also participate in keeping the place clean and preparing wholesome meals. Lydia has minimal funds. That's why it would be ideal to charge only a modest boarder fee, to cover the cost of groceries and a portion of the energy and telephone costs. Not many people look for room and board around here. On top of that, partially looking after a senior woman wouldn't be an attractive situation for most. Yet for the right person, it's an opportunity of sorts."

"You're right," agreed Margo. "It's not a one-size-fits-all possibility. But... I don't think I should refuse to look into it. I'd like to meet this Lydia Harms... you know, check her out. If we like each other, it just might turn out to be a win-win situation."

Muriel let out a great sigh. "You do surprise me, young lady. I didn't think it was the kind of arrangement that would interest you."

They planned to call on the octogenarian the following afternoon for a visit over a cup of tea. It wasn't a long walk from the Wirts' Fourth Avenue residence to her tiny bungalow on Third Avenue. Soon after they knocked on the commonly used back door, they heard the padding of slippered feet coming to let them in.

Muriel hadn't described Lydia's appearance and Margo hadn't thought to ask. Upon seeing the comical figure of Lydia Harms, Margo turned her face aside to control herself from laughing outright.

Mrs. Harms kept her white hair pulled back in a tightly wound bun at the nape of her neck. The top was loose enough to admit a single wave. A multitude of short hairs stuck out, mostly along each side of her face, producing the effect of an airy lion's mane. A pair of wire-rimmed reading glasses lay parked on top of her head. Bright, steely blue eyes peered out from a soft, wrinkled face that included a few coarse hairs, distinctly noticeable, under her nose and on her chin.

Lydia's stature was short, not more than five feet tall, and she had the plump shape of a traditional grandmother. She wore a clean but faded apron over a chintz housedress. A blue, unbuttoned cardigan covered her arms. Her hands, somewhat gnarled, bore several liver spots. Beige leotards clothed her legs, which appeared as thin as a bird's. Slouched around her ankles were men's grey work socks, the kind that had white toes and heels and a red strip beneath a white band. These were tucked in well-worn, moccasin-like slippers that fit loosely, creating a clapping sound when she shuffled across the floor.

Cute was the word Margo thought of when she and Muriel were invited inside.

"So nice of you to think of spending a little time with an old hen like me," prattled Lydia in the kind of shaky voice often characteristic of seniors.

"It's a delight, for our part," Muriel assured her. "I've brought some banana bread we made recently, so the flavour should be ripe and moist."

"No need, but that's awful nice of you." Lydia accepted the small loaf. "My daughters were here last week. And before they left, they filled up the fridge and icebox. I b'lieve I have enough food to last me until the second coming!"

Muriel chuckled. "Does that mean the good Lord has shared the secret date with you?"

"No, He hasn't, not even in a dream," tittered Lydia before turning her sights on Margo. "So who have you brought with you? I don't b'lieve I know this young lady."

"This is my friend, Margo Owens," introduced Muriel. "She's been staying with us since January. Now she's thinking of making her home in Minitonas."

"Iz zat so?" Lydia took another appraising look at Margo. "Where did you live before?"

"I moved here from Dauphin," answered Margo politely.

"Dauphin, hey? I used to know someone from there. But that was many years ago. Could be dead now."

She ushered the two women into her compact, eat-in kitchen and beyond to the small living room.

Although Margo hadn't seen the interior of many houses over the years, she instinctively understood, generally speaking, that the way women arranged their homes suggested a lot, not only about their taste but also about their personality.

She wasn't sure what this place represented about Lydia, however. The living room was crammed with furniture lining every wall as close as beads on a string. A riot of assorted colours assaulted the senses, and every surface was cluttered with ornaments, collectibles, and framed photographs. A circular shelf unit constructed from black metal rods stood in front of the picture window; it showcased a large Christmas cactus and at least a half-dozen African violets. An upright piano, ornamentally carved, dominated the room. The turquoise sofa usurped most of the wall opposite, and its armchair mate took up the corner between the plant shelf and piano, obstructing the seldom-used front door. An old, glass-doored cabinet displayed a large collection of colourful bird figurines, numerous pairs of salt and pepper shakers, and a small set of fine china. A predominantly pink wingchair with a smattering of aqua highlights stood opposite a television parked in the far corner. Beside this chair rested a side table and lamp bearing an untidy array of miscellany, including a tissue box, Bible, and magnifying glass. A short bookshelf had been squeezed in between the side table and cabinet, and a coffee table in front of the sofa made for narrow aisles to traverse the room.

Margo took a seat in the armchair while Muriel seated herself on the sofa nearest to Lydia, who took possession of the wingchair, obviously her centre of operations in the house.

"Have you been cleaning, Lydia?" asked Muriel cheerily. "Do I discern the scent of household cleaners?"

"Well now, you prob'ly do," said Lydia. "Katie and Lorraine tore apart the house washing all the walls down and windas and curtains. Said they were going to do an early spring cleaning for me. They wanted to paint the walls in here and the kitchen, too, but I put my foot down on that. I like my mauve walls and I think my yellow kitchen is cheerful. But they washed out all the kitchen cupboards and took away lots of things they claimed were outdated. So if it seems a little bare in here, it's because my girls went through the place like a hurricane. It was all I could do to keep them from cleaning me out altogether!"

Margo raised her eyebrows at this but out of courtesy made no comment.

"I see you've managed to retain your favourite collections," acknowledged Muriel. "Tell me, Lydia, how are you feeling? Is the cold weather hard on your arthritis?"

"Well now, some days are better than others, but on the whole I'm in good shape for the shape I'm in." Lydia smiled at her own wit. "I won't complain. There's others who suffer much worse than me. I'm thankful for the Lord's care. I have everything I need and more."

"That's a wonderful attitude, sister."

"Good gracious! Where are my manners?" expostulated Lydia. "I should have put the kettle on first thing and here I am waxing on and not looking after my company. I'd forget my head if it wasn't attached!"

"Now, now, don't you worry none. Let me get it." Muriel got her feet. "You stay put and tell Margo about yourself. After all, you've led an interesting life and I'm sure she would enjoy hearing about it. I know where the kettle is."

"That's good of you, Mrs. Wirt." Lydia's eyes followed the pastor's wife as she got up and returned to the kitchen. "The teabags are in the cannister on the counter marked TEA!"

Lydia turned her attention to Margo, poised sedately across the room.

"What brought you to Minitonas?" asked Lydia directly.

"A major change in life circumstances," answered Margo vaguely before firing back a question of her own. "Have you always lived in this town?"

"Not quite. I grew up in Renwer, which isn't so very far from here. My husband brought me here shortly after we were wed. He got on with the railway and worked at that for a few years. Later he went to work in the lumberyard, which suited him much better. Good gracious, but that was a long time ago."

Margo leaned forward, interested. "How long have you been alone?"

"My Henry passed eleven years ago. He was a good man, humble and kind, and a good father. I'm used to him being gone, but I still miss him. Where are your parents? Dauphin, I suppose."

"My parents died in a motor vehicle accident three and a half years ago," answered Margo without emotion.

"How unfortunate. I'm sorry for your loss."

Muriel re-entered the living room bearing a plate of sliced banana bread and set it on the coffee table. "I can serve tea, if you'll tell me where you've hidden a tray."

"It should be lying on top of the refrigerator." Lydia shifted in her chair. "If it's not there, then Katie or Lorraine have put it elsewhere, in which case your guess is as good as mine."

Muriel found it as suggested and soon returned with the tray on which three cups and saucers, full of hot tea, emitted swirling columns of steam.

As the conversation continued, they heard about Lydia's love of gardening, her career teaching a one-room school for two years before marrying the ten-years-her-senior Henry Harms, and the history of the house she yet lived in, which was built by her husband while he was employed at the lumberyard. They also learned she had once been a good pianist who played for the church congregation and taught piano lessons to children, had served with the Ladies Aid Society, and after that had become a member of the Minitonas Women's Institute.

After Henry died, she'd lost interest in participating in community committees, though. She no longer possessed the drive and energy for such things.

"It's time to let the younger people step up and put in their two cents," added Lydia firmly. "I've done my time."

"So what did you think?" asked Muriel after she and Margo had left.

"I think she's a hoot," replied Margo. "She's very direct, to the point of being nosy, but somehow it doesn't get under my skin. She's cute and funny and doesn't realize it. I like her… and I'm going to seriously consider boarding with her."

∽

Pursuant to Muriel's advice, Margo asked her boss for more hours. At first Bev demurred, although she later relented. Margo could work more if she was willing to clean, not only in the kitchen but in the café itself. She also was willing to train Margo in the art of serving tables, so there would be a backup when their regular waitress was ill or resigned.

Margo left the café a happier girl.

On the way back to Wirts' place, she stopped in to see Lydia.

"Come in!" called Lydia in a shrill voice.

Margo let herself in and upon entering the kitchen saw Lydia standing on a kitchen chair, trying to look through some items on the topmost shelf of a kitchen cabinet. Margo hurried to steady the chair, since it appeared Lydia was reaching farther than was safe.

"Can I help you get whatever it is you want?" asked Margo breathlessly.

"I don't know if it's up here." Lydia sounded cross. "Since my girls overhauled my kitchen, I can't find anything. Probably got thrown out. They complained I saved too many empty containers and kept cracked dishes that ought to be gotten rid of. 'Let things go, Mother,' they said. I was told I've become a hoarder. I don't believe 'not wasting' is hoarding."

Lydia panted as she slowly got down from the chair. After she had safely stepped aside, Margo got up onto the chair.

"Okay, what am I looking for?" asked the younger woman, peering into the cupboard.

"Well now, just a minute here… Oh, for Pete's sake… if that don't beat all. It appears I've clean forgotten what I was after. I'm sure it will come to me as soon as I sit down," said Lydia sheepishly. "Memory isn't in the brain, you know. It's in your behind…"

$\sim$

Margo giggled all the way back to the Wirts' place.

"Lydia's daughters are right," declared Margo to Muriel after she had regaled the story of her encounter with Lydia. "She shouldn't be left too long on her own. I think I can work at the café and look after her, too."

"You're sure?" pressed Muriel. "Seniors can be an utter delight, as well as a trial. It's well known how set in their ways they can be. Even so, they should have our deepest respect and be treated with kindness. How will you handle it when your wills collide?"

"I understand and I'm not worried. Dealing with difficult customers was something we had to cope with quite often at the fashion shop. I've learned a thing or two about diplomacy that should come in handy if necessary."

~

A flurry of phone calls ensued. Muriel telephoned Lydia's eldest daughter, Katie. Katie then contacted her sister. The siblings started a conference call and interviewed Margo over the phone. When everyone's questions were asked and answered, expectations clarified, and various details agreed to, it was determined that Margo should go to live with Lydia as both boarder and assistant.

"Has your mother already agreed to all this?" Muriel asked.

There was a long pause.

"I'll call back after discussing it with her," Katie said.

A half-hour later, Katie exuberantly invited Margo to take up residence at the Harms house that very weekend. As soon as Lydia had understood it was Margo who had applied to board with her, she had been most happy to oblige. In fact, the very air had seemed to sparkle with happiness all around.

~

On Saturday morning, Margo repacked her large travel bag, then cleaned and prepared the guestroom so it was ready for its next occupier. Muriel appreciated her thoughtfulness.

In the afternoon, she unpacked the same piece of luggage in the spare room of Lydia Harm's house. It occurred to her that since she was putting down roots in Minitonas, having no other ready options, she ought to retrieve more of her clothing from Hugh and Ellie's storage shed. She would look into that.

When the last item was hung in the closet, Margo folded and then slid the bag under the bed. As she sat on its edge, she was aware that she had very mixed feelings. On the one hand, she anticipated that living with Lydia would begin a new chapter in her life. On the other hand, having previously lived independently, she couldn't help but reflect on the reality of her near destitution.

A single tear slid down one cheek.

"Buck up, girl," Margo scolded herself. "You're safe and you're warm. You'll begin again a wiser woman. Hugh did it and now he's doing well. So will you."

Ten

"**WHAT SHOULD WE** say to the woman who organized this luncheon and is the last one to get here?" asked Darcey amiably to her neighbour and friend.

Cynthia sat across from her in their favourite booth at the front of the café next to the window that looked out onto the street.

"She's only ten minutes late," Cynthia remarked. "Maybe something came up."

They ordered coffees to sip while waiting for Ellie to make her appearance. As soon as the mugs were brought to the table, the café door opened and the third member of their party blew in with a rush.

Seeing her friends already occupying a booth, Ellie broke into a wide but apologetic smile and slid in next to Cynthia.

"Sorry I'm late," panted Ellie breathlessly. "I lost track of time."

"Do tell," said Darcey. "What could so occupy your attention that you would fail to remember a luncheon with your best friends… and that you organized, I might add?"

"Dreaming and planning our future family home," replied Ellie.

She would have added to her story had not the waitress come by to take their order. Darcey and Ellie ordered the noon special—corn chowder and a fresh roll—but Cynthia merely asked for dry toast. Darcey stared at Cynthia hard and long, obviously waiting for an explanation.

Cynthia squirmed and looked away trying to hide a tell-tale smile.

"The only time I eat dry toast for lunch, and maybe supper too, is when I'm newly pregnant," observed Darcey with a knowing look. "Have you got something to tell us, Ms. Cynthia?"

"Oh Darcey!" exclaimed Cynthia in mock annoyance. "I was going to tell you both, but later. So, yes, I'm expecting and the morning sickness doesn't exactly stop at noon. If it doesn't end soon... then this isn't the fun ride I thought it would be."

"Congratulations!" exuded Ellie. "When are you due?"

"Mid-September."

"Nice, but you may find summer miserable for getting through the last trimester," Darcey noted with the voice of experience. "How did Brent react when you told him?"

Cynthia shrugged. "Happy. Scared. Back to happy. Then scared again."

"That's typical for first babes, I think," said Darcey. "What's he scared of?"

"Scared we can't afford it. Scared he won't be a good parent. Worries the baby will arrive flawed... all kinds of silly apprehensions." Cynthia faltered. "And I'm temperamental, too. I'm so happy and yet I cry at the drop of a pin."

Suddenly, her eyes started welling up in tears.

"You poor dear." Ellie reached over to pat her friend's arm. "I'm sure it will pass."

Darcey snorted lightly. "It usually passes after three or four months. Then you'll feel great until the ninth month. That's when you feel as big as an elephant, waddle like a duck, and won't recognize yourself in the mirror because of all your physical distortions from the eyebrows down."

"I'm sure that was meant to encourage me," said Cynthia dryly.

"It very much is." Darcey smirked. "Because soon after that you'll deliver the child with enough pain to wish you could simply die and go live with Jesus. And then the nurse will put the wee thing in your arm—or in my case, not very wee—and you'll fall instantly in love with complete amnesia for what you just endured to bring forth the fruit of your womb. Before you leave the maternity ward, you'll be wanting to discuss with your husband how soon you can work on the next one. Trust me, I know how this goes."

Ellie and Cynthia giggled along as Darcey expounded on the joys and travails of childbearing.

With their meals delivered, the subject changed. The women asked Darcey what was new.

"Abby's cut more teeth and crawls herself into all kinds of trouble," Darcey replied. "Carrie is acing Kindergarten and Lainey can talk the hindleg off a donkey."

Cynthia and Ellie looked at each other and then back at Darcey in perfect synchronization.

"We weren't asking about your daughters. We were asking about you," said Ellie.

"Oops, I guess there is a difference. Well, let's see. I tried a new recipe last Friday that none of us were impressed with. Won't be making that again. Tony built a beautiful chest to keep the toys in after 7:00 p.m. There might be a playmate in the oven for Cynthia's baby. And I ordered some bigger slacks from the Sears catalogue this morning, which was no fun. I may be losing my girlish hourglass figure forever, and I do mind, in case you're wondering," said Darcey in her typically blunt style.

"Wait a minute," interjected Ellie. "Did you just say you're pregnant again?"

"Shhhh," Darcey held a finger over her mouth. "I'm not sure yet. I'm late, but I haven't been to my doctor to confirm it."

"That would be number four for you," said Cynthia, rather awed.

"I do believe Tony will keep them coming at least until he gets a son. He's not scared of begetting more kids. His was a family of nine and he believes the more the merrier." Darcey looked across the table. "What about you, Ellie? I thought you were aiming to be in a family way."

"I am… but so far it hasn't happened," she admitted freely and then added, "Not for lack of trying."

Darcey sighed. "Ahh, well, you're not married long. It probably won't be much longer until you're puking up your breakfast and trying to subsist on dry toast yourself."

"I want to know about the house plans you're drawing," Cynthia said to Ellie. "Did you bring them with you?"

"No. I never thought of it," replied Ellie. "I've been working at it since January and I think I've finally got it nailed down to something *both* Hugh and I are happy with."

"Sounds like you've had a few arguments," intoned Darcey.

"I wouldn't go straight to *arguments*, but it has taken a while to satisfy each of our wants and needs."

"What does Hugh want, and what do you want that calls for compromise?" asked Cynthia.

"That's easy. I want a big house with beautiful character in the details, like something from the Victorian period or the grand old houses in England and Europe. Hugh wants simple, and not too big because he doesn't want a large mortgage. I get it, but I don't want the house to be lacking in style, and fancy details cost extra. So we've had a few intense discussions."

"Describe your plans to me," bade Cynthia. "It's so exciting that you get to build your dream home."

"Well, that's just it," said Ellie. "We only get to do this once, so I want it to suit all the stages of our lives from newlyweds to retirees. And I want to love it, to enjoy every room for its function and beauty."

She reached for a paper napkin and began to draw lines to represent the various rooms. All three women bent their heads together as Ellie explained the two-storey floorplan.

"I love it!" chimed Cynthia. "The furniture you have so far will look wonderful in it."

"Of that I have no doubt," agreed Ellie. "What I must do now is get a rough estimate from a builder. If it fits within the budget Hugh set— which, by the way, is based solely on his income—then I can get the plans drawn up. If not, I guess I keep whittling away at it."

"Why just on Hugh's income?" asked Cynthia perplexed.

"Because once our babies start coming, I'll reduce my working hours at the hospital to casual for the sake of maintaining my license. But the contribution to the household budget will be negligible. I don't want to work just to hand over my earnings to a babysitter. And I want to be the mama who raises my children, even in this age of loud feminism."

"I get that totally," Darcey said. "The budget at our place is set based on Tony's income as well. If I bring in a few extra dollars from crafting or whatever, it's considered gravy that can be put towards something we want. As for the build, Hugh's right. You see that, don't you? I understand the importance of beauty, but it has to be subject to financial affordability. Good for Hugh to force you to make those two principles come together neatly. Even Jesus confirmed the principle of estimating the cost before beginning to build a tower."[2]

"I know, I know," granted Ellie. "It's what makes us a good pair. I'm the dreamer and visionary, while he's the practical implementer. He works out if it can be done as envisioned. But sometimes it seems like he wants to skip the beauty aspect altogether. He balks at bay windows or grand staircases."

"Is it a difference of preference, do you think?" asked Cynthia. "What I consider beautiful and what Brent thinks is lovely are often two different things. I favour art deco while he prefers traditional. Usually he yields to me, though." She chuckled. "It boils down to 'If mama ain't happy, ain't nobody happy.'"

"That's an indisputable truth!" confirmed Darcey with conviction.

"Hugh doesn't seem to have much of a gift for imagining how something will look before it comes together," Ellie said. "But he likes everything I've done, so I don't think his reservations are about that. I think he fears money problems more than anything else. Right now he's better off than he's ever been in his life and he wants to make sure it stays that way. No backsliding allowed if it depends on us."

"I don't mean to be nosy, but are you in danger of that?" asked Cynthia.

---

[2] Luke 14.

"No. I don't think so. It's an attitude of prevention. I'm sure it comes from his youth. He grew up poor and it's made an indelible effect on money matters ever since."

"Plus he's still new in the faith," added Darcey. "Practical wisdom is good and necessary; after that, we trust the Lord with our needs. He'll come to it and you'll help him get there, Ellie. You've both got good heads. You'll work it out right, I'm sure."

"What about your holiday?" asked Cynthia. "I mean your honeymoon. Have you made travel plans?"

"The travel agent has our details, but she hasn't finalized things yet. We intend to go to Niagara and the Toronto area for a week or so, but we're not sure when is the optimal time. Hugh wants to go as soon as the snow has gone in April, because of his plans to put up his new shop and Quonset this spring. He wants the build to begin the day after the frost has gone out of the ground, since the project will begin with pouring concrete floors and foundations. But I want to go when the magnolia trees are in bloom, which is usually May, so…"

"Stick to your guns, girl." Darcey was emphatic. "The building projects will always be here. Anyway, spring is a crapshoot for the kind of weather one needs to pour cement. Your holiday to Niagara is a rare event. Even Hugh should see that. Do you want me to talk to him? You know, set him straight on a few things?"

"Thanks, but no thanks, Darcey dear," answered Ellie. "He would see that as poking your nose into what's not your business. We'll work it out. I told him we could get my brother Rob to supervise some jobs if it really meant missing steps that would otherwise get seriously delayed by our absence. He'll come round. He just needs a bit of time to think it out."

Cynthia gazed out at the street, looking philosophical. "Marriage… strange, isn't it, that such wonderful and satisfying companionship also comes with clashes that strain the vows with which we promised to stay together for life?"

"True enough," said Ellie. "My Aunt Ruth would say that it serves a good purpose, though. If two people always agree on everything, one of them is unnecessary. It's more like steel sharpening steel. And of course friction isn't pleasant… until you get to the right conclusion."

"I remember reading some author write that disagreements, and even fighting, is inevitable in marriage. The trick is to do it right so the relationship remains intact," appended Darcey. "I daresay Tony and I have worked out the bugs in our partnership so serious disagreements are rare. They usually come as a result of some underlying worry."

"Us too," agreed Cynthia. "Brent and I have learned each other's personalities so well that our disagreements don't come around too often. Lately it's more about my unpredictable, moody feelings. I'm the problem, not Brent. He's just trying to make sense of his new, fickle wife."

Ellie looked wistful. "Obviously you two are way ahead of Hugh and me. But I'm sure we'll get there. He really is my very own Prince Charming after all is said and done."

"Oh please! It's not necessary to go all mushy and maudlin." Darcey rolled her eyes. "Let's keep it realistic."

The waitress came by just then and carried away their empty dishes. She returned with a steaming pot and asked, "More coffee, anyone?"

Ellie and Darcey placed their mugs near the edge of the table so she could refill them easily. The waitress then looked up questioningly at Cynthia.

Cynthia eyed her nearly full mug. "No, thank you. It's not agreeing with me today. A glass of cold water would be great, when you get a minute."

"How about dessert?" asked the waitress.

"Not for me." Cynthia shook her head. "I'll have another order of dry toast, though."

"Do you want to share a piece of pie?" asked Ellie, directing her question to Darcey.

"Only if you want one bite," she retorted with a chuckle. "It's the only piece of dessert I'm allowing myself this week. I won't be short-changed."

Ellie sighed. "In that case, I'll just have a dish of jelly," she said to the waitress. To her friends, she added, "Feeding Hugh is adding pounds to my own hourglass figure. Ha!"

Soon the waitress returned with a tray bearing everyone's order. The ladies were quiet while she laid out the toast and desserts.

"When does it end?" asked Darcey dolefully as she gazed down at her piece of pie.

Ellie looked up. "When does what end?"

"The all-consuming quest to maintain the lithe and shapely figure of a young woman," her friend answered. "Why can't we just live normally with food and accept the body that comes as a result? Why do we feel it's a mark of womanly success to always look like we're in our twenties? When was it decided that beauty means being thin and curvaceous, like a fashion doll? Who decided that grey hair is automatically ugly... except for men, since apparently it makes them appear distinguished! And why is makeup preferred over a more natural look?"

Ellie and Cynthia exchanged glances.

"She's having one of those days when she gets all philosophical," said Cynthia as if she were having a private word with Ellie. "You just have to help her work through these spells."

"Right. But it's a worthwhile discussion," Ellie said. "Why are we as women so preoccupied with our appearance? Does it come from our men? Our selves? Our culture? And what brought this on, Darcey?"

Darcey was plainly perturbed. "I'm looking at this lovely piece of homemade apple pie and feeling guilty about eating it, because I'm not yet down to my pre-pregnancy weight before Abigail. I wonder if I ever will be again, and I wonder if it matters. I feel like there are a myriad of people out there who would judge me as a tall, fat woman who ought to be discarded because she'd failed to keep her slender, youthful appearance."

"Darcey, you know it's unrealistic to think that we'll cheat the process of time," rejoined Ellie. "You're lovely."

"I'm big."

"You're merely taller than average."

"I'm big and running to fat."

"Nonsense. You look healthy. Skinny women often appear sick-ly, or witchy, which is as bad or worse. I once heard a man say that plump women are more attractive than skinny ones. Most men want some flesh to put their hands on! By the way, what does Tony say about your appearance?"

"I did ask Tony not so long ago if he thought I looked heavy," admitted Darcey.

"And...?" plied Cynthia.

"He said I looked fine. To me, that's code for a little dumpy. But he knew enough not to say so."

"Or it means he is content with your appearance," insisted Ellie.

"Well, I tried to push him. You know, to get him to be more spe-cific. And finally he said, 'Look, I wouldn't like it if you let yourself go and got so heavy you could hardly get around and had to wear a tent instead of a dress. But you're not anything like that, so it's all good. You look like a mother, and there's nothing wrong with that.'" Darcey still hadn't taken a bite of her pie. "Somehow being told I look like a mother doesn't have the same effect as being told I'm still beautiful in his eyes."

"Men!" fumed Ellie. "Maybe I should have a talk with Tony and educate him on the importance of complimenting his wife periodical-ly." She turned to Cynthia. "What about Brent? Does he remember to tell you you're lovely from time to time?"

"Actually, he's pretty good," answered Cynthia. "He does it with cards and sometimes brings me flowers, even when it's not my birth-day or our anniversary."

"Very nice." Ellie turned back to Darcey. "On Tony's behalf, I will tell you that you're beautiful. You're not fat, and you still wouldn't be even if you gained a few more pounds. Actually, I think when he said you looked like a mother he was saying you're especially beautiful because you're committed to bringing up his children healthy, clean, educated, and obedient in a well-kept home and if it wasn't for you, there would be no purpose to life. Tony adores you, even if he hasn't two brain cells to rub together to tell you so."

Cynthia smiled. "I think Ellie's right. You look great. And you're a wonderful mom."

"So it's okay to eat this pie?" asked Darcey, brightening.

"Enjoy every well-deserved bite," assured Ellie.

They each went their separate ways shortly after that, promising to get together again soon. There was nothing as therapeutic as talking things out with other women who were kindred spirits.

Back in her own home, Ellie buzzed around the cottage sweeping the floor, putting away odds and ends, and tidying the kitchen after she prepared supper—a pot roast surrounded by chunks of potato, carrots, and onion.

She had time to do a little reading before Hugh arrived. It was hard to concentrate, however. Her thoughts frequently went back to the discussion with her girlfriends, particularly Darcey's fretting about gaining weight.

~

Hugh's favourite time of day was coming home to his wife and a hot home-cooked meal when the workday was done. It was all he could do to refrain from accelerating on the highway and risking a speeding ticket. What kept him from disobeying the speed limit was the thought of wasting money by having to pay the fine—money that could purchase something useful for his new garage come spring.

At last he turned up Road 150W, the final stretch to reach home. He rolled into his driveway and parked alongside Ellie's car.

After getting out of his truck, Hugh quietly stepped onto the veranda that stretched across the front of their house. Before he went inside, he paused for a moment to practice a little habit he had created in recent weeks. He liked to stop and look through the window and see what was going on within. Outside it was dark, but inside the house was warmly lit with soft lights; the scent of a fine supper met his senses. Ellie was standing at the counter with her back to him, fixing a salad, as he could see by the greens. Music played on their stereo. It was like looking at a TV screen of his life before he came on the scene to participate in it.

Hugh's heart ached with joy. What had he done to deserve such a great home and a beautiful, talented wife to boot? Man, God was good!

He stepped away from the window, ready to take his place in the life transpiring inside.

"Hi, honey!" greeted Ellie cheerfully as Hugh entered.

Hugh hung his jacket on the coat tree, took two steps across the room, and planted a passionate kiss on Ellie's mouth.

"Ummmm, what's that about?" asked Ellie sensually, appreciating the particular musky smell of her man.

"The nights·when I come home to the house with the soft lighting and you're here and supper's on and the music is playing… man. That's what makes life worth living."

"Awww, I love you, too."

They enjoyed their pot roast supper and later snuggled together on the couch, watching a couple of TV shows. Yet sometimes Ellie's thoughts still strayed to the matter of weight gain. The bee in her bonnet was pestering her, so she finally put it to Hugh.

"The bathroom scale tells me I've put on a few pounds since our wedding," she said nonchalantly. "Do you think I look fat?"

Hugh looked at her as if he hadn't heard right. "What?"

"Do you think I look fat?" repeated Ellie.

He did a quick scan of her body before answering. "No, I think you look fine."

Ellie sighed. Darcey was probably right again. If your husband tells you you look fine, it likely means he thinks you're a bit pudgy but doesn't want to get hooked into a discussion about it.

Eleven

GETTING TO KNOW her landlady and part-time charge was Margo's main focus during her first couple of weeks living with Lydia Harms. Adjusting to the woman's peculiarities was sometimes delightful and other times trying, just as Muriel had suggested it might be.

The first supper Lydia proudly prepared for Margo consisted of warmed-up spaghetti (out of a can), cold bologna, sliced cheese, and a few commercially prepared mustard pickles. Margo looked down upon this meal with a forced smile and silently wondered what tasty meal was laid out on the Wirts' supper table.

A few minutes into the meal, Margo piped up with an ingenious suggestion.

"I have a great idea, Lydia," said Margo. "Muriel has taught me quite a lot about cooking, and so has Mrs. Illichman at the café. I propose that I make our supper every other day. That way, you get a break, and I get to stay in practice with what I've learned."

Lydia looked up and away, contemplating Margo's offer.

After a moment, she replied. "Well now, that seems like a fair and square idea. I made my daughters take their turn at cooking and baking back in the day so they would make good wives and mothers after they married. Makes sense to train you for such an eventuality, too. So I'll agree to that." Lydia nodded, then added, "Mind you, you need to think economical like. We'll go grocery shopping together sometime and I'll show you how it's done. When it comes to a budget, it's not for nothing we say 'Look after the pennies and the dollars will take care of themselves.'"

"I understand completely," said Margo. "Muriel Wirt lives by the same philosophy. I'm quite acquainted with that piece of practical wisdom."

"Very good. Of course, that's at least what we would expect of a preacher's wife."

The next afternoon, Margo browned a pound of minced beef in the frying pan along with a chopped onion whilst cooking noodles separately in another pot. With Lydia looking on, she built a layered casserole starting with the browned meat and noodles, adding canned tomatoes, a tin of mushroom soup spread, and finishing with a generous sprinkle of cheddar cheese.

"Well now, I've haven't seen a combination quite like that before, but it sure do look good," declared Lydia. "Mind you, it's likely to take us a week to eat it all, and that we have to do because I don't hold with allowing food to go bad."

"This recipe is delicious, I promise you," returned Margo. "Even reheated as leftovers, it's every bit as good as the day it was made. I predict you'll be sorry when it's all gone."

"Hmmpf." Lydia grunted and then left the kitchen while Margo tidied up.

The octogenarian indubitably had her entrenched habits, such as the strict and specific order she liked to keep certain items. She drank coffee or tea from a mug of the day, and between her hot beverages the mug was parked next to the kettle, which in turn sat beside the toaster, which was set after a pair of tin cannisters marked COFFEE and TEA respectively.

Not yet knowing many of Lydia's habits and preferences, Margo saw the cup sitting on the counter. Upon noticing it wasn't clean, she carefully rinsed it out and returned it to the cupboard. She then sat at the kitchen table with a new pen and notebook she had purchased from the community store and proceeded to write out recipes from memory she had observed from watching Mrs. Illichman prepare her splendid soups, pies, buns, and other savoury dishes from the café's menu. The venerated cook was getting on in years and it was easy to see that retirement would come sooner than later. Margo had taken a notion to record the chef's best dishes so the café would have the means to keep things going. It crossed her mind that she might like to carry on the traditions of Mrs. Illichman and perhaps introduce a few new menu items.

Sometime later, Lydia came into the kitchen to plug in the kettle for an afternoon cup of tea. Automatically she inserted the prongs into the electric socket—and then stood stock still, staring at the counter.

Frowning, she looked to the left and then to the right, then back and forth again.

"What is it, Lydia?" asked Margo, glancing up from the table.

"My cup has vanished!" Lydia sounded highly perplexed. "Now why would anyone want to steal an old woman's cup?"

"If you're talking about the mug you used at breakfast, I washed it out a little while ago and returned it to the cupboard."

"Oh." Lydia retrieved the cup from the cupboard and continued to fix her cup of tea in deafening silence.

"Is there a problem?" ventured Margo delicately.

"I suppose not. Not compared to real problems all over the world like starving children and how everything is getting so expensive, and such like."

Margo prodded. "But something is bothering you..."

"Well now, I ought to tell you that I have my ways and my mug of the day is one of them."

Margo raised her eyebrows. "You have a mug of the day?"

"Yes." Lydia proceeded to explain with a teacher's patience. "Whatever mug I take for coffee with my breakfast is the one I use throughout the day when I make a cuppa whatever else I have a fancy for. And I keep it parked next to the kettle so it's handy. I wash once a day after the evening meal when there's enough dirty dishes to warrant filling the sink with soapy water."

"I see." Margo exhaled with her own exaggerated forbearance. "Is this about conserving water then? I thought we were on the town's water and sewer system."

"Of course we are," agreed Lydia quickly. "Even so, there's no need to be wasteful with it. When I was a girl, we got our water for cooking, washing, and bathing, bringing it in by the pail from an outdoor well. Them were the days, let me tell you, and we learned not to waste water unnecessarily. It's a practical skill the youth don't seem to be taught these days. Everything seems to come so easily to our young people that they don't even appreciate it. They see it as a right, not a privilege to be thankful for. What do you think, Miss Margo? Aren't I right about that?"

"Well… um… I see your point, Lydia," admitted Margo dryly. "However, I also think we've made lots of progress since the days of water wells, kerosene lamps, and woodstoves. We should happily take advantage of those better and easier ways to live. I for one am very thankful we have running water without limit in our homes. I think we live cleaner, healthier lives for it."

Lydia sighed. "Yes, you're right about that. I'm also very grateful for the modern conveniences. The good Lord knows I would have a hard time collecting well water at my age today. But the point I was trying to make was not to be wasteful of food or water or anything else. It's just not right."

Taking her mug of afternoon tea, she padded back to her sweet spot in the living room, leaving Margo to watch her quit the kitchen with an audible sigh.

～

Midweek, the café's regular waitress brought in a half-dozen eight-week-old kittens in a basket, hoping she could find new homes for them from the clientele. They were adorable and had a lot of variety in their colouring. Margo fell in love with one that was mostly white with black splotches and took it back to the Harms' house with her.

"I've brought you a present," chimed Margo to Lydia.

She stood before the elderly lady in the living room with her hands behind her back. Lydia was seated, as she often was, in her pink wingchair trying to read from a book using a magnifying glass.

Lydia set her book aside. "Well now, a present you say. What for? It can't be my birthday yet. That's not until the summer."

"It's a no-occasion present meant to bring you company and a bit of cheer," said Margo, smiling. She brought her hands around and deposited the little kitten onto Lydia's lap.

"Good gracious and for the love of Pete, what have we here!" said Lydia with surprise.

The kitten stretched, yawned, and then began to purr as Lydia held it up for a closer look.

"He's a cute little guy, isn't he?" crooned Margo, happy that so far the kitten hadn't been rejected.

"That he is. But then all animal babies are fetching." Lydia stroked the little thing to its utter pleasure. "The problem is, he'll grow up t'be a big cat that'll claw the furniture, jump on the kitchen counter, and chew at whatever food is laying out there, and meow half the night, too. And that's only the half of it. They shed, you know. Pretty soon there's cat hair all over the furniture and on your clothes and floating in the air so that it gets on your food and you're wiping it off your face so it don't get up your nose. Cats can cause trouble enough to make a preacher swear..."

"I think he's young enough to train," protested Margo gently.

"Well now, cats can't be trained exactly. Dogs will learn to do and not do what you want of them. Not so with a cat. They're stubborn, hoity-toity critters that stay bent on their own ideas for living in a house. So I don't think, Miss Margo, that we ought to keep him."

"I think there's another way to look at this. He's a living critter that needs to take up his place in the world, too. All living creatures have their purpose, don't you think?"

"Well now, are you saying we need a cat? What for? I got no mice in the house." Lydia nuzzled the kitten under her chin; the kitten, in turn, meowed demurely.

"Besides keeping guard against mice ever becoming a problem, he could be like a living teddy bear," countered Margo. "Something to cuddle and to have as company instead of being alone so much."

Lydia replied in a sage tone of voice. "Now you're wrong about that. I'm never alone. The good Lord is with me always and His Spirit lives in my heart. No cat, pretty as this one is, can comfort me like the Saviour does. And that's a fact."

"In that case, can I keep him as *my* cat? I could use a bit of comforting now and again, especially in the evenings when I do feel lonely sometimes. He could be my living teddy bear, if that's okay with you."

Lydia studied Margo over top of her wire-rimmed glasses. "Well now, I suppose if it means that much to you. Mind you, I expect you to take full responsibility for him. That means you buy the cat food and litter and whatever else is claimed housecats need nowadays."

"I will," vowed Margo happily.

"And you do all the cleaning up after him."

"I promise."

"And you make sure he doesn't get into our meat thawing on the counter."

"Yes, ma'am."

Lydia pursed her lips tight. "So whatcha gonna name your cat?"

"I don't know yet," answered Margo, taking it from Lydia's hands. She sat on the sofa adjacent to the pink recliner and petted the kitten, who stretched and purred under her strokes.

"We had a white and black cat like that when I was a girl." Lydia watched the critter with continued interest. "We called him Fritz."

"Fritz..." Margo held the kitten up at eye level. "Are you a Fritz?" The kitten meowed in response. "Then Fritz it is."

Lydia nodded with satisfaction for the chosen name.

Margo stood up. "Do you mind looking after the young Mr. Fritz while I go to the community store and get what I need for cat supplies?"

"Not at all," said Lydia, reaching for the kitten.

While Margo donned her winter coat and boots in the back porch, she heard Lydia cooing and clucking over the little cat.

"Well now, aren't you just the cutest little thing on God's green earth… I mean white earth. It's winter, you know. You'll be a good little cat and behave yourself now, won't you? Gosh darn if you don't look like the spit of my own Fritzy when I was a little girl. Lord, that was a mighty long time ago. Imagine that I still remember it! Maybe he's your great-great-grandpappy…"

Margo left the house smiling and shaking her head.

It was beginning to bother Margo watching Lydia struggle so hard to read the books and magazines she kept near her. Although she wore her glasses, on top of that she had to use a magnifying glass. Even so, it was still slow going for the senior woman.

At last, a big pang of sympathy led Margo to speak up. "Mrs. Harms, how about I read to you so you can give your eyes a rest?"

Lydia paused and looked up at Margo over her spectacles. "Well now, that's very kind of you. I suppose my old eyes could use some time off as you say."

She handed Margo her book, a well-worn copy of the King James Bible. It was opened to the Gospel of Luke, chapter six.

"You can start at the beginning of the chapter," she said in her slightly shaky voice as she passed the book over to Margo with hands that also tremored a little.

Margo received the black-leathered volume. After adjusting herself on the sofa to sit more comfortably, she began to read aloud. To her credit, Lydia listened patiently, albeit painfully, as Margo read through the verses as mechanically as someone might recite the figures of a bank statement.

When she came to the end of the chapter, Margo looked up at Lydia. "Do you want me to keep on reading or is that enough for today?"

Lydia was slow in answering. "That will be enough, thank you," she said in an odd tone of voice that Margo picked up on immediately.

"What's wrong now?"

"Not wrong, exactly. But something I only suspected before is now clear as day to me," said Lydia. "You don't know the author of that book."

"Oh my goodness, of course I don't. It's an ancient book, even older than Shakespeare with all it's ye's, thees and thys," exclaimed Margo, casting her eyes upward.

"That book in your hand may be old, but it's different from every other book, too," shot back Lydia. She sounded more like her normal assertive self. "This is a living book... alive with truth that is both as practical and comforting today as the day the words were put into writing however long ago that was. It's timeless and ageless, and just like Jesus, it's the same yesterday, today, and forever. But never mind that. You don't know the author, which is the good Lord Himself. He breathed His Word through the prophets and godly men of old so we could know Him and what He requires of the people He created. Why, I bet you don't even know that He loves you and longs for you to belong to Him!"

Margo attempted to say something, but Lydia was on a roll. She couldn't get a word in edgewise.

"Being as you've become like a daughter to me, Miss Margo—or maybe a granddaughter, more like—I think I should speak to you freely as a mother would, which is straight up, bare naked truth. No beating around the bush. And what I have to tell you is that this world is not our home. Like an old song says, 'We're just passing through.' But this earthly journey is for the express purpose of making a choice: choose Jesus as your Saviour, on account that you need one, or forever suffer the consequences, which is to burn forever in the lake of fire."

"Like I told Muriel, religion makes no sense to me," interjected Margo. "I think it's all poppycock!"

"Well now, what do you even know about it?" asked Lydia tartly. "I'm thinking you have no idea what is written in the Bible, but you're throwing out the baby with the bathwater anyway. And that is the worst kind of foolishness. Supposin' I was to give you a gift and I gave it to you in a box wrapped up real nice, but instead of opening the present to see what was inside, you just tossed it into the garbage because... because you decided all those kinds of boxes were empty and contained no gift at all. And you decided that without first looking inside. How is that not obvious and outlandish foolishness, tell me?"

Margo opened her mouth to protest, but no sound came out. Lydia's argument had hit a nail on the head and she had no comeback. It was true, after all, that she had never made any effort, ever, to look into the matter of religion, Christianity, or whatever it was called, and therefore had no honest reason for rejecting it.

"Look, I'll admit I don't believe in the Bible like you and the Wirts do. You have your opinion and I have mine. And that's what it's all about: opinions."

"Oh." Lydia suddenly sounded sad. For a moment, neither of them said anything. The air in the room felt awkward. "So you have an opinion about something you know nothing about. Well, I guess I know what my purpose is in my old age while I still have breath."

Lydia rose stiffly out of her chair.

"I'm afraid to ask, but... what would that be?" asked Margo, truly curious.

"To pray for you, that's what." Lydia seemed annoyed. "I'm going to pray that the Spirit of God will convict you of your sinful condition. And I'm going to pray that the hound of Heaven will chase you and nip at your heels until you're exhausted with your carnal life and turn to Him who alone can save you."

"That doesn't sound very nice," said Margo wryly.

"On the contrary, it's an act of love." Having risen, Lydia turned to go in the direction of her bedroom. Then she paused and turned again to look at Margo. "I told you true. I've come to love you like one of my own granddaughters. And the idea that you might not be with me in eternity... well, the pain in my breast is almost more than I can bear. So I will pray that you come to see the light and not resist it."

After that she padded off to her bedroom and closed the door while Margo stared after her without another word, stunned that Lydia had so neatly nailed her for rejecting the Bible, and all things to do with God, on ignorance.

⌒

"Coming!" cried Muriel as she raced across the house as fast as she could. Whoever was ringing the doorbell was rather insistent and impatient about it. "Why Margo! What a surprise. Is everything all right?"

"Yes, everything is fine. At least I hope so," said Margo breathlessly as she entered the Wirts' house. She removed her parka and hung it on a kitchen chair.

"But this doesn't seem like a random friendly visit. I can tell you're agitated about something," said Muriel with intuitive assessment. "Does it call for a cup of tea?"

Margo nodded vigorously. "A cup of tea is most definitely in order."

Muriel soon had two china mugs filled with steaming sweet-spiced herbal tea. The two women sat across from each other in the living room, just as they had when Margo had lived there.

"What's this all about?" asked Muriel candidly. "Are you finding Lydia more than you can handle?"

"No, it's not that. To be honest, she's a very interesting house-mate. Every day is different. Sometimes she's the funniest thing, a real hoot. Other times she's a brilliant and wise woman. Then there's the times when she's as simple and naïve as a child. She forgets lots of things in the present but can tell you with detailed accuracy an experience she had as a little girl. You never know what she's going to come out with."

Margo relaxed into the rocking chair. She stopped talking and looked away through the living room window, gazing out onto the darkened street, lit only by streetlights.

"But...?" Muriel encouraged, knowing very well that Margo couldn't be pushed into revealing personal details on a matter.

"But in all cases she is very blunt, to put it mildly," added Margo with pursed lips.

"Has Mrs. Harms offended you then?"

"Not exactly offended me," replied Margo slowly. "Ohhhh, all right. Fine, I'll tell you how my intentions of doing a good deed went south."

Muriel then heard the unabridged story of how reading the Bible to Mrs. Harms had resulted in the older woman cornering Margo on her negligible Bible knowledge, declaring her unbelief nothing but foolishness.

"No doubt you side with Lydia, since you also are a Bible nut," said Margo. "No offence meant."

"None taken." Muriel smiled. "But how can I help you?"

"I guess I need to read the Bible for myself so I can argue my case intelligently. The thing is, Lydia's Bible reads like Shakespeare. It's tiring. Hard to follow. I hated literature class in high school, too, so reading this stuff is a real chore. I was wondering if the Bible is available in modern English."

"It is. I don't have a copy of one in the house, but I believe there are a few in Leland's office. He likes to pass them along when an enquiring person shows an interest. If you wait here, I'll run over and get one for you." Muriel hesitated for a moment. "Before I go, may I ask you something?"

Margo braced herself. "Probably. I guess so."

"I'm curious to learn how you came to reject Christianity. What brought you to that conclusion?"

"I wondered that of myself after Lydia walked away from me," began Margo, relaxing again. "I believe the answer is I was brought up to it. Religion was pretty much forbidden in our house. I'd say my mother was indifferent, but my father was very opinionated on the subject. He used the word God for swearing at things and people, too. Lots of times he would go on a rant against Bible-thumpers and churchgoers. I remember once him threatening my sister Diane and me. 'If I ever catch you girls going into a church, I'll tan your hides so you can't sit for a week!' he shouted while shaking his index finger in our faces. Of course, he was drunk at the time. Still, we grew up with the understanding that religion was something stupid… and that God was an imaginary idea like Santa Claus and the Easter rabbit. I never gave it any serious thought."

"I see," said Muriel. "I have to agree with Lydia. You should have proper information before spouting an opinion as well as rejecting what many have found to bring them inner peace and a purposeful life."

"You ladies have made your point," said Margo wryly. "I've already moved from not remotely interested to mildly curious. I hope that's good enough for you to let me borrow a readable Bible."

"It sure is." Muriel rose to get a copy.

Twelve

AS FOLKLORE PREDICTS, if March comes in like a lamb, it goes out like a lion, or the other way around. The last couple days of March were miserably cold compared to its early days, but April 1 was lovely and mild with the promise of spring fragrant in the air.

It was Wednesday, but Ellie wasn't scheduled to be at the hospital, affording her an opportunity to lounge in bed for as long as she felt lazy. Hugh had long since gone to work, leaving her to think through her dreams and anticipations without interruption.

At about 9:00 a.m., Ellie had had enough dillydallying and got up to begin her day with a shower. She opened the drawer to withdraw some fresh underwear and—

A not-so-little garter snake peered up at her.

Ellie screamed and slammed the drawer. Shocked and shaken, she fell back onto her bed. How was it possible for a common prairie snake to get into their snug, well-built cottage, and while there was yet so much snow lying around? They should have still been hibernating.

Slowly it dawned on her that it was April Fool's Day. Most likely, Hugh had put a fake one in her drawer as a prank.

"Well done, Hugh-morous," said Ellie with a broad smile. "You got me good. Now I wonder what I can come up with to return the favour."

Before entering the shower, Ellie fetched a pair of tongs from the kitchen and very slowly reopened her underwear drawer. The snake lay there just as it had earlier and she lifted it out with the tongs… just in case it *was* real.

Of course it wasn't, but it was a pretty good fake, certainly convincing at first glance.

To keep the game going, she tossed it into Hugh's undies drawer, hoping it would give him a bit of a jolt, too.

Throughout her shower and afterwards, top of Ellie's mind was to think of an April Fool's prank of her own. By the time she had gone through the cottage with a dust cloth and vacuum cleaner, and tidied the kitchen, she had an idea.

With the house in tiptop shape, it was time to refill the pantry and refrigerator. For this, she opted to buy her groceries at the community store in Minitonas. Although the grocery store in Swan River was considerably larger and had more variety, supporting the local business, or else lose it altogether, was important to her and Hugh.

While in town, she also picked up the mail and stopped in to visit Darcey for a few minutes before heading back to her place. She'd been away approximately two hours.

Turning into her driveway, she saw a car parked in front of their house that seemed somehow vaguely familiar. It was nevertheless a surprise, since she hadn't expected anyone.

As she drove around it to park under the carport, Ellie quickly noticed no one waiting within. That was strange, since she was pretty sure she had locked the house before she left.

Bringing the groceries, Ellie went to her house harbouring uneasy feelings. The door was locked, just as she remembered.

She left her purchases in the kitchen and went back outside to peer into the deserted car. The keys hung from the ignition and a large, thickly stuffed manilla envelope lay on the passenger seat. The back seat and floor held several cardboard boxes in assorted sizes.

Ellie looked all around, thoroughly puzzled.

And then it came to her. This was Margo's car!

So where was the driver? Presumably Larry must have delivered it. In which case, he must have convoyed with another vehicle and driver to take him back to Dauphin. But why not wait until she or Hugh had returned to make the drop-off? Even more curious, why hadn't he called first to say he was coming with Margo's things?

The more she thought about it, the angrier Ellie became. By all appearances, Larry had come and left in a cowardly way. Not only was he gutless, he was rude and devious to boot. What she wouldn't give to deliver an earful of rebuke to that man.

Back in the house, Ellie fussed and fumed while she put her groceries away. After that, thoroughly rankled, she called Hugh.

"Whoa, babe," said Hugh patiently. "Slow down. Begin at the beginning…"

$\sim$

When Hugh returned home from work, he first looked into Margo's car before going inside for supper. Ellie came out to meet him.

"It's just as I saw it when I came home from Minitonas," she said. "I haven't touched a thing."

Hugh didn't respond but opened the driver's door and sat inside. He picked up the large and bulky manila envelope, saw that it was sealed, and re-laid it on the passenger seat. Then he popped the hood and went to investigate the motor.

"Good Lord! This thing is practically out of oil. And what's here is blacker than tar. I'd say it missed more than one oil change." Hugh whistled through his teeth, fully annoyed. "Before we get this thing to Margo, I'd better give it a full checkup and change the oil. Could use a thorough cleaning, too. I'm sure she'd like to have wheels again, but not as is. It wouldn't be safe."

"I'll help you get her car roadworthy, but after our supper. We're having burgers tonight," said Ellie, shivering.

Hugh clamped down the hood and followed Ellie inside.

At the table, Ellie set out plates of burgers and French fries. Hugh quickly asked the blessing over their meal and then lifted the burger stacked with lettuce, tomato, and onion already dripping with meaty juices.

"You make the best burgers. Better than the burger shops in town," he said before taking a large bite.

"Aww, thanks love." Ellie smiled broadly and then took a generous bite herself.

Hugh's face took on a puzzled expression as he chewed and swallowed hard. Frowning, he peered into his meat patty and soon noticed the irregularity.

"Your April Fool's prank?" he asked as he pulled a piece of cardboard from the centre.

"Hmmm." Ellie just kept chewing. "But it didn't bring on the effect I was hoping for. You would have been proud of the scream I produced when reaching into my undies drawer."

Hugh smiled guiltily. "Dang! So sorry I missed that."

After supper, Ellie set out small dishes of jelly with a side of store-bought cookies on the table.

"The dessert is okay, right?" Hugh lifted a suspicious eyebrow. "You didn't mess that up, did you?"

Ellie reseated herself. "Everything is edible, I promise."

Hugh ate some of the gelatine and was satisfied that nothing was amiss. Confidently he bit into a cookie and almost immediately realized he'd been had again. This time, he went to the sink and spat.

"Toothpaste?"

"You're so clever. Can't get anything past you."

"It's a good thing April Fool's Day only comes once a year," Hugh remarked dryly.

As they concluded their meal, they decided to take Margo's car to the repair shop where Hugh worked so he could give it a proper checkup and oil change in a heated environment where all the applicable tools and parts would be on hand. Ellie offered to come along to clean the inside. The idea was to return the car to Margo with the added blessing of it being freshened up and in top condition.

But the drive into Swan River soured Hugh's mood considerably.

"This car needs more than an oil change," he muttered. "It has no get-up-and-go. I'm starting to worry there's trouble brewing under the hood. Do you hear that ticking sound?"

"No, I don't," answered Ellie after a few seconds of listening. "I think it's one of those sounds only a mechanic picks up on."

Hugh grunted.

While Ellie cleaned the vehicle with a vacuum and a wiping down, Hugh went over the entire motor. Besides the oil change, which produced another round of muttered criticisms for Margo's neglect, he replaced a belt as well as the battery. Two tires were also seriously bald. He installed used tires in better condition. Everything else was either cleaned, tightened, or passed inspection.

It was late before Hugh deemed the car ready to return, but it was too late to deliver that same evening.

~

The next evening, Margo and Lydia were at their supper when they noticed a male figure walk past the kitchen window, followed by a rap on the back door.

"I'm not expecting anyone, are you?" croaked Lydia, puzzled.

"Nope, but I'll see who it is." Margo rose and answered the door with a fork still in her hand. "Oh. It's you." She broke out in a wide smile. "What's up?"

She stepped aside so Hugh could enter.

"I'm on my way home after work," he said warmly. "Maybe I should have called first, but I want to bring you home with me. There's a surprise waiting for you at our place."

"Surprise? Like, what do you mean?" asked Margo, her face scrunched up in a half-frown.

"It won't be a surprise anymore if I tell you, but I think you'll be pumped."

"Well, I'm just in the middle of my supper. Can you wait a couple of minutes until I finish scarfing it down?" Margo gestured for him to follow her into the kitchen.

"Sure. But I was hoping to share my supper with you, too," said Hugh. "Ellie left a stew simmering in the crockpot before she left for work. They're usually pretty good."

"I'm sure you're right, but the invite is a little late." Margo took her place at the table. "Lydia, meet my brother Hugh. Hugh, this is Lydia Harms."

"Pleased to meet you, ma'am. I'm sorry to barge in on your supper."

"Well now, that's quite all right. No harm done." Lydia looked directly at Margo. "There's still a helping left here, so why don't you get him a plate so he can join us?"

"Oh no, Mrs. Harms," said Hugh quickly. "I've got supper waiting for me at home. I came to bring Margo with me for a spell."

"You don't say. So you're her brother. Can't say I see the family resemblance, though." Lydia looked back and forth between the siblings. "Do you have the same parents?"

The blunt question took both Hugh and Margo aback, but Hugh responded with a light chuckle. "Yep. Same ma and pa. Margo resembles our mother more than I do."

"I suppose that means your brother gets his good looks from his father then?" Lydia put the question directly to Margo. "I may be old, but I still know a handsome man when I see one," she added with a wink.

Hugh blushed. He wasn't quite sure how to respond.

Margo understood completely yet enjoyed his discomfiture. "Yeah. Now that you point it out, Hugh is pretty good-looking, but growing up with him I only saw a skinny, pimply faced beanpole. I don't think he turned anyone's head back then."

"Well now, everyone seems to go through whatcha call an 'awkward stage,'" said Lydia with conviction. "Anyhow, what do you do for a living, young man?"

"I'm a motor vehicle mechanic, ma'am, and I've got the greasy hands to prove it."

Hugh held out his hands and Lydia quickly examined them.

"Good for you!" she said with a satisfied smile. "I don't think the world can have too many Mr. Fix-It types. Got no car anymore for you to look after. How about plumbing? Do you know anything about fixing leaks or plugged pipes? Sometimes I have need for such a one. What about fixing the lid on a pot? The black gripper broke not so long ago on my potato and porridge pot, and now it's hard to use. Can you make a new pot knob, do you think? Or is it only cars and truck motors you know your way around?"

"Well… uh… let's have a look," answered Hugh slowly. He felt somewhat bemused.

Lydia rose stiffly on account of her arthritis, went to the kitchen sink, lifted out a pot lid, and handed it to Hugh with a doubtful look on her face. Hugh quickly saw the hole in the centre of the lid where a screw had once held a finger knob.

"If you let me take this home with me, I think I can find a way to make it usable again."

"Well now, that would be mighty fine of you," said Lydia, beaming. "My daughters think I should just get rid of my pots and pans and buy a new set. But what for? I expect I'm not long for this world so I'd rather just make do with what I have. And anyway, my pots are experienced. New pots don't add anything to the flavour of things, if you follow my meaning."

"I do follow your meaning, though I have to admit I never thought about pots being 'experienced' before. I suppose it's like a good pair of shoes that are broke in. They're a heck of a lot more comfortable than new shoes, for sure."

"Margo, your brother is a smart man and that's something no one can take for granted in a body nowadays." Lydia, pleased that Hugh understood, saw that Margo had finished her meal. "You best be going, young lady. I'll tidy up so you don't keep your brother waiting."

"Are you really going to fix Lydia's pot lid?" asked Margo when she and Hugh were on their way.

"Sure. A little piece of wood with a bolt and nut will make it functional again. Won't be fancy, but it'll work."

"She likes you, obviously, and she's liable to glom onto you for any number of favours if you let her," warned Margo.

"I don't mind helping her out. And besides, isn't that what you're doing, looking after her as part of your room and board arrangement?"

"I suppose so, but in my case it's also a matter of scratching each other's back. I'm just saying, I didn't know you were so considerate."

"I'm pretty sure there's a lot you don't know about me," said Hugh as he was about to turn into his driveway.

"Wait! Is that my car? It is, isn't it?" Margo let out a whoop as she scrambled out of Hugh's truck. "I can't believe it! Larry even washed it before bringing it to me."

"Not Larry. I washed it," Hugh corrected her. "Ellie cleaned the inside. The truth is, sister, I don't know how Larry got it here without it breaking down on the highway. It was way overdue for an oil change, tires were bald, the battery was on its last legs, and a belt needed replacing. I did a complete overhaul and checkup last night. It's clean and safe to drive now. And you're welcome!"

"Wow. I suppose I owe you a bunch of money now," said Margo, her spirits suddenly less excited.

He stood with hands on hips. "Nah. I did it for love. I did it so you could drive around safely. Seriously. It was about to die or blow up."

"I don't know what to say except thank you," said Margo humbly.

"That's fine." He smiled crookedly. "Just look after your vehicle and it'll look after you."

Sensing that the lecture was over, Margo returned her attention to the car itself. Frowning, she opened the rear door to see what was inside the boxes. One seemed to be full of dishes. Another had pots and pans. A smaller one contained her high school yearbook and other papers relating to achievements and matters once important to her. These boxes contained the evidence of a life she had recently thought prosperous, but now she realized they contained the leftovers from sundry foolish decisions.

Margo blinked back the tears beginning to fill her eyes, not wanting to arouse Hugh's attention.

She noticed the thick manilla envelope lying on the passenger seat and instinctively knew it held copies of the divorce papers and other legal documents relative to her parting of ways with Larry Owens. She hoped it was sealed; it appeared to be. It was just that she didn't want Hugh or his wife to know the final details of her many failures. They already knew enough to keep her embarrassed for the rest of her life.

"I have no use for any of these things while I live with Mrs. Harms." Margo indicated the boxes to Hugh, who waited on the steps. "Can I store them here until I decide what to do with them?"

"The shed is crammed full with my stuff, wedding gifts, and your clothes," replied Hugh doubtfully.

"Right! The rest of my clothes. I meant to sort through them at Lydia's house. What if I make a swap...?"

"Yeah, sure. I'll help you make the switch."

The exchange took about fifteen minutes. The clothing boxes took up considerably more room in the car than had the housewares. One box, which contained a dozen or more purses and a few pairs of shoes, was emptied only to stuff the items behind, underneath, between, or on top of the other cartons.

In the end, there was only enough room for Margo to get in as driver.

"You better hope a cop doesn't catch you driving like that," cautioned Hugh. "No way you can see out of any window other than straight ahead or to your left."

"I get it. It's a good thing I don't have far to go. Maybe I'll wait until it's dark. Less noticeable..."

"That's okay by me, because I have more to tell you." With that, Hugh led her toward the house.

"Now what?" asked Margo suspiciously.

"Now I eat first. I'm starving."

Once they were inside, he served himself a bowl of steaming, mouth-watering stew.

"What I have to tell you is that I picked open the lock on the trunk not long ago," he said. "Inside are some letters Ma wrote to the three of us kids. It also contained a collection of the better items that were in the house. We're supposed to divvy these up between ourselves to remember her by."

The unexpected announcement caused Margo to freeze; she stared back at her brother, frowning with a lack of comprehension. "What did you say?"

"I said the trunk is open and there are letters inside that Ma wrote to each of us, and also instructions to split up her possessions," he repeated as impassively as before.

He nonchalantly took another bite of his supper.

"Did you read them?" she asked in a rush. "What did they say? What kind of stuff did she pack? I can't imagine any of this is good news."

Hugh set down his spoon and met Margo's eyes directly. "The letters are hard… I'm not gonna lie. She had reached a desperate point in her life and wrote it out on paper. Not only was she lonely as blazes, but she was at the end of her rope trying to cope with Pa. She didn't come out and say it, but it's a good guess that she did something to cause the accident that killed them."

Margo sat fully erect. "So… now you want me to read those letters?"

"If not now, then sometime before too long. We'll have to get Diane out here to do the same and choose her mementos."

"Good Lord, that's two big surprises in less than an hour. I'm not sure I'm up for the second one. Or maybe even the first." Margo sighed. "I saw the sealed packet in the car. Pretty sure it doesn't contain good news either."

Her eyes fell on the top of the trunk. Since it also served as a coffee table, Ellie had set a pottery bowl atop it filled with clay replicas of fruit. Beside it lay a paperback copy of the Good News Bible with the corners of the pages beginning to curl.

"Well, looky here!" she said with a hint of disdain. "Did you get this from the Wirts? Muriel gave me one, too. I'm trying to read it so I can argue intelligently about why religion is nothing but twaddle."

"Oh yeah? How's that going for you? What have you read so far?" Hugh smirked, then got up to refill his bowl with more of the savoury stew.

"Not a lot yet. I read the first bit, where God supposedly made everything on earth in six days. That seems rather unbelievable…"

"Unless you're the almighty creator God," Hugh remarked. "Then one could ask, what took Him so long?"

Margo rolled her eyes. "So you believe it then?"

Hugh released a short laugh. "I didn't always, but I do now. And from what I've learned so far, it fits with God's all-powerful character."

"Right. Muriel said you got religion. And apparently it was Ellie who got you to believe in it," said Margo, crossing her arms.

"It's true that Ellie played a part in leading me to believe and trust in God. But it was the family I stayed with in Winnipeg who first intro-duced me to religion, as you put it. I saw the good effects of it in their lives, although I didn't get involved until after I started hanging out with Ellie."

"Was that so you could win the girl's heart? We've always known the Baumans were a strict religious bunch. Pa always made a point—"

"Pa was wrong about the Baumans… and most other things, too."

Margo reared back defensively. "Sorry! You don't have to be so touchy."

"For the record, the Baumans are pretty incredible people," Hugh replied firmly. "Kind and generous, not to mention they're my family now. I won't let you keep thinking badly of them."

"Well, I wouldn't know about that, would I? I just remember Ellie being one of the stuck-up girls in high school who hardly seemed to notice Diane or me, even though we rode on the same school bus."

"Yeah, well, I wasn't there to see that, but I bet your choice of friends didn't overlap with hers. And if you were as biased against her back then as you still seem to be today, I doubt you were open to a friendship." Hugh got up to put his empty bowl in the kitchen sink. "Be honest."

"I don't want to talk about Ellie anymore," sniffed Margo. "I'm curious why you took to religion. How did you become convinced there was something to it?"

Hugh didn't answer immediately. He took a minute to tidy the kitchen before seating himself in the armchair adjacent to the sofa. He put his feet up on the trunk and briefly twiddled his thumbs across his belly.

"Do you remember how it was for me up to the day I ran away on my sixteenth birthday?" asked Hugh, staring off into the distance.

"Of course I do. Including what Pa did to you for wanting to play on the basketball team."

These were bad memories. Margo sincerely hoped this conversation wasn't going to sidetrack into a rehearsal of the bad old days. She leaned into the sofa, pulling her legs up and around, bracing herself for what Hugh might come out with next.

Hugh sat quietly without speaking, his mouth slightly agape. His concentration seemed focused elsewhere, as if he were all alone in the room.

After what felt like several minutes, Margo called out: "Yoohoo!" She waved a hand to catch his attention. "You look completely zoned out. What's the matter with you?"

"Nothing. I was just thinking... testing myself..." Hugh snapped to attention and returned his gaze to his sister with a pleased smile. "You asked how I became convinced there was something to religion. My answer is simple—because of my own changed life. I ran away from home because I couldn't take Pa's abuse anymore. I believed it was only a matter of time before he would kill me. It seems I was his scapegoat... or at least he refused to recognize me as his kid. It was to do with some kind of row he and Ma had before I was born. Aunt Gertie told me about it. Anyway, I left angry and scared that Pa would try to find me and finish the job. You know the story of how I ended up being unofficially adopted by that truck driver who picked me up as a hitchhiker? You must have met Marcie and Brian Turner at the wedding."

Margo nodded. So far he hadn't said anything new.

"Living with them brought me an immediate change of lifestyle," continued Hugh. "For a long while, I still looked over my shoulder regularly to see if Pa had caught up with me. But for the most part I was able to bury all my bitterness and live a happy life with the Turners and friends I made while finishing high school. But after I got my mechanics license, moved out on my own, and started working full-time, things began to get to me again. If a customer questioned my work or quibbled about the cost of repairs, I got very annoyed, irate enough to get the boss involved. And that didn't go well. It was like all the anger I had suppressed was still smouldering. Even though I wasn't consciously aware of it, it came out sideways through whatever crack it could find. I was asked to resign and work elsewhere."

"Somehow I find a bit of comfort in that," Margo remarked, listening intently.

"At the time, I justified myself. I thought everyone else was stupid and out to take advantage of me… in other words, *they* were the problem, not me. In some cases, that might have been true, but I'm now aware that I was as much the problem as anyone."

Margo shifted uneasily but didn't interrupt.

"Close to a year ago, trouble came again at the last garage I worked at in Winnipeg. I excused myself, thinking I just wasn't a people person and that I'd be better off living alone, possibly with a dog for company. I got the idea that I should come back and take over the family farm since Ma and Pa were gone and couldn't trouble me no more."

"And yet I was still surprised you would ever want to come back here," said Margo.

"I'm sure if a better idea had presented itself, I wouldn't have. I see it differently now, in hindsight. God led me home to deal with my past and offer me a good future."

"Okay. I'll bite. How did you come to terms with your... your issues?"

"Ellie called me out on a whole bunch of hints I didn't mean to drop," he said. "She very directly told me that if I didn't forgive the people who had wronged me, I would wind up a bitter, mean, shrivelled-up excuse for a human being. I was surprised as all get out that she could read me like an open book. It produced a furious outburst that made me see, in a snap vision, that my insides were burnt out. All I had was a black, sooty cavern beneath my ribs that had been eaten away for years by smouldering hate. That vision passed almost as instantly as I saw it, but the truth of it scared me. Even so, the idea of forgiving Pa was totally impossible, not to mention undeserved, as far as I was concerned."

Hugh paused for a moment, remembering that unasked-for discussion with Ellie as if it had only just happened.

"Then she started to go on and on about needing to invite Jesus into my life, otherwise I wouldn't heal from past wounds, nor would I have what it takes to forgive those who wronged me. I had a bit of knowledge about religion, because the Turners had wanted me to attend church with them. At first I found it curious, but I couldn't get into it. It seemed like it was all about weird little rituals. It was just so boring. Like you, I thought it was pretty much all nonsense."

"Thought... as in past tense," noted Margo. "But somewhere along the line you changed your mind...?"

"That's because Ellie talked about knowing God in a personal way, not through religious ceremonies," he said. "She drew me a sketch of the human condition—my human condition—being separated from a pure and holy God by my sin. I think that sketch is still tacked up on the wall of the shed in the corner where I slept. She explained that there was no way I could be friends with God unless I repented of my sin and accepted the gift of Jesus dying in my place."

"Wait!" Margo put her hand up. "What are you talking about? What you just said makes no sense at all."

Hugh sighed. "It's too bad Ellie isn't here to explain it. She does it a lot better than I can."

"No, I want to hear it from you."

"Look. Everybody is a sinner… or as Ellie usually puts it, everyone is broken."

"I'm not broken."

"You've never lied? Stolen something? Hurt someone?" asked Hugh with raised eyebrows. "All it takes is one instance of wrongdoing to prove that you're a wrecked product in need of repair."

"Why does it prove that? Nobody's perfect!"

"Exactly!" exclaimed Hugh. "But the first man and woman God created *were* perfect. They had the Spirit of the living God within them, the God who had created them to live beautiful, creative, and happy lives with purpose—that is, until they both disobeyed God's one and only rule. That act cut off their perfect, seamless relationship with Him. They were instantly broken, like the severing of a telephone wire."

Margo leaned forward in interest. "If God is so powerful, why didn't He just replace the wiring, as it were?"

"He did, but in a way that didn't compromise His character. Perfection and purity cannot tolerate wickedness in its presence. Therefore, with God, a person guilty of sin has to die. No exceptions. The only way for Him to save humanity was to have a sinless person die in humanity's place."

"If that's the rule, no one qualifies," observed Margo. "Not if everyone sins at least once."

"You're a smart cookie and exactly right." Hugh was relieved that she understood his bumbling explanations. "So, enter Jesus."

"Right. Jesus. I knew He had to fit in somewhere."

"Remember, He's the Son of God, meaning that He *is* God and was sent to dwell in a human body for more than thirty years. He passed the test of committing no sin in all that time, therefore qualifying to die in our place. He actually volunteered to pay the price of death, which He did on a cross by crucifixion. But the beauty of it is that Jesus didn't stay dead. He rose on the third day and shortly after returned to His place in heaven. Because the debt of sinful, separated man was paid, all any of us has to do is agree that Jesus died in our place and accept Him as our saviour. Then God gives us the gift of the Holy Spirit to dwell in our lives and we're back to having all the elements of life that Adam and Eve originally had. Do you follow me?"

Hugh searched Margo's eyes.

"I think so," she answered slowly. "But what did you mean earlier when you said you were testing yourself?"

"The promise is that when the Holy Spirit comes to live inside you, your sins are washed away and you become a brand-new person. Your life is made new... the old things pass away. And the proof, to me, is that when thoughts of Pa cross my mind, I no longer react with overwhelming hate and anger. Mostly I feel sorry for the old skunk."

Margo stared at Hugh, as if trying to catch him in a lie, but all she saw was the genuine article.

"You do surprise me, brother," she said. "I never thought I would hear that kind of talk from you. I honestly don't know what to think. But I'm sure not ready to forgive him for what he put us through."

"Did he... did he hurt you?" asked Hugh delicately, fearing the worst.

"No. I mean, he didn't beat me and he didn't... well, you know. But it came close once. It was late at night and Di and I were in bed. He opened the door to our room and just stood there in the doorway. He didn't come in. It was like he was trying to decide what to do. I hadn't fallen asleep yet, so I was well aware and planned to fight him off with tooth and nail if he tried something." She shook her head, trying to banish the memory. "Something caused him to turn away. Ma came out of their bedroom and asked what he was doing. 'Nuthin,' he said and pushed past her to get into their own bed. It never happened again..."

Margo set her feet back on the floor.

"Shoot," she grumbled. "I haven't thought about that memory for years. It's going to bum me out all over again."

"Do what I did," urged Hugh. "Invite Jesus into your life and become a brand-new person inside. He'll wash you clean of everything sinful, like He did with me."

"What you've told me is very interesting, I admit that. But I need to turn it over in my mind. Somehow I'm not ready to buy into it yet. You had to think about it a bunch before you came around, didn't you?"

"Yeah, I did. I wasted several more weeks before I came to my senses. We Fishers are a stubborn lot—and that's nothing to be proud of."

"Phffff," snorted Margo as she got up to return to Minitonas.

Thirteen

"COME ALONG, DOGGIES," called Ellie to Ruby and Ruff. "Let's go for a walk through our bit of scrubby forest. I want to see how far the river is from our yard."

The pair of mongrels given to Hugh and Ellie as eight-week-old puppies were now about half their expected full-grown size, yet they were still delightfully playful and handsome to look at. Although their breed was an indiscriminate Heinz 57, those knowing something about dog types would suggest a strong bent towards collies with their sharp noses and longish hair.

Throughout the winter, both their masters had been putting in effort to train them in obedience. "Come," "Sit," "Down," and "Stay" had been practiced with moderate success. Ellie now wanted to add leash training while she scoped out the bush between their yard and the East Favel River. Remembering her startling encounter with a young cougar the previous fall, she thought the dogs, although young, might add a measure of protection in case other unexpected surprises wandered in.

Her first goal was to visit a small natural pond a couple of hundred yards away from the main farm buildings. The once tall grasses, wild weeds, and flowers lay flat on the ground, making them relatively easy to trample. Much of the snow had already melted, but here and there mounds still lay in undulating drifts, no longer white but laced with black snow mould. The grassy area around the pond was bare, thickly littered with fallen leaves and a few broken branches. The pond itself was still largely frozen, although she wouldn't allow the dogs to test the strength and thickness of the ice.

The dogs strained at their leashes in a desire to explore and sniff out the unfamiliar area.

"No, you guys, I want you to learn to stay with me," admonished Ellie. "We'll explore the place together."

The dogs showed no sign of understanding anything she said, nor did they seem to care.

Even though none of the trees had yet leaved out and all was dead brown, Ellie thought the spot was beautiful, even more so that it represented the place where Hugh had so creatively proposed marriage. She promised herself to return soon with a rake to tidy the area and also cut and maintain a walking path from their house to this very spot.

Looking around, she imagined a gazebo set near the tree line, or at least a couple of Adirondack chairs by the pond to accommodate times of personal reflection and prayer.

Ellie continued trekking through the woods until she came to the area where she and Hugh had discovered the three vintage vehicles that had since been dragged out and taken to the home yard for him to eventually restore. The ground still bore the messy signs of that operation. It was also where she had encountered that young cougar, an experience that had been both frightening and exhilarating.

She watched the dogs excitedly sniff the trees and stones, tangling their leashes. Yet they went about it calmly, unalert to the scent of any wild critters nearby.

Relieved, Ellie untangled the ropes and carried on farther west than she had ever ventured. The brush scratched her as she climbed over fallen trees. It was too difficult to lead the dogs on their leashes, so she released them to find their own way.

Suddenly she came to the river's edge. It lay below a short drop-off of about three feet. The water had been very low when it froze for the winter. Here and there, stones poked up through the ice and Ellie knew for certain she had nothing to fear, even if she broke through.

Childlike curiosity caused her to hop down to explore further. The puppies whined and yelped, afraid to jump down what seemed to them a steep cliff.

"C'mon, you rascals. Where we go one, we go all."

She lowered Ruby first, and then Ruff.

The uneven, stony, and slippery surface made walking precarious. It was the dogs' noses that chose to track the river to the left, and now Ellie followed their lead. The East Favel River wasn't wide, hardly more than a creek, yet it wound around like a girl's hair ribbon dropped on the floor.

Pretty soon, Ruby, Ruff, and Ellie rounded a bend and were surprised to see something of a clearing atop the bank. Even more puzzling was a stick about four feet long stuck in the ground. Hung at the top was the remains of a tattered red T-shirt.

"How odd," remarked Ellie. "We haven't gone far, so I'm sure this must still be on the edge of our property."

Curiosity led her to hoist her pups onto the top of the bank and scramble up after them. Immediately the pair walked around in circles, their noses to the ground while Ellie looked around. She stood in a grassy patch she guessed must be located about thirty feet away from where she had originally come upon the river. It was edged with shrubbery, beyond which grew thick natural vegetation characteristic of all Manitoba's woods.

Nothing appeared amiss, yet she began to feel apprehensive. The dogs were still exploring nearby as she examined the stick with the red T-shirt. Clearly it was meant to be a marker of some sort, but for whom? And for what purpose? By all appearances, it had been there for some time, judging by the fading of the red cloth and the bark falling away from the stick.

A mystery indeed, yet she had no way of knowing whether it represented current activity or some leftover relic from the past.

She looked up, realizing that the pups had found something. She could tell by their selfish growls that they were fighting over some object. They were only a few yards away when she saw they had dragged out some kind of package from beneath a fallen tree.

"What have you got there, Ruby? Move over, Ruff, so I can have a look."

The pups yielded their discovery to Ellie. It was a well-worn backpack in grey and black, not heavy, but neither was it empty. It also didn't have the faded, deteriorated appearance of a forgotten item that had been lost for several seasons. That realization doubled Ellie's anxiety. It had to mean someone was lurking about, and that translated into someone being up to no good. What else could it mean?

Suddenly she just wanted to go home and sit in her safe little cottage and wait for Hugh. He would know what to do about this. She would take the backpack as proof, but leave the red T-shirt so she could find the spot to show Hugh later.

"C'mon, time to go home," she commanded the dogs.

Having a pretty good sense of direction, Ellie faced east and began to walk. She'd taken only three steps when a man stepped out in front of her. The dogs began to bark furiously but stayed close to Ellie's side.

Ellie recognized the guy but couldn't recall his name.

"I've seen you before," she said coolly, hoping her fear wouldn't betray her. While she couldn't remember his name, his olive skin and long, tied-back black hair, topped with a timeworn black cowboy hat, seemed familiar.

"You were here before with Tipper."

"You have a good memory. That backpack you're carrying belongs to me. I want it back."

Slowly she handed over the backpack. But as he reached out to take it, she didn't let go.

"I want to know what you're doing here," she said with more confidence than she felt. "By prowling around our property without permission, you're trespassing. We can have you arrested for that."

"Save your threats," he replied dryly. "I was just walking up the river, and no one owns a river even if it runs through their property."

"Now I remember. You're Chiclets. At least that's one of your names. Well, you're not on the river now. You're on my property. So once again, what are you doing here?"

The dogs resumed their barking.

Chiclets stared at her, as if trying to decide how he should proceed.

Finally he answered, "I was looking for my kin."

Ellie's eyes went wide. "Are you saying there's someone else wandering around here?"

"No. That's not what I'm saying." Chiclets pulled his backpack out of Ellie's hands and strode past her to the edge of the bank and hopped down to the ice-covered river.

Thoroughly shaken, Ellie watched him head downstream.

"C'mon, doggies. Let's go home."

She soon found the area where the ground was ripped apart and from there made her way back to the cottage in just a few minutes.

An idea came to her.

With her fear under control, Ellie jumped into her car and drove north up the road. In less than two miles, she came to the small country bridge that spanned the East Favel River. Nearby, halfway into the ditch, sat Chiclets' faded navy pick-up—the same vehicle in which he had brought old man Tipper to make good on an old deal with Hugh's late father.

Tipper had claimed that the farm held secrets, and together she and Hugh had discovered a few of them. But with Chiclets prowling around, obviously there must be more. That didn't sit well with Ellie and she knew it wouldn't with Hugh, either. But what to do about it, she hadn't a clue.

Slowly she returned home, with some of her previous anxiety returning with her.

"Aunt Ellie? Can I come home with you and spend the afternoon at your place?" pleaded Charlotte.

Church had been let out and as usual most people hung around the foyer and parking lot, getting in a quick visit before going home to lunch and a Sunday afternoon siesta.

"I'd like to say yes, but Hugh just told me he invited the Moore brothers over for lunch and I only have four chairs, sweetie," replied Ellie ruefully.

"Then I'll stand and eat my lunch at the island. I don't mind, I really don't. It's a glorious spring day and I just want to be away from home for a while," the girl replied. "Besides, it's been a long while since we had a woman to woman talk."

"A woman. To. Woman. Talk," repeated Ellie with a half-frown. "How old are you again?"

"Almost fifteen."

"Going on twenty, I think." Ellie grinned. "Okay, kiddo. You can come, crowded though it will be."

Not many minutes later, they were back at the Fischer place. Charlotte immediately began to set the table while Ellie assessed the chicken roasting in the oven and got the potatoes and vegetables boiling on top of the stove.

Hugh greeted Jeremy and Ladd shortly thereafter.

"The cookin' smells awesome in here, Ellie," said Ladd. "I bet you're one of the best cooks in the whole valley."

"That's a little thick, Laddie." Ellie grinned. "Flattery will get you nowhere, but keep trying!"

Having prepared the entire meal as much as possible before going to church, it was quickly transferred to serving dishes. Before anyone could say "Jack Robinson," they were seated at the small square table with Hugh offering thanks for their dinner.

The conversation was soon dominated by the three men. Anticipation for Hugh's new shop, including an autobody paint bay to be built in a month, made them positively giddy with excitement. The brothers had now gotten the motor running on the 1938 Chevrolet their grandfather Moore had originally owned. They were pumped to continue its restoration with a new paint job. The original colour had been black, but Jeremy wanted to cheer it up with a bright red hue.

Ladd and Hugh simultaneously objected.

"An authentic restoration means it's supposed to be restored to its original features," Ladd said with a grimace. "Therefore, it stays black."

"He's right," added Hugh. "At the very least, you want to use a colour they used that year. I don't think bright red was in their palette."

Jeremy was undeterred. "Who cares! The idea is to get it roadworthy again and then add some pizzaz. At least that's my goal."

"He makes a worthwhile point," Ellie said. "Quite often at a vintage car show you'll see an old-timer vehicle painted in especially bright colours, like canary yellow, hot pink, or screaming orange. They aren't original colours, but they do add pep... and they draw attention, which no doubt the owner is seeking."

"Since we share that old car, buddy, we have to come up with a colour we both agree on," Ladd said. "And I don't agree to bright, fire-engine red. I still think classic black is the way to go. It'll look like a mafia car or something, and that's cool, too."

Jeremy shook his head. "More like a funeral hearse if you ask me."

"I think Jeremy's idea to paint the antique car bright red is... is wonderful!" chimed Charlotte from her standing position at the little barnwood island.

Everyone stopped talking and looked to see where the voice had come from. All that attention suddenly made Charlotte feel conspicuous and she smiled nervously.

She was not to be cowed, however. "My mother says men's cars and trucks are like an extension of their personalities. A bright red vintage car sounds sexy. And I'm sure a sexy-looking car is something any guy would want."

The s-word produced a sudden awkwardness amongst the company. Hugh raised his eyebrows and smirked. Ladd coughed to cover a measure of embarrassment. Ellie's mouth dropped open, somewhat stunned.

Jeremy blushed. "I hadn't thought about bright red being an extension of my personality, or sexy. I just thought it was the perfect colour to represent the rebuilt motor and reintroduce its timeless style in a new era."

"And I think you're right!" insisted Charlotte.

Ellie rose. "Anyone want more helpings? If not, I'll bring out the dessert. It's going to be a few weeks yet before you need to settle on a paint colour. It will be striking, whatever you decide."

That pretty much ended the discussion.

After inhaling Ellie's delicious bread pudding with caramel sauce, Hugh herded the guys outside. They took measurements and pounded in stakes where Hugh intended his three-bay garage to be erected.

Meanwhile, Ellie put away the leftovers and then washed dishes while Charlotte dried. At first their conversation concerned the mundane matters of teenage life. In answer to Ellie's questions, Charlotte replied that she was doing well in school, enjoyed the youth group at church, and looked forward to getting her driver's learners permit soon.

Then, like the flip of a switch, Charlotte changed the subject with a question of her own.

"Aunt Ellie, don't you think Jeremy is the most handsome, adorable young man in the whole Swan Valley?"

Ellie looked up in surprise. "Jeremy? Jeremy who? Do you mean Jeremy Moore?"

"Of course I mean Jeremy Moore! What other Jeremy do you know? At least around here?" replied Charlotte sharply, crossing her arms.

"Well… I suppose he's good-looking in your average, Canadian country boy kind of way, but to my mind he's not jaw dropping man-beautiful," said Ellie in a matter-of-fact tone. "What makes you think he's so handsome?"

"I just love the natural curls of his hair and his dreamy blue eyes, not to mention his trim, athletic build. And every time he speaks, he sounds so smart—like he knows what he's talking about."

Ellie tried not to smile. "Hmmm. How well do you know the Moores?"

"Not well personally," answered Charlotte as she returned the dried plates to their place in the cupboard. "I just know them as regulars who come to church. Jeremy has always been ahead of me in Sunday school classes. Now he's in the college and career group, while I'm still in the youth class. But I've noticed and admired him for quite a while. Mind, you're the first I've admitted this to, and I'm trusting you'll keep this confidential."

"Sure. I can do that. I remember noticing and admiring a few guys when I was your age. But why Jeremy? What about the other boys, like the high school guys? There must be at least a couple of them worthy of a girl's admiration."

"Nope! They're all so immature, it's pathetic. I can't imagine a single one of them wising up to be men worthy of taking for a husband. That is, with the possible exception of my brother. Trevor is an idiot a lot of the time, too, but occasionally I see him being smart about something, just like Daddy. So there's hope for him. But that doesn't help me. After all, I can't marry my brother!" She cast her eyes heavenward.

"Whoa girl!" exclaimed Ellie with a chuckle. "It's a lot too soon for you to be thinking about marriage. You should be examining yourself and trying different ideas on for size regarding the kind of career you're suited for."

"That's what my mom says, too." Charlotte sighed. "We have to decide whether I'm going to finish high school in the academic or general programs. Without being exactly authoritarian about it, I know my parents want me to take the academic program so I'll be ready to continue on to university. But I honestly don't know what I'd like to do for a career. That's why I wanted to talk to you. How did you know you wanted to be a nurse?"

"Oh. So that's what this is all about," said Ellie, somewhat relieved. "I don't honestly remember how I settled on that profession. I believe it was mostly the desire of your grandmother that I become a nurse. She thought I was a good fit for that role. I didn't disagree, but I was more pumped about getting away from here and living in the big city than chasing after a profession. Mind you, I'm thankful my parents saw to it that I got the training. It's been a rewarding career thus far. And to their credit, they were right. Nursing has been a good fit for me."

"But what about me?" implored Charlotte. "I can't tell what I'm a good fit for. The idea of being a schoolteacher doesn't appeal to me. Being someone's secretary is even less appealing, despite the fact that I get good grades in typing. Selling stuff sounds like it will be boring after a while. Cooking and baking sound okay, but not as a career. I've been wondering about airline stewardess and interior decorating, but Daddy has pointed out that being a stewardess is simply another category of waitress. Interior decorating often means you end up selling furniture, or paint and wallpaper, draperies and ornamental things. I'm not sure about nursing, either. I can't stand the smell of puke and lots of blood makes me queasy, too. I can sew pretty good, but the idea of sewing all the time already makes me sick of it. Honestly, Aunt Ellie, I think the Lord made me to be a wife and mother. That's an honourable vocation and includes a bit of everything women do for careers in running their households."

Ellie was rather amazed. "Wow! It sounds like you've been giving this a lot of thought. And you've concluded your chosen *career* should be marriage. You've even picked out your husband-to-be. Fascinating. I wonder what Jeremy Moore would think about that."

"That's a good question, since so far I don't believe he's noticed me," said Charlotte glumly.

"After your little contribution to the table talk today, that might have changed." Ellie chuckled. "But then again, who knows? What I know about the Moore brothers is that they're car and truck crazy. I mean *nuts*! They're all about motors and gears and transmissions and sparkplugs. I'd be surprised if they ever took time out of their day to think about women. If any girl were to catch their eye, she'd have to be a grease monkey same as them."

Suddenly a lightbulb seemed to go off in Charlotte's head and her mouth stretched into a thin, thoughtful smile.

"But Charlotte, you don't want to be thinking about marriage yet," continued Ellie. "You should take some time to have some adventures, maybe do some traveling, try your hand at different things before you settle down for good. And… you should meet other men. Jeremy isn't the only good guy out there. There's lots more fish in the sea. What about Bible school? A couple of years there will help to ground you in the faith and you'll meet other young people from all over the country. It's not nicknamed bridal school for nothing—"

"Yeah, Momma thinks I should do that before career training, and she thinks I should consider a nursing career, same as you."

Ellie raised her eyebrows. "And that doesn't appeal to you…?"

"I just don't know," whined Charlotte. "Why does life have to be so complicated? Why can't it just be simple… and living simply?"

"Now that's good insight from a mature teenager." Ellie nodded in approval. "Tell you what. I'll ask our head nurse if I can bring you to work with me on a weekend shift so you can see firsthand what hospital nurses do. Maybe we can dress you in some candy-striper clothes for the day so you can visit with some of the patients. That ought to help you decide. Beyond that, you should try your hand at different things. Experience and exposure will allow you to discover your natural bents and talents."

"Yeah, I suppose you're right," said Charlotte softly, looking out of the window and watching the movements of Hugh, Ladd, and Jeremy. "But I still think Jeremy is the cutest man I've seen in my life so far."

This time it was Ellie who cast her eyes heavenward.

⌒

"Good job, guys! Thanks for your help," said Hugh with appreciation after the Moore brothers had marked the four corners where the shop was to be built. "Can you spare me some more time to mark out the parameters of the Quonset?"

Ladd and Jeremy looked at each other. "Sure. Got nothing else planned for today," answered the elder brother.

They walked over to the vicinity where the old, sagging barn had stood until Hugh demolished and burned it the December before. The snow was gone but the ground remained very moist.

Right away Hugh noticed a disturbance in the dirt and ashes on the west side of the area. He frowned and went to take a closer look.

"Looks like someone was doing some digging here and I know it wasn't me," Hugh commented. "Or Ellie either."

"You're thinkin' you got a trespasser?" suggested Ladd warily.

"Yeah. That's exactly what I'm thinkin'," answered Hugh with rising anger. "Ellie went for a walk with the dogs down to the river a few days ago. She saw some questionable markings where our property meets the river and then ran into an old buddy of my pa's. He told her he was looking for his 'kin,' though what that means I don't understand, because he also let slip that no one was with him. I thought that meant he had a look around and that was it. Over. Done with. Now I'm not so sure… I don't like the idea of a prowler—particularly if I'm away and my wife is home alone. I mean, the dogs aren't old or savvy enough to protect her much."

"How about we take a look around before we mark out your other build?" Jeremy peered into the bushes. "We keep a shotgun behind the seat in our pickup. We could bring it along in case we run into trouble."

"Nah," countered Hugh. "I'm all for exploring the bush between here and the river, but I doubt we need a gun. Ellie said he wasn't armed."

"Let's go!" Ladd took some steps towards the wooded area.

Hugh and Jeremy immediately joined him. They spread out a bit but saw nothing to raise suspicions as they wandered about, dodging some yet unmelted piles of snow here and there.

"Come with me. I have a hunch where this particular trespasser might have done some snooping," said Hugh after a few minutes.

He headed over to the pond, which was well on the way to melting back into water. A frosty-looking iceberg floated in the centre. There were no footprints in the open area around the large flat rock. But there was more recently disturbed ground in the bush a little to the east.

"Looks like someone was digging here," observed Ladd.

Hugh pursed his lips. "It do that."

"Why here?" asked Jeremy. "What could the guy be looking for?"

"My pa had a shack tucked in the woods back here. No doubt our trespasser thought he might find something of interest to him in the same place. They were buddies, after all."

Ladd looked around, curious. "Do you think he found what he was looking for?"

"Doubtful. But you never know. Another of Pa's former associates told me this place is riddled with secrets. He's dead now, so I can't ply him with questions." Hugh couldn't suppress his worry. "Let's check out by the river. Ellie said there was a stick there with an old red T-shirt hanging off it. I want to see if it's still there."

They tramped through the woods easily and noted some boot-sized footprints. Following them to the edge of the river, they came to the stick with the faded rag of a T-shirt plunged into the ground. Hugh angrily yanked it free, then threw the stick as hard as he could. It flew across the river, which was little more than a few yards. He wadded up the remains of the T-shirt into a ball and took it with him to be burned with the trash after he returned home.

They took a different route back to the farmyard, passing through the area where they had originally discovered the Plymouth and Studebaker as well as the antique McCormick-Deering tractor. There were no other old relics around other than the remains of what most likely had been a winter sled, given its ski-type runners. In the olden days, it would have been the norm to travel into town in winter for supplies, drawn by a horse. Hugh took note to mention it to Ellie in case it would be of interest to her, but it didn't mean much to him. And because it didn't involve a motor, it also didn't attract the notice of the brothers.

"So whatcha going to do about your trespasser?" asked Ladd when they eventually got back to the farmyard.

"I don't know what I can do, really," Hugh replied thoughtfully. "First I'm going to put up NO TRESSPASSING signs on every side of our property. After that, I have to catch him in the act before I can bring charges. But unless he does real damage or actually harms someone, I can't see that going anywhere. If only I knew what he was after. Then I could beat him at his game and end the problem another way."

"My pop says he knew your pa a bit before your folks had that accident," ventured Jeremy. "I don't mean no offence or anything, but he said your pa was a shady sort of character. No one trusted him really. Do you s'pose that's a hint for what your trespasser is after?"

"I know very well what my pa was, and no offence taken." Hugh sighed and then added, "Absolutely there is some kind of link there for our prowler, but I'm gobsmacked to figure out what it is. I suppose I just have to be patient until the truth comes to light, because I'm sure it eventually will. But knowing a bit about Pa's band of cronies, I doubt it can be anything good. Makes me kind of nervous about what I don't know."

"If we can help in any way, you just have to call," offered Ladd.

"Thanks. Who knows if I won't someday take you up on that."

Fourteen

"A NICKEL FOR your thoughts."

Margo jumped, thoroughly startled. "Gosh! You scared me. How long have you been standing there?" Her question was directed at her boss.

"Not long," answered Bev. "But long enough to notice you were miles away from Minitonas."

Margo sighed from both relief and embarrassment. It was after the lunch rush and at the moment no one sat in the café. She had grabbed a broom to quickly sweep the floor and reset the tables in preparation for the afternoon coffee break. After concluding that task, she'd looked around and for the hundredth time indulged in imagining…

"Actually I wasn't miles away. I was right here in this very space," said Margo, leaning on the broom.

"Wait, have you taken your break yet? Tell me what you were thinking over a cup of coffee. I'd really like to know."

Bev reached for a pair of coffee cups. She filled them with the joe on the coffee maker, which emptied the carafe, and quickly set it up to brew a fresh pot a bit later. She motioned for Margo to join her in one of the booths.

Margo first emptied the pan of sweepings and put the broom away.

Bev spoke first. "So you don't feel I've called a meeting to complain about your work, I want you to know that so far we're very pleased with you. I'm particularly happy with how well you've learned from Mrs. Illichman. I do believe that if she couldn't make it to work, you could cover for her and none of our customers would notice the difference in cooks."

Margo beamed. "Really? Thank you!"

"So what were you thinking when it looked like you were having an out-of-body experience?"

"I'm not sure I should tell you." Margo slowly looked down into her cup of coffee.

"Why ever not?"

"I might hurt your feelings, or possibly make you feel insulted," said Margo, looking away.

"Oh posh! Are you saying you were thinking nasty thoughts about me?" demanded Bev teasingly.

"Oh no! I was playing what-if with myself."

"My goodness, I think I can handle that." Bev drummed her fingers on the table. "But what if... what?"

"What if this was my restaurant? What would I want to change, and what would I want to keep the way it is?"

"You don't say. Well, now I'm curious. How did you answer yourself?"

"Every time I play this game, I picture something different. For one thing, I would change the décor. Not only repaint, but I'd choose a theme and decorate accordingly. Then I'd make sure the menu offered dishes along that same theme. I'd also change the restaurant's name..."

"Fascinating. You really have gotten a thing for the restaurant business, haven't you! And you haven't been here all that long either," said Bev with surprise. "We have to get back to work soon, but give me an example of one of your *themes*, as you put it."

"One that I thought of is nautical and the décor would be all about ships, nets, oars, anchors, and that sort of thing. The menu would need to have a seafood section and the restaurant could be called Fisherman's Grub Café or something else with an oceanic gist." Then she added, second-guessing herself, "Probably not a great idea for an area that's mostly about farming, though."

"Only from the standpoint that it might be difficult to keep in seafood supplies—and that, affordably. People like to eat out, but they don't like to pay a lot," said Bev dryly. "What else have you thought of?"

"It could be staged in antiques and country décor and called Grandma's Kitchen. Or we could pick a colour and do everything from tablecloths to dishes in shades of that one colour. For example, purple. Then we could call it The Purple Diner."

"We? Not me, we," objected Bev quickly. "I'll agree the place looks pretty tired, but folks around here don't like change. The seniors rather fondly remember the Millers, who started this restaurant in the early 1950s and named it Lindy's Lunch after the proprietress. She sold it to me because they wanted to resume life in the warmer climes of the Okanagan in B.C., as well as retire there. That was all of fifteen years ago. Time sure does fly. You might have some good ideas, but I'm not interested in spending money on such ventures. I think I can get a few more miles out of the way things are, outdated as they may be. But… since you seem to have gravitated to the restaurant business, let me give you some free advice. Learn everything you can about all the roles it takes to run a café and know how to do them yourself. And then learn everything you can about running a *business*—that means taking a course. Then come talk to me about this time next year."

"Why? What's there to know about next year?" asked Margo, puzzled.

Bev lowered her voice and leaned in. "I'll tell you something if you promise on pain of death not to repeat it."

"Of course I won't."

"Pinky swear!"

Cautiously, Margo linked her smallest finger with Bev's.

"I'm serious. I'll break your finger if this gets out before I'm ready to speak of it," said Bev softly and conspiratorially. "Next spring, my husband is up for retirement. I'm thinking of giving up the restaurant, too, so we can do some traveling together. You know… see the world. In which case, perhaps the next owner of this outfit should be you with all your big and fancy ideas. Save up your dollars to become a businesswoman. Think about it."

Margo was shocked. "I don't even know what to say!"

"For the time being… absolutely nothing," warned Bev. She smiled to reinforce their secret.

~

"What on earth are you bringing in all those boxes for?" charged Lydia in sharp dismay. "There can't be any space left in your room to get around."

"I'm almost done," said Margo, panting. She tried to add the latest box to one of the stacks on the floor but couldn't manage to get it high enough. Huffing, she backed out of her room and deposited it in the middle of the short hallway.

Lydia looked on, hands on hips, frowning.

"What's in all those boxes?" she asked, wary over the sheer volume of cartons being brought into the house.

"Clothes. Shoes. Stuff that girls wear."

"Good Lord! You must have enough stock to open up a clothing store," noted Lydia with a mixture of awe and disapproval.

"I'm not going to keep it all, but I do need to sort through it," Margo looked around with forced patience. "The mess won't last longer than a few hours. Promise."

Lydia tsked, then turned on her heel and returned to her recliner in the living room, muttering under her breath about the excessiveness of young people these days.

After Margo brought in the last few items from her car, she went into her room and closed the door behind her. She stood with her back against the door for at least a full minute, taking in the scope of the mess of boxes in front of her. Dread, curiosity, and weariness converged, making it difficult to determine how she should proceed.

An image of Muriel Wirt crossed her mind. She easily imagined the good woman saying, "Face your problems head on, young lady. Don't run from them."

"Yes, Muriel," said Margo under her breath before adding, just as softly, "The way to eat an elephant is one bite at a time."

She opened the closest box first to find that it contained mostly sweaters and cardigans. Frowning judiciously, she began to assess and sort.

It took several hours and was well past midnight before Margo had divvied up the clothing into three groups to her satisfaction.

Just about all the items that still had the price tags attached were repacked with the intention of sending them back to the clothing store in Dauphin. Those two cartons were carefully taken to Lydia's basement and set on a table.

Another three boxes were filled with clothing, shoes, and purses that she would put out in a yard sale at some point in the springtime. These, too, were transferred downstairs to be out of the way for the time being.

The rest, practical items as befitted her new page in life, were hung in the closet and filled every drawer in her room. It was still a lot, but Margo reasoned she wouldn't have to buy new clothes for a long time, thus enabling her to save every red penny, nickel, and dime that came her way.

Bev's secret disclosure had birthed the notion that she could start anew and make something out of her life. She had no idea what sum of dollars might be needed for a downpayment for a small-town café, but the idea fully captured her imagination and provided a goal to strive for.

As Margo readied herself for bed, her eyes fell on the thick manilla envelope she had recently received from Larry. Yesterday she hadn't possessed the courage to open it. She was sure the money coming to her after the sale of the house in Dauphin and the settling of all their outstanding debts would amount to a paltry sum.

But now, with her thoughts quickening for the future, she was keen to know just how much she could add to her yet diminutive bank account. With trembling hands, she picked up the small package, sat on her bed, and carefully ripped one end open. Ignoring the sheaf of papers, she focused on the small envelope that was taped shut.

A few coins fell on to her lap as she ripped one side open. It contained several twenties and some smaller bills as well as a folded statement. Opening the statement first, she read the final summary of their financial status. Showing the credit from the sale of the house, and the list of debits that had been outstanding and were now paid, the leftovers amounted to $137.23.

Not a single tear escaped Margo's eyes, but her heart cried out in despondence. Lost. Lost! So much had been lost through pride and foolishness. She wished she could believe in God and that He could help her start over from the mess she had made of things.

Hugh claimed that God had helped him and, in fact, had made a new person out of him. Was that true? Could that happen to a person?

In the wee hours of the morning, Margo realized with a clarity she would not have admitted to anyone that she, too, needed a makeover—and she was *not* thinking of another way of applying makeup or a new hairdo.

And yet… how could believing in God really make a difference like that? Seriously. The idea defied all logic.

Just then, she remembered Bev's words. Learn everything you can about the different jobs in the restaurant and take a course. Learn how to run a business.

The door to Margo's bedroom was ajar. Fritz the kitty slipped through and jumped up on the bed, aiming for his mistress's lap.

"There you are!" cooed Margo. "Just what I need right now."

She returned the papers and manilla envelope to the top of the highboy, gathered up the young cat into her arms, and slipped under the covers.

"I gotta change my life, kittycat. Gotta learn more stuff, like how to run a business, and change the course of my life, ya know? Gotta pull myself up by the bootstraps and make something outta myself. Gotta take charge of my destiny. What do you say, Fritzy?"

The kitty purred while she stoked his back and scratched his neck, but he didn't like being held in confinement. After a short meow, he left Margo's embrace, hopped off the bed, and left the room.

Margo sighed before pulling up the covers and soon fell asleep.

The last of the lunch crowd had finally paid for their meals and left, freeing Margo to tidy up the café without interruption or regard for the patrons. She went to each booth to refill salt and pepper shakers and reload the napkin holders.

Suddenly the door flew open and a young, light-haired man rushed inside.

"Hi Rory," Margo said with a smile. "Looking for late lunch or early coffee break?"

Rory was a regular at the café. Bev joked that you could set your watch by the young strawberry blond farmer, since he seldom failed to show up at least once a day unless it was seeding time or harvest. At those times, all the farmers set aside their kaffeeklatch routine to put in, or take off, their crops.

"Late lunch," said Rory hurriedly. "What's ready to eat in the kitchen? I haven't time to wait. I hafta get to Dauphin before the close of business."

"I think there's still some soup of the day in the pot."

"What is it today?"

"Cream of potato and cauliflower."

Rory took a stool at the counter. "That will have to do."

In just a couple of moments, Margo returned with a bowl of soup and a side plate holding a crusty bun and pat of butter.

"What's in Dauphin for you?" asked Margo as she set his food in front of him.

Rory buttered his bun. "Need a part to fix my seeder, and I'll have it faster if I get it myself than wait to have it shipped to me."

"You know, you might just be an answer to prayer, as the saying goes." Margo leaned on the counter nearby. "Is there any chance you could do a drop-off for me in Dauphin? I have a couple of boxes that need to be delivered to a store on Main Street. Would you be able to do that?"

"I suppose I could," he replied unenthusiastically.

"I could give you some gas money for your time. After all, I was planning to send them by bus. But if you're going right away, it's that much faster…"

"Nah. It's not about the money. How big are these things? How much time would it take? Are they ready to go?" fired Rory between spoonsful of soup.

"Two good-sized boxes and they're ready to go. I can have them on your truck in five minutes. And I'll write out the address for you."

Rory lay down his spoon and rose. "Fine. Let's get 'er done."

Joyful as well as thankful, Margo settled the tab and promptly directed Rory to Lydia's house. In short order, the boxes were retrieved and securely placed in the back of his truck.

She handed him a slip of paper. "Drop these off in the back alley by the door at this address, and just before you leave, ring the doorbell. You don't have to wait and speak to anyone. Someone will answer the buzzer, see the boxes, and take them safely inside. It's how all shipments are handled."

"Seems a bit weird to me, but all right. If you say so." With a shrug, Rory climbed in behind the steering wheel.

"Thanks, Rory," called Margo as he began to drive away. "I owe you bigtime!"

Relief seemed to flood every fibre of her being as she watched him drive to the end of the street and turn north to meet up with Highway 10 to Dauphin.

Yet with every step she took returning to the café, Margo's doubts worsened. By the time she reached the rear door, which led to the kitchen, her arms were shaking and her breathing was irregular.

"What in heaven's name is wrong with me?" demanded Margo. "I did the right thing, after all. Didn't I?"

Fifteen

HUGH LEANED ON the horn of his truck so it conveyed his impatience.

"Good Lord, woman!" he grumbled to himself. "You've had more than four months to get ready for this trip. What in tarnation is taking you so long?"

It was easily a full minute later before Ellie exited their cozy cottage, checked to make sure the door was truly locked, and got into the half-ton carrying a bulky satchel.

"Hold your horses, Hugh-manoid!" said Ellie, mildly annoyed. "I realize you're pretty eager to get this show on the road, but we've got lots of time."

"We told Brian and Marcie we'd be at their place midafternoon. If we keep dillydallying, we'll be late for supper."

Hugh gunned the motor as they sped off their property.

Ellie looked his way. "You're really looking forward to seeing them, aren't you?"

"I am indeed! In a way, it will be like going home for a visit with the folks."

"I get it. I really do." Ellie patted his thigh, then gave him a sideways glance. "But you're not more excited to visit with them than to honeymoon with me, now are you?"

Hugh grinned but didn't say anything.

"There's only one right answer," teased Ellie, pinching his arm.

"I'm glad I get to do both."

Ellie settled in for the long ride. "I suppose that's close enough."

The trip was uneventful and they arrived at Brian and Marcie Turner's Charleswood address in Winnipeg in less than five hours, thanks to Hugh's heavy foot. As anticipated, they greeted each other with whoops and hugs.

The Turners ushered the newlyweds into their home, where they were met with the mouth-watering odours of roasting ham. Ellie paused to take in the scene, as this was the first time she had been in their house. The traditional furnishings in classic neutral colours and their arrangement lent a comfy and welcoming atmosphere. It was easy to feel instantly at home.

They were shown to Hugh's old bedroom to spend the night.

"This room has changed," Hugh remarked as he surveyed the space with nostalgia. "It's a lot tidier and no longer bears the telltale signs that a guy lives here."

"Nor the smells, either!" Marcie laughed. "Sometimes I miss the company of my boys, and that includes you, Hughie, but not the stink of clammy runners or fusty sweatpants and T-shirts!"

Hugh and Ellie set down their luggage and followed Marcie back to the front room where she invited them to sit on the sofa. There was some chitchat about the fine spring weather they were having as well as enquiries about the impending builds to the farmyard.

"Are you still game to go antique shopping with me after we get back from our honeymoon?" asked Ellie of Marcie.

"Most definitely. I'm looking forward to it!"

Smiling broadly, Marcie rose a moment later to check on the roast in the oven. About halfway to the kitchen, though, she stumbled and reeled, reaching out to the closest wall to keep from falling.

Ellie and Hugh noticed and looked back at Brian, confused. His face appeared grim, but he offered no comment.

"Don't mind me," said Marcie, quickly composing herself. She offered a light-hearted chuckle when she saw they were all staring at her. "Occasionally I walk with two left feet. Only God knows why."

She carried on to the kitchen without further incident.

~

Their plane was scheduled to leave shortly after lunch and the Turners made sure the couple got to the airport in plenty of time to check in without necessitating any rush. It would be Hugh's first flight and Ellie's second. Their nervous excitement was as much about taking the rare opportunity to see the earth from a bird's eye view as it was to experience the sites upon arriving at Pearson International Airport.

The flight did not disappoint. It was fun to try and follow the changing geography, corresponding to the places they saw on the map in front of them.

Upon arrival, they took a shuttle to their downtown hotel near Toronto's city hall. They quickly settled their things. Their room was near the top of the building and provided a panoramic view of the city's core.

A nearby restaurant served up a delicious steak for Hugh and a seafood plate for Ellie. By the time they had returned to their hotel afterward, darkness had descended over the city. Hugh and Ellie stood quietly side by side gazing out at the colourful sparkling lights.

"What do you think, Ella Rose?" asked Hugh softly. "Is it beautiful… or… eerie?"

Ellie understood. "It reminds me a bit of Christmas, the way they're multicoloured and seem to twinkle as though they mean to celebrate. On the other hand… it also reminds me of that song, 'The City Never Sleeps at Night,' which makes me realize how much restlessness so many people live with. The night seems to be just as hustle-bustle as the day. Not exactly a picture of peace and tranquillity, is it?"

"No, not at all. One wonders why the traffic doesn't slow down. It speeds to its destination as if it can't get there fast enough. Why the hurry? It feels a bit ominous. Perhaps it was the same in Winnipeg when I lived there, but I didn't notice it." He suddenly wore a thoughtful expression. "But now that I think about it, I fit in with my surroundings because, in a way, they were an extension of myself. That's it, isn't it, babe?"

He turned to his bride and pulled her close.

"Our living environments reflect what we're like as people," he continued. "In this case, busy, restless, and apparently hurried. I might already miss our simple country home."

Hugh planted a tender kiss on Ellie's forehead.

"Now who are you and what have you done with my husband?" Ellie playfully turned up her face to nibble on his chin. "My Hugh doesn't usually wax on all philosophical like."

"Isn't a honeymoon supposed to be when newly married couples discover all sorts of previously unknown things about each other?" queried Hugh huskily.

"Well... when you put it that way... I'm totally up for learning new and wonderful things about you. I hope I never get to the end of those discoveries."

She began to undo his shirt button by button.

"Just as I hope to never lose my fascination for you," said Hugh as he covered her mouth with his own.

~

They slept well. Upon waking, the pleasure and satisfaction they had enjoyed the evening before was still with them. Ellie arched her back in a cat-like stretch, then rolled over to face her husband. He was awake, staring at her contentedly, leaning on one arm.

"Hungry?"

"Honestly, I'm still full from last night," she purred. "Doubly so, I might add."

Hugh wriggled his arm so he could read his watch. "What time are we supposed to meet David in the lobby?"

"We agreed upon 9:00 a.m.," answered Ellie, snuggling into his chest.

"Whoa! That means we need to be downstairs in twenty-eight minutes." Hugh suddenly pushed away. "Seeing as you need more time to gussy up than I do, you'd better shower first."

Ellie quickly threw back the covers and bounded for the bathroom. Yet despite her damp hair and rushed application of makeup, she was ready to leave their room at the same time as Hugh.

They arrived in the hotel lobby at precisely 9:00 a.m. No David Johnson was there to meet them, however, and they stood around the entrance, feeling a little uneasy with each passing minute.

"Are you sure you have the time right?" Hugh finally asked.

Ellie responded with barely concealed irritation. "I checked my notes before leaving our room. He said nine."

At twenty minutes past nine, David sauntered through the grand entrance. He seemed surprised when Hugh and Ellie greeted him immediately.

"Good to see you again." Hugh grinned as he shook his cousin's hand and clapped his back with the other.

Ellie took her turn next, greeting him with a hug while whispering in his ear, "You're late!"

David withdrew from the embrace, blushing a little. "I'm not used to women being on time, so you'll have to forgive me," he retorted. "I was trying to give you a few extra minutes to do whatever it is women feel they must when they ready themselves."

Ellie's eyes flashed. "I'll have you know I was in time for my own wedding. And it was you who made me appear late!"

David grinned sheepishly and turned to Hugh. "I hope you have what it takes to live with this one. Every time I have an encounter with her, she seems rather exacting."

"I think I've got the hang of it," joked Hugh.

"That's enough," broke in Ellie with a low chuckle. "What have you got planned for us? I'm ready to see the great sites of Toronto."

David began to lead them to his car. "Not sure where your interests lie, but there's a few things we can do."

When she saw the car awaiting them at the curb, Ellie cooed enthusiastically. "Oh wow! A convertible!"

"Your '69 Cutlass Supreme!" Hugh said approvingly.

"Yup. And she runs smooth as silk." David's pride was obvious. "For this evening, I've made arrangements to see the vintage car collection of a colleague and friend. Thought you'd enjoy that, seeing as you've got a start on your own collection."

Hugh smiled. "Cool! I'm sure I will."

Within a few minutes, they were driving down the busy street.

"In the meantime, I've got something special lined up for your lady." A couple of blocks later, David added, "That's the building of the law firm I work for, and a few blocks away is my apartment complex."

Ellie watched their surroundings with genuine interest. "Will you show us your apartment? I'm sure Aunt Gertie would like to hear a firsthand description."

"No, for several reasons. One of them being that I think it's better for my mother to happily *imagine* what my bachelor's pad looks like than be disappointed with the reality. It's basic living quarters—nothing fancy. For another, my cleaning lady hasn't been by recently and I'd rather not deal with your disappointment in my decided lack of housekeeping skills."

"I see how it is, but it's still too bad," said Ellie. "She'll be disappointed, too."

"Trust me. You aren't missing anything. On the other hand, I hope you'll be impressed with touring our first stop. I thought you might enjoy a walkthrough of Casa Loma, Toronto's own authentic castle. It was built to echo the fine classical medieval homes of Europe's aristocracy."

"No kidding! A real castle? Or do you mean a grand Victorian home?" Ellie sounded rather doubtful.

"Well, you tell me." David pointed ahead and slightly to the right where the tops of the chimneys and towers of Casa Loma poked above the treetops.

"Oh wow! I didn't think Canada was an old enough country to feature an honest-to-goodness-castle!" said Ellie, marvelling.

"It's not all that old actually," David said. "It was built a little less than seventy years ago. But the builder, Sir Henry Pellatt, had his architect design it along the same veins as castles in Europe. It's said that at one point it was the largest private dwelling in Canada. I don't know if that distinction is still true."

They found a parking spot conveniently near the entrance. Ellie was all smiles as she slipped her hand into Hugh's. The trio walked up to the great front door, feeling dwarfed by the sprawling edifice.

Once their fees were paid, armed with a brochure which showed the floorplan and brief descriptions of the major rooms, they began their tour.

Because they were among the first tourists to arrive for the day, there was no waiting to see the different room displays. It felt like they had the whole place to themselves, and thus their exploration didn't take as long as it might have had the place been crawling with visitors. Here and there, Ellie expressed a few oohs and aahs but didn't linger long in any one room.

Hugh was just as glad. The place was interesting for sure, but not so much as to make a whole day of it.

Eventually they found themselves back on the main floor, near where they had started. Hugh saw an opportunity to use a public lavatory and excused himself. While waiting, David and Ellie wandered back to the lovely conservatory for a second look.

"My powers of observation suggest this might be your favourite room in the whole palace," said David with a tilt of his head.

"It is lovely, that's for sure," agreed Ellie. "What's not to love about the light filtering through the coloured glass? The beautiful, airy ambience? It's easy to see why this is so frequently chosen for weddings and private events."

"Wouldn't you like to live in a place like this if you had the chance?"

By his tone of voice, he seemed to assume she would answer yes.

"Oh no," replied Ellie quickly. "Don't get me wrong. It's a beautiful place, but it's not my style at all."

David raised his eyebrows. "Really! I'm surprised. I thought every woman would seize the opportunity to live in finery like this, if it came their way."

"I doubt that, seriously. It's... it's too much!" Ellie made a grand sweeping gesture with her arm.

"Too much? Too much what?" asked David, intrigued. "If I lived in a place like this, it would mean that I'd *arrived*. That I'd become an elite... someone prestigious."

Ellie looked at him oddly for a few seconds. "Is that, like, a goal or something for you?"

"I believe it's everyone's desire to make a difference in this world." David spoke with an air of magnanimity.

They began to walk back to the area where they had left Hugh.

"I'm sure you're right on that point," continued Ellie. "But I hardly think achieving great wealth, to the extent that one could afford to live in and maintain a castle like this, is a criterion for making a difference in this world. You're no doubt aware of Mother Teresa. She's poor as any church mouse, yet she's also a household name and a shining example of someone who's making a remarkable difference."

David sighed with forced patience. "I don't dispute that, but it's also true that wealthy people wield power and influence. It comes with the territory. And usually their place of residence is a quick indicator of the level of... of the influence they wield. I see it all the time in our law office. And often it's better to be the one putting out the influence than being on the receiving end."

"Hmmm." Ellie glanced at him sideways. "Sounds like you have a few stories to tell."

"Actually, I'd rather go back to talking about how you liked visiting this castle," said David, neatly changing the subject. "Was bringing you here a winner or a bust?"

"Winner! It was great to see how the upper class lived once upon a time. It's totally an interesting site. But as beautiful as this place is, for me it's not cozy. Everything screams, 'Don't touch me!' And then there's the thing about Lady and Sir Henry Pallett having separate bedrooms. I wonder what that was all about." She paused, then continued in a light and airy tone. "It would take so much time, money, and responsibility to look after a home like this. I'm quite content with a much simpler lifestyle, living someplace where I can curl up on the sofa and put my feet on the coffee table."

"You make a point."

David turned his head in response to movement on his left. Hugh had returned to join them.

They left Casa Loma a little before noon, with David suggesting that they grab lunch at the Eaton Centre. He explained that it had opened about three years earlier and was considered one of Canada's largest and most prominent shopping malls.

Hugh and Ellie listened with interest while trying to take in the passing downtown sites as David drove along. It seemed like miles of endless stores and businesses. So much fast-moving traffic. The sidewalks were filled with smartly dressed people strutting purposefully, and some obviously poor folk, too.

"Sounds like something worth seeing," admitted Ellie brightly at the suggestion of visiting the mall. "But just so you know, I'm not going to be much of a shopper."

"Every woman I know should have Shopper for a middle name. It's their biggest past-time. I know this about the gender." David turned to look at her with a smug smile on his clean-shaven face.

Ellie pursed her lips. "You need to remember we came here via airplane and our suitcases are full. Can't take a whole lot back with us."

"If you don't leave the mall with your arms full, I'll... I'll..." David snorted as he slowed down to obey a red light.

"I'd advise you not to wager on Ellie." Hugh chuckled. "If nothing else, it will become a motive to prove you wrong. If you get to know her well enough, you'll eventually uncover a vice or two, but unrestrained shopping isn't one of them."

Ellie shot a look of mock shock and disbelief at Hugh. "What kind of vices do you think you've discovered?" She attempted to poke him in the ribs, but he skillfully evaded her efforts, grabbing her hands instead and holding them fast.

Hugh gave her an exaggerated wink. "Let's just say your secrets are safe with me."

"Some of my living is made from the discovery of people's embarrassing and sticky secrets," commented David as he turned into the Eaton Centre's parking lot.

"I don't doubt it." Ellie gave him a sidelong glance. "The unfortunate truth is that we all have some. I'm not about to divulge mine, but I admit to being curious about yours."

"And I'll never tell..." David offered a rather mysterious crooked smile.

Because the parking lot was full, it took a few minutes to find a spot, and a few minutes more to walk to the main entrance.

It was an exhilarating experience to enter the enormous space. Ellie looked up, amazed at how high and airy it felt, especially with the likenesses of Canada geese poised overhead. It seemed like this indoor street of shops, lining both sides of the thoroughfare, went up several levels. Ellie counted four.

"Just how many shops are there?" wondered Ellie, wide-eyed.

"Well over two hundred."

The three of them had a little discussion to allot the necessary time for lunch in the food court and walking around the shops. They agreed on lunch first, to forestall being caught in long lineups when the anticipated noon crowd showed up.

They each settled on a different meal. Hugh chose a traditional burger and fries, David had a plate of Asian food, while Ellie opted for a fresh salad and chicken strips.

It took only fifteen minutes to consume their lunch and get back up to walk through the mall. It was Hugh's idea to begin on the top level and work their way down.

But David demurred. "I suggest we only scope out two floors. I still want to take you two to the CN Tower for a view of the lake and city before dinner. After that, we have that appointment I told you about."

"Sounds like a smart plan," agreed Ellie, while Hugh nodded in agreement. "I wasn't kidding when I said I didn't come to shop. But having a look around will give us bragging rights when we tell others about this place."

That settled, they began to walk along, slow enough to note the window displays but quick enough not to dawdle. Occasionally Ellie remarked on an outfit she thought appealing or particularly untasteful. Her gentlemen escorts shrugged in response, conveying ignorance in the matter of ladies' fashions.

When they passed a popular men's clothing outlet, David went inside to take advantage of a two-for-one sale in solid-colour shirts.

"I need a clean shirt for Monday," he explained when Ellie raised her eyebrows at the unexciting purchase.

"I see," she replied. "Will we need to look into getting men's underwear then, too? Eaton's is just ahead."

David returned her teasing tone. "My supply of underwear is greater than my shirts, so I'm good for a while yet. And you can tell my mother, should it come up in conversation, that if I have an accident and end up in hospital, my drawers are clean, intact, and of the highest quality! They even match my suits!"

Not to be left out, Hugh added, "I get the navy blue ones to match my jeans. It's not just girls who know how to dress styling."

Ellie pursed her lips, rolled her eyes, and moved on down the mall. There was only one shop she entered, to the shock of both men. It was a maternity store.

"Is she trying to tell us something, do you think?" asked David, puzzled.

Hugh looked nervous. "I sure hope not. I'd be okay with the news, but this isn't how I wanted to find out about it."

They took a seat on a bench across from the store. Hugh bounced his knee impatiently while David smiled, clearly amused.

Moments later, Ellie returned to find both men boring holes into her with their eyes. "What?"

"Are you trying to tell me something, Ella Rose, going into a shop like that?" asked Hugh quite seriously.

David looked away.

"You mean, because I went in to look at maternity fashions? Heavens no! I'm not pregnant... not that I know of, anyway," declared Ellie. "I just wanted to compare the fashions pregnant women wear with what regular women wear. That's all. Believe me, if I was in a family way, I'd tell you privately—and likely with a lot of celebration."

Ellie patted Hugh on the shoulder, then slipped her hand into his and continued walking along the mall avenue.

Back on the first floor, Hugh went up to the kiosk selling a variety of fudge and purchased two slabs: chocolate with nuts and a creamy butterscotch. He offered pieces to Ellie and David, which they accepted and enjoyed.

After that they concluded their tour and continued on their way to the CN Tower.

It wasn't a long ride from the mall to one of Toronto's more recent tourist attractions. On the way, David bragged that it was the tallest free-standing structure on the planet.

"Just how tall is it then?" asked Ellie interested. She was sitting in the front seat, actively peering all around and taking in the city. In the back seat, Hugh was less inquisitive. He exhibited a more laid-back pose, an if-you've-seen-one-city-you've-seen-them-all kind of attitude.

David answered proudly. "Five hundred and fifty-three meters, plus change."

"I'm old school," Ellie said. "What's that in feet?"

"More than eighteen hundred. The viewing decks aren't that high, of course, but they're still what you'd call 'dizzying heights' for a lot of people."

"Do great heights bother you?"

"Nah. It's all built very safely. Rather exhilarating, actually," replied David. "What about you?"

"Not sure. The highest I've been is probably our hotel room. And that hasn't bothered me or my honey. Right, Hugh?"

Hugh jerked to attention. "What was that?"

"We're talking about heights, and whether being way up high gives you the heebie-jeebies," she repeated.

"Not so far." Hugh leaned forward to more ably participate. "The high altitudes of our flight weren't troublesome either, so I think we'll be okay."

David pulled into the parking lot. "We're about to find out."

"Oh my gosh." Ellie craned her neck to see the top of the tower as they walked towards the entrance. "From here, it really does seem like it pokes through the sky and into outer space."

"It's tall, but not that tall!" chuckled David with a playful roll of his eyes.

After they bought their tickets, David led them to the glass elevator, which allowed them to view the landscape as they ascended. It was fun at first, but about halfway up Ellie's stomach began to feel tentative. She grabbed Hugh's hand and he squeezed it reassuringly.

As nonchalantly as she could, she looked around the elevator, hoping it would cancel the odd, prickly sensations her body produced as it left the familiar steadiness of the ground.

David noticed and smiled but didn't razz her about it. Truth be told, he'd had a few problems himself the first couple of times he had visited the site. It took a little getting used to, and he respected that.

At last the elevator doors opened to the viewing deck and they walked out to join a rather crowded space. The hum of chatter was quite loud. Ellie noticed several different languages being spoken. Listening carefully, she picked out German, French, Chinese, and British-accented English. There were other tongues as well, but she couldn't identify them.

They walked around the circle of the viewing chamber, courteously waiting for a gap to open so they could have a closer look. The great Lake Ontario was truly great. It might have been a sea or an ocean for its immensity. A ship could be seen in the distance.

Additionally, it felt odd to perceive the tiny details of the city below and feel safe doing so. Her stomach had settled back down by now — that is, until she inadvertently stepped onto the glass floor. Immediately all the cells in her body felt disconnected from each other, like a tub full of cottage cheese. She quickly stepped off the glass, feeling unsteady and queasy. Not far behind, Hugh grabbed her quickly, as it looked very much like she might faint.

"You okay, babe? You're looking rather pale…"

"I am now that I'm back on solid ground," she replied weakly. Embarrassment kicked in. "I guess I'm a big baby, after all… I mean, it's just as solid as the floor we're standing on. Silly me."

"No, you're not." Hugh reassured her with a squeeze around her shoulders. "It was an experience of fake danger. I saw the glass floor and knew I wouldn't like the sensation of looking through it. So I moved to the side. I thought you saw it coming and were intentionally going for the full-meal deal."

"Nope! I never looked down. Just tried to keep pace with the traffic in here and not bump into someone or step on their toes. Where's David?" Ellie looked behind, and then all around. "I'm sure he would have enjoyed my discomfiture immensely, if he saw it."

They finally found David twenty feet away engaged in conversation with a couple. It was obvious they were acquainted. While politely waiting for him to conclude this random meeting, Ellie and Hugh agreed not to share with anyone the story about Ellie nearly losing her cookies or wetting her pants by inadvertently walking onto the floor's transparent inset.

Fifteen minutes later, they returned to the ground floor via an internal elevator. While they didn't have to contend with fluttering stomachs on the descent, it was so crowded that Ellie was sure she could name the aftershave lotion of the gentleman who had been all but pressed against her.

It was now late in the afternoon and time to think about supper. The men deferred to Ellie.

"How about Chinese food?" she suggested. "Haven't had that in ages."

"I know just the place," gushed David, pleased with her selection. "It's not fancy, but the food is excellent!"

Hugh smiled. "That's what matters."

As it turned out, there was an authentic Asian diner within a block of David's apartment building. Upon entry, the proprietor greeted David warmly.

"First name basis!" Ellie said, impressed. "Must mean you're a regular here."

"I am. That's why I know the food is great—and reasonably priced, too."

David introduced Hugh and Ellie to Feng, the owner, and then asked for recommendations for their evening meal. In charming broken English, Feng said that he would fix them something special—a little of this and a little of that.

They weren't disappointed. In all Feng brought them eight bowls to share, including shrimp, lemon chicken, ginger beef, tasty whole vegetables, noodles, fried rice, and some mystery dishes neither Ellie nor Hugh recognized but enjoyed just the same. By the time they finished, they were stuffed to the gills and very satisfied. Hugh paid for the meal and left Feng a generous tip.

Feng bowed several times. "Thank you, sir, and your beautiful missus. Come back soon and I make you something tasty. Some of Feng's specialties."

The supper hour had the effect of giving them all a rest, putting the three of them in touch with how tired they felt after a full day of being out on the town. Nevertheless, David wanted to show Hugh his friend's vintage car collection, claiming it would be worth every minute—especially because he had come from far away and couldn't see it any old time. The newlyweds were ready to kick off their shoes, but David's fervent exhortations convinced them to finish the day with this one last tour.

It took close to forty-five minutes to drive out beyond the suburbs to the five-acre property. A fine redbrick house with classical white pillars and Victorian style finishings materialized after they turned into the rather long driveway, lined on both sides by extraordinarily tall spruce trees. Although it was dusk, Ellie quickly noticed that the lawn was neat with numerous clumps of budding peonies. Beyond the stately house stood a long, plain garage clad in simple white siding. David pulled up to this building and, seeing a light on through a small window, pressed a short, friendly toot of his horn and then cut the motor.

"Prepare to be impressed," said David to Hugh with a wide smile.

All three opened their doors and stepped out of the car. They had barely stretched their legs when a white-haired gentleman exited the garage through a side door and stood smiling with his hands stuffed in the pockets of his trousers. Ellie pegged him at approximately seventy years old, his lightly wrinkled face already tanned around a thick, bushy moustache. Friendly, crystal-blue eyes peeked out from underneath combed yet fluffy eyebrows. A Toronto Blue Jays cap sat tipped upward on the back of his head. His mostly red and green argyle knit pullover covered an unbuttoned-at-the-neck beige shirt atop green twill pants. Heavy, brown brogue shoes covered his feet.

For a senior, Ellie thought him striking to look at and imagined he had been quite the dreamboat as a young man, likely turning the heads of all women who crossed his path.

"Thought you'd be here an hour ago, Davy Crocket," said the handsome senior.

"Yeah? Well, we opted for a nice sit-down dinner and it took longer to eat than a burger on the go." David reached out to shake his hand. "Let me introduce you to my cousin and his wife. This is Hugh Fischer and his bride Ellie. Ellie and Hugh, this is my good friend Ian McCallum."

They exchanged firm handshakes and then Ian led them into his well-lit garage.

Hugh hadn't been sure what to expect, but the private collection of shiny vintage vehicles parallel parked on both sides of the building—he counted twelve in total—wasn't it. His mouth dropped open in unabashed delight, as did Ellie's.

David had been watching for Hugh's first reaction. "Told you." He grinned with satisfaction. "Worth the effort to see these beauties, right?"

"This... this is amazing!" said Hugh in wide-eyed admiration. "Do they all belong to you, or do you store some for other owners?"

"They're all mine except the one that belongs to Davy Crocket here. Well, make that two. My wife owns one of them and makes sure I don't forget it." Ian chuckled lightly.

"Don't tell us which ones they are." Ellie was all smiles. "Let's see if I... I mean, we... can guess. I have a tentative guess which one might be Mrs. McCallum's."

Ellie panned the space a couple of times. One in particular stood out in her mind.

"Oh sure," Ian said amiably. "Games are usually fun. Every vehicle here has a story to go with it."

"Let's hear them," implored Hugh. "They look as new as when they were first manufactured."

"They do, don't they. I've tinkered on every one of them, but I'm not a mechanic by trade. I don't even have much of a natural bent for fixing motors and revitalizing autobody. And because I need extra help with the trades, which can be quite costly, I can't afford to retire just yet. It's an expensive hobby. But Dave and I have inadvertently created a vintage car club. It began with 'I know a guy who knows a guy who can help me solve my problem.' Then they catch the bug for wanting to resurrect an old classic, so we're always trying to scratch each other's back... the results are pretty rewarding."

"What do you do when you're not working on an antique car?" asked Ellie.

Ian smiled and stroked his chin, as if considering which personal details he should divulge. He glanced at David, who shook his head slightly, enough to indicate that he hadn't gossiped.

"My career has been devoted to law," said Ian. "And I've spent the last fifteen years presiding as a provincial court judge."

Ellie nodded with understanding. "Of course. I should have guessed."

"So what's the story with this Oldsmobile?" asked Hugh, bringing the subject back to the matters at hand.

"That's the auto that got me started on this hobby." Ian turned his full attention to Hugh and his collection. "I bought this 1951 beauty from a neighbour twenty years ago when he was liquidating all his stuff to move into a retirement home. Paid $500 for it and it was in pretty good shape. Mostly needed a little bit of refreshment, but I kept to its original colours and overhauled the motor. Purrs like a kitten..."

One by one, Ian guided them through each classic vehicle. The collection included an orange and white Chevrolet Belair hardtop, a 1937 Plymouth Roadster, a 1959 Impala four-door hardtop, a 1922 Duesenberg Model A doctor's coupe, a powder blue 1957 Volkswagen Beetle, a red and black 1936 Chevrolet half-ton, a 1949 Ford Station Wagon with wood panelling, a green 1940 Ford Tudor, a 1942 Studebaker President Land Cruiser, a 1938 Lincoln Zephyr convertible coupe, and an especially elegant 1928 Falcon Knight Roadster that had been meticulously painted in pastel shades of pink, mint green, and cream; the inside was every bit as wonderful with a creamy interior and rosy pink upholstery.

"This must be Mrs. McCallum's car," declared Ellie.

"What gave it away?" asked Ian with mock surprise. "You're right, of course."

"You don't strike me as being the pink type," she replied. "I never think of cars as being beautiful, but this one is quite exquisite. I believe I'm lusting a little for this one..."

Ian laughed. "In fact, I usually defer to my wife when it comes to the paint and upholstery. She has a better eye for what suits them. She says it's their colour that communicates their personality."

"I daresay she has a point." Ellie smiled broadly.

"And which do you think is my collector's item?" asked David with a tilt of his head.

"Ummm. I suppose the red and white Impala," said Ellie slowly after scanning them all a second time.

David turned to Hugh.

"I'll guess the Chev Belair," Hugh guessed. "I can see you being excited about that one."

David shook his head. "Wrong, both of you. Mine is the powder blue Volkswagen Beetle. I bought it at a yard sale for a hundred bucks. The motor was seized up, but it didn't take a lot to get it running again. And then I got into restoring the rest of it to its present pristine condition."

"I am surprised," said Ellie. "Wouldn't have thought you were the Beetle type, but what I'm learning is that this hobby is hinged on chance opportunities... lucky finds."

"Often it is," agreed Ian.

David nodded. "And if word gets out that you're interested in vintage vehicles, people start calling you with offers. But they usually want way more than they're really worth for the condition they're in. I got a guy trying to get me to buy his 1947 Indian motorcycle... for the price of a new Harley! And it needs tons of work. I told him to come back when he's ready to have a reasonable discussion."

Ian turned to Hugh. "I hear you have some old-timers lined up for restoration."

"Yes, I do. I found some relics in the bush of our farm: a 1939 Plymouth PT half-ton in pretty good shape, and a 1942 Studebaker that will need lots of TLC. I've also got a real old tractor I don't know what I'm going to do with yet. But I'm pumped to bring these items back to beauty and function. Seeing your collection inspires me! Thanks loads for the private tour."

"You're most welcome," said Ian genuinely. "In your case, you have an advantage over me. You're actually a mechanic who knows his way around motors. I'm just a tinkerer who needs to depend on the expertise of skilled tradesmen. I expect your restoration projects won't require as much cash outlay as mine do."

They left shortly after that and the return trip to downtown Toronto was filled with chatter and reviews over the splendid old-timers they had seen. Hugh truly was excited about the prospects of restoring his Plymouth and Studebaker. He wished he could return home at once to erect his garage as soon as possible so he could get to work on them.

Hearing this, Ellie fell silent. The men didn't notice, so wrapped up were they in their excitement over car restoration. It didn't bother her enough to cry about it, but it did dampen her spirits a bit. It wasn't the first time she had felt in competition with Hugh's additional interests.

However, she hadn't expected to have to reckon with them on her honeymoon.

Sixteen

AFTER A LEISURELY Sunday breakfast at their hotel, Ellie and Hugh got into their rental car armed with local maps of the city and beyond. They took a deep breath and backed out of the parking space, off to explore the area and get a good look at the mighty St. Lawrence River. The evening before, they had invited David to come along, believing his knowledge and familiarity of the region would prevent them from getting lost—or getting involved in an accident, with the speed of traffic being so much higher here than back on the prairies. However, David graciously declined, citing the "homework" he needed to do in preparation for going into the office on Monday, not to mention certain household chores that could no longer be neglected.

Leaving the city wasn't as complicated as they feared and eventually they got used to the pace of fellow travellers, which, by taking the scenic route on Highway 2 instead of the freeway, was plenty slow enough for sightseeing. Southern Ontario was already in bloom on account of the warmer temperatures. Many of these plants couldn't have survived in the much cooler and shorter season of the central provinces.

Neither Hugh nor Ellie spoke much as they made their way out of the city. But after a while, Ellie ventured an observation.

"There are a *lot* more grand old houses and character homes in these parts than we see back home on the prairies," she said thoughtfully. "Makes poor old Manitoba appear plain and dowdy by comparison."

"I know what you mean." Hugh glanced back and forth between the road and the sights to his left and right. "The houses you see along our country roads aren't often as classic or handsome."

Ellie took a thoughtful moment to consider that. "Except for barns. There are some wonderfully grand barns gracing rural Manitoba. I still wish the original barn at our place could have been salvaged and renovated."

"If it didn't represent so many awful memories, I might have been open to it."

He looked over at Ellie, who peered intently out of her passenger window. His heart felt like it would burst from the rush of love he suddenly felt for her. The surprise of it brought tears to his eyes, and he quickly blinked them away in embarrassment.

Ellie hadn't noticed his private moment of deep emotion, for which he was somehow relieved. It wasn't that he thought himself unmanly; it was more about how he was suddenly put in touch with how quickly his love could reduce him to something like soft, mushy pudding. It seemed too bare and sensitive, and it made him feel strangely afraid.

When the moment passed and he had collected himself, Hugh reached over to hold Ellie's hand. She responded with a reciprocating squeeze and flashed a sweet smile in his direction before returning her gaze to the passing scenes on her right. They were getting their first glimpses of the St. Lawrence River between the steady stream of houses, restaurants, shops, and boat launches.

"Liking what you see?" asked Hugh nonchalantly.

"Oh yes," replied Ellie without hesitation. "I was thinking how this river has witnessed so much history. If it could talk... well, some of the history we studied in school would probably need correction and updating."

"Hmmm. You're thinking about Canadian history and I'm thinking hot and heavy of getting you naked and pinning you down under my bare chest and—"

"And then what?" queried Ellie wide-eyed with faux innocence. She no longer gazed upon the river but bored into her husband intently, daring him to speak aloud that which usually remained unmentionable and private.

"Why don't I just show you." Hugh spoke in a sensual tenor, seeming to look around for something resembling a private lane that might lead to an inconspicuous glade where he might love on his bride in keeping with the idea of a honeymoon.

"Seriously? Here?" Suddenly Ellie felt alarmed that Hugh's teasing might actually lead to a truly mortifying situation in broad daylight.

"No, not here." Hugh sighed. "But I would if I knew a suitable getaway close by."

Ellie received his loving, hungry looks with happiness. "Yeah. It's a lovely idea you have there. Just hold on to that thought for later, okay? For now, how about we just enjoy seeing part of our homeland we can't readily visit? We'll always be together, but only God knows if we'll ever come this way again."

Hugh pulled her hand up to his face and kissed it. "Love you, babe."

"Love you, too." Ellie then turned to gaze upon the mighty St. Lawrence again.

They arrived in Cornwall early in the afternoon. Hungry again, they found a fish and chips diner and ordered takeout so they could eat by the shores of the great river.

They found a small park that had benches on which to sit facing the water.

"According to the map, it's not a whole lot further to drive into Quebec, or even as far as Montreal," Ellie said. "We could then return to Toronto on the much faster 401 freeway. What do you think, love?"

"Not gonna lie, I'm getting tired on driving. I'm ready to head back as soon as we're done with lunch."

Ellie didn't push it.

While the trip along the four-lane highway back no longer offered glimpses of the monumental river, it did afford pleasant views of crops and vegetation unique to eastern Ontario. By the time they got back to their hotel, both felt they'd had a well-rounded tour.

A short time later, Hugh delivered on his earlier declaration to his wife.

⌒

Monday morning was their last for the Toronto leg of the vacation. They had time to leisurely pack up their belongings, do a walkabout through the hotel's neighbourhood, and eat a delicious epicurean lunch before boarding a special tourist bus that would deliver them to their hotel at Niagara Falls. The less than two-hour bus ride showed off the region's density.

As before, neither Hugh nor Ellie said anything as they took in the views left and right barrelling down the QEW freeway.

At length it was Hugh who said, "Pretty sure I wouldn't like to live here. Too many people. Too much traffic."

"Me neither," agreed Ellie. "I'm suddenly in touch with how much of a country bumpkin I am, even after living in the heart of Winnipeg for ten years. Still, I'm glad we've come to see more of our country firsthand."

Their hotel wasn't far from the falls themselves. Their room, on one of the top floors, granted them a vista that included the cascading water as well as the mist that perpetually obscured it. As soon as the couple had registered with the hotel, they deposited their luggage, turned on their heels, and left the building. In under fifteen minutes, Hugh and Ellie stood beside the metal fencing, wondrously gazing at the water crashing against the rocks below. The spray and mist felt refreshing on their cheeks, the roar of the rushing water in their ears speaking to the awesome and fearful marvel of the site. Paradoxically, it coincided with the sweet peace arresting their spirits.

"So glad we came," shouted Ellie over the roar. "There's nothing like this where we come from. It's a feast for the eyes and soul."

Hugh squeezed her hand in return. "I'm right with you, honey."

Over the next four days, they made daily visits to the falls, experiencing them in a variety of ways. The *Maid of the Mist* provided an exciting opportunity to see the see the falls from the river below. On another occasion, they stood behind the falls along a fenced ledge.

Ellie eventually claimed these visits as the highlights of each day. Hugh agreed that it was an interesting place, but he wouldn't have gone so far as to consider it a mystical experience.

Much to Ellie's delight, and as she had hoped, the magnolia trees along the Niagara Parkway were in bloom, their sweet fragrance captivating the senses. Their rental car made it possible to drive along this scenic stretch of road and see many of the other famous sites nearby, including the whirlpool further downstream. They also saw part of the impressive Welland Canal that linked Lake Ontario with Lake Erie. They were lucky enough to watch an enormous ship from a European country go through the locks. Hugh was especially fascinated by the engineering and mechanics involved in the process.

While roaming about the southern peninsula, they took in some of the fruit orchards and fields of grapes, including wineries.

Ellie enjoyed poking around in some of the boutique shops in St. Catherines and Niagara-on-the-Lake, choosing the occasional unique piece of pottery and handcrafted knitted wool sweaters. They also visited antique shops. Despite discovering some wonderful pieces, though, Ellie didn't make any purchases. The cost of shipping them home to Manitoba was substantially more than she was willing to pay.

On Friday, they nervously anticipated the last full day of their vacation. With helpful information from some seniors in Minitonas who remembered Rudolf and Huldah Fischer from the homesteading days of the 1920s and 1930s, Ellie had successfully made contact with Hugh's Aunt Renata and asked for a meeting between the long-lost relatives.

Renata's initial shock soon gave way to curiosity and an enthusiastic desire to meet her estranged, and now deceased, brother's son and his new wife.

Hugh's unacquainted relatives lived approximately a half-hour away in the small town of Grimsby. While Hugh made the necessary arrangements through the hotel concierge, Ellie carefully packed a tote bag with two photo albums, a gift-wrapped box of chocolates, and a few miscellaneous papers she and Hugh had found in the pair of trunks from the old homestead. She also tucked in another gift-wrapped item, this one large and flat along one side.

Thus outfitted, she descended to the main floor via the elevator.

"Nice car," admired Ellie approvingly of the late model sports car they were given when they went out to pick up their rental car.

A smile tipped up Hugh's right cheek as he consulted the map. He then turned over the navigation to Ellie while he exited the parking lot and made his way to the QEW, heading north. No chatter passed between them, partly because their eyes were peeled to watch out for their exits—and partly because the closer they got to their destination, the more excited, as well as anxious, they became to meet their unfamiliar relatives.

Aunt Renata had provided a Main Street address, which they thought odd until they realized how many beautiful homes graced the primary roadway as they drew closer to the centre of town. The house numbers weren't all that easy to spot, so Hugh slowed down as much as he dared, to the annoyance of the drivers behind him who often sped past rudely tooting their horns.

"Here it is!" exclaimed Ellie.

The number they were searching for was elegantly displayed on an oval disc welded to a black Victorian style metallic fence that began at the entrance of the driveway and presumably enclosed the property.

Hugh turned in and immediately stopped the car. His demeanour suddenly changed. Both hands gripped the steering wheel, white-knuckled. Uncertainty and trepidation took over the expression on his face.

Thankfully, Ellie was quick to understand. "It's going to be all right," she assured him. "No doubt your lost and found relatives are feeling a tad nervous as well. This is an exciting opportunity, honey. Let's make the most of it."

She reached over and laid her hand on his arm.

Hugh nodded, then slowly brought the car up to the stately red-brick house with white wooden trim. He parked near the front entrance in an area designated for guest parking. Both exited the vehicle at the same time with Ellie carrying her purse and the tote.

Walking up the steps to the veranda of the gorgeous colonial residence, the grand oak front door opened before they could apply the knocker. The smiling woman who met them was tall, slim, and shapely, smartly dressed in a crisp white shirt with the collar standing up behind her neck, accessorized with a colourful scarf at the throat over perfectly fitted navy slacks. Her pale blond hair had been meticulously coiffed in a short wedge cut that exposed sparkling diamond stud earrings. Stylish flat-heeled Italian leather shoes clad her feet.

Ellie was profoundly grateful that she and Hugh had had the foresight to dress up for this occasion. First impressions often lasted a long time.

They each stood for a couple of wordless seconds, taking each other in.

Renata spoke first. "Oh. My. God. Are you sure your name isn't Fredrich Fischer? You look exactly like the brother I left behind close to forty years ago." Her eyes blurred with tears as she reached out to embrace her nephew.

Hugh tentatively stepped into her embrace. "Hugh Richard Fischer. At your service."

"And this must be your bride," cooed Renata, turning to Ellie.

"So pleased to finally meet you, Aunt Renata." said Ellie warmly. They also exchanged cursory hugs.

"Yes, well, do come in and welcome!" Renata stepped aside to let them in. "Aunt Renata, is it? This is the first time I've been thus addressed. It feels a bit strange, but I suppose I'll get used to it."

The entrance led to a generously sized central hall. Beyond that stood the grand staircase padded with a luxuriously thick burgundy carpet runner. The walls were partly oak-panelled and wainscoted. The handcrafted plastered walls were painted a crisp ivory. Large, nature-themed artwork hung in elegant frames, adding to the magazine-like perfection.

Ellie was wide-eyed, trying to take it all in at once. "What an absolutely beautiful home you have," she gushed.

"Thank you," returned Renata. "It has taken us many years and a *lot* of money to restore this home to its former elegance while incorporating necessary modern amenities. But the mission is finally accomplished and now we're wondering whether we should downsize, since it's a lot of house for an empty-nested couple. Well, not quite empty-nested. Mother—that is, your grandmother—occupies a small in-law suite in one wing of the house."

She led them through window-paned pocket doors on the right into a spacious living room furnished with high-quality antiques. Hugh and Ellie opted to sit in a pair of red plaid wingchairs, leaving Renata to seat herself across from them on the slightly curved sofa upholstered in what appeared to be white linen.

Ellie looked around the room, drinking in the beauty of a bygone era. "We saw Casa Loma a few days ago. It was lovely, and elegant, but this..." She waved her arm to encompass the whole house. "This is a lot closer to what I would call my dream home. It's beautiful but has enough informal elements to infer comfort rather than intimidation. I so hope you'll give us a tour before we return to our hotel."

"Perhaps later." Renata turned her focus to Hugh. "Right now I'd like to learn about my long-lost nephew and be brought up to date on my brother's life. After I left Manitoba, and especially after my mother left following my father's passing, it was like Fred fell off the edge of the world. Mother wrote. I wrote. But he didn't reply even once. Eventually we just gave up. And now you're here looking like his identical twin! You said he died in a vehicle crash three and a half years ago along with his wife? There are a lot of stories to catch up on. I'm impatient to hear them."

"You said my grandmother still lives and resides with you," said Hugh cautiously. "Shouldn't she join our conversation?"

Renata tensed. "I did, and that's true," she began hesitantly, "but now that I've seen you first, I think she may be very shocked and distressed. Your finding us after so many years has stirred up many unpleasant memories for my eighty-year-old mother. I'm just not sure how she'll react."

"Is she well?" asked Ellie, concerned.

"More or less, yes. However, we're noticing occasional mental lapses lately and suspect Alzheimer's or dementia. The point is, if she gets peculiar, I may have to speak for her or take her back to her room."

"We have all day, if need be, to catch up on each other's lives," Hugh said with a resolve that took him by surprise. "You know, we can take our time filling in the blanks. But I have questions. I need a few answers."

"We have questions, too," returned Renata frankly. "Would a cup of coffee be welcome? I'll come back with a tray... and let Mother know you're here."

"That would be lovely," replied Ellie.

Renata got up and left the room, giving Ellie a few moments to admire the handsome fireplace and other touches around the room. Hugh shifted in his chair, signalling his uneasiness. He started drumming his right leg with his fingers.

It was hard to sit patiently. Ellie wanted very badly to walk around and explore the gorgeous, antique-filled rooms but felt it would be rude to do so without Renata's consent.

She pulled out the two gift items and set them on the coffee table.

Eventually they heard muffled talking in some distant part of the house. Soon after came a pair of footsteps: one confident and sure, the other with the rhythm of lameness and a cane.

Renata entered first and set down a large wicker tray on the low table. It contained a steaming coffee pot, mugs, cream and sugar, and a plate of sliced poppy roll. Immediately she turned to the very short, grey-haired woman standing in the entrance. The woman was puzzling over the strange guests.

"Komm rein, Mutter. Treffen Sie Ihren Enkel, Friedich's Sohn und seine Frau," said Renata as she steered the elder woman towards Hugh.

Hugh stood immediately, and so did Ellie.

Hugh's grandmother stared at him for several seconds, blinking with a furrowed brow. "Ist das nicht Friedrich? Ist er endlich bekommen, um seine Mutter zu sehen, bevor ich weitergehe?"

"Nein. Er is Friedrich's Sohn und Ihr Enkel, der Sie besuchen kommt," restated Renata patiently. "Kommen Sie. Setz dich bitte." She patted the seat beside hers on the sofa. "Lass uns einander kennenlernen. Ist es nicht wunderbar, einige von Friedrich's Familie zu treffen?"

Hugh and Ellie resumed their seats. Grandmother Fischer sat but didn't take her eyes off Hugh.

Hugh returned the stare but addressed Renata. "Sorry, but I don't know a word of German. I take it she's confusing me with my pa since there's a lot of resemblance. Does she speak only German?"

Renata turned to her mother with a sly smile. "Oh no, she understands and speaks English well enough. German is used when we don't want Englishmen to understand what we're saying. Mind you, it is her mother tongue and she reverts to it more and more as she ages. Don't you, Mother?"

The grandmother nodded slightly, with only a hint of a smile. She kept her gaze upon Hugh.

Renata poured coffee and passed out the mugs and snack while Ellie and Hugh continued to assess their newfound relatives. Remembering what they had learned from the Bredins and Kleins in Minitonas, it appeared that Huldah Fischer hadn't changed too much over the years. She was still petite, with a face that brought to mind a mouse, given its small, sharp features. Her pewter-shaded hair was short and styled primly. Attired in a purple, polyester pantsuit with pink blouse beneath, she emitted an air of sophistication. Walking with a cane suggested hip problems, but that did nothing to dampen her air of self-assuredness; it bordered on pride, if not outright arrogance.

Hugh recognized the trait at once, having seen it in his father all his life. He saw it in Margo's personality, too, though not so much in his youngest sister Diane. Nor in his mother, whose spirit had been knocked out of her soon after teaming up with her ill-matched husband. He wondered how much of this tendency to pride he himself displayed. What lasting impressions did he leave on others when they first met him? He would have to remember to discuss this with Ellie sometime.

"Are these gifts for your grandmother?" asked Renata, referring to the wrapped packages Ellie had set out.

Ellie smiled sweetly. "They're for all of you to enjoy."

"That is so thoughtful of you." Renata passed the top package to her mother and then proceeded to open the second one herself. "Your wedding portrait! How absolutely lovely!"

Renata peered closely at the photograph and then passed it to Huldah.

"Sehr gut, danke," said Hugh's grandmother approvingly as she held up the box of chocolates. Upon seeing the picture, she frowned, however, and looked questioningly to Renata.

"Nicht Friedrich, Mutter." Renata comprehended her confusion. "Dein Enkel und seine Braut." She indicated Hugh and Ellie sitting across from them.

The elder woman looked from the photograph to the couple and back again before nodding that she understood.

"Do I have cousins?" asked Hugh.

"Yes. We have two daughters." Renata set down the photo. "The elder is Cassandra. She's a doctor in Toronto, specializing in cardiology. The younger is Emily and she has a degree in interior design. She has a flourishing business in St. Catherines. I daresay she was bitten by that bug as we redid this house. She followed the interior designer we hired around like a puppy."

"Nice. Married? Children?"

Renata chuckled uneasily. "Oh no. They consider themselves too modern and liberated to engage in such old-fashioned traditions. However, they each have a significant other they share their lives with. But no children. Careers first, you know."

"Yes, I do know," put in Ellie. "I had that same mindset for a few years, until it burned me good. I came back to tried and true traditions, as well as the faith of my Christian parents. And honestly, I regret those so-called enlightened years."

Renata's eyes went wide upon hearing this but made no comment.

"I heard you ran away from Minitonas to elope," said Hugh in an offhanded tone.

"That's true," said Renata, smiling yet surprised. "Did your father tell you that?"

"No. I remember my sister Margo once asking Pa at the supper table whether we had grandparents or relatives on his side. He said, 'Nope. All dead.' And that ended the discussion. Last summer, though, I discovered an aunt on my mother's side. She ferreted out some seniors from Minitonas who had known the original homesteading Fischers back in the day. From them we learned about you, your elopement, and a bit about my grandparents." He smiled broadly at his grandmother.

"That's rather amazing!" More to herself than her guests, Renata added, "I wonder why Fred claimed we were all dead. Mother and I sent him letters regularly."

"Where is your husband, by the way?" Ellie asked.

"Your Uncle Mervin, that young lover with whom I eloped a long time ago, is out showing clients a house. He's a realtor with his own business. He knows you're here and may walk in at any time, depending on how things go."

Ellie sat forward, feeling curious. "Why didn't you and Uncle Mervin stay in Minitonas?"

"That's easy. We were both looking for an exciting life in the big city with all its possibilities. Toronto sounded perfect. It was a little tough getting started, but we stuck to our goals, worked hard, and made a good life happen. I started out as a salesclerk but eventually got a job with a florist, learned the trade, and in due course established my own business here in Grimsby. Mervin got started in real estate and climbed his way up. He has four other agents working under him now. After my father's passing, Mother moved in with us. She helped with my babies and then worked with me in the flower shop, which gave her something to do that she enjoyed as well." She fixed her eyes on Hugh. "I want to say that neither Mother nor I dropped Fred from our lives. Rather, he dropped us. And to this day, I don't understand why."

Ellie and Hugh exchanged glances.

"How would you have described my pa when you knew him as your kid brother?" asked Hugh cautiously.

"Oh my goodness, that was a long time ago. Let's see… He could be pretty funny. Also a prankster. I recall he and my parents argued a lot. Dad saw him as undisciplined and wild-hearted. He wanted him to get a good education and make something of himself. Fred didn't care what my father wanted for him. He was all about having a good time and following his own path, not one forced upon him. I suppose I saw my kid brother as a spoiled brat. His circle of friends and mine didn't overlap. That's about all I remember. What can you tell us about him throughout the missing years?"

Renata leaned comfortably into the sofa. Huldah, however, continued to sit on the edge of her seat. Thus far she hadn't contributed a word to the conversation, but her eyes remained fixed on Hugh.

During the ensuing pause, it became clear just how ill at ease Hugh felt.

"It's not a pretty story," he said at last. "To tell you what it was like for my family and I to live with him would likely spoil any positive memories you still have." He turned to Ellie then and asked, "What do you think I should tell? I don't want to ruin this visit just when I discovered I have living relatives…"

Ellie's response was quick. "Always tell the truth, honey. In this case, break the news gently."

"Wait just a minute here," broke in Renata. "You're making it sound like he was some kind of monster or something."

Hugh met her gaze. "That's not far off."

Renata exhaled slow and long. "If it's bad news, like your wife says, break it to us gently."

"I brought along a few pictures we came across that were stowed in an old trunk. Let me show them to you and you can ask questions." Ellie reached for her tote bag and pulled out a pair of photo albums.

Renata shuffled to the middle of the sofa and Ellie scooted across to sit next to her.

The first page showed images of Friedrich's and Alice's wedding. Renata poured over them closely with Huldah also leaning in as near as she could get.

"When did they marry?" asked Renata.

"September 1948," answered Hugh flatly.

Renata looked up. "When were you born?"

"October 29, 1949."

"Your mother looks happy," noted Renata, returning to the wedding photos.

"I'm sure she was on her wedding day, and perhaps for a few weeks or months after that."

Renata looked up sharply. Hugh returned the look with a steady gaze.

His aunt looked down at the album again. "This photo of three little kids…"

"A rare photo of my sisters and me," Hugh replied.

"Where are they now?"

"My next sibling is Margo. She moved back to Minitonas in January following a divorce and is currently working at the local café. My youngest sister is Diane. She's married, lives in Yorkton, Saskatchewan, and is bringing up two kids."

The photos changed to images of the old buildings Ellie had taken before Hugh tore them down. Renata once again pored over them.

"These are of the farm, are they not?" she asked, uncertain.

Huldah pulled the album onto her lap to get a closer look for herself. Hugh nodded. "Yes, ma'am."

"They look awfully dilapidated. Did Fred not keep the farm?"

"He kept the farm. He just wasn't interested in putting up much money to maintain the buildings. The farm is mine now and it's where we live. I pulled down almost all the old buildings last summer and fall. Only the big garage remains, and I'll tear that one down, too, as soon as I have the replacement built. By the end of this year, I should have all new buildings and none of the old left. Nothing to trigger bad memories."

Renata nodded with understanding. "A fresh clean start. I can relate to that."

"I can show you drawings of the main house we plan to build this summer," said Ellie eagerly. She opened the second album, which held images of the yard plan, house, and outbuildings slated for construction upon their return to Manitoba.

"Very nice," said Renata sincerely. "I wish you all the best. So you are a farmer then, Hugh?"

"No. I'm a mechanic for a dealership in Swan River. I rent out the land to Ellie's brother, who farms next to our place."

"I see." Renata looked doubtful. "So far I'm not seeing how this adds up to my brother being some kind of monster."

"That's because I haven't yet told you that my father was an alcoholic who became meaner and more abusive as time passed. Made life hell for my mother and us kids. The last time I saw him was on my sixteenth birthday. I lit out to Winnipeg before he could beat me to death, which seemed to be where it was heading." Hugh spoke in a rush. When he paused, he looked into the shocked faces of his aunt and grandmother. "Sorry. I hadn't planned on telling you that. Don't know why I did."

He looked to Ellie for some direction. Her face was blank, but she nodded slightly.

"Well, indirectly at least, I asked for it," said Renata, the shock still evident on her face.

Huldah became restless. "Was hat er gesagt? Von wem sprach er?" she asked, poking Renata on her knee.

"Er sagte, Friedrich sei ein Alkoholiker und er habe seine Frau und Kinder geschalgen."

"Nein, nicht unser Friedrich."

"Warum nicht?" Renata replied. "Papa war so geneigt oder hast du es vergessen?"

Huldah clicked her tongue in continued disbelief and looked around the room with an angry look on her face.

"She's having a hard time believing such an evil thing about Fred," explained Renata. "But as I think on it, I can possibly believe it. My own father was so inclined himself. He held his liquor well, but he drank an awful lot of it. We made our own wine back then, too. I won't say he beat us, but he was very strict and could be harsh. It contributed to my decision to run away with Mervin to live our own lives far away from Manitoba. Oh my gosh. I haven't thought of these things in a very long time."

"I'm sorry to upset you, Aunt Renata," said Hugh apologetically. "Like Ellie said, it's best to know the truth about things. I'm thinking Grandpa Fischer read my pa pretty accurately as a young man. But I'm glad to know I have living relatives, and you don't seem to be riddled with the kind of problems that plagued my father."

"Well, I'm not an alcoholic," returned Renata with self-assured pride. "I may not be perfect—no one is, of course—but I don't have that vice." Renata had recovered from her shock and ill-ease and resumed her composure. "You said, when you called from Manitoba, that Fred and your mother died in a motor vehicle accident. Was it drunk driving then?"

"It's at least possible that was a contributing factor," began Hugh. "We found some handwritten notes by my mother that strongly suggest she planned to do something to end her life with Pa. Their truck was found upside-down in the Roaring River and neither were alive."

"I don't know what to say," stammered Renata, visibly shaken. "I'm sorry for your loss."

"I'm sorry for the loss of my mother. I wish I had done more for her when I was able to do so. Mind you, I was pretty messed up myself for a long while, and it's only by the grace of God and the love of my good wife that I'm doing as well as I am today. But that's a story I'll share another time."

Renata picked up the coffee pot to pour another round. "I'm sure you have an interesting life story."

Huldah Fischer seemed to have made up her mind about something. Abruptly she stood and crossed the room to Hugh. He stood out of respect. She suddenly threw her arms around him. Bewildered, Hugh bent over and lightly returned the embrace.

"Friedrich, Friedrich," moaned Hugh's grandmother mournfully, clutching at his sports jacket. "Warum hast du deine Mutter so lange vergessen?" She pulled back to look into his face. "Aber es ist jetzt in Ordnung. Endlich bist du gekommen. Du bist ein gutter Mann. Ich glaube nicht an die schlechten Geschichten, die uber dich erzahlt warden. Jetzt kann ich in Ruhe schlafen, weil du endlich zu mir gekommen bist. Es ist alles gut... alles gut." Huldah concluded her speech by patting his chest.

Hugh was painfully uncomfortable and looked to Ellie first and then his aunt for direction. Concerned, Ellie also turned her focus, seeking guidance from Renata.

"So sorry, Hugh," said Renata in a troubled and frustrated tone. "I was a bit worried this meeting wouldn't be all peaches and cream. She's stuck on the notion that you're her long-lost son, here to make amends for the long silence. I might as well admit that she's been asking about Fred quite often in recent weeks. When I told her he had died following your phone call a few weeks ago, she wouldn't believe it. She said it wasn't possible because they had to see each other to clear the air between them."

Renata shook her head, uncertain as to what to do next. She stood and then tried to pull her mother off Hugh.

"Come, Mother," she said firmly. "We need to let Hugh go. He has a plane to catch and can't stay any longer."

"Nein, bleib bitte mit deiner Mutter," wailed Hugh's grandmother. "Du bist gerade erst angekommen."

"Mutter," barked Renata with sudden sharpness, "Er ist nicht Fredrich! Er ist nur sein Sohn! Komm jetzt mit mir. Hugh und Ella mussen in ihre Heimat zuruck gehren."

Renata managed to worm her way between Hugh and Huldah. Grasping the elder woman by the arm, she steered her out of the room and down the hall.

Shortly thereafter, they heard a door close loudly. Ellie returned the photo albums to her tote, expecting to soon be dismissed.

Renata came back wearing a troubled look on her face. "I'm so glad you came, but because Mother's upset we'll have to connect another day. Now that I've seen you, I have a thousand questions burning in my mind…"

"So do I," interjected Hugh. "I'm also glad to meet the family I didn't know I had."

"You're really leaving in the morning?" asked Renata, her tone rich with regret.

"Unfortunately, yes." Ellie sighed. "But we can keep in touch with letters and phone calls. After our house is built, you can come and stay with us. Sometimes going back to our roots has the effect of healing old wounds."

"Or reopening them," added Renata dubiously. "We'll have to see…"

Seventeen

ELLIE AND HUGH left soon after, making promises to stay connected. No sooner had they pulled out onto the street and started driving back towards Niagara, though, than Ellie wanted to talk about what they had seen and heard.

Hugh covered his lips with his finger, then picked up her hand and kissed it. "I can't talk about it yet," he said quietly while watching the traffic. "I need some time to process."

"I think we should talk about it while it's still fresh in our minds," she protested. "I have a number of observations about your aunt and grandmother I'd like to discuss."

"And we will… when I'm ready."

They travelled back to Niagara in silence. Even small talk couldn't coax Hugh into any meaningful conversation after they got back to the hotel. They ate a light supper in a nearby Asian restaurant and then walked along the falls one last time before packing up their belongings in preparation for the trip home.

~

They were met at the Winnipeg airport by Brian Turner.

"Where's Marcie?" asked Ellie, looking around for the man's wife.

"She didn't come with me." Brian paused before adding cryptically, "But I'll take you to see her."

Before Ellie or Hugh could ask more about this, he wanted to know how their holiday had gone. They answered at exactly the same time.

"Wonderful!"

"It was okay."

Ellie looked at Hugh doubtfully, but then turned back to Brian and expanded upon her answer. "The Niagara Falls are stunning. The Great Lakes and St. Lawrence River are truly impressive. And we saw a lot of other memorable sights as well. I had a fantastic time."

"Yeah, it was good," agreed Hugh with less enthusiasm. "Saw lots of cool stuff. And now I'm ready to go home and get back to work."

Neither paid particular attention to the route Brian was taking as they left the airport—that is, until he turned into the parking lot of the Health Sciences Centre.

"What do we have to do here?" Ellie asked, surprised to be arriving at the hospital.

Brian answered patiently. "This is where you get to see Marcie."

"Oh my gosh, what happened?" Ellie was wide-eyed with concern.

"Now, now, don't fret," admonished Brian. "She had a couple more of those spells similar to when you were with us a few days ago. I insisted she seek help and took her into emergency. The doctor decided to keep her to run a bunch of tests. So that's what is happening. She's having tests done and they're monitoring her movements. Basically she seems to be fine. She's eager to see you, by the way."

Brian wasted no time leading the couple up the elevator, down halls, and finally into the room that held his wife. She was perusing a magazine and lit up like the proverbial lightbulb when they walked in.

Beaming with joy, Marcie closed the magazine and set it aside while simultaneously swinging her legs over the edge of the bed to rush at Hugh and Ellie with arms open for hugging. She ran for Hugh first.

"So tremendously glad to see you! I so hope your holiday was everything you hoped it would be." Marcie hugged him hard.

Hugh squeezed her back. "Yeah, we had a good time. But seeing you in here doesn't exactly pop my cork. What's going on?"

Marcie turned to embrace Ellie. "Brian seems to think I have a worrisome condition that needs looking into and my doctor agreed. My spells of weakness have been showing up oftener and we're trying to get to the bottom of it."

"I'm glad to hear that." Ellie released Marcie. "Have you got any results?"

"So far, we know what it's not," replied Marcie casually. "I don't have heart problems. My ticker beats well, thank God. Blood tests also don't show anything to be concerned about. We're now investigating my nervous system, so we'll see." But she seemed insistent on changing the subject. "Tell me about your honeymoon."

"It was wonderful!" declared Ellie. "The Niagara Falls are awesome and do not disappoint. And the sights around Toronto and the southern part of Ontario are also very interesting. Quite different from what we have in Manitoba."

"And you?" inquired Marcie, turning to Hugh. "What was your favourite part?"

He replied after just a moment's hesitation. "Hmmm. My wife."

"Good answer," chimed in Brian, and they all laughed.

"Seriously, it was all very interesting. While it was good to get away, it's great to get back, too. Now I'm pumped to get home and build my projects. I've discovered that I'm basically a home guy. Pretty sure I don't have a bone that itches to travel."

Hugh's eyes met Ellie's, holding an expression of apology. She received it with a weak smile and nearly indiscernible sigh.

Marcie and Brian asked for more details of their trip, so the next half-hour was filled with anecdotes for the sights they had experienced. When the nurse came bearing Marcie's supper, they said their goodbyes with promises to keep in touch and Brian proceeded to take the newlyweds back to his home.

Once they arrived, Hugh blurted out his desire for a change in plans.

"You don't need to entertain guests right now, and I'd just as soon get back to Minitonas," he said. "If we leave now, we can be home before midnight."

"I was hoping to check out some antique shops with Marcie before we went," protested Ellie.

"And now she's not available. Besides, the house isn't going to be built until midsummer. You have lots of time to shop later and not have to worry about storage in the meantime."

Crestfallen, Ellie ceded. Strictly speaking, it was true. But more than that, Hugh had basically declared that the holiday was over and she could see that trying to push him would only lead to mutual frustration.

Shortly thereafter, their pickup was loaded with luggage and they were on their way home.

~

Sunday morning, Hugh and Ellie slipped into a pew near the rear of the church's sanctuary, where they sat next to Jeremy and Ladd Moore. The brothers were surprised yet happy to see them, but as the service began there was no time for chitchat.

The choir director led the congregation in a rousing rendering of "All Hail the Power of Jesus' Name," the organ adding full-throated energy with all the stops pulled out. During the third verse, Ellie noticed movement on the far side of left and automatically looked to see what it was.

She nearly dropped the hymnal. Elbowing Hugh in the ribs, she pointed to the couple being ushered to a pew about halfway down the far aisle.

"Well, paint me green and call me a pickle," said Ellie, shocked.

Hugh looked where indicated, frowning until he recognized the pair, and then broke into a crooked grin. Rory Lange stepped aside, indicating that Margo should precede him in occupying the open space. He followed and sat next to her. Beyond curious, it was hard for Ellie to concentrate after that.

When the worship hymns were concluded, announcements were made for the upcoming week's events. Ellie barely heard them, so focused was she on the strange sight of Margo and Rory together.

But she did hear the final one. The youth, including the Baptist churches of both Minitonas and Swan River, had chartered a bus to attend a retreat in Edmonton later that fall, and it would include a Michael W. Smith concert. The congregation was asked to help with the expenses so no young person who wanted to go would be left out.

A lightbulb went on in Ellie's head. Rather than draw attention by whispering in Hugh's ear, she wrote a note in the margin of the bulletin and passed it to Hugh.

I have a great idea for how we can help.

Hugh looked puzzled for a moment, but then dismissed the note to concentrate on the next item of the service. After that Pastor Leland delivered a fine message from the Gospel of John.

When the concluding hymn was called for, Rory and Margo rose as if cued and, with heads bowed so as to avoid making eye contact with anyone, slipped out of their seats and quickly left the sanctuary.

Ellie was about to follow them, but Hugh grasped her elbow.

"Leave them alone," he whispered hoarsely. "It's obvious they don't want to talk to anyone."

Feeling chagrined for a second or two, Ellie gave in to Hugh's wishes, acknowledging that he was likely right.

But when the last amen was pronounced, she dashed out to the parking lot. There was no sign of either of them.

"What do you think it means?" asked Ellie animatedly on the drive home. "I mean, we've all been hoping and praying for Margo to take an interest in spiritual matters, but Rory? How does he, of all people, fit into this picture? You don't think they're dating, do you?"

"No, I don't. I can't imagine she's anywhere near over her divorce. Besides, I hardly think he would be her type. Mind you, I can't say I know him either. We shouldn't jump to any conclusions. And don't push Margo. She'll just get mad and back off. Be patient, and eventually she'll likely tell you what possessed her to give church a try. Maybe she did it to please Muriel. Or maybe Mrs. Harms challenged her to attend. Possibly Rory simply offered her a ride. Let's just be glad she showed up and pray that the pastor's message struck a chord."

"I suppose you're right," acknowledged Ellie. "But I'm so curious I can hardly stand it."

"It's not bothering me. What I'm curious about is your note. What's your great idea for helping the young people with their fundraising? I mean, I don't mind throwing twenty bucks into the pot if that's what you're thinking. Is that what you're thinking?"

"Nope." Ellie shook her head. "No one has shown any interest in the old combine and disc tillager parked at the south end of the yard. Why don't we donate them to their trip? Then one of the parents who has a large flat deck trailer could take them to the scrap metal place and the money would go towards the costs of the youth retreat."

Hugh didn't say anything for a moment while he turned the proposal over in his mind. "It's a good idea, Ell-igator. You're right. No one wants to buy those outdated dinosaurs. But I don't know of anyone, including your brother, who owns a big enough flat deck trailer to haul them away. Somehow I doubt any appropriate scrap metal yard would be close by. The time, labour, and expense might make the notion impractical."

"But we'll make the offer, right?" asked Ellie, hopeful. "It seemed like such a win-win when the idea came to me."

"I can imagine the look on Rob's face when I make the offer. I doubt he'll be interested."

"Well, in that case, maybe I should be the one to pitch it to him." Ellie had a gleam in her eye. "As my mama used to say, 'Where there's a will, there's a way.' It's for a good cause. He wouldn't do it for us, but for his kids and the rest of the youth group? He'd try to make it happen, I think."

Hugh sighed. "Okay. Make the offer, but please don't insist. I want us to stay in his good graces. He's helped me… us… a lot. I don't want him to feel presumed upon."

Ellie sent him a deprecating look. "I'm insulted you think me capable of anything less than perfect decorum, Hugh-perboly."

"I wonder if Otto Hoffman, or my cousin David, would have something to say about that," said Hugh with a smirk.

Ellie blushed… just a little.

Margo waved goodbye to Rory as he continued his way and then quickly entered the Harms house. While removing her jacket, she heard Lydia begin more paroxysms of coughing and wheezing. The older woman had come down with a nasty head cold.

"I'm back, Lydia," announced Margo, making a beeline for the living room.

The poor old woman looked positively miserable. Her eyes were red from constantly tearing up and her lips appeared chapped and sore.

"Where did you go?" croaked Lydia. "I didn't know you were gone. Thought you were sleeping in, as is your Sunday usual."

She let out another string of ragged coughs.

"Not this time, ma'am." Margo stood straight and proud. "You'll be pleased to know I went to church this morning."

"Well now, you don't say," said Lydia, stifling more hacking. "What made you decide to try it out? Something Muriel said?"

"No. I got roped into going by Rory Lang, believe it or not. We got into a little discussion about religion yesterday afternoon at the café. He bet me fifty bucks that if I went to church, not only would I like it, but I would learn the answers to the meaning of life and gain the peace of mind every human longs for. I laughed out loud but agreed to go. Suddenly I had dollar signs in my eyes. Winning fifty bucks helps me grow my savings account in order to finance some extra education this fall."

Lydia wiped her eyes for the umpteenth time. "I see. I daresay the young man isn't wrong. Neither would it hurt to get more learning."

Even this short speech sent her into another paroxysm of deep chest coughs.

The coughing fit alarmed Margo. "We can talk about this another time. Right now I'm going to make you a cup of tea to hold you while I fix us some homemade chicken noodle soup. They say it's a sure cure for anything that ails you. If you get any worse, we're going to have to call the doctor. In the meantime, you might like to read this."

She placed the church bulletin on Lydia's lap.

"Thank you, dear. I don't have the energy to argue any points with you today," said Lydia, coughing again.

Ten minutes later, Margo brought Lydia a cup of tea sweetened with honey and a slice of lemon. She also brought a small plate of buttered toast since it would require the better part of an hour to assemble and cook the soup before it was ready to eat. While it simmered, she quickly baked some plain biscuits.

Working busily in the kitchen didn't prevent Margo from processing her first church experience. On the one hand, she had surprised herself by enjoying it. But she reasoned this was only true because she had gotten to know Pastor Leland personally and therefore knew him to be an honest, caring man who wouldn't spout lies from the pulpit.

She'd also had another new experience. By all recollection, this was the first time she had clearly heard Pa yell at her in her mind.

"What in tarnation are you doing in a church, for cryin' out loud? How many times have I told you that religion is for sissies and dolts? Nobody with any brains believes there's a God. I don't want any daughter o' mine fallin' for that crap. Do you hear me?"

The voice of Fred Fischer in her head was so clear as to be almost audible. Margo looked behind her, expecting to see her pa standing in the doorway. It was empty, of course, but Margo answered anyway.

"Shut up, Pa. I'll make up my own mind."

"What's that?" called Lydia from the living room. "I couldn't make out what you said."

"Nothing. Just yelling at the cat."

Shortly thereafter, she served the homemade soup and hot biscuits. Lydia should have enjoyed it, and tried to, but instead she complained that she couldn't taste anything. It reminded her of the smell of dishwater.

Given that Margo was unsettled in spirit, it was difficult to be patient with the senior despite her being genuinely ill.

After lunch, Lydia went to her room to lie down, much to Margo's relief. Having some time to herself, she realized that she wanted to talk to someone. Someone who could listen to her thoughts objectively.

She could think of no one. Certainly not Muriel and Leland or Hugh and Ellie or even farmer Rory. They were nice people, but they also had a bias for wanting her to convert to Christianity.

Suddenly, Margo felt utterly lonely. Another dismal truth of her nearly thirty years was that she was essentially friendless. She knew lots of acquaintances, yet she had no one in her life to name as a personal friend... a kindred spirit.

A tear slipped unbidden from her eye. As she wiped it away, she recalled the words of Pastor Leland only a few hours earlier.

"Jesus calls all who belong to and follow Him friends. Are you one of Jesus's friends? All those who put their trust in Him..."

Margo couldn't remember what he had said after that, because she'd realized the service was coming to a close and wanted to skedaddle before anyone could stop her to explain herself.

Lydia had lain the church bulletin on her side table. Margo rose and picked it up to read the order of service and found the information she wanted. The pastor's message had been based on John 15.

She set the bulletin back down and went to her room, softly closing the door behind her. She picked up the Good News Bible and eventually found the chapter in question. Starting from verse one, she read until she arrived at the verses that spoke of being friends with

Jesus. She didn't understand much about the part concerning vines and branches, but she got the message about Jesus and friends. It made her heart ache with such deep desire that her chest felt tight with the pain of it.

"But are you really real?" cried Margo, rocking on the edge of her bed, the Bible pressed against her bosom.

A vision of Muriel crossed her mind. The pastor's wife was utterly and completely convinced of the reality of Jesus and God and the living truth of the Bible. She lived by it, too. Muriel was one of the kindest, most generous, and caring persons she'd ever met. Apparently living by the Bible turned one into that kind of person.

For that matter, it had changed Hugh similarly. Margo found her resolve to resist and dismiss religion breaking down. She wanted what Muriel and Hugh had and it was becoming increasingly clear that a person couldn't effect much change for the better themselves. One needed help. One needed the likes of Jesus, who offered His friendship with the deal.

Suddenly, another vision of Pa Fischer replaced the image of Muriel in her head. Margo imagined him visibly enraged.

"Yer doing it again! Yer falling for them religious lies. I ought to thrash yer arse good so you'll learn to mind what I tell ya."

"Stop it right there, Pa!" hissed Margo. "Truth is, you're no longer real. You're dead and buried. You can't do nothin' to me. You can't tell me what to do either! Maybe it's you who is filling my head with lies. I'm not gonna listen to you anymore. Get away from me! I'll make up my own mind!"

With that, the vision disappeared at once, like a crow flying away. The vision of Muriel disappeared, too, and Margo couldn't make the experience return.

Sighing, she set the Bible back on the dresser and stole out of the house to take a walk in the warm sunshine. She needed to clear her head.

Eighteen

"I'M REALLY HAPPY for you." Ellie snuggled up to Hugh under the covers. "You'll soon be able to move in and set up your dream shop."

He was beat, burning the candle at both ends from putting in a day's work and then passing another four hours or more at home working at the new workshop. The building crew had been paid to put up the main structure, metal siding, roof, and Gyproc on the interior. An electrician and plumber looked after the wiring and waterworks so a building inspector would be satisfied that all was up to code. To save on coin, Hugh had opted to finish the interior himself. Presently he spent his evenings mudding the seams of the drywall, a tedious but necessary job. He took his time because he didn't want the results to look like a hack job.

"I prefer to think of it as *our* shop," said Hugh tiredly. "After all, you had a hand in the final design of it."

"And I'm right, aren't I? The addition is going to be a bonus once everything is set up and you get going on your projects. It's not out of the question you'll eventually run a business out of there, if only a hobby business."

Hugh slid an arm under Ellie's neck and drew her close. He kissed her forehead. "Having an office space isn't what sold me as much as the wisdom of having a restroom at hand. And it'll be great to have a designated space to meet with the guys. A stroke of brilliance, honey."

"You know I was thinking selfishly, don't you?" murmured Ellie. "I just wanted to keep as much grease and grime out of the house as possible. If you install a bit of a kitchen—"

"I know. You've argued the point more than once. It's a good idea to have a place to store lunches in the fridge or warm up some food, or put on a crockpot of chili. I get it. You think of everything. You're a good partner. Can we go to sleep now?"

But Ellie wasn't yet ready to quit the pillow talk. "Pretty soon. I want to know what you think of Charlotte more or less attaching herself to Jeremy."

"Now that you mention it, she does seem to get next to him a lot. Not sure if Jeremy has noticed it, though," responded Hugh with a yawn.

"I agree. But then I don't think either of those Moore boys are given to noticing girls. They've been brought up to eat, drink, and sleep farming and mechanics. Also hunting wild game, as I recall. Their mom, while a dear soul all around, isn't exactly a model for femininity. I doubt she encourages them to add women to their lives."

"Couldn't tell ya. The subject of women has never come up, so maybe you're right. And you know what else? I don't care. It's not my problem. Anyway, they're both still pretty young. They haven't missed the boat or anything. It's all about waiting for the right girl to come along."

"Right." Ellie suddenly giggled. "And you didn't hear it from me, but I happen to know that Charlotte has a huge crush on Jeremy. So it's funny to watch her try and gain his attention while he remains totally oblivious to her overtures."

Hugh chuckled softly. "I'll have to pay more attention, I guess. But Ellie?"

"What?"

"Stay out of it. Let people find each other by themselves." Hugh yawned again, then withdrew his arm.

"But of course. Good night, Hugh-bert." Ellie kissed him on the shoulder before turning over on her side.

Occasionally the evenings drew visitors interested in the new construction going up at the Fischers' place. Rob Bauman had just finished seeding his last fields, the rented acres from Hugh and Ellie, and after putting away his equipment he stopped in to see the new garage before heading home to his wife and family.

He found Hugh inside, masked and covered in white powder.

"Sanding drywall is a heck of a dirty business," acknowledged Rob while taking a cursory look around. "It's quite a place you got here. Got time for a short tour?"

"Can do."

Hugh, with evident pride, showed Rob the most southerly bay first, explaining that it was meant to be used for autobody work. The middle bay was intended for long-term projects like the restoration of vintage vehicles. The first bay was for relatively short-term projects like replacing sparkplugs, changing tires, oil changes, or a carpentry project.

Rob indicated the most northerly end of the building. "And what are these rooms for?"

"They're Ellie's contribution. She got to thinking long-term and thought I should add space for an office and restroom, as well as a space that could be used for a lunchroom or meeting room."

Rob nodded and walked in and out of each space. He wore an approving expression, which pleased Hugh. Rob's opinion meant a lot to him.

Just then Ellie walked in, all smiles.

"Just the guy I wanted to see," she said cheerfully. With a sweep of her arm, she indicated the whole building. "It's great, isn't it?"

Rob nodded. "Sure. It's well thought out and should serve you well."

"So has Hugh spoken to you about our proposal?"

Hugh and Rob exchanged glances.

"No, I don't think so," answered Rob. "Make it short. I haven't had my supper yet."

"We'd like to make a donation to that youth retreat the young people are raising funds for," said Ellie.

"That's nice." Rob remained impassive. "You can do that directly at the church."

"We want to donate the old combine and disc tillager." She smiled sweetly. "Our donation would be whatever cash they can get for them."

"I see." Rob removed his cap, scratched his head, and then replaced his cap. "And this involves me how?"

"We suppose those old pieces must be transferred on a large flat deck trailer, and we don't know who in the church has one. Thought you might." Ellie crossed her arms.

Rob furrowed his brow. "Where are you thinking they need to go? Why not the scrap metal place in Swan River?"

"I took truckloads of small metal scraps there last fall," Hugh said. "It didn't seem to me they took in large items like that."

"Have you asked them?"

The obvious question suddenly made Hugh and Ellie feel a bit foolish. They shook their heads.

"I'm fairly sure they *do* take large items," continued Rob. "They likely don't keep them hanging around long, or they take them apart. If I'm wrong, take the thing apart yourselves and get it down to them piecemeal. Suddenly it's all small stuff. Know what I mean? Does the combine still run?"

"Well, yeah," Hugh admitted. "I drove it to where it's parked."

"You're a mechanic. Make sure it's roadworthy enough to make the miles to Swan River. Since it's for the church youth, get Trevor involved. He has his driver's license and no doubt would be tickled pink to drive it into Swan for you." He looked at Hugh and Ellie in turn and then smiled crookedly. "Glad I could help. Nice shop you got here, by the way. See you later."

Rob grabbed the door handle to let himself out.

"That was neatly done," said Ellie, feeling slightly embarrassed. "Ball is back in our court."

Hugh shrugged.

~

Walking up the steps to the cottage, Hugh heard the telephone ring. Hurrying, he answered the call with a joke. "Harry's armpit. How can I help you?"

He enjoyed the brief silence while the caller processed the gag.

"Oh, it's you, Margo. How are you?"

He listened with the telephone receiver tucked under his chin while he built a crude sandwich with leftover beef from the fridge.

"Sure, you can come down," agreed Hugh genially. "I'm alone this evening. You can keep me company. Just so you know, there's something I want to watch on television about forty-five minutes from now. We can watch it together."

The conversation quickly ended and Hugh continued building his sandwich, slathering it with mustard and then adding sliced onion, tomato, and some semi-wilted lettuce he found.

He had barely wolfed it down when Margo showed up ten minutes later.

"Wow! That's no little shop—er, garage—you put up," exclaimed Margo, upon leaving her car.

Hugh smiled broadly, appreciating the support. "A dream come true, that's for sure."

Like all the other interested persons who had dropped by, he gave her a tour of the building with explanations from one end to the other.

Margo listened, nodding her head here and there.

When she had seen it all, she smiled at her brother with sincerity. "It's great, bro. Really it is. I'm proud that you're making something good and decent out of this place. I can't believe this is the same spot where we grew up. It looks and feels so different."

Margo swept the yard with her gaze from south to north.

Suddenly she froze. "Something's missing. The hydro pole that used to be near the barn... where is it?"

"You noticed! I'm impressed," replied Hugh without any edginess. "I had a talk with Manitoba Hydro and they agreed, given our building plans, to erect a new pole in a more suitable place. They did it just a few days ago. They even took down and carried away the old one for me. You'll understand, I felt a few pounds lighter after that."

"Yes, I do understand." Margo followed Hugh into the cottage. "With all the clean-up and changes here, I wonder if our folks are rolling over in their graves."

"I doubt Ma would be. She'd be proud, I think. And I never wonder what Pa would think about anything." He went over to the fridge and looked inside. "Can I get you a cola? My TV show is about to start."

"Sure." Margo made herself comfortable on the sofa. "What are we watching?"

"A rare TV special called *The Billy Graham Crusade*," answered Hugh, taking the armchair and placing his feet upon the trunk.

"Never heard of him. What is his claim to fame?"

"He's an evangelist... a preacher. He goes around the world preaching the gospel to tens of thousands of people at a time. And thousands respond, too. Ellie saw that he was on tonight from the *TV Guide* and told me not to forget to watch it. She's very disappointed that she has to miss the broadcast because of work."

He glanced over to Margo, watching for a negative response. None came.

"Goodness, if he can draw a crowd like that, he must be pretty good," she replied instead. "Let's hear what he has to say."

This crusade was convened in a large football stadium. The program began with music that included a choir made up of local volunteers, a special appearance and song by Johnny Cash, a personal testimony from a well-known public figure, and finally a stirring rendition of "Until Then" by George Beverly Shea.

Then Billy Graham stood behind the pulpit. From the first words he uttered, his seasoned and commanding voice delivered a compelling sermon featuring the biblical Jonah, who had run from God's will in disobedience and rebellion only to bring more and deeper sorrow upon himself and others. He also addressed the matter of choice, pointing out that we make numerous choices daily and they account for the direction we take in life. He urged people to choose Christ, for that was where life's fulfilment and purpose lay.

Drawing the message to a close, Billy called on the audience to make a decision for Christ, by which he meant to conscientiously believe in the sacrificial death of Jesus on behalf of all humanity's sin, and by faith receive His Spirit into oneself to live for Him going forward.

At once, the camera showed streams of people making their way down the slim aisles of the grandstands. They quickly filled the playing field to take their place before the stage where Billy stood waiting to lead them in a prayer to receive Christ. The choir earnestly sang a well-known hymn: "Just as I am without one plea…"

Hugh had yielded to Christ eleven months earlier, and it was his beloved Ellie who had assisted him in his first ever prayer. Even so, the call as expressed from Dr. Graham pulled at his heart irresistibly. He understood it wasn't necessary, but in the privacy of his heart and mind he responded anew.

Yes, Lord, he prayed. *I come to You with all that I am…*

Without being obvious, Hugh looked over to Margo out of the corner of his eye and saw the tears quietly streaming down her cheeks. Her lips quivered.

"Don't fight it, Margie," he said softly. "If you do, it will be like Billy said. Your heart will harden and—"

"I know what he said." Margo sniffed. "He nailed me, Hugh. I saw it: my rebellion… my sin… and the consequences in everything he preached."

Hugh answered as delicately as he could. "Are you willing to give it up so you don't end up like Pa?"

Margo flashed a shocked look in his direction. "Funny that you should mention Pa. I've heard his voice yelling at me several times recently. He's been shouting at me to stop listening to preachers and church folks, saying that he would tan my hide if I gave in to them."

"I've had similar experiences. They started soon after I got here. It's not really him, you know. The Bible speaks of the devil going about like a lion seeking whom he may devour. I believe he thinks he can prevent us from turning to Jesus by using our fear of Pa. It's a lie, Margo. And most of what Pa warned us about religion is a lie, too."

"I know." Margo wiped away more years. "At least, I know that now. But where do I go from here? What did all those people coming towards Billy Graham have to do?"

"They had to begin a conversation with Jesus. In this case, that's called prayer," began Hugh patiently. "To accept Jesus into your heart, your first prayer should include agreeing with Jesus that your sinful condition keeps you separated from Him, and that you need His forgiveness for that. Then thank Him for making a way to walk in friendship with Him through His death on the cross which paid for all our sins, including yours. Follow this with an invitation to come into your heart to guide you in all your ways. Then thank Him for the gift of eternal life."

"I don't know what most of that means," said Margo, puzzled. "I just want to have forgiveness and peace in my heart, like Billy talked about."

Hugh smiled and got on his knees next to the trunk. "C'mon. Kneel with me. I'll help you like Ellie helped me." Still teary, Margo knelt beside Hugh. "Repeat after me…"

Hugh led Margo in an unsophisticated version of the sinner's prayer, including all the elements he had mentioned earlier. Margo concluded with an "Amen" of her own.

Suddenly, as though a dam had burst within Margo, she sobbed with utter abandon. Hugh hadn't expected that, but he soon understood the need of it.

"It's all right, Margie." He collected her in his arms. "Cry it out…"

Margo didn't resist and laid her head against his chest. The onslaught of tears made a large wet spot on his shirt, but he didn't care. Soon he was softly weeping with her. Crying could sometimes be contagious, he reflected.

But there was another reason. He knew very well the strain of a lifetime of wounds, distress, and trouble. Many of their plights had been shared, having been raised in the same miserable home. Pent-up feelings needed to be let out... or burst.

He rocked his sister as he held her, murmuring soft words of encouragement and sympathy. After what seemed like many minutes, the sounds of intense sobbing reduced to the occasional snuffle.

At last, Margo pulled away. Hugh released her and both stood up.

"Are you okay, now?" he asked gently.

"Yeah. I don't think I've ever cried like that in my whole life."

"You needed to... just like I needed to when things came to a head for me last summer. Ellie helped me get through my breakdown. Crying like that is cleansing... and healing."

Margo gave him a crooked smile. "I suppose if anyone understands, it's you. I feel like I have my brother back."

"I've been back, as you say, for longer than just today. You just weren't having me yet."

"I feel... I feel..." Margo struggled for words.

"Empty inside?"

Her eyes filled with wonder. "Yeah... that's part of it."

"Peaceful? Unfamiliarly calm?"

"Yes. That's the right word, I think: peaceful. And you're right, it's a new feeling," responded Margo with a sense of wonder. "I feel really tired now, too. I should go home and to bed."

"Crying hard can be exhausting," he granted. "I had to rest so I could recover from my breakdown as well. By the way, don't keep your decision to follow Jesus a secret. Tell someone about it as soon as possible. I'm sure Muriel and Pastor Leland will celebrate with you. I imagine Mrs. Harms will be pretty pumped, too."

Margo prepared to leave. "Ain't that the truth. I will, I promise."

⌐〜

Margo stole into the Harms house quietly so as not to wake Lydia, who usually retired around nine o'clock in the evening. That the living room lamp was lit was no surprise. Lydia often left it on purposely so Margo would have light when she came in.

The surprise was that Lydia was still up, dressed in her night-clothes and chenille housecoat, sitting in her favourite chair with a half cup of tea cradled in her wrinkled hands.

"Oh dear. Are you up on account of me, Lydia?" Margo immediately felt bad and plopped down on the sofa across from the older woman.

"Oh no. I stayed up to watch the Billy Graham crusade on the tele-vision." Lydia's voice was laced with regret. "That's a rare treat, you know. And he didn't disappoint. He preached a fine sermon on Jonah. I was only sorry you weren't here to watch it with me. Mr. Graham explains the gospel so well, it would have helped you to understand the importance of getting saved and following Jesus."

"I went to visit my brother this evening to see the workshop he built, and he invited me to stay and watch some television with him. And guess what, Lydia?" Margo smiled broadly. "We also watched the Billy Graham crusade. To be honest, I've never heard anything like it. And it seemed like he was talking to me personally. The short of it is, I said the prayer that invites Jesus to live in my heart. Hugh helped me with that."

"You don't say," said Lydia much surprised. "That's the best news I've heard in a long time. I wonder if the good Lord will give me some credit for it since I've prayed for you every day for the past few months."

"I have a lot to learn about how the good Lord does things, but it sounds fair to me, whatever that's worth."

"Well now, that's what's next for you, Miss Margo. Learn God's Word inside and out, and live for Jesus. And now that you're safely in

His kingdom, I b'lieve I'm free to go to my true home… my heavenly home." Lydia swallowed the remainder of her tea.

"I don't think you need to talk so depressing," objected Margo. "You still have basically good health for a senior. I shouldn't think you need to worry about dying just yet."

"I'm not worried about dyin' at all. It's just that I'm so tired. Tired of this evil world that's getting worse by the hour." Lydia sighed. "Tired of living. Just bone weary. All I want now is to be done here and go to live with my Lord…"

"You wouldn't just will yourself to die, now would you?" Margo grew concerned about the train of Lydia's thoughts. "I am rather fond of you. You're the grandmother I never had. Please don't leave just yet."

"Don't you worry none, Miss Margo. I'll be here as cantankerous as ever until the Lord calls me home. And when He does, the time will be right and I won't look back."

Lydia rose stiffly and crept to her bedroom with a decided limp that reflected the arthritis in her joints.

Margo turned out the lights and followed suit. The glow of inviting Jesus into her heart remained with her, but that space was shared with a small amount of worry for Lydia's desire for her own demise.

Nineteen

"HURRAY!" HUGH SHOUTED with great enthusiasm as he hung up the phone.

He practically skipped to the door to greet Ellie, who had just arrived home following her hospital shift.

"Welcome home, sweetheart," he said with a quick embrace. "Got good news. You get three guesses."

"Wow. It must be good news if you're that cheerful. Let's see..." Ellie hung up her cardigan. "You found some hidden money."

"Nope. Try again."

"You got a big raise in your salary."

"Nope, but good try."

"I don't know... a call from Brian perhaps, saying that Marcie is back to being in good health?"

"That's close enough for a bingo! I *was* talking with Brian. Marcie is home. The doctors still don't know what causes her strange bouts, but she's booked off the rest of the school year. Brian wants to use up some banked days off, so they're going to come up here for a week or so. He wants to help me finish off the shop so I can set up my tools. Isn't that great?"

"Of course it is," chimed Ellie. "Where will they be staying?"

"Brian said they would be fine at the hotel in Minitonas, but I'm hoping Rob won't mind if they stayed in the farmhouse."

"I hope he doesn't mind either. I don't see why he would."

As it turned out, Rob was more than agreeable to the Turners spending their nights at the Bauman farm. A house needs people to keep it from deteriorating, he said.

The Turners arrived the following evening.

~

With all the interior painting completed in basic white, Brian and Hugh laid down the mottled grey and black floor tiles in the office, washroom, and meeting room. Working together, they accomplished this job in a day. As much as Hugh wanted to get to building workbenches and the shelves to hold his power tools and sundry equipment, they instead completed the finishing trim around windows, hung doors, and installed the washroom fixtures so the women would be free to finish outfitting those rooms however they desired.

Hugh's Aunt Gertie and Uncle Ed had been amongst the visitors to drop by the week before, and Ed had offered them the use of an old oak desk the bank no longer had use for. Ellie and Marcie had taken Hugh's half-ton to fetch it. The gift included a couple of oak swivel chairs and oak filing cabinet.

"A double-sided desk?" Hugh asked as they now unloaded the monstrously heavy piece of furniture. "Are you sure we want this?"

Ellie looked sheepish. "I felt it would be rude to turn it down. And as my mother often said, beggars can't be choosers."

After a lot of grunting, groaning, and complaining by Hugh, the enormous desk was finally reassembled and placed next to the northside window of the office. They parked the filing cabinet in a corner.

While Hugh and Brian got started on building a workbench to line the back wall of the first bay, Ellie and Marcie went to Minitonas to look at some old cabinets the Ungers had offered following a kitchen upgrade Tony had built for his mother. Although very dated, Ellie determined that they would look nice, once reconfigured and repainted white, in the shop kitchenette.

However, all that effort took time, which is why Ellie served supper later than usual that evening. They had barely consumed their meal when Ellie's Aunt Ruth and Uncle Herb drove into the yard with their grain truck.

"I brought you my kitchen set and the chesterfield I told you about when we dropped by last week," said Aunt Ruth.

"Right! I'd forgotten about that," said Ellie.

All hands were on deck as they unloaded a dark brown couch and armchair upholstered in the nearly indestructible frieze. In fact, it appeared almost new, other than the telltale detail that this style had been popular back in the sixties. Aunt Ruth also brought her grey formica and chrome kitchen table set. The pattern had worn off in places, but otherwise it was sturdy and there weren't any rips in the plastic upholstered chairs.

Ellie gave her aunt a hug. "This is all so very generous of you."

"I'm glad to help," replied the plump woman. "And I'm glad for the opportunity to buy something new for myself." With that, she flashed Herb *the look.*

Herb spoke through pursed lips. "And I don't see why we have to buy something new when the old is still perfectly useful and in good shape."

"Because a woman gets sick and tired of the same old thing for what seems like the last hundred years!" Ruth threw up her hands.

Herb shook his head and stuffed his hands in his overalls. He glanced over at Hugh and Brian, looking for some support.

"If you want the good cookin' you're used to, Herb Wagner, you won't give me grief over this," warned Ruth in a faux pleasant tone.

Ellie quickly intervened. "I think we should all take a coffee break. I have some chocolate cake—your recipe, Aunty Ruth—that would hit the spot, I think."

"Oh no, don't trouble yourself," said Ruth, unruffling her feathers. We'll drop by another time to see what it's like when you're all set up."

They left shortly thereafter.

Hugh hesitated. "I hope you know what you're doing bringing all this old stuff home. Why do we have to use castoffs to outfit a brand-new building?"

"Wouldn't you rather spend money on tools and such? Do you really want new things to get messed up with the grease and grime that goes with the territory of a shop like this?" asked Ellie pointedly. "As a matter of fact, I wasn't sure if I liked the trend that was emerging either. Yet all these things add up to a charming retro look. Trust me in this."

"Don't I always?" Hugh smirked.

Just as anticipated, Muriel was ecstatic with Margo's account of responding to the gospel by putting her faith in Christ. She insisted that they go and share the story with Leland, who was in his office at the church. He, too, received the news with delight. Together, they prayed over Margo—that she would grow solidly in the faith and be guided by the Spirit of the Lord as her life unfolded.

"I'm sure Lydia must have been joyful," said Muriel on the walk back to the manse.

"Yes. She was," admitted Margo tentatively.

Muriel frowned. "There is a 'but,' isn't there?"

"She said that now that her prayers for me are answered, she wants to go to her true home, meaning heaven. She said she's tired of living in this worsening wicked world. I don't know what to make of it. I'm worried she might will herself to die or something crazy like that."

"I see…" Muriel trailed off slowly. "It's not unusual for seniors to express a desire to pass into eternity. Daily living is tough when one's bodily functions start to deteriorate, the sort of thing we so often take for granted. On top of that, it's easy for them to feel like they no longer have purpose, that they're just taking up space and being a burden on the family and community. Worse, they can feel like they no longer have value, that only the young are beautiful, desired, and celebrated."

"I told her that she's the grandmother I never had," Margo said. "And that I want her to stick around for a long while yet."

"Did you mean that?"

"Of course I did!"

"Then treasure her knowledge and wisdom, Margo," advised Muriel. "Ask her to share her life story and what she's learned about marriage, parenting, getting through hard times, and handling disappointments and hurts. Find out what she knows about stretching a limited budget, preserving food for a prairie winter, and having to mend and make do when money is tight."

Margo nodded. "I'm getting the picture, Muriel. Can I tell you something? If Lydia Harms is the grandmother I never had, you're the mother I never had."

"That is kind of you, and I'm grateful I had the opportunity to speak into your life. But you did have a mother and she should be honoured. From what I can glean, she tried to do her best with unusually limited resources, and I'm not just talking about money. I hope you can forgive her for her shortfalls. It seems to me it was all she could do to keep upright for the sake of her children. We all have a story… a history… We need to remember to be kind to one another."

⁓

By the end of the week, the new shop was outfitted. With the help of the menfolk, the repainted pieces of selected vintage kitchen cabinets were installed between a used red refrigerator—Ellie found it among the classified ads in the newspaper—and matching stove. A single stainless-steel sink completed the kitchenette.

The brown sofa and chair were set in place along the north wall under the window, positioned perpendicular with each other, with a square end table sitting between them and holding an ashtray… in case a smoker dropped by, Ellie reasoned. The retro table set took up the centre of the room. The remaining unadorned wall offered spots to hang a monthly calendar and the unfavourable teapot clock Ellie had received at her wedding shower.

A large Coca-Cola clock she had delightfully found at the thrift shop was claimed by Hugh who hung it where it could be readily seen in the main part of the garage. With Brian's assistance, all of Hugh's tools were carried over, unpacked, and stowed in their designated places in the garage, whether pegboard, drawer, or shelf. A strong sense of satisfaction and accomplishment filled them all.

Additional excitement that week came with the arrival of the crew from the Quonset company. However, all Hugh had to do was show them the designated area and they took over the pouring of concrete and erecting the arched metal building.

⁓

"Stay longer," Ellie urged Marcie. They were fixing supper in the cottage but planned to eat it in their new facility to inaugurate the *staff room*, as Ellie named it.

"I wouldn't mind if we did," responded Marcie warmly. "It depends on Brian and if he feels he can postpone returning to work a few days longer."

Ellie carried over a hot pan containing roast pork surrounded by chunks of potatoes, rutabaga, carrots, and onion. Marcie followed with a bowl of salad and a jug of iced tea.

Upon arrival in the kitchenette, Ellie set down the food she'd brought and looked around for Marcie, who was no longer just behind her. Frowning, Ellie retraced her steps and found Marcie only halfway to the new shop. She appeared to be frozen in a strange posture and her face wore an expression of great distress.

"Oh no!" Ellie dashed to the distraught woman and took the jug and bowl from her. Thus relieved, Marcie clung to Ellie's arm and lurched to the new shop like someone fully inebriated.

Once inside, the woman literally fell into the armchair and began to sob.

"I was doing so well," lamented Marcie through tears. "I dared to hope I was okay, after all. Then, without warning, my sense of balance left me. If I had continued walking, I believe I would have crumpled to the ground and ruined the food I was carrying."

"That would have been the least of our worries. Can you think of anything that might have triggered this spell? I'm wondering about fatigue. You worked hard for us this week. Perhaps too hard."

"And I enjoyed every minute of it," Marcie reassured her. "I have no idea what brings these episodes on. It frightens me that they come about without forewarning. Because of that, I fear I am a danger to others, let alone myself."

The tears continued to flow.

Ellie sat close by on the sofa and laid a hand on Marcie's arm as a gesture of comfort. "I can only imagine how upsetting this is for you. I just wish I could help in some way…"

"I wish I could talk about it candidly," sniffed Marcie. "I don't mean with Brian, or even my doctors. They just want to address my problem like a mechanic fixes a knock in a motor."

"I know what you mean. You want to be able to talk things out in a way that helps you process your distressing experiences… to think out loud with someone who will simply listen and perhaps help connect some clues."

"Yes! That is what I wish for."

Ellie reached over to hold her hand. "I'll listen, if you're willing to share your thoughts and fears."

"My doctor asked me if any of my relatives displayed similar symptoms," began Marcie with a faraway look in her eyes. "At the time, I said no. But the more I think about it, my grandfather might have had similar problems. I was only a very little girl, but I seem to recall he occasionally swayed and reeled from one point to the next. I remember the oddness of it making me uncomfortable with him. My granny assured me that Grandpa would be all right in a little while and not to worry. Now I'm thinking I have some genetic defect that no surgery or medication can rectify… and from now on, I'll be *that* woman people whisper about… the weirdo who suddenly, and without notice, wanders about like the proverbial drunken sailor… or the poor woman who has fits now and again and can't control herself."

Marcie broke out in a fresh wave of tears.

"The people who know and love you won't think that way about you," noted Ellie kindly.

"People will pity me, and that is almost as bad," cried Marcie with a trace of bitterness. "I feel my life is about to get very small. No more driving alone, no more shopping on my own, no more time to myself because someone has to keep an eye on the crazy lady—"

"You are not crazy, Marcie. Did the doctors have no idea at all to explain your mysterious malady?"

"The best hypothesis they have is that I have a tiny glitch somewhere in my brain. When my brainwaves come across it, I stumble until it's passed and I can carry on normally again." Marcie took a moment to compose herself. "It's not a common ailment, but they did promise to look for literature that may discuss the affliction."

Ellie squeezed her hand. "Let us hang on to hope then."

"Oh to be young and healthy again, like you." Marcie sighed. "When I was your age, I believed no illness would ever debilitate me. I was too strong and healthy for such nonsense. I vowed to look after myself such that I wouldn't fall prey to the big health issues that deteriorate, or kill, people."

"Maladies run the gamut," replied Ellie quickly. "Plenty of young people struggle and suffer with all kinds of problems. It's not a domain belonging only to the aging."

"Intellectually, I know this. But did you say that as a nurse, or from personal experience?"

"Both," answered Ellie, and instantly regretted it. She had certain worries she didn't want to admit to anyone, including the sweet, motherly Marcie Turner. "Even children and youth struggle with cancers, heart problems, deformities, and everything else under the sun." She hoped these generalizations would divert attention from herself.

"I understand that, but in what way are you struggling personally?"

Marcie's genuine kindness caused Ellie's eyes to well up in tears, but she remained quiet.

"Sorry, I didn't mean to pry," said Marcie apologetically. "Should we call our men in for supper?"

"I have my fears, too," blurted Ellie in a rush. The unbidden tears escaped and slid down her cheeks.

"Oh my dear girl, what's troubling you?" Marcie moved to sit next to Ellie on the couch and put an arm around her shoulders.

For a couple of minutes, Ellie didn't speak, but the quiet, intense shaking of her torso communicated deep sadness.

Pulling herself together, she finally spoke. "After five months of marriage, I thought I would be well into a family way. Instead I cannot seem to get pregnant. I'm worried that I'm barren..."

"I shouldn't think that's a fair deduction after only a few months. What about a doctor's checkup? He could provide the reassurance you need."

"I keep putting it off... because I'm afraid he'll tell me what I don't want to hear."

"Do you have reason to suspect you aren't altogether healthy? That you aren't able to conceive?"

"I believe myself to be in fine health," said Ellie, suddenly confident. She wiped the tears from her eyes with the back of her hands and then stood. "There is nothing preventing us from conceiving. That's why I'm so surprised that I am not yet with child. I'm sure you're right. I need to be a lot more patient. Please don't tell Hugh I fretted over this."

"Of course not," agreed Marcie, though her eyes held a doubtful look. "I take it Hugh doesn't share your concern."

"I've kept it to myself. I don't want to rain on his parade. His new garage is the only baby that means something to him. At least at this moment. I don't want him to worry over nothing. I'm just being silly."

"Hmmm," mused Marcie thoughtfully. "If you say so..."

Twenty

THE TURNERS LEFT after the Quonset had been constructed. Brian had assisted Hugh in transferring the old Plymouth into the middle bay of the new garage. He also helped move the old-timers, tractor, riding mower, farm truck, and other miscellany into the new Quonset.

While Hugh practically danced from building to building and around the yard, Ellie grew more subdued—partly because the new facilities made it possible for him to work on projects that had been deferred, reducing the amount of time he spent together with her. Hugh didn't seem to notice this. Ellie purposely brightened up for him while they shared meals and discussed the events of the day. As soon as he left her presence, though, the dark clouds reformed and hung over her like a heavy weight.

She was grateful for work. Putting in shifts at the hospital at least four days a week distracted from her worry and the emotional baggage that came along with it.

But today had been hard.

A friend from the First Baptist Church had come in during the night and put in sixteen hours of labour before giving birth to a beautiful little boy. Ecstatic, her husband had sought out Ellie in the post-surgical wing to share the good news. She felt genuinely happy for her friends yet privately grieved her own stubbornly empty womb.

When her shift was over at 4:00 p.m., Ellie raced home, shed her scrubs, and donned jeans and an old T-shirt. She had decided there was no human on earth with whom she could bare her heart, not even Hugh. Thus, she felt a great longing to talk things over with her deceased mother, and with Jesus-sitting-on-the-sofa.

She traipsed up the road to the Bauman farmhouse.

Before going inside, Ellie walked around the house, noting the purple irises in bloom and the peonies in bud. Weeds filled the spaces between the perennials. She made a note to come back soon and tidy the flower borders to honour the memory of her mother.

The first thing she noticed upon entering the kitchen was that it no longer smelled like home. Of course it didn't. It was now over a year since her mother had passed away. Still, it added to her sadness.

She ambled over to her father's favourite armchair. Its soft, worn upholstery surrounded her just as it had when she'd returned to Minitonas, making it her favourite chair as well.

Her losses assailed her afresh. She felt the full force of grief and anxiety.

As she had before, she imagined Jesus sitting at the far end of the sofa, patiently waiting to hear what was on her heart and mind. She envisaged her mother sitting nearer to her on the other side. The irony was that Ellie wouldn't have bared her heart to her had she been alive; rather, she would have kept her secret as securely as ever.

Ellie instinctively knew, even now, that if she spoke of her abortion to family and church friends, they would thereafter view her differently. They would give her words of forgiveness and compassion yet whisper behind her back. A barrier would be raised. Trust would be broken. She would *feel* their disappointment, certainly for having intentionally ended the life of an innocent child, but also for having secretly led a life regarded as immoral.

The rub was that although the Bible assured her she was forgiven upon confession of sin, she no longer *felt* forgiven. Her vacant womb convinced her she had somehow been damaged during the procedure. Guilt nagged at her spirit, telling her she was being punished in kind. Sin could be forgiven, but that didn't remove all consequences, she recalled a pastor preaching somewhere along the way. Her heart wasn't in agreement with what she knew to be true in her mind, resulting in a raging war within her soul.

The comfort, peace, and reassurance she sought seemed non-existent. They were luxuries for those who hadn't sinned as seriously as she had.

"No!" cried Ellie aloud, rebutting the speeches in her head. "'As far as the east is from the west, so far does He remove our sins from us.'[3] Stop lying to me, Devil!"

She brought her legs up to her chest, wrapped her arms around them, and buried her face in her knees. She wanted very much to cry, but her eyes remained dry.

"Mama," wailed Ellie as she unfolded herself. Her thoughts were full of things she wanted to say, but she couldn't articulate them. "Jesus, I need You!"

She wanted to say a lot more, to pour out her heart, weep, and plead… but the words couldn't seem to get past her lips.

"Help me talk, Jesus. I need to talk. I want to bring You my burdens like You told us to."

Strangely, her tongue remained tied and the peace for which she pined proved as elusive as ever.

She happened to glance at her wristwatch and saw that it was well after five o'clock. Hugh would be home by now and probably wondering where she was, looking for his supper.

Ellie rose, squared her shoulders, and left the house. By the time she reached their cottage, she had manufactured a happy disposition and greeted her husband in her usual sunny manner.

The weekend had come and at 9:00 a.m. the yard at the Fischer place was teeming with the youth group from the First Baptist Church.

[3] Psalm 103:12, GNT.

Guys and gals alike had come to earn dollars towards the coming retreat in Edmonton. Some of the guys were tasked with dismantling the disc tillager into small pieces and loading them onto Hugh's vintage farm truck to be taken to the scrap metal site in Swan River. The others were assigned the duty of tearing down the decrepit machine shed and carrying the boards to the burn pit. Many hands made light work. A lot was accomplished amidst easy chatter and laughter. Indeed, the demolition work was fun.

Ellie contributed by setting up an iced tea and cookie station available throughout the day. Lunch was a wiener roast followed by platters of cupcakes. Overall, the youth had a good time.

In the afternoon, Trevor got to drive the obsolete combine into Swan River while Ladd, one of the supervisors on the scene, followed behind in Hugh's scrap-metal-filled farm truck.

After they left, Jeremy took the opportunity to go into the new garage to look over Hugh's vintage Plymouth half-ton.

Charlotte, who always kept an eye out for Jeremy, noticed this. She set aside her prybar and nonchalantly sauntered into the shop a couple of moments later.

The hood was up on the Plymouth and Jeremy was pouring over the rusty, seized-up motor, fingering some of the parts as if to assess their viability.

Charlotte moved in close beside him and similarly bent over the motor. "This old truck is really cool, isn't it? I sure hope Uncle Hugh can get it going again."

"Yeah, it's a great find. It will take a lot of work, but he should have a fine collector's item when all is said and done." Jeremy was somewhat surprised that a girl would admire an old vehicle like this with apparent sincerity.

Charlotte leaned in further. "These are sparkplugs, right?" she asked, touching one.

"That's right."

"This is called a fan belt, isn't it? And that is where a battery is supposed to go, correct? Is this the distributor cap?"

Jeremy nodded, impressed. "Yeah, it is."

Charlotte leaned a little closer to him. "What do these wires do?"

"Couldn't tell ya. We'll find out when we disassemble the motor one piece at a time."

Their heads were close together. On impulse, Charlotte turned slightly and kissed his cheek. Jeremy jerked back as though stung by a wasp.

"Ho! What did you do that for?" he snapped rather loudly, his hand covering the kiss on his cheek.

Charlotte straightened as well and backed away a step. "I don't know..." she said tremulously, her face registering shock and confusion.

"How old are you?"

"Fifteen," answered Charlotte quickly and anxiously.

"Fifteen! I can't imagine deacon Bauman would be pleased to know his daughter goes about kissing boys."

"I *don't* go around kissing boys, not even my brother! I just... I just... I don't know why I did it." She then started to cry.

"Oh, don't cry," pleaded Jeremy, clearly nonplussed. "You just surprised me, is all."

Charlotte wiped tears from her eyes with the sleeve of her shirt but continued to appear distraught.

"Never mind. No harm was done." Striving to be gentle, Jeremy reached out and put his arms around Charlotte. This confused Charlotte even further. The mutual stiffness of their embrace might have made it one of the most uncomfortable ever.

Still, he didn't pull away but began to pat her back lightly, the way a mother might pat the back of her baby so it would burp. A couple of minutes later, Charlotte stopped crying and relaxed a little in his arms.

"You know... uh... if something... uh... were ever to develop... uh... between us," stammered Jeremy, "you would have to finish growing up first."

"I know," said Charlotte weakly, blushing with embarrassment.

He released her awkwardly and they exited the garage.

Charlotte returned to her prybar with mixed feelings. On the one hand, she felt the burn of mortification as a silly, immature teenager. On the other hand, she was pretty sure she had finally gotten his attention. She glowed from the suggestion that something could... might... develop between them. And he was the one who'd said it!

∿

A bet is a bet, Margo scolded herself as she swept the floor of the café. No customer was in the diner at the moment. Doing routine work during a quiet afternoon permitted ample opportunity to process her thoughts—and right now, Rory Lang loomed large in her reflections.

They'd had discussions about Christianity, mostly when he came in for a late lunch and no one else needed to be served. He had tried to convince her that faith in Christ was the most important decision a person could make, and she had resisted the argument wholesale. He'd offered to bring her to church, saying that she should at least have enough knowledge to make an informed decision.

When he had put fifty bucks on the line, Margo had seen it as easy money to add to her slow-growing bank account. All she had to do was go to church and somehow resist becoming a Christian.

The trouble now was that she *had* become a Christian. Dr. Billy Graham had preached past her defences and reached into the corners of her heart and mind where the rubber met the road. She had seen the truth of her condition as a wretched sinner in need of a saviour and responded to the love and forgiveness God offered. She had no regrets about that, even now as she contemplated her predicament with Rory.

But gee, handing over fifty bucks would make a big dent in her measly savings account, especially at a time when she needed every red penny to pay for courses she would have to take if she wanted to become a businesswoman and make the downpayment to buy the café from Bev one day.

You have to do it for the sake of integrity, she argued with herself. *You can't risk being thought of as dishonourable or untrustworthy.*

She wouldn't do it in the restaurant. Sunday, after church, would be best.

Although the church experience was still new, Margo found that she enjoyed going. The music had a nice ring to it and Pastor Leland's message this week was down-to-earth and compelling, as usual. She hung on every word.

Some of the other congregants were patrons at the café, and a few greeted her warmly as they filed out of the sanctuary afterward.

Rory offered to drive her home when the service ended. It wasn't necessary, since the Harms place wasn't far, but she accepted.

"Do you want to go out for lunch?" he asked as he slowly drove out of the parking lot. "Swan River has some places that are open."

"Sorry, no. I need to fix lunch for Lydia. Thanks anyway." Then Margo opened her purse to retrieve the bills. "Here. I owe you this," she said, setting the bills down in the space between them.

Rory frowned, uncomprehending. "What's this for?"

"You win the bet."

"What bet?"

"The bet we made over accepting Christianity. I became a Christian after hearing Billy Graham preach on television. I lost and am making good on the wager."

"No kidding," Rory said. "You want to tell me about it?"

"Maybe another time." Margo prepared to depart. "I should get back to Lydia. She seems to be on the decline. She can't get around and do for herself as much as she used to. I'd better go."

"Are you working the tables tomorrow?"

Margo stepped out. "Yes. Thanks for the ride."

∽

On Monday, Rory came into the café later than the lunch crowd. He went straight to his favourite spot, the rearmost booth, with a newspaper under his arm.

Margo approached him as usual. "What will you have today? We still have some of the Chicken a la King special if you're interested."

"Sounds good. What about dessert?"

"There's a fresh lemon meringue pie, and also some triple layer chocolate cake we made this morning."

"I'll go with a piece of pie."

Rory consumed his meal while paging through the newspaper. No other conversation passed between them.

At last he came to the counter to settle his tab. "Have a good rest of your day," said Rory as he left the café.

"Thanks, same to you."

She went to the booth to carry away the dirty dishes—and under the plate lay her tip: a crisp fifty-dollar bill.

∽

"Ellie, could you settle our next patient?" The head nurse handed her the chart. "This woman broke her wrist and hit her head. The doctor wants to keep her overnight for observation to make sure she doesn't have a concussion."

Ellie cheerfully accepted the chart. "Happy to."

She read the name on her way to the ward where personnel from the emergency department had just wheeled in their latest patient.

Suddenly, she stopped short.

"Ruth Wagner! My aunt?"

She waited patiently while the woman was gingerly transferred from the gurney to the hospital bed. When the orderlies completed the transfer and left the room, Ellie approached the woman. Although her eyes were closed, it was indeed her relative. Her left wrist was encased in a cast from her palm to her elbow. A multi-shaded blue and purple bruise over her left eye had swelled to the size of an egg. There were also some minor scrapes on the cheek.

"Oh dear," Ellie whispered. "Whatever happened to bring about this sad state of affairs?"

Ruth's good eye fluttered open. "Is that you, Ellie? News travels fast if you've already come to visit me. You always were a thoughtful girl."

"I hope I'm a thoughtful girl, but you've been assigned to the part of the hospital where I nurse. I should check your vitals first, and then you can tell me the story."

Ellie got down to business. She popped a thermometer into Ruth's mouth and proceeded to take her blood pressure. Ruth lay still while her pulse rate was taken and Ellie listened to her heartbeat via stethoscope.

When all these duties were carried out, Ellie hung the chart on the foot of the bed. With a loving smile, she approached her aunt on her good side.

"You look like you've been in a fight. Did you at least win?" teased Ellie.

"No, I lost to a patch of ice," retorted Ruth in the same spirit. She then gasped with a throb of pain.

Ellie frowned in confusion. "Ice? In June?"

"Oh. Is it June already?"

"The chart said you tripped over a garden rake and fell headlong over a stepping stone. I guess that explains the damage to your pretty face."

"Who told you that?" snapped Ruth. "It was a patch of ice. I know a rake when I see one."

Ellie went into pacification mode. "Of course you do. It must have been Uncle Herb who told the doctor you tripped over a rake.

Whatever it was, you broke your wrist right and proper. It'll be a while until you get to use your left hand again."

She smoothed the blanket over her aunt and attached the call button to the rail of her bed.

"They said I could go home tomorrow," said Ruth. "You don't have to tell your mother or anyone else where I am. I won't be here long enough for visitors. If they want to see me, they can come to my place."

Ellie looked at her aunt strangely. "Of course. That makes perfect sense."

"I'd like to sleep now. Is there something I can have to put me out quickly? The bruise over my eye is paining pretty good."

"I'll see what I can do," said Ellie. "In the meantime, try to relax as much as possible."

When Ellie had returned to her station, the head nurse walked up to her. "Did she settle in nicely?"

"Yes… and yet…" started Ellie slowly. "I know this woman and understand why the doctor wants her to be observed for concussion. Her speech seemed strange, addled, and out of character. I truly hope a bump on the head explains it."

Twenty-One

"**PHONE FOR YOU**," said Ellie breathlessly. She had run from their house to the garage where Hugh was at work disassembling the motor of the Plymouth. "It's your Aunt Renata. It seems your grandmother is out of sorts."

Hugh raised his eyebrows, grabbed a rag to remove the grime from his hands, and hurried to the house.

"Hullo. Aunt Renata?"

"Hello, Hugh," she began in a rush. "I'm sorry to bother you, but I may need your help in a matter going on here."

"Ho! Not even any pleasantries to start with," said Hugh jokingly. Yet he wore a frown.

"My apologies." She paused. Her tone was less frantic but forced somehow. "How are you and Ellie?"

"We're doing well, thanks for asking. How about yourself and the others?"

"Not so well. That's why I called. I've got a situation here. I'm hoping you can bring relief."

Hugh felt apprehensive. "Okay. I'll try. What is this about?"

"Your grandmother is obsessed with making amends with Fredrich. She goes from moaning to crying and then to nagging that he come and spend time with her before she passes. We're going crazy with her constant fixation on Fred. I'm just about ready to have her committed to a seniors care facility so *they* can deal with her."

"Two questions. Is she really at death's door? And how do you think I can help?" asked Hugh, genuinely puzzled.

"She seems to think so. I've heard about people having premonitions regarding their deaths, so who knows? She isn't quite bedridden but does have serious heart issues and has slowed down a great deal over the past few months. As for your second question, I hope you will agree to pretend to be your father and talk to her so she gets off her chest the guilt and burden she's been carrying since she left him and Minitonas behind."

"I see several problems with that, Aunty," he replied slowly. "For one thing, I don't speak German. For another, I have no idea what happened back… what was it… thirty-five years ago, if not more?"

"You don't need to speak German. She understands English very well."

"Well, what do you know about it? She came to you, after all. She must have given you her reasons for not returning out west."

Renata sighed. "She told me she hated the country life. Especially the primitiveness of it. She was highborn in Germany and married beneath her station. Coming to Canada to homestead sounded like wonderful fun and a great adventure, but she soon missed the refinement of city life… the concerts and social events. Mother had been used to having servants take care of the mundane details. Suddenly she had to learn skills taken for granted by other women. Besides all that, your grandfather proved to be a proud and unsympathetic man. Living with him wasn't easy." There was a hard edge in her tone now. "I should know. I was his daughter."

"I can relate to that part," put in Hugh dryly. "What was her reason for leaving her son without warning? Were they not getting along?"

"Truth be known, I may have played a part in it."

"I'm listening…"

"When she came east, the timing couldn't have been better," began Renata. "I had just given birth to Cassandra, my first daughter, and she was a wonderful help to me. Our house was large enough for Mother to have her own room. After a month had gone by, she began to talk about her dread of returning to the farm. There was nothing there to draw her back. She had no close friends to speak of. With my father gone, she felt she had the freedom to live according to *her* preferences. What she wanted was the city life. I might have encouraged her to stay with us and leave the farm to Fred."

"So he wasn't involved in the decision. What if he didn't want to farm?"

"He could have sold it and pocketed the money."

"Am I right in surmising he was given the property but no capital with which to run it?"

There was a short pause before Renata replied. "I suppose that would be a reasonable deduction."

"My theory is that gaining a good chunk of real estate without any means of operating it put a real sour taste in his mouth," Hugh said. "Like being gifted a car but with missing parts. Where's the gift in it if you can't run it? And how old was he? Twenty? Can't imagine him having any savings to the tune of running a farm." He drew a long, deep breath. "Here's another thing. Ellie and I met up with my mother's only sister last summer. She scrounged up some seniors from Minitonas who remembered the original Fischers back in the day. According to their recollections, Pa... Fred... felt abandoned by her. Her decision not to come home wasn't discussed ahead of time and he had no reason to expect it. I suspect he felt hurt and resentful. Probably took it personal."

"We wrote him letters!" insisted Renata. "Everything was explained in our letters. He never wrote back or tried to get in touch with us."

"The seniors I mentioned suggested the mother and son were close, but not the father and son. You said that much yourself. So I can imagine Huldah, leaving him the way she did, caused him to feel abandoned and betrayed. He thought he'd had her support. That would have been enough to make him hopping mad. Pa was a bitter, angry man who held on to grudges and that's a fact. He trusted no one. It wouldn't surprise me if that's when it started."

"We wrote letters…" maintained Renata tremulously. "It wasn't our intention to end the relationship. We should have been able to continue communicating, to talk things out through correspondence. If that's truly what the problem was, Mother might have extended him a loan or something."

"It sounds to me like mother and sister didn't really know Fred at all."

Hugh felt that the conversation leading into territory he didn't want to enter, that he was being driven against his will.

Renata hesitated. "At the time of Mother's parting, I'd say we knew him."

"Did you know that my father never accepted me as his own son? That he believed me to be a bastard because my mother went to a party without him and spent the night at her sister's place shortly after they were married?"

"That's ridiculous. You are the very spit of him."

"So everyone says, but he took a notion and no amount of truth or reason would shake him from it. Why? Probably because he wasn't the faithful type himself, so why would he think anyone else would be? The point is, when Pa made up his mind about something, he stuck to it like tar to a front wheel bumper. The seniors I talked to said he had a drinking problem, from his youth, and Huldah may have contributed to it by giving him alcohol as a medicine to cure everything from toothache to a sore throat, even insomnia."

"She did the same for me, and I don't have a drinking problem."

"All I'm saying is that the whole Fischer story is a hopelessly tangled web and I doubt I can help my grandmother with her dying wishes," said Hugh drearily. "Your stories help me understand Pa better, but my family suffered badly under him. My mother and I had the worst of it. I ran away on my sixteenth birthday because I couldn't take it anymore. I honestly don't think I can pull off a stand-in for Fred."

There were a few moments of uncomfortable silence.

"You'll at least think about it, won't you?" persisted Renata.

Hugh let out a long sigh. "Yes, Aunty, I'll think about it. Goodbye for now."

He hung up the phone and slumped onto a kitchen chair across from Ellie, cradling his head in both hands, dejected.

Ellie had been sitting at the kitchen table throughout the phone call. "I can follow the gist from what you said. What does Renata want of you?"

"She wants me to pretend to be Pa to my grandmother. Apparently Huldah is carrying a lot of guilt for the way she left. I'm guessing Pa provoked that guilt on purpose, his way of punishing her for leaving him high and dry. Knowing him the way I do, instead of being grateful for his substantial inheritance, he felt double-crossed. No one double-crossed Freddie and got away with it. But back to the question… Renata wants to set up a meeting so my grandmother and Pa can 'reconcile,' allowing her to pass peacefully from this world."

"I know something about the restlessness people experience before they pass," said Ellie, trying to be helpful. "We took a class about it during my nurses training. If there's unfinished business or amends to be made, the dying person often actively and restlessly resists parting from this world until those outstanding matters are dealt with. That is, if there is a willingness between all concerned."

"Sounds reasonable, but it's too late for that. Pa's gone. Standing in for him amounts to a deception. When is that ever a good thing? What do you think I should do?" The appeal in his voice carried tones of confusion and anguish.

"I get the part about lying. Beyond that, I don't understand why she needs to involve you. Wouldn't any man do for a telephone meeting?"

"I suppose she's trying to stay as close to the truth as she can, and at least keep it within the family." Hugh sighed. "Huldah is convinced that Pa came to visit them when we were on our honeymoon. No amount of insisting that it was the grandson makes any difference. Stubborn stupidity is a family trait."

"Oh no, stubborn stupidity is a *human* trait. You don't own the corner on that. I think it's naïve of Renata to believe a pretend conversation with Fred will make your grandmother's passing, whenever it happens, so much more peaceable."

"Why wouldn't it? I can see Renata's viewpoint on this."

"Because we believe the Bible, and it explains the truth about humans and the experience of death."

"You're preaching to the choir, Ella Rose."

"Maybe. But hear me out. At death, our bodies decompose back to dust. Our spirits, sometimes referred to as souls, continue in the eternal realm. The Bible teaches that the default realm for sinful, separated-from-God humans is hell. To be rescued from automatically spending eternity in that realm, we have to take the way out that God paid for and provided by claiming Jesus's death on our behalf. That's the ticket to peace with God and in our souls."

Hugh cast his eyes upward impatiently. "I. Know. All. This."

"I know you do. My point is, your grandmother is screaming for peace from the wrong source. And it's obvious to me that Renata is clueless as well."

"So… what do you want me to do?"

Ellie proceeded uncertainly. "Do you think there's any chance they'll listen to your story about your own restless misery and how you came to Jesus?"

"I dunno… doubtful. When we were there, I had no sense they were religious people."

"She might not have the patience to hear your story over the phone, but what if you wrote it out in a letter? If you throw in a bunch of your family history, you're likely to have their full attention."

"It just might work," said Hugh. "Having said that, I can't fault Renata for wanting to help her mother come to a place of peace."

"That's fair."

Hugh stroked his face as he looked around the room, considering. His eyes fell on the steamer trunk. "There might be a clue in there. Let's unpack that thing."

"Finally!" erupted Ellie. "I thought you were *never* going to show an interest in its contents." She quickly removed the magazines and ornamental dish gracing the top.

Hugh lifted the lid carefully. He picked up the sheaf of handwritten papers and handed them to Ellie. "Make two sets of photocopies of these please, for Margo and Diane."

Ellie took them from him and stowed them safely in a drawer where they kept their important papers. The shallow tray held only the wedding dress. That, too, was set aside. Beneath that, they unpacked an eight-place setting of fine bone china featuring red roses; crystal wine glasses, vase, and bowl; a wooden box of tarnished silverware; four silver candle-stick holders; two blue and white serving platters; and a matching soup tureen.

Ellie showed interest in a few antique linens that had been used to keep the dishes from breaking. Hugh was more interested in the concertina, a gold pocket watch on a chain, a small telescope, and a compass included in the mix. Ellie gravitated to the mantle clock, but Hugh reminded her that he had never seen it keep time.

The bottom of the trunk was lined with a few small books written in German, a packet of report cards from Hugh and his sisters' school days, a paper bag holding a few age-old and meaningless photographs, and a crushed shoebox.

His eye caught something else wedged between the books. He pulled it out and smiled broadly.

"Look at this! My little red toy truck. Not lost after all!" Hugh rolled it across his thigh. Some of the red paint had flaked off, but otherwise it was completely intact and brought him a jolt of nostalgia.

"Nice," said Ellie, smiling as well. "I wonder if Aunt Gertie would remember giving it to you."

"She might, especially if she saw it."

He set it on the end table next to the lamp. Then both returned their attention to what remained in the trunk.

"I have a hunch what I'm looking for is in here," said Hugh, pointing to the shoebox.

"Do you want me to look first?"

"I think I can handle this one."

Hugh rose and removed the litter of newspaper wrappings from the armchair. He sat down, resting the shoebox on his lap. He glanced over at Ellie, then lifted the squashed lid and peered inside to discover a stack of mail. The envelopes, once white, were yellowed with age and brittle. Hugh fingered through them, noting that they were organized according to date, the oldest being in front.

He withdrew the first envelope, saw that it had been opened, and removed the letter. The creases cracked the paper upon unfolding it.

"Drat! It's written in German," he complained. "The return address is in Ontario. This has to be the letter Renata told us about. And look here. The other letters behind this one haven't ever been opened. They all have the same return address."

"I'm sure we could find someone proficient in German to translate for you."

"I'll admit I'm a bit curious as to how they announced my grandmother wouldn't be returning and the details for transferring the property over to Pa, but I don't think I want anyone else to know about our dirty laundry just for the sake of translation. I believe Renata's version of what transpired, but we can work out the probable reasons Pa responded how he did. What seems to matter, at least to Huldah, is that they somehow have an opportunity to reconcile with the past. I still don't think I should be dragged into it."

"We can think and pray about this before you reconnect with Renata," said Ellie sensibly. "In the meantime, what should we do with all this stuff?" She panned the room with her arm.

"We should do what my mother wanted… distribute these amongst her children. I'll keep the guy stuff and this box of mail. Someday I could be interested in learning more about our family history. What would you like to keep?"

Ellie shook her head. "Oh no. I'm not expressing an interest in anything. I've heard so many stories of families that fought and split over the remaining stuff of dead people than you can shake a stick at. Choose what you will. It's your inheritance, not mine."

"Well then, in addition to the concertina, pocket watch, telescope, and compass... I choose the mantle clock, even though it doesn't work, and the blue and white platters and tureen." Hugh read Ellie's face for signs of approval.

"You chose very well," replied Ellie with a broad, knowing smile. "Though I can't imagine either of your sisters would be interested in the linen tablecloths. Those are delicate items you can't just throw in the washing machine."

Hugh grinned. "Then I should be the one who looks after them for posterity, right?"

"I've always known you to be a responsible man." Ellie winked.

"I'm just that kind of guy. If that covers my obligations, we can pack up the rest of this stuff and my sisters can go through it on their own time, whenever. And for the purpose of clarification, are we done with the mysteries of the trunk now?"

"Check. We are done with the mysteries of the trunk, Hugh-spit-able."

Twenty-Two

IT WOULD BE all of another month before the construction crew began the task of erecting the Fischer's new house. In the meantime, Ellie set about developing the yard while Hugh mostly kept himself occupied with projects in the shop. The Plymouth lay in pieces in the middle bay. Reassembling the motor would take a long time, what with parts no longer being readily available; he would have to improvise. That's where the Moore brothers came in handy. They seemed to be masters of improvisation.

Having tidied the main yard, Ellie set about making a clear walking path to the pond a few hundred feet away in the bush west of the home yard. Using the lawnmower, she created a grassy sward alongside the huge flat rock that bordered the water. A pair of Adirondack chairs were set there to facilitate times of intimate conversation and quiet reflection.

When this was completed to her satisfaction, she cut another meandering path, this one leading to the East Favel River. Here, too, she mowed a strip of foliage along the riverbank large enough to accommodate a park bench. The babbling river soothed mind and soul, she found. It gave her great pleasure to create these walking paths and it had the good effect of distracting her from the worry that constantly threatened to throw her into deep depression.

Next Ellie turned her attention to the home yard. There was no use creating flower borders until the big house was built, but she had another idea. She wanted to create something more appealing with the big boulder they had unearthed and rolled to the corner at the entrance of the driveway. If she added other large rocks and positioned them in an interesting arrangement, she could add dirt between them and rock garden plants. She had in mind hens and chicks, assorted sedum, and a certain hardy variety of cactus. The cacti she had seen flowering in their climes stunningly resembled roses.

Having donned her shabbiest jeans and T-shirt, and gloved her hands, she attempted to move some of the bigger stones from the rockpile. The ones she wanted were too heavy to lift, however, and there was no way to proceed on her own. She'd have to ask Hugh for help.

"Hello darlin'," she said, greeting him mushily where he was hammering at a piece of metal on the workbench.

Hugh paused and looked up at her suspiciously. "That's not your usual tone. Methinks you want to ask me for something I won't want to do."

"Probably, but I need you and your big strong muscles to help with my project."

"Hmmm. Trying to win my service through flattery. What project is this now?"

"I want to create a rock garden by the big boulder. I'm not strong enough to move the rocks I want over there."

"Oh, so you want me to be the one to have back problems!"

"It shouldn't take too long if you bring the tractor over and we load a few at a time in the bucket," she pleaded. "As Rob would say, 'Don't work hard, work smart.'"

"Does it have to be right now?" asked Hugh reluctantly.

She smiled sweetly. "I would appreciate it if you would… right now. I'll make it worth your while…"

"Oh yeah? How?"

"Not sure yet, but I'll think of something."

"Okay, but you owe me, Mrs. Fischer," he teased.

He set aside his hammer and went to start up the tractor while Ellie headed in the direction of the rockpile. She was standing on top when Hugh slowly approached and used hand directions to indicate where the bucket should be positioned so the big stones could be more easily rolled in.

Once the bucket was set in place, Hugh shut down the motor, clambered up the pile, and began to roll rocks into the bucket as Ellie pointed them out. The first load carried six over to the giant boulder and were deposited along its backside. They went back for a second haul and this time got eight hefty stones in varying shapes. Determining that this was enough for now, Hugh descended the pile and took his place in the driver's seat. Meanwhile Ellie thought she could fit in one more smaller stone she could handle by herself. She squatted to lift the thing by the strength of her legs. Once she had placed it in the bucket, she turned and looked back at the spot where she had lifted the rock. Her eyes went as wide as humanly possible as she let out a bloodcurdling scream.

The sound caused Hugh's heart to lurch in sheer terror. Startled, his first thought was that she had uncovered a snake den or possibly a wasps' nest. As fast as he could, he fled the tractor and scrambled up the rockpile to see what Ellie was screaming about.

The sight made his insides freeze. There lay the smashed remains of a human skull. It was still attached to neck bones inside a filthy shirt collar.

Hugh grabbed Ellie and pulled her to himself. She clung to him crying and gasping by turn.

"Shhhhh, listen to me," said Hugh with as much rational calm as he could muster. "We're going to get off this pile and go into the house and call the cops."

Ellie's legs suddenly didn't seem to work properly. Hugh helped her down as though she were a child and supported her all the way back to their cottage.

Once inside, she sank into the nearest kitchen chair. Her crying had stopped, but she shook like the proverbial leaf.

Hugh remained extraordinarily cool as he called the Swan River police station, carefully reported how they had come upon the human remains, and then waited for their arrival.

Ellie gradually stopped shaking and composed herself.

"If that isn't Tipper's big secret, then I don't want to know what it is," she said to him once he was off the phone. "I had no idea what it could be, but I *never* imagined this."

"Come here." He sat on the sofa. "Let me hold you."

Ellie gladly went to him. Neither said anything for a couple of moments. Then Hugh spoke in the same calm tone he had used earlier.

"I had no idea what the big secret would turn out to be either, but I'm not totally surprised. This fits with the company Pa kept." He sighed audibly. "It's not necessarily murder, you know. Any number of things could have happened here, but it doesn't look good any which way you slice it."

Hugh's uncanny calm was effective in settling Ellie down. She stopped shaking and her breathing returned to normal.

When the police showed up, Hugh released Ellie and went outdoors to meet them. He led them to the rockpile and showed them the skull. The area was taped off to establish an official crime scene.

At first Ellie had no wish to watch the cops at work, yet she didn't want to miss anything either. When she finally decided to go back to the scene, she found she could only watch from a distance. That suited her fine.

Very carefully, the police extracted the skeletal remains and gathered them into a body bag. More of the rockpile was taken down as the officers searched for a murder weapon, but nothing of further interest was found.

Hours later, two police officers joined Hugh and Ellie inside to record their statements. During this time, Hugh recalled the strange conversation he'd overheard in the Swan River restaurant a few months earlier concerning his father and a big secret. Ellie added some details about

Chiclets having trespassed on their property claiming to be looking for "his kin."

"Chiclets is the street name for Ronald Addy," said one police officer to another. "He's well known in the district as a brutal fighter."

"I know. I've had to break up some fights he's been involved in. I don't know why some guys take him on. They usually leave pretty damaged," concurred the second officer. "Based on these statements, we'll have to bring him in and see what he knows about it."

That being enough excitement for one day, Hugh and Ellie ate out and then retired earlier than usual. Emotional exhaustion had claimed them.

On Sunday morning, the sun shone with a magnificent brightness that hurt the eye, yet Ellie wanted nothing more than to soak up its rays. Flowers bloomed in practically every yard in Minitonas. Birds sang in praise and worship outside the First Baptist Church. Pastor Wirt delivered a thought-provoking sermon from the book of Romans. After its conclusion, people gathered in the foyer to catch up on each other's lives. Some made plans to get together soon.

Sarah invited Hugh and Ellie to join them for Sunday dinner, to which Ellie immediately agreed. Then Ellie saw Margo helping Lydia Harms descend the front steps.

"I fixed a casserole at home," Ellie said to her sister-in-law. "If I brought it along to add to the table, would you be all right with inviting those two as well?" She indicated Margo and Lydia.

"Of course," Sarah agreed. "The more, the merrier."

Sarah approached the two women while Ellie hurried away to retrieve her casserole.

At first Margo demurred at the invitation, but Lydia brightened at once.

"We would love to come," said Lydia before Margo could further decline. "I b'lieve the good Lord made Sunday mornings for worship and Sunday afternoons for food, fellowship, and afternoon naps. Food and fellowship go with merriment, and that's good like medicine according to the good book. We could do with some of that merriment on a fine day like today."

"I couldn't agree more." Sarah chuckled. "We'll see you at our house shortly."

When Hugh and Ellie arrived at Rob and Sarah's place with their casserole, the house was a beehive of activity. Trevor and Rob had extended the table and Charlotte spread a tablecloth over it. She and her little sister Beanie then went about setting the table for nine. Sarah had pots of potatoes and vegetables cooking on the stove and was occupied making gravy from the drippings of the roast chicken. Rob carved up the meat, leaving Trevor to entertain the ladies in the living room, something he wasn't quite comfortable doing.

Thus, when Hugh entered the room, his relief was plain.

"Hello, ladies," greeted Hugh.

Lydia turned to Margo. "This is your brother, is he not?"

"Yes," Margo said. "Good for you for remembering."

"What's new in your camp?" asked Hugh politely.

"Well now, not much," Lydia replied. "One day tends to run into the other without anything more exciting than switching the TV channels."

Margo put a hand on the older woman's shoulder. "We held a yard sale yesterday. Don't you remember, Lydia? I made a few dollars selling some of my extra clothes."

"And I made a whole dollar on a pair of salt and pepper shakers I no longer had use for," grumbled Lydia. "T'wasn't worth the effort to set up the table."

Rob announced that dinner was ready to be served and invited his guests to come to the table. He asked the blessing over the meal.

As soon as the amen was said, Trevor spoke up. "Uncle Hugh, will you play on my baseball team at the FBC picnic day next Saturday?"

"Wasn't planning to go this year," answered Hugh while spooning mashed potatoes onto his plate. "Ellie is scheduled to work that day."

"Aww, come anyway," Trevor pleaded. "I'm still short a couple of players."

"We'll have to see. No promises."

Sarah turned to her guest. "How are you getting along these days, Lydia?"

"Better now that the warm weather has arrived," she answered. "The arthritis in my hips is less troublesome."

"I'm happy to hear that. How about you, Margo?"

"Not badly," she replied. "I'm still enjoying my work at the café."

"Good for you," commented Sarah. "Haven't seen you in a while, Ellie. What have you been up to lately?"

"Well, apart from my hospital shifts, I've cut some walking paths through our bush as far as the river. Now I'm working on creating a rock garden near the entrance of the driveway. It was going great until we discovered a skeleton under the stones of our rockpile. I decided to take a break then."

Ellie said this as nonchalantly as reciting the alphabet. She didn't skip a beat as she passed the bowls of food along.

Beanie screwed up her nose. "Peugh!"

"Are you serious?" asked Charlotte, wide-eyed.

"Very funny," piped up Trevor disbelievingly. "Haha. Good one."

Sarah appeared nonplussed, and Rob looked over at Hugh with a bland expression on his face.

"What? You don't believe her? It's the truth." Hugh looked around, sensing that everyone was expecting him to repudiate his wife's words as a silly joke.

"All right, I'll bite." Rob speared his fork into the chicken. "What's the story? You found a Hallowe'en decoration or costume?"

"Nope," said Hugh. "Ellie roped me into helping her move some boulders from the rockpile behind our house with the tractor. We weren't working very long before she uncovered a bashed-in skull. She screamed loud enough to wake the dead. Sorry, let me rephrase that. The skeleton we uncovered did not wake up. But she screamed loud enough for her to be heard all the way to Winnipeg. We stopped working and called the cops."

"I can imagine what a shock that was!" Sarah put her fork down. "Gives me the willies just thinking about it."

"Are you saying there was a murder at our farm?" asked Margo, stunned and dismayed.

"No one knows yet what happened," continued Hugh. "I believe the cops are planning to have the remains examined by a specialist to determine the cause of death. The skull was crushed, but it's unlikely whoever it is was alive when that happened."

"How can you be so unruffled about it, Aunt Ellie?" Charlotte sounded incredulous. "If it was me, I think I'd fall apart at the seams!"

"I did fall apart," Ellie said. "When I stumbled on it, I screamed to high heaven, just like Hugh said. Then I felt like all my cells became disconnected from each other. I got so weak in the knees that Hugh practically had to carry me back to the house. Eventually I got over the shock. Sort of. But I doubt I'll ever forget that initial sight. Still gives me the shivers."

"How long do you suppose it was there?" asked Margo.

"Years, though I have no idea how many," answered Hugh coolly. "Obviously sometime before Ma and Pa's accident."

Margo drew a slow breath. "Then Pa must be implicated."

"Of course. Not that he'll answer for it, being beyond the reach of the law."

"I can't believe you're so cool about this," spluttered Charlotte. "I think I would be undone for weeks if I had stumbled upon something like that."

"I was shook up," agreed Ellie. "I'm still bothered by it, but I expect I'll return to centre again. My rock garden project is on hold until I do."

"Did the police find anything else of interest as they went about their business?" asked Rob carefully.

Hugh offered a grim frown. "They did take apart the remainder of the rockpile, looking for evidence that would explain what went down. I don't believe they found anything."

Rob nodded. "Do you, or the police, have a theory?"

"I'm guessing it's a fight that ended badly." Hugh sighed. "It had to be covered up."

"You're awfully quiet, Lydia," said Sarah gently. "What do you think about this rather shocking revelation?"

"I'm trying to remember something I haven't thought of in a long while," said the elder woman. "You say the body was buried under a heap of stones? There's an old saying that goes, 'Whatever you bury, you bury alive.'"

Trevor regarded her with scepticism. "Are you suggesting the guy, whoever he was, was buried alive?"

"No, that's not what she meant," put in Rob quickly. "I've heard this saying before myself. It means that when people bury their problems instead of dealing with them, they don't stay buried forever. Eventually there is a day of reckoning. Am I right, Lydia?"

"Well said, deacon Bauman," said Lydia with a smile. "And I do b'lieve it's the truth."

"Hugh has firsthand experience with that proverb," Ellie remarked.

Hugh eyed her sideways. "Oh, and you don't?"

"My point is that unresolved issues don't go away just because they're buried. They fester and haunt us until they're dealt with. I was thinking about your grandmother."

"Our grandmother?" said Margo quickly. "I haven't heard about this."

"I don't want to go into a lot of detail, but apparently she's troubled by her lack of relationship with Pa, which unintentionally ended when she left Minitonas after our grandfather died." Hugh shook his head sadly. "That was a problem buried alive that's now screaming for reconciliation."

"That saying you quoted about burying stuff alive has layers of meaning then, like the layers of an onion," said Charlotte, thinking hard.

Rob met her eyes. "Yes. It does."

Sarah looked dazed. "Oh my goodness. I had no idea this sunny, cheerful day was going to produce such a troubling discussion. Does anyone have some positive news to share? Something we could celebrate?"

"I'll be positive if Uncle Hugh agrees to be part of my ball team next Saturday," piped up Trevor.

Twenty-Three

"I THOUGHT I'D stop by and see how you're doing," said Ellie upon visiting her aunt. She had taken a notion to drive the long way home after work and look in on Ruth, who was still mending from her broken wrist. "Is your garden off to a good start?"

Ruth lit up at the sight of her niece. "I saw beans, beets, and the hairs of carrots. My wrist seems to be mending fine, too. It's so nice of you to drop by."

"Well, I care about you, I hope you know. It must be hard for you not to be able to cook, bake, and do yard work like you're used to."

"It's not so bad. There is lots to choose from in the freezer. Your Uncle Herb is keeping the weeds down in the garden. We're managing just fine."

"Great! I've got time for a cup of tea if you do."

"It will have to be a quick one," said Ruth. "I'm presenting a Tupperware party this evening and I haven't yet prepared myself for it."

Ellie furrowed her brow. "A Tupperware party? I thought you retired from that years ago."

"Now where would you get an idea like that?" Ruth sounded annoyed.

"As I recall, you quit selling Tupperware about the same time I graduated from high school. So where is the party going to be this evening?"

"Ahhh… Swan River," replied Ruth, thinking hard. "The exact address is written in my appointment book. Don't you worry, Ellie. I've got everything under control."

"Of course you do…" Ellie eyed her aunt strangely. "Can I get the kettle boiling? Or do you have some of your delicious Russian tea on hand?"

"No, there's none of that, but I have some peppermint tea that's lovely."

"Sounds perfect!"

A few moments later they were enjoying the refreshing tea and oatmeal cookies. Ruth reminisced about the good old days when telephone calls were carried out by operators, clothes were washed in wringer washing machines, and pastors paid regular visits to their parishioners. Ellie listened happily, enjoying the anecdotes of late relatives and friends from a bygone era. Most of the stories she had heard before, but she didn't mind hearing them again. They were as comfortable and affirming as a soft old quilt. Aunt Ruth's memory seemed to be as sure as any historian… until Ellie rose to go.

"I'd better get on home and put supper together. Hugh doesn't like to eat late," she said, setting her teacup on the counter. "Besides, I don't want to make you late for your Tupperware party."

"What Tupperware party?" asked Ruth with a surprised frown.

"The one you said you're doing in Swan River this evening."

"You need to look after your memory, young lady. I retired from selling Tupperware years ago."

Five minutes after Ellie got home, Hugh pulled into the driveway. He spent a couple of minutes playing with their dogs, who responded joyfully to the attention.

When he came into the house, he threw a packet of foolscap on the table.

"What's that for?" asked Ellie while setting the table for supper.

"It's to write out my testimony for Aunt Renata," replied Hugh. "It was your idea, remember? And I think it's the best way for me to try and make her and Grandma Huldah understand how things were, and are now, from my perspective."

"Good for you, honey. I think so, too."

Following their meal, Ellie cleared the dishes so the table was available for Hugh to use as a desk. Instead he donned his cap, picked up the packet of foolscap, and headed for the door.

"Where are you going now?" she asked in surprise.

"To the office in the garage. I think I need a quiet place with no distractions for this assignment."

"Oh. I guess that's fair. I'll miss you," she said with a half-smile. She reached up and kissed him lightly on the lips.

Hugh smiled as he closed the door behind him. "Like I said… no distractions."

Suddenly, with Hugh gone, the house seemed empty, and the evening stretched out before her. It came to her that if Hugh was going to write out his story for his newfound relatives in an environment that facilitated concentration, she should do the same with the matters troubling her own heart. It had been months since she had recorded her thoughts.

Ellie looked for her journals in a seldom opened drawer and found them. She made herself comfy in the armchair, curling her legs up around her. The smaller of the two journals was the one she had used to assign herself topics for reflection. The larger one contained questions she had felt the Lord Jesus asking of her, as well as her heartfelt answers, arrived at through long processing and returning to the faith.

Browsing these journals revealed how much progress she'd made and how the Lord had blessed her with healing and love from family, friends, and a good man to call her husband.

Yet here she was, stewing again. Writing things out prayerfully had helped before, so it seemed prudent to try again. In the small journal she wrote:

Identify your worries and fears.

Because these exercises were supposed to reflect the naked truth as she felt and thought them, she took her time recording her responses.

I worry that I'm unable to conceive. I fear being childless.

That was all she wrote, though. She couldn't think of anything else to add.

The weight of this concern caused her eyes to swim, but she wouldn't give in to weeping. Hugh might come in at any time and she didn't want to complicate the evening with her worries. It would be heavy enough for him to concentrate on his family's difficult history. Besides, there was always a chance she was worrying needlessly…

Ellie tried to pray, but her words came out disconnected. They seemed to evaporate as soon as they left her mouth, not even reaching the ceiling, never mind the throne of heaven.

She didn't bother trying to make another entry in the bigger journal. Instead she put on a cassette tape of music played by a stringed orchestra. It soothed her low spirit.

Hugh made several false starts before he got into the stream of writing. Even then, he crossed out many words and replaced them with better ones, hoping he was being true and tactful at the same time. When he was satisfied, he recopied the whole thing afresh so it was clean and coherent.

At ten minutes before midnight, he walked back into the cottage, letter in hand.

Although she had changed into nightclothes, Ellie hadn't gone to bed, having stayed up to receive her husband, thinking he might return very glum considering the nature of his mission. He might need her encouragement.

She had been dozing, however, and her eyes flew open at the sound of the door.

"Why are you still up?" said Hugh. "You didn't need to wait for me."

"I thought you might need to talk a bit before calling it a night." Ellie stifled a yawn. "It's taken you quite a while, so I assume it was a hard job."

"Not as hard as I expected, but I wanted the words to be right and kept revising as I went along. Had to rewrite the thing just so it isn't a mess to read. You can look it over if you want."

Ellie rose quickly. "I would love to do that, just as soon as I come back from the bathroom. Nature is calling me."

While she was gone, Hugh picked up her small journal, mildly curious about what sort of book it was. It opened easily to the page of her last entry. He read the few words she had written before realizing it was meant to be a private diary. He quickly returned the item to its former position just in time before Ellie came back. She picked up his sheaf of papers and began to read.

Meanwhile, Hugh got ready for bed.

"This is beautiful, Hugh," praised Ellie after she was done. "You've written respectfully and clearly. If Renata and your grandmother don't hear the love in your tone, then they have hard hearts indeed."

"Thanks, babe." Hugh yawned. "I won't mail it immediately, though. It needs to rest for a few days. That way, when I look at it again, I'll know if I need to add or change anything. But I'm done for tonight. Time to hit the hay."

"Say, my mother-in-law invited my girls over for some grandma time," Darcey declared as soon as Ellie picked up the phone. "I'm free to kaffeeklatsch if you are."

"I would love to chinwag with you!" exclaimed Ellie. "Come on over!"

Ellie hung up the phone and immediately put on some coffee and brushed her hair. Darcey's van rolled into their yard shortly after that and Ellie went out to meet her.

"You've made page two of *The Swan Valley Star and Times*," said Darcey as she approached her friend with a newspaper in hand.

"Really? I haven't seen the article."

"It says here in this tiny column that a human skeleton was uncovered buried under the rocks for years. Apparently an investigation is underway to determine its identity," Darcey said, following Ellie inside. "When were you going to tell me about this?"

"The very next time I saw you, but I wasn't going to do it at church."

"Fair enough. That must have been exciting, though."

"Shocking is a far more accurate word. I still haven't had the courage to walk through the area where we uncovered it."

Darcey raised an eyebrow. "Why? Is it gory or something?"

"Oh no. It's just that that spot now kind of gives me the creeps."

"Oh piffle," poo-pooed Darcey. "Show me where this happened. The most exciting thing that's happened to me recently is that Abigail fell down the steps and scraped her forehead. Didn't even require stitches."

"Thank goodness for that."

Ellie poured herself and Darcey some fresh coffee and then led her friend out to the back bush where there used to be a rockpile. Now stones of every size and shape were strewn all over, making any attempt to walk through them an invitation to trip and fall.

Having Darcey along helped a lot to diffuse the creepy feelings Ellie had referred to. Other than a rocky mess, there was nothing sinister or gruesome here.

Heartened, she took Darcey on a tour of the path she had created to the pond.

"This is lovely." Darcey settled her tall, generous frame in one of the Adirondack chairs.

Ellie took the other. "It is, isn't it?"

Both women briefly closed their eyes and drank in the earth-scented air.

"So this is what peace feels like... sounds like... smells like..." observed Darcey softly.

"I suppose it does... usually." Ellie reclined with a stretch of her shapely legs. "Are you in need of a peaceful repose?"

"That and more. I need a break. Some me-time. Ever thought of adding some goldfish to this pond, and perhaps planting some water-lilies?"

"Given that I hope to take a swim here on the really hot days of summer, I don't want water creatures nibbling at my legs. So I think I'll pass. It would be pretty, though." Ellie stood. "Let me show you what else I've done."

She led Darcey along the walking path that continued to the river. Once there, they deposited themselves on the park bench overlooking the stream. It was running low now that the torrent of spring runoff had passed.

Darcey thoughtfully stared at the babbling water. "You're rich, you know."

"In what way do you mean?"

"Owning property with these beautiful bits of heaven included. A rare amenity, I hope you know."

Ellie nodded pensively and then murmured under her breath, "Beauty for ashes..."

"What's that? I didn't hear what you said."

"I was just thinking that while Hugh's family lived here, these beautiful spots weren't appreciated and enjoyed like we are now. But I agree; we do have a wonderful property. You can come for a retreat as often as you want."

Darcey took a final swig of her coffee. "Thanks. I may take you up on that."

"Are you okay? You seem a bit off today, girlfriend. Is something troubling you?"

"No. Not troubling. More like the soda pop has gone flat."

"Care to expand?"

For a moment, Darcey didn't say more. She just looked out, studying the river, and Ellie wisely didn't push. Their silence amplified the rippling sound of water running lazily over the stony riverbed. A song sparrow sang a phrase of spiky notes and trills nearby. It fed the soul.

Darcey sighed deeply. "I'm a busy mom from morning until night. I cook, clean, help Tony with his building, train my daughters daily, help out my neighbours occasionally—and that includes my mother-in-law—make beds, mend clothes, and… well, you get the picture. On the one hand, I *know* this is a right and good use of my time and energy. On the other hand, I find myself asking if this is all there is…"

"I've never heard you talk like this before," said Ellie, surprised.

"Don't you ever feel as though life boils down to a rather boring routine? Sleep, eat, work, and then sleep, eat, work all over again. Occasionally something happens to spice things up a bit, but the routine stays generally the same."

"I guess I haven't really thought about it like that before. There seems to be enough *spice*, as you put it, to keep me on my toes. I'm grateful when life is slow enough to settle into a regular routine."

"Don't get me wrong," said Darcey. "I love my husband and my kids and I appreciate that we have a good life without any real hardships to navigate. It's just that in my heart of hearts I long for more… Sometimes I feel that longing so keenly I could weep." Her voice quavered.

Ellie placed her hand on Darcey's arm. Darcey put a hand over Ellie's, expressing her appreciation for their camaraderie.

"Sorry. I shouldn't have dumped on you," apologized Darcey. "Being out in this beautiful spot of nature kind of triggered my longing anew."

"When you put it that way, it gives me a hint where this is coming from."

"I think I know what you're going to say, and I don't disagree. It's a longing to be with our Creator where the environment isn't compromised, right? No same old boring routines there. Or at least we'll have a more intimate relationship with Him."

"We don't sing 'This World Is Not My Home' without reason," answered Ellie. "I'm thinking the Lord must be so very blessed to hear you long for Him as you do."

"You don't think I'm weird or crazy?"

"Only a little. Just kidding. I think you're an amazing mother and a wonderful friend. I also know you to be a sincere and genuine follower of Jesus. Your admission of longing for a more purposeful and meaningful existence... well, this yearning you have for more of Jesus inspires me." After a pause, she continued. "I do remember wanting more meaning to this life when I sought to get over my depression. I can say that the Lord ministered to me through His Word. It's still the best way for me to find my centre again. Anyway, one of the reasons this world is worth living in is because you're in it, dear Darcey. You can take that to the bank!"

Twenty-Four

THERE WAS NO help for it. If Ellie wanted to be done with the endless fretting, she would have to see her doctor for a full checkup. She made the appointment on one of her days off.

She got to his office slightly early and, after reporting to the nurse receptionist, took a seat in the waiting area. She could see that there would be a couple people ahead of her. Picking up one of the magazines lying on the side table, she began to browse the colourful photos.

A door opened and closed and someone began to exit through the room. Automatically Ellie looked up…

…and locked eyes with Hugh. He returned the stare for a second and then continued his way out without a word.

Ellie suddenly felt hot and flustered. What was he doing here? He hadn't mentioned any complaint. Was he ill in some way? Then again, he might be wondering the same about her, since she hadn't said anything to him about seeing a doctor either.

⁓

"You're in fine health, Mrs. Fischer," said her doctor briskly after he had completed the exam. "We can have your blood tested to make sure, but I don't hold any suspicions or concerns in that regard."

"Are you sure my reproductive organs are functioning properly?"

"Yes, from what I can discern. The PAP test will reveal if there's something to worry about."

"I've been trying to conceive since the top of the year. So far, I've had no success," said Ellie. "I just want to be sure all is well with my body."

"In my professional opinion, there's nothing to be concerned about. My advice is not to try so hard. Relax. Get a hobby. Establish some other goals to pursue. And don't be surprised if pregnancy shows up when that's the last thing on your mind." The doctor gave her a wry smile. "That's often the way it goes. Babies have a way of entering the picture when you aren't planning for them."

Ellie left the doctor's office relieved and encouraged.

However, unexpectedly running into Hugh at the doctor's office bothered her. Why hadn't he said anything? What in the world would he want to see a doctor about?

Ellie sighed. Some little piece of women's intuition implied a discussion was on the horizon—and it was going to be a touchy one.

She had some free time before Hugh came home from work. She decided to continue making progress on her rock garden. Now that the stones were lying everywhere, she could pick out the manageable ones, hoist them into a wheelbarrow, and cart them over to their designated spot. The project was slow going, but it still felt like progress.

She only managed to accomplish a couple of small loads before Hugh arrived. He passed her on the driveway, parked, and then bounded up the steps into their house without waiting for her.

Ellie followed a moment later. Instead of a warm, affectionate greeting, he appeared antsy.

"Is there something ready to eat?" he said hurriedly. "I want to go to the Moores' place tonight."

"The casserole in the oven should be about ready," said Ellie. "What's the rush? Are you okay? I was surprised to see you at the doctor's office."

"Yeah, I'm fine. Can't say I was expecting to see you either. Why were you there?"

Ellie drew in a breath and replied evenly. "I haven't had a full physical exam since before I left Winnipeg. I wanted to make sure I was in good health."

"And are you?" Hugh's tone was crisp.

"Doctor says I'm fit as a fiddle."

"Good."

"What took you to see the doctor? Did you get hurt at work or something?"

"Nope. I haven't had a checkup since... I don't know when. Thought I should make sure I'm sound from head to toe."

"And are you?"

"Doc says I'm healthy as a horse."

"Glad to hear it."

Ellie quickly laid the table for two and set the casserole between the settings. Hugh removed his cap and took his seat. The silence that followed, and lasted a couple of minutes, didn't feel right.

"I have this feeling that you're mad at me about something. What is it?" probed Ellie tentatively. She spooned some food onto her plate.

Hugh replied evenly. "I'm not mad..."

"You're something," insisted Ellie. "Talk to me, please."

"Why should I? You don't talk to me."

"Oh for Pete's sake! What's this about?"

"Do you think I haven't noticed how mopey you've become? But you haven't spoken to me about it. I think you did to Marcie, though, because before they left she came to me private like and said, 'Be extra thoughtful to Ellie. She's feeling sad.' Now why would she say something like that? What have you got to be sad about?"

Ellie felt cornered. "I didn't want to worry you with my fears until I was sure I had something to worry about."

"What fears are you talking about? I think I should know." He laid down his fork to hear her answer.

"I was becoming seriously worried about the fact that I wasn't yet pregnant," said Ellie, her eyes brimming with tears. "I was afraid I was damaged because of... well, you know why."

Hugh softened a little. "I suspected as much, so I went to see the doctor to find out if I was the problem."

"You! I never once considered that my apparent infertility had anything to do with you. Never!"

"Okay. Fair enough. But I have a question burning in my head I want to know the answer to. What if, Ella Rose... what if it turns out for some strange reason we can't have kids? I want to know if I'm enough for you... just me. Just the two of us. Or am I just a babymaker to you?"

"You're being ridiculous!"

"Am I? I need to know how you really feel."

Ellie looked away, tears brimming in her eyes, unspeaking.

"Holy smokes! You have to think about this?" stormed Hugh, suddenly angry. He pushed himself away from the table, donned his cap, and left the house, slamming the door behind him.

Ellie ran after him. "Where are you going?" she demanded in an anguished tone. She stopped on the veranda.

"Someplace where I can think about things," retorted Hugh. "Since you need to think, I guess I do, too!"

He jumped into his half-ton, revved the motor, and spun the tires as he raced out of the yard.

"You pompous, self-centred, irrational jerk!" shouted Ellie after him. Then she slumped to the floorboards and began to sob, unrestrained. Ruby and Ruff rushed to her side, doing their best to comfort her with licks and short whines.

~

Even before Hugh got to the corner of Highway 10, he realized he had blown it, bigtime. But pride was having its way. Rather than turn around, he went left and began to cruise east.

He didn't go far. He turned north on the Lenswood Highway, driving as far as the 587 before veering left again and driving to the Craigsford corner. He then aimed south towards home via the 366.

The whole drive took maybe half an hour, but it was long enough for him to cool down and feel bad about ditching his bride for not answering his question *tuit de suite*. In a way, it still irked him, and he knew why. It still hadn't been right or fair to jump ship and not listen to her explanation.

About a mile from his place, he pulled over and cut the engine. Chagrined, Hugh rubbed his hands on the steering wheel.

"Lord, I need help." There was a moment of silence. "I don't know what to do."

The next thought was clear. *Go home.*

"And then what? I'm still new at this husband thing."

Listen to her.

"Okay. Anything else?"

Comfort your wife.

The thoughts were so clear, they might as well have been audible.

Hugh started the engine. As he slowly drove the last mile home, he began to prepare a speech. An apology would be the place to start, he figured.

He parked next to her car, glad to see it there. It meant she hadn't taken off for somewhere, which wouldn't have surprised him.

She wasn't in the cottage, however, and that made Hugh uneasy. He tried to think where she might have gone. Back to the Bauman farmhouse, perhaps? Maybe to sit in her dad's former armchair that had been her retreat a year ago? He'd go there if he failed to find her at their own place. Not that he thought it likely.

To exhaust the home yard, he checked the rooms of the new shop and Quonset, just in case. No Ellie.

Perhaps the pond then. It was a favourite spot for her just as it had been, and still was, for him. He followed the new path Ellie had mown, appreciating the interest she had shown in making their property so parklike. That Ellie was something of an artist in whatever she put her hand to wasn't lost on him. Love began to swell in his heart.

As he neared the pond, he heard her before he saw her. She was talking to someone.

For a moment, his heart fell. Now was not the time to interact with a third party. He almost turned around to wait for her in the house when he overheard what she was saying.

"...Lord, I'm sorry I fell off the rails and made it about me and not about You. I accept Your will for my life. And if that means no family, then so be it. Not my will, but Yours... Amen."

Hugh edged in closer and saw that she had been kneeling on the ground with her elbows on the Adirondack chair. She was getting up slowly when the nearby dogs caught his scent and announced his arrival with excited barks.

There was no backing out now.

Hugh came forward. Before sitting in the adjacent chair, he bent over to kiss Ellie. But she leaned away from him and said nothing. Her face was still splotchy and red from much crying. The expression on her face didn't spell anger. It was worse; it read mistrust.

"Ell, I'm sorry," he began clumsily. "I've been a cad."

"Correction. You are a pompous, self-centred, irrational jerk." She didn't say it with malice.

"I'm trying to apologize. Are you intending to make this hard for me?"

"No," she replied, kindlier. "Let's hear it then."

"Do you want to know why I got so bent out of shape at the supper table?" He laid his hand on her arm, but she didn't, wouldn't, respond to his touch.

"I'm listening," said Ellie coolly.

"If someone had asked what you meant to me, without hesitation I would have said you're the best thing that ever happened to me. You're the sun in my sky... the fizz in my cola... the jam on my toast."

Ellie looked at him sideways as if she disbelieved he had just said those things.

"When you hesitated, it came across to me that you didn't feel the same way about me and I was hurt. It felt an awful lot like the rejection I endured growing up. I couldn't stand it. Especially since I've poured out my life to you."

"Okay, not only are you a sometimes jerk, but an idiot as well." A glint was returning to Ellie's eyes. "Apparently we've been like two ships passing in the dark. None of the things that have been worrying me of late were a reflection on you. I thought I'd be in a family way a long time ago, and when it wasn't happening I worried that maybe damage had been done to me when the abortion occurred. I went to the doctor for a full body exam and asked expressly if my reproduction organs were healthy and intact. When you asked about whether you'd be enough for me should it turn out we couldn't have children, I had a sudden epiphany. I was reminded of a conversation I had with Darcey a few days ago when she expressed a longing for more meaning to life. I suddenly realized I had let my priorities get screwed up. I wanted a child… a family… as my number one desire, but I believe that our personal fulfillment is realized when we put God first. Then comes husband and family, with friends and relatives coming after that. But you ran off and slammed the door before I could articulate any of those things."

"I'm sorry Ell-overa, for real. I thought I was done with my issues only to find out, when a test came along, that I haven't made as much progress as I thought," said Hugh ruefully. "It's discouraging."

He picked up Ellie's hand and kissed it. This time she didn't rebuff his gesture.

"It's not so much different for me." Ellie sounded glum. "I've been floundering in guilt for the past few weeks, even though I *know* the Lord has forgiven me. Multiple scriptures promise this. Yet I've been harbouring the idea that my lack of conception means I'm being punished. My head knows better. Logically speaking, I know the punishment for our sins was paid by Jesus when He hung on the cross. We still may face consequences for making bad decisions, I understand, because consequences and punishments aren't the same thing. It's like my head and heart are quarrelling. My head knows the truth, but my heart is susceptible to lies."

A moment of comfortable silence passed between them.

"That reminds me of what Pastor Wirt preached on not so long ago," said Hugh thoughtfully. "It was about how the apostle Paul spoke for everyone when he said that he wanted to do right and good but didn't, and the thing he didn't want to do he did.[4] Sounds like the same kind of quarrel you're talking about. Not to mention the trouble I'm having with myself."

She nodded. "You're right. I see the similarity. What it means to me is that we're going to have to overcome the lies that assail us over and over again as long as we're alive. The enemy doesn't give up easily. I get weary of the battle, though. I want my victories to be once and for all, but... apparently not." She gave him a pointed look. "To answer your question, however, yes, you are enough. You're all I ever hoped for and wanted in a husband. Having said that, you need to conquer the urge to flee whenever you start feeling insecure. I want my man to face his trials bravely."

"Right. And I want my woman to be open with me about what troubles her," said Hugh, matching her tone.

"Like I said, Hugh-gemony, I didn't want to broach the subject until I was sure I honestly had an issue and wasn't merely imagining it. And I didn't want to be a sourpuss and rain on your parade. Not when you were so happy and excited over your new garage and Quonset."

"Listen. I'm happy and proud to have these new facilities, not gonna lie. But they aren't nearly as important to me as you are. Don't ever think otherwise."

Dusk was falling around them, so they rose and strolled back to their tiny house holding hands.

"Fizz in your cola? Jam on your toast? Seriously? Where did that come from?"

---

[4] Romans 7:18–21.

Twenty-Five

"**ARE YOU SURE** you're ready for this?" asked Bev.

"Yes," answered Margo in a firm tone of voice. "I believe I can prepare the dishes on the menu as well as Mrs. Illichman."

"I've watched you help and cover for her, and I think so, too. She wants to resign as of this fall. Before winter sets in. We'll put you in her place as head cook." Bev gave her a knowing smile. "You can expect a healthy raise then as well."

"Thank you! Thank you so much!"

The good news had Margo practically floating on cloud nine for the rest of the afternoon.

Later she waltzed into the house excited to share with Lydia what she considered to be a big promotion.

"Guess what, Lydia?" Margo crossed the kitchen. She saw the elder woman's grey-haired head above the top of the recliner where she regularly roosted.

She came around and saw that Lydia was sleeping with a contented look on her face. Her Bible was open on her lap and the magnifying glass lay on top of it.

"I'll tell you my good news later," whispered Margo. "You keep napping while I fix your supper."

She gently removed the Bible and set the book and magnifying glass on the side table. A short while later, after warming up some leftovers, Margo went to wake Lydia. It was unusual for the senior to doze for so long. She ordinarily only took catnaps.

Margo tapped Lydia on the shoulder and got no response. Only then did she notice that the woman wasn't breathing.

Panicked, she immediately called Muriel. "You need to come at once. Lydia won't wake up!"

Pastor Leland and Muriel let themselves in less than ten minutes later. It was Leland who took charge of the situation and confirmed Margo's fears.

"Lydia Harms has gone to be with the Lord," he said gently after checking for a pulse.

Margo whimpered. "It must have happened just before I got home. She just looked like she fell asleep with the Bible still on her lap. I didn't even notice she wasn't breathing."

"That sounds like the perfect homegoing to me," said Muriel tenderly. "What a blessing that she had the privilege of passing without going through a season of pain and suffering. Not many get that. We'll have to let her daughters know. Do you know where she keeps their phone numbers?"

After they had notified Lydia's family, Leland took charge of calling the police. The death was legally pronounced and a funeral home called to pick up the body.

"Are you comfortable staying here tonight?" asked Muriel.

"Where else could I go?" cried Margo. The reality of the situation was sinking in. She had to think about finding somewhere to live now that the situation had changed.

Muriel took her hand. "You're welcome to stay with us at the manse until another situation opens up for you."

Relief registered on Margo's face. "Can I come tonight? Somehow I think it will be too lonely and strange here by myself."

"Yes, dear. I understand."

"Can I bring Fritz?"

"You mean the cat?"

"Yes."

Muriel sighed. "I'm not much of a cat person, but neither am I one to break up a family. Bring your kitty."

~

Within two days, both Katie and Lorraine had arrived together with their husbands and their families. There was a bustle of activity as they made funeral arrangements and once again combed through Lydia's material possessions. The family also held meetings concerning the will and distribution of Lydia's worldly goods.

One of those meetings happened at the manse.

"Besides reviewing the funeral service with the pastor, we wanted to meet you in person," said Katie.

The salt-and-pepper-haired woman resembled her mother in facial features but was notably taller. Her generous hips recalled a pear shape. Her smile was genuine and so was the brief hug she extended to Margo.

"Yes, we wanted to be properly introduced to the young lady our mother frequently referred to as her honorary granddaughter," added Lorraine kindly.

The younger of the sisters was petite, like her mother, but the resemblance ended there. She wore dark-rimmed glasses under a short bob of silver hair. Her shape reminded one of a cylinder, the waist being as thick as her hips and chest.

The women's husbands had come along, but they deferred to their wives in the present matter.

"I'm happy to meet you as well," said Margo warmly. "Lydia spoke proudly about her family."

The order of service was quickly agreed upon, and then Katie turned her attention back to Margo. "My son will deliver the eulogy, but he is looking for more material, particularly more recent anecdotes. What stories can you add from the time you spent with Mother?"

"Well… she could be pretty opinionated. But I'm sure you already know that. She despised waste and hated to part with anything that might, even remotely, have a future use."

"How many hundreds of times did you have to hear complaints of things we threw out after we cleaned her house last winter?" chuckled Lorraine.

"Only two."

"Twice only?"

"Only two hundred times," corrected Margo, smiling broadly. "But usually I found it funny. I didn't know seniors could be such a hoot. Her complaining was never nasty. It was more like an opportunity to have something to say. Almost like something to do."

Katie sighed. "It's kind of you to see it that way."

"Did you notice a point when mother began to decline?" asked Lorraine tentatively.

"Actually, I think maybe I did." Margo surprised herself by the recollection. "It was after I told her I'd accepted Jesus into my life. When I first came to live with her, she soon figured out I wasn't religious and was, in fact, very resistant to it. She made it her personal mission to pray for me daily—until I repented of my foolishness, as she put it. I paid her no mind, not believing there was any power in a person's prayers. But when I came home a few weeks ago and told her I had made the decision to receive Christ, she made a point of saying that her earthly work was done, that she was ready to leave this wicked world and go to her heavenly home. I didn't like the sounds of that, but now I'm wondering if she meant it."

Katie appeared pensive. "Hmmm. I remember her saying something similar to me, now that I think about it, during one of our telephone visits."

"Did she seem… different to you, earlier in the day before you found her… gone?" Lorraine's voice quivered reflecting grief for her loss.

"Not really," answered Margo truthfully. "I had fixed her oatmeal for breakfast, adding lots of brown sugar and only a ration of cream, just the way she liked it. She asked me what my job was going to be that day: cooking, cleaning, or waiting on tables. I replied that it would probably be a little of everything. Her last words to me were: 'Well now, remember that whatever you do, do it heartily as unto the Lord.'[5] I smiled and left for work."

"Those were probably her last words to a living soul." Katie's eyes brimmed with tears. "Thank you for sharing that, Margo. It's a wonderful way to remember the final hours of our mother's life."

The meeting didn't go on much longer after that.

Because Lydia Harms had lived in Minitonas all her married life, most of the town knew her. On the day of her funeral, the First Baptist Church was filled to capacity. Although the situation contained some sadness, as befitted someone who had passed away, the service was more of a celebration of a life well-lived.

Margo was surprised by this, having expected something far more sombre and solemn. She couldn't help but compare this to the burying of her own parents a few years earlier. She had overseen that occasion without any ceremonial observance whatsoever.

It was what they would have wanted, she reminded herself.

Pastor Leland addressed the congregation by reminding them that those who died in Christ were not truly dead, as many suppose, but are merely asleep while awaiting the last trump of God to rise again.[6] In the meantime, their souls were with the saviour, because to be absent from the body is to be present with the Lord.[7]

This was all good news to Margo, who was considering such things for the first time. She felt strangely comforted, receiving the pastor's message as hopeful and promising. Hitherto she had assumed that when humans died, they simply ceased to exist.

---

[5] Colossians 3:23.
[6] 1 Thessalonians 4:16–18.
[7] 2 Corinthians 5:8.

The next day Margo returned to the café. The business of work kept her from brooding over Lydia's passing and thinking too much about her next steps.

Even so, it was a surprise when midafternoon Leland and Muriel walked into the diner.

"Coffee break time?" asked Margo, brightly picking up a freshly brewed pot of coffee and intending to pour them each a cuppa.

"The Harms sisters are requesting another audience with you," said Muriel.

Margo frowned and returned the pot to the hot plate. "Why? Am I in some sort of trouble?"

"Oh no," Leland assured her. "They simply want to conclude some business. We agreed to come along as witnesses."

"Witnesses? To what? I'll have to check with Bev, at any rate."

"Already done." Bev came through the double swinging doors. "I'll cover for you while you're away."

Leland and Muriel escorted Margo to Lydia Harms' house, a mere few minutes away. Respectfully they knocked on the door and waited.

Soon Lorraine appeared and invited them inside. She led them to the living room where Katie, their husbands, and a strange man wearing a navy double-breasted suit were comfortably seated.

Katie rose to greet the new arrivals and indicated places for them to sit. As the elder daughter and executor of her mother's will, she took the reins and chaired the meeting.

Margo stirred uneasily.

"Why, you look as frightened as a bird. It's all right, Margo," Katie said soothingly. "We hope that what we have to tell you will be received as good news."

"I'll go first." Lorraine looked around the room at all the faces before addressing Margo. "We want to express our sincerest gratitude to you for caring for our mother so kindly and generously. It made possible one of her most adamant wishes, which was to stay in her home until she passed. Thank you for looking after her needs, and for providing some companionship in what was a lonely widow-hood."

"You're very welcome," replied Margo quickly. "It was all my pleasure."

"Mother's will leaves the house to Lorraine and me," said Katie. "But she started a conversation with us a few weeks ago expressing her desire for you to have the house after she died. We've talked about it thoroughly since then and the bottom line is this: we'd like to give you her house as your own."

Margo blinked and then frowned, as though she didn't comprehend the words.

"You'll notice many things are missing. We allowed our children to take some keepsakes to remember their grandmother by," spoke up Lorraine. "Katie and I have taken what's meaningful to us as well. But there's enough here for you to continue, functionally speaking."

"But... but why?" stammered Margo. "Why don't you want to keep it for yourselves?"

Katie and Lorraine exchanged glances and broke out in smiles.

Katie's husband spoke up. "Let me tell this part. Our families are both well looked after. None of the grandchildren are interested in living in Minitonas, and Lydia relayed to us a bit of the difficulties you endured of late. She desired to help you face the future."

"Lydia didn't change the will," Lorraine's husband said, picking up the ball. "She left it up to us—that is, her daughters—to discuss the matter and agree. And we have."

"We've all agreed to honour mother's request to pass along the title of this house to you," said Katie firmly.

Margo felt dazed. "Well now... I don't know what to say."

They all broke out in laughter. "It seems Lydia left her mark on you, Margo," said Muriel after she'd stopped chuckling.

"A simple 'yes' would be sufficient, my dear," advised Lorraine with a broad smile. "Then you can sign the papers this fine solicitor has drawn up and we'll depart for our own homes, leaving you the keys."

Margo searched the faces of Muriel and Leland.

"This isn't a joke," said Muriel, answering the unasked question. "It seems to me the Lord has supplied for your needs in a most wonderful way."

"I can't believe it's true." Margo gulped. "I do not deserve this!"

"If it comes to a question of deserving," added Leland sagely, "none of us would have anything. Yet this is one of the finer examples of grace I've ever witnessed."

A multitude of papers were produced, signed, and signatures witnessed. Once the lawyer was satisfied that everything was in order, he politely left their company.

Katie and Lorraine hugged Margo warmly, repeating their sentiments of gratitude before handing her the house keys and making their departures.

Muriel and Leland left, too, after Margo asked to stay behind for a while longer to take in the change in her fortunes.

After everyone was gone, the house was so quiet that Margo could hear the refrigerator hum. She looked in the kitchen cupboards to see what was left. It didn't seem like much had been removed at all. A peek in the fridge showed plenty of groceries remained, and the yellow chrome and Formica kitchen table and four chairs had been left behind.

Lydia's bedroom had been cleaned out, which didn't surprise Margo. It had contained a handsome, solid wood bedroom suite that anyone who knew fine furniture would have appreciated at once.

Margo's previous bedroom appeared to be just as she'd left it.

The living room still bore the turquoise sofa and matching armchair, but Lydia's personal throne and side table had been taken, as had been the antique corner cabinet holding the multitude of salt and pepper shakers and bird ornaments. The TV and its stand were also gone, although the upright piano still dominated the room. Margo wondered what she would do with it—and a moment later, an idea came.

She nodded to herself. *Yes, that just might work...*

The house felt comfortable. Without Lydia's personal stuff lying around, it seemed that the place had managed to let go of the past and readied itself for change.

It's waiting to see what I will do with it.

Margo took a seat on the sofa, the same place where she customarily sat when reading or talking with Lydia.

"If you can hear me from your place in heaven, I just want to say thank you for passing your house on to me," she said aloud. "That's a mighty generous gift. I've already got a plan. Since this house is about to launch a new chapter, I want to paint all the rooms white, as a symbol of my fresh start. I'll add colour by and by as life takes on its new flavours. You don't mind, do you?"

Margo was still, as though listening for a response.

She chuckled. "I think I just heard you say, 'Well now, it's to be all white next, is it? I thought you had more imagination than that, Miss Margo.' Just be patient, Lydia. I don't know yet what the colours will be, except they won't be mauve or yellow…"

She fell quiet again, studying her surroundings, and then gave credit where she believed it was due.

"Jesus, it's You to whom all my thanks ultimately go. You are the One who preserved my life through all its crazy twists and turns… who kept me going when the bottom fell out… who set me back on my feet again through loving people like Muriel and Lydia… and my brother… and, okay, his wife, too. Anyway, I'm deeply grateful for all You have done for me. Not just in earthly terms but also for saving my soul. I need guidance going forward. Show me what to do with myself. Make me wise and good like You. Amen."

A tear escaped one eye, and then the other. She cried a little for missing Lydia, in gratitude for the goodness of God and the Harms family, and for the peace that suddenly overwhelmed her. In that moment, her soul had never felt more satisfied.

"Oh, it's Margo. Did you know she was coming?" Ellie watched through the window as her sister-in-law's car drove up to their house.

Hugh looked on as his sister slowly exited her vehicle. "No, I didn't. It doesn't look like she's upset or in a hurry, though."

Margo panned the yard in a 360-degree turn before ambling up the steps.

Hugh opened the door before she could knock. "Hey sis! Are you just dropping by or—"

"I came to tell you the good news in person, and also to pick up the rest of my stuff," answered Margo before he could finish.

"Perfect. I'm always up for good news," commented Hugh.

She came inside and briefly scoped the room before seating herself on the sofa. Margo and Ellie exchanged cheerful pleasantries.

"Is this supposed to be a private chat between you and your brother?" Ellie asked. "Because I can—"

"Oh no. I want you to hear my good news, too." Margo drew a deep breath. "Believe it or not, I'm a homeowner again! To make a long story short, Lydia Harms asked her daughters to give me her house, and they did. The keys were given to me yesterday. That's why I'm here to get the rest of my things."

"No kidding!" Hugh said with great enthusiasm. "That's amazing!"

Ellie smiled warmly. "Congratulations!"

"It's small and old, but it has everything I need to live comfortably," Margo added. "In time, I think I can turn it into a cute little place."

"I'm sure you can," said Ellie wholeheartedly. "Is it furnished? I'm sure we can come up with some pieces to help you out."

"They left a lot behind, so I'm not in need of anything important. In time, and as I can afford it, I would like to replace most, if not all, of the furnishings. In fact, there's a piece I'd like to pass along as soon as possible, because I'll never use it and it takes up tons of space."

"Interesting. What would that be?"

"Lydia's piano. It's a fine antique and I thought you might like to have it in your new house, Ellie. I know you have a thing for antiques."

"And so I do. Hmmm. I did take piano lessons as a kid, but I didn't keep it up during high school. My parents sold the piano after I moved to Winnipeg to make room for the big stereo unit that still sits in the farmhouse. It might be nice to tinker on a piano again. Would it be all right if I came to look it over before I commit myself?"

"Don't I get a say?" interrupted Hugh in a dark tone.

Both women looked at him as if they had only just realized he was in the same room.

"What say would you like to have, Mr. Fischer?" asked Ellie, surprised.

"What if *I* don't want a piano?" The dark tone took on a thread of humour.

"Oh gosh. Who knew you cared?"

"Why wouldn't I? It's my house, too, isn't it?

"Yes… it's as much your house as your new shop is my shop. If I get a say in what equipment you buy and where it goes, you can have as much say in what furniture we collect and where it will be placed. Deal?"

Hugh sprouted a smile. "Just pulling your leg, Ell. I know that a house is a woman's nest to feather to her liking. I didn't know you once played the piano, though. What else am I going to find out about you?"

"If I play my cards right, you'll never reach the end of the mystery that is me."

Margo listened to this banter with interest. "I never had this sort of fun with Larry. If we ever laughed together, it might have been at the same line in a movie or something. I guess it's time I admit that I appreciate everything you guys have done for me since you rescued me the day after your wedding. I apologize for the awful way I've treated you—especially Ellie."

"How do you mean?" asked Ellie, her brows knit together.

"Truth is, I've carried a lot of resentment towards you. In my eyes, you were everything I wanted to be but wasn't. Not to mention how smart and capable you are at just about everything. On top of that, you stole my brother's heart. It bugged me that he was so devoted to you. I'd never seen anything like it. How stupid is it to be jealous of a brother's wife? But I kind of was. I was wrong, Ellie, and I'm sorry for it. You told me once that you were happy to finally have a sister. I've been a rotten sister, but I hope you'll give me another chance to not only be real family but a friend as well."

The confession brought tears to Ellie's eyes. "I don't know what to say…"

"Please, just say you forgive me."

Twenty-Six

AUGUST BROUGHT THE building crew to Hugh and Ellie's place. At last the new house was being erected.

While it was exciting to watch the progress being made every day, it wasn't easy to cope with the dirt and mess that necessarily came with it. Intermittent rains halted the work, too. With all the building projects taken on since spring, the yard was often muddy.

Hugh began to fuss and plan for a lot of gravel to be brought in to rectify that problem. Ellie pointed out, not that she needed to, that there was no use laying down gravel until the building was complete and the tradespeople had finished their work. Otherwise all the extra traffic would soil the gravel, and the improvements would be negligible.

Although Ellie called for patience, she was hard-pressed to practice what she preached. She hated the dust and noticed dirt being tracked into the house as much as anyone.

With the tractor and bucket, Hugh brought over a few more large stones to the new rockpile. But Ellie soon realized that having too many projects going on at the same time was an exercise in futility. Instead she poured herself into the myriad of decorator magazines loaned by her good friend Cynthia, pledging to gain the best, most doable ideas for wall colours, window treatments, kitchen cabinets, furniture placement, and interesting accessorizing.

Sometimes she would show Hugh pictures of stunning room arrangements. His refrain was invariably the same: "Yeah, that looks nice. Do whatever you want, babe, so long as you stick to the budget."

Ellie's response would also be predictable: rolling her eyes, sighing, and continuing to pore over the illustrations.

$\sim$

The phone rang midmorning while Ellie was trying to narrow down the finalists from the dozen or so paint chips laid out across the table.

"Hullo," she greeted distractedly.

"Ellie?"

She brightened. "Yeah, it's me. This sounds like Cynthia."

"Right on. Say, I have a proposal for you. Would you be interested in a second sofa and chair to go with your plaid set? You know, for your new house?"

"I haven't gotten that far in my plans, but I'm listening."

"A customer brought me their old set for recovering. We went so far as to buy the fabric before she backed out, having been won over by a new set. She's willing to give the furniture away if someone would be willing to reimburse her for the price of the fabric. I thought of you since I think it would go well with the sofa I recovered for you last year."

She immediately felt tempted. "Hmmm. Can I come and have a look?"

"I'll get a kettle boiling for tea if you come now."

"I'm on my way."

Minutes later, Ellie was entering the front door of Cynthia's home.

"Goodness, you look like you're about ready to pop!" Ellie remarked, closing the door behind her.

"I wish I would, but supposedly I have three weeks to go by the doctor's calculations. And that's if I'm not overdue, which I'm told is common for first-time mothers. The baby kicks me so hard I wake up at night!" Fatigue showed on Cynthia's face. "But never mind me. I'm excited to show you the pieces in my workroom."

Cynthia led Ellie into the repurposed garage. There sat a boxy, old-fashioned couch with navy, tufted upholstery that resembled damask. The velvet-like finish had worn off over the years, but it was easy to see that this had once been a handsome piece. There was some wooden adornment on the front of the armrests, typical of the period.

"Wow!" Ellie said. "I see what you mean. Not exactly a match to what I have, but similar... like family resemblance."

"I thought so, too. But it gets better. Look at this."

Cynthia pulled out a bolt of heavy fabric, laid it on the sofa, and unfolded the end, stretching it over the back of the sofa. The vintage print was similar to paisley in deep, rich colours. Then she draped a remnant of the same classic plaid with which she had recovered Ellie's furniture months earlier. While the base colour of the paisley was a lush red, it related beautifully with the tartan.

"A marriage made in heaven, don't you think?" said Cynthia, looking up at Ellie.

"It is very, very beautiful. It also looks very expensive. Can I afford this?"

"Consider that the furniture itself is free. If you're not in a rush, and I can work on it whenever I have spare time, I'll do the job for free and call it your housewarming gift."

"That's very generous of you, girlfriend. It sweetens the pot, but you'd better show me the bill before I agree. You seem to be dodging the question..."

Cynthia disappeared into her house and was back in a trice. She showed Ellie the bill of sale.

Ellie's shoulders sagged at once. "That still puts a huge dent in my home outfitting budget... to which Hugh is holding me very strictly." She sighed.

"I understand. I'll only say that if it was me, I'd consider this a once-in-a-lifetime opportunity. I'd take advantage of it by putting off another purchase for later."

"Is there any chance your customer would accept a lesser price?"

Cynthia looked surprised. "How much less would you take if you were in her shoes?"

"I'd hope for a full refund, of course. But if there were no takers, I'd settle for whatever I could get."

"You're the first person I've offered this opportunity. So we can't talk about that kind of discount yet. If you're willing to risk this chance going to someone else—"

"Oh never mind. I used the splurge-and-save principle while setting up our cottage and I can do it again. I'll take it. I can see that it will be a stunning addition to our living room." Ellie's shoulders slumped. "Maybe I can work some extra shifts."

"That's great! I'll tell my aunt her hopes came true."

Ellie frowned. "Your aunt? You didn't tell me that."

"Why would I? I'm pretty sure you don't know her. And besides, what difference would it have made?"

$$\sim$$

Ruth Wagner shook her grey-haired head in disgust. Her slippers had gone missing, and that was a fact. Slippers didn't just walk off on their own! As far as she was concerned, there was no other explanation other than someone had come into her house during the night and taken them. But who would do that? She had always trusted her neighbours, and not one of them did she suspect even now.

Other things had mysteriously disappeared, too. A birthday card for Ellie that she had lain on the table so she would remember to put it in the mail. It had disappeared that very night. Herb insisted that he hadn't moved it, that he hadn't even seen it. Yet it had vanished.

Missing, too, were some new kitchen tea towels and dishcloths she had purchased on sale. She would have sworn on the Bible that she had added them to the drawer where the rest of her kitchen linens were kept, yet they were nowhere to be found.

And that wasn't even the most brazen theft. Someone had come in the night and replaced the toilet in the bathroom. Suddenly the seat was so low that she could hardly get up again. How had they had gotten away with it without Herb or herself hearing the disturbance?

Ruth thought there were other items as well, but she couldn't recall them immediately.

Now, on top of all that, she couldn't find the recipe card her sister Elizabeth had written out for her. It was enough to make a preacher swear! How was she to prepare the poppy filling for the kolaches she wanted to make?

The obvious answer was to call Liz and ask for it again. With an annoyed sigh, Ruth rummaged for a pen and slip of paper. Upon gathering these items, she dialled the Bauman farmhouse phone number from memory.

It rang several times and then an automated voice announced that the number she had dialled was no longer in service. Ruth frowned at the receiver in her hand. No longer in service? Impossible!

Ruth redialled, paused, and then angrily hung up the phone when it produced the same result.

Without further contemplation, she looked down a handwritten list in search of Ellie's number. Finding it, she carefully dialled the numbers.

On the third ring, Ellie answered with the customary greeting. "Hello."

"And hello to you too, dear." They exchanged a few pleasantries before Ruth came to the reason for her call. "I tried to call your mother, Ellie, but the telephone company is trying to tell me her number is no longer in service. Did your mother get a new phone number? And if she did, why wouldn't she have told me?"

There was dead air for a few seconds.

Ruth found herself growing anxious. "Ellie? Are you still there?"

"Yes, Aunty, I'm still here," answered Ellie slowly. Then she added, "Mama is gone…"

"Gone where? When will she be back?" Ruth continued on with barely concealed annoyance. "I want her to give me the recipe for a poppy filling. I seem to have lost it somehow."

"Aunt Ruth... Mama lives with Jesus now. Don't you remember?" asked Ellie gently.

"Lives with Jesus... you mean... she's passed?!"

"Yes, Aunty. It happened a little over a year ago."

"Well, why on earth didn't you tell me?" Ruth cried out, clearly shaken. "I'm her only sister, for heaven's sake! I would have come to the funeral and grieved with the rest of the family. Oh my! Lizzie's gone and no one thought to inform me! That's not right, Ella Rose!"

Ruth's growing anger was now mixed with an onslaught of grief.

"Aunty Ruth... you *were* at the funeral. You wept buckets because the stroke that took her came unexpectedly. It's not like you to forget something like that." Ellie spoke with obvious concern. "Are you all right?"

"Of course I'm all right! It's just that... I mean... Liz has really died? I... I..."

The phone suddenly clattered, leaving only the sound of the dial tone.

~

Ellie sprinted to the shop where Hugh was bent over the Plymouth.

"Hugh, will you come with me?" she panted. "I want to run out to Aunt Ruth and Uncle Herb's place. I just had the weirdest conversation with her and I need to tell my uncle about it."

Hugh looked up, frowning. "Now what?"

Ellie repeated as much as the conversation as she could remember. "I want to get Uncle Herb aside and tell him about this. Your job will be to keep Aunt Ruth's attention elsewhere. Get her to show you her flowers or garden or something."

"Right now? This can't wait?"

"I'm worried right *now!*"

A few minutes later, they were headed towards the Bowsman district. Driving into the Wagners' yard, they saw Herb and Ruth sitting leisurely on a bench outside the house, just right of the back door. Ruth lit up like a lightbulb upon recognizing the young couple.

"If I'd a known you were coming, I'd have made a big supper to share," she said to Ellie.

"Oh no. We didn't come to eat. I have a question I want to ask Uncle Herb this time." Ellie smiled pleasantly. "Something you wouldn't be interested in."

Hugh was at his most charming. "I hear you grow an amazing garden, Aunty, and I've never seen much of your property. How about you show off your yard to me?"

"Well, lots of it has been harvested and put away. But sure, I can show you around."

When they were out of hearing distance, Ellie turned to her uncle and repeated the story of the strange conversation she'd had with her aunt. Herb listened carefully, showing no emotion.

"I'm worried, Uncle Herb. I first noticed she wasn't quite right when I took care of her in the hospital. Every time we've crossed paths since, she's dropped an odd comment that makes me wonder if…"

"If she's got the Alzheimer's… or what's the other thing they call it?"

"Dementia," supplied Ellie unhappily.

"She's been slipping for some time now." Herb rubbed his large hands on the knees of his overalls as he quietly looked off into the distance. "The first time I noticed it was in the spring, but I told myself everyone gets forgetful now and again. But lately the mistakes are troubling. Guess I'll have to get her to see a doctor somehow. That won't be easy. She's otherwise a healthy lady."

"Consider seeing the doctor yourself first to explain the situation. That way, when you get her there, he'll already know how to go about assessing her."

"I suppose I could do that," said Herb thoughtfully.

Hugh and Ruth were circling their way back to the house. Before they came within earshot, Herb turned to his niece and said, "Don't get old, Ellie…"

～

"I've managed to get the armchair done," said Cynthia to Ellie over the phone. "Do you want to come and see it?"

"Already? I thought you were going to take your time. Maybe by Christmas, you said." Ellie sounded surprised. "Of course I'd like to see it. Would tomorrow morning be all right? I don't have to go to work until after noon."

"Perfect!"

Midmorning, Ellie showed up bearing a gift of ten homemade chocolate chip cookies. Her mother used to make six loaves of homemade bread at a time and always gave away a loaf as a blessing to others. Ellie seldom made bread, but she tried to maintain her mother's tradition through whatever baking she did. On this occasion, it was cookies.

"Oh yum! Brent will love these. I haven't spent much time in the kitchen lately. With this belly, I can't actually get close to the counter."

"You must be due any time now."

"Yes, and the show can't get on the road soon enough." Cynthia gestured for her friend to follow. "Come on. I want to show you how gorgeous the armchair turned out."

Ellie followed her into the workroom. Parked in the middle of the space, the chair was the first thing she laid eyes on. Her jaw dropped with pleasure.

"It's positively stunning. The paisley-like pattern suits the set famously. You're so good at your craft." Ellie looked over at Cynthia and noticed the stricken expression on her face. "Oh no. What's the matter?"

"I'm fine. It's just that these Braxton-Hicks contractions are no fun."

"Are you sure they're Braxton-Hicks and not the real thing? I don't have firsthand experience, but I seem to remember reading they're not as painful as true labour."

"I've been to the hospital twice in the past week, and each time they sent me home assuring me I was merely experiencing Braxton-Hicks. I felt like a silly schoolgirl. So I'm not going back until I'm absolutely positive the baby is on its way."

They left the workroom and went into Cynthia's kitchen. Another contraction gripped her and she clung to the counter for support.

"I honestly think your time has come for real," Ellie said, highly concerned. "Do you want me to call Brent?"

"Not just yet…"

But then another contraction overpowered her and she sank to her knees on the floor with a groan. That's when Darcey walked in carrying fifteen-month-old Abby on her arm.

"I saw your car in the driveway and thought I'd come and see what you girls were up to." Darcey then realized Cynthia was on her knees. "Whoa, what have we here?"

"She thinks she's having another round of Braxton-Hicks contractions, but I think it's the real thing," replied Ellie nervously.

"We're all girls here," began Darcey, taking charge. "Do you mind if we have a look? Ellie's a nurse and I'm an old hand at this business. Abigail, you sit here and *don't* move."

Abigail was parked on a kitchen chair. She didn't move.

Cynthia complied by lowering her slacks and undies, groaning between the contractions which were now coming less than two minutes apart.

"Cynthia, dear, I believe you're fully dilated," Ellie said, using her nurse's tone of voice. "I can see the baby's head, but also that your water hasn't yet broken."

As if on cue, her waters broke then and there, creating a sizable puddle on the floor.

"Okay then," announced Darcey. "No time to get you to a hospital. You're having a home birth perforce. Don't worry. You're in good hands. Between Ellie and me, we've got you covered. Now relax as much as you can between contractions. Try to work with them, not resist them."

"I want my mother," moaned Cynthia in distress.

"We'll call her, if you like, when the job's completed. We need towels. Where will we find clean towels?"

"Hall closet." Another contraction gripped Cynthia, causing her to cry out. "Don't use the best ones!" she added when the pain subsided.

Darcey looked through the stacks in the hall closet and came back with three terry towels that didn't look brand-new. She situated herself in front of Cynthia while Ellie moved towards Cynthia's shoulders to offer support from that end.

"The baby has crowned," Darcey said. "With the next contraction, help it along with a little push."

"Are you sure we should be doing this? Shouldn't we be rushing her to the hospital?" asked Ellie anxiously. "I really have no experience with this. I haven't been in an obstetric unit since a brief practicum during my nurses training."

"Most of the time, birthings are nothing to worry about. It's a natural female function. Only when there are complications does it get a bit dicey. So far, this appears to be a very normal birth. If it were breach, I'd want to see her in a hospital, too."

Another pain assailed Cynthia.

"Just give it a little push." Darcey spoke with gentle confidence. "That's a good girl, Cynthia. You're doing great. Okay, the head is born. Now with the next contraction, push with everything you've got."

Darcey opened the towel and placed it ready to receive the baby.

The next contraction rose up and Cynthia pushed hard while Ellie supported her head and shoulders. Out slid the newborn into the towel.

"Good job, Cynthia, baby is here," announced Darcey joyfully.

"Well done!" added Ellie.

Cynthia looked up tiredly. "What is it?"

"Don't know yet, give me a second," answered Darcey. "We'll wait until you expel the placenta. It's important that it's all in one piece."

While she was talking, the infant began to cry lustily.

"Good strong lungs!" Darcey opened the towel and rewrapped the baby snuggly. "You've got a son—a beautiful baby boy!"

"Oh, Brent will be thrilled!" Cynthia rose on her elbows to catch a glimpse of her newborn.

Darcey placed the little one in his mother's arms. "Here's your little boy."

Gently, Darcey pressed against Cynthia's belly. Another, lesser contraction came on and the placenta slid out. Before retrieving it, Darcey fetched a large plastic bowl.

"As far as I can tell, it's all apiece," announced Darcey, relieved, and laid it carefully in the bowl. "I need string and a very sharp knife."

"In the drawer next to the fridge, and take your pick from the knife block on the counter," replied Cynthia frankly. Then she wailed, "I can't believe I had my baby on the kitchen floor! And Brent missed it. He wanted to be present for the birth."

"On the other hand, the good Lord saw to it that your friends were on hand to see you safely through," said Darcey as she rifled through the what-not drawer. "This will do!"

She held up a small ball of white string.

"Think of it this way, Cynthia," said Ellie from behind. "This birth story is going to outrank everyone else's humdrum hospital story. An unforgettable memory just happened here. And as for you, Darcey, I think you've missed your calling."

"How so?" asked Darcey as she cut two pieces of string.

"I think you'd be great as a midwife."

"Hmmm. Never crossed my mind, but I'll give it some thought."

Darcey tightly tied the string around the cord in two places a couple of inches apart and then neatly severed the cord.

"And that's all there's to it." Darcey smiled proudly. "Well done, Cynthia, and congratulations on your new son."

"Yes, congratulations," added Ellie. "Although I would suggest we run you into the hospital now anyway. It would be good if you and baby were checked over."

"Yes, I'd like to do that," agreed Cynthia.

"Then I'll hold baby while Ellie helps you to the bathroom. You can tidy up a bit before going in." Darcey glanced over at Abby, who had sat remarkably still through the whole event. "You can come to Mommy now, Abby. See the new baby?"

Darcey let Abby look at the tiny face exposed in the swaddling terry towel. Abby didn't seem to know what to make of it and clung to her mother's neck.

Ellie stopped at her place first to pick up her scrubs before heading to the hospital so she could go straight to work after depositing Cynthia and baby.

"Feeling all right, Cynthia?" asked Ellie once they were on the road.

"I'm feeling the whole gamut of what just happened…"

Ellie chuckled and patted Cynthia's lap. "I think maybe I am, too."

Twenty-Seven

SEPTEMBER CLOSED THE summer season with its characteristic mix of beauty and sense of ending. For most farmers, the harvest was in. The vegetable gardens were reaped, flower borders bore the signs of frostbite, and trees had transformed their greens into stunning red, gold, orange, and yellow hues.

The new house was looking more and more like a classic Victorian era home. Clad in deep red clapboard siding, the two-story bay window suggested a turret. A partial wraparound covered porch connected the grand front door with the common use side door, upheld with five pillars. The windowpanes looked as though they, too, came from an older period. All the trimming was white and the dark grey roof added to the traditional impression.

Inside, fewer features relayed the vintage look, but an oak banister graced the staircase with timeless elegance. The antiquated dining room chandelier had been purchased cost-effectively from a second-hand store. It had looked pretty shabby when she'd brought it home, but after Ellie cleaned, polished, and outfitted it with pointed bulbs, it looked fantastic.

Word of mouth had led them to a rare stone mason to build a fireplace in the living room using the small fieldstones that had been part of the recently dismantled rockpile.

At first Hugh had objected. "Why do you want a common stone fireplace instead of a fancy mantelpiece like we saw in Renata's house?"

"Well... for one thing, we don't have to pay for them, which extends the budget. For another, I like the fact that these stones are related to a mystery with regards to the family saga."

"What? I would have thought you'd do everything possible to forget that chapter of our history. You screamed yourself into a basket case at the time, and now you want to glorify the incident? Sometimes I just don't get you, Ell-ter Skelter!" Hugh shook his head, baffled.

"I know you don't, and sometimes I like that, too. Wouldn't want to bore you, after all." She winked. "Thirdly, he's going to add a thick wooden mantle to the front, adding functionality to the beauty in common rocks. You'll see, Hugh-stanoff. It's going to be the star feature of the house."

All their spare time was now spent on the finishing tasks. Occasionally Hugh would grumble about the jobs Ellie pointed out that needed doing.

"It's not like doing the dishes, you know," she said, growing tired of his complaints. "This only has to be done once."

"Yeah, but your list of once-only jobs looks to be an eternity long!"

About the third week of the month, Hugh found that his letter to Renata hadn't yet been mailed; it lay where he had left it to rest atop the TV unit, covered by the telephone book they seldom consulted. Annoyed with himself, he quickly reread it, added a note, and then made a special trip to the post office to send it on its way.

Suddenly, September was over. The thirtieth fell on a Wednesday and it was with a shock that, while driving home from Swan River, Ellie realized exactly a year ago Hugh had proposed marriage to her in the most romantic way a girl could hope for.

It seemed like they should celebrate that anniversary, but how? Another banquet featuring rock Cornish hens? Too late to pursue that now. She wondered whether Hugh remembered that today held special meaning.

Hugh's truck was parked on the yard, meaning he was home. And given the hour, he was probably busy painting a room in the new house or hanging over his Plymouth in the shop. Ellie decided she would shed her scrubs before she went looking for him.

She saw them almost as soon as she stepped into their cottage: a dozen red roses, mixed with asparagus fern and baby's breath, standing in a lovely vase in the middle of their kitchen table. Propped against it was a card that read:

If I had to do it all over again, I would in a heart-beat.
Thank you for loving me and agreeing to be my wife as of one year ago.
All my Love, Hugh-everafter

"Awww, he remembered! He remembered better than me…"

Ellie wondered again what fun thing she could do to bless him likewise. Then came a lightbulb moment. At her wedding shower, one of the items of advice to the new bride had been to keep their intimacy spicy. She remembered the suggestion to occasionally greet her husband wearing nothing but saran wrap.

Well, tonight would be the night she tried that.

Ellie brushed out her hair and left it unbound and loose just the way she knew Hugh liked it. Next she refreshed her makeup and added some sparkly earrings. Wrapping herself in saran started off easily enough, but eventually it became difficult to reach around back and bring it to the front again.

Patience won the day, and at last she was satisfied with the results. The see-through garb, styled in a passable halter-top pencil dress was ready for showtime. A pair of white high heels completed the salacious outfit.

Ellie strutted over to the shop uneasily, since stilettos don't do well in soft earth. Nor was walking made easy in a literally skintight dress.

She made sure the door slammed shut behind her after she entered the shop so she would immediately garner his attention.

Hugh looked up, down, and then up again in a doubletake. Frowning, he appraised Ellie's see-through appearance and began to chuckle softly. Ellie took that for approval and sashayed towards him.

When she got near enough, he reached out and pulled her close with one arm. "What's this about? Are you trying to seduce me?"

"Is it working?"

"Not really?"

"Oh, come on. Why not then?"

"Well… you're inviting me to a party but then all I can do is look through the window. There's no fun in that at all."

"Oh. The idea, I think, is that you will be moved to get to the party by breaking the window…"

"Ahhh. This cowboy would have found you more irresistible if you had waltzed in here stark naked with only your housecoat on. Now *that* would have been exciting."

"Well, since my efforts have bombed, I guess I'll just have to go back to the house and break the window myself," said Ellie, disappointed.

"Wait. I got the message, and I'm on your page. I'll be in to party with you shortly. You'd better skedaddle before the Moore brothers get here."

"No!" cried Ellie in a near shriek, her eyes as big as dinner plates. "Are you expecting them tonight?"

"No, but they seldom call first. I'd pay to see the look on their faces with you in that getup," said Hugh, chuckling again.

"This was meant for your eyes only."

"Right, so don't take chances, okay, hon?" He kissed her long and sweetly. "That's just to get us started…" He sent her out the door with a light slap on the bum.

"Let's go for a drive," pleaded Ellie on their way home from church. "I need a change of scene and a break from working all the time."

"What did you have in mind?" asked Hugh good-humouredly. "I'm rather sick and tired of going back and forth between a wrench, hammer, and paintbrush."

"What about paying Diane and Bill a visit? We haven't seen or heard from them since our wedding."

"That's a two-hour drive," hedged Hugh. "Each way."

"That's four hours of relaxation."

"For you... not the driver who has to look out for wildlife and reckless motorists," Hugh reminded her. "I don't have a better idea, so sure, give her a call. I'd hate to show up and them not be around."

They ate a quick lunch. While Ellie made the call, Hugh put the remaining boxes of steamer trunk heirlooms in the back of the truck to take along. Ellie jumped in the cab moments later and they were off.

"It was a weird conversation," began Ellie while settling in for the long ride. "It wasn't until I mentioned we would bring the things Alice had set aside for her children that she brightened up a bit."

"You mean she doesn't want us to come?" Hugh sounded perplexed.

"I don't know what I mean. But there wasn't much enthusiasm, that's all I can say."

It was the ideal Sunday afternoon drive. Although chilly, the sun was bright and the fall colours at their peak. They didn't talk much. Instead they let the radio drone on as they watched the scenery pass by.

It dawned on them that it was almost exactly a year ago that they'd made the first trip to Yorkton to share the news of their engagement.

"I guess that explains why things don't look any different than the last time we came this way," remarked Ellie.

They pulled up to Diane and Bill's address midafternoon. Each carrying a bulky box of Alice's heirlooms, they rang the doorbell. They heard a scurry of feet and then Diane opened the door, her children looking on curiously from behind her.

"Hi guys. Come on in. Are these the so-called heirlooms you were talking about?" asked Diane, gesturing to the rather large boxes Ellie and Hugh brought inside.

"Yes. And they're all for you at this point," said Ellie. "Hugh has chosen his items and so has Margo."

"What's in the boxes then?"

"An eight-place setting of fine china, some stemware, and miscellaneous dishes of the nicer kind used when entertaining."

"In other words, stuff I'll never use, just like Mama," said Diane indifferently. "I don't need to look now. I'll do it another time."

"Sure. Whenever you like."

Before they could get further inside, they heard a hoot and a holler from the living room. "Yahoo!"

"That must mean Bill's team scored a touchdown," said Diane, smiling. "We're watching a CFL game. Come and join us. It's the play-offs. Teams are vying to see who will play for the Grey Cup."

Hugh and Ellie followed her into the living room. Diane sat next to Bill, leaving a space that Hugh took, while Ellie sat in a separate chair.

"Hello, you two," greeted Bill. "Everything all right in your camp?"

"Yeah, we're doing fine," replied Hugh. "How about you?"

"Still standing upright. Can't complain. Can I get you a beer?"

"I'd do better with a cola, thanks."

Bill turned to his wife. "Have we got any cola, Di?"

"Might have… what about you, Ellie?"

"A glass of water would be great, thanks."

Diane got up and left for the kitchen. She returned momentarily with a can of cola for Hugh and a glass of water which she handed to Ellie. Then she retook her seat beside Bill.

"So tell us what's new with you," asked Ellie conversationally.

Diane and Bill were focused on the game and didn't reply right away. Ellie made eye contact with first Mandy, and then Sean, but this made them self-conscious. Sean scooted to his mother's lap and Mandy ran to hide in the hallway.

When a commercial came on, Diane answered. "What's new with us? Nothing really, other than we're all a year older. Same old, same old. What's new with you guys?"

"The rest of the old farm buildings are gone," said Hugh. "I put up a new garage and storage shed this spring."

"We went on our honeymoon to Niagara Falls, and we're almost finished building our new house," added Ellie.

"Sounds nice." Diane glanced back at the TV.

The game was still on commercial. "So... who's your favourite football team?" threw out Bill.

"Sorry, I don't follow football." Hugh shifted in his seat. "A little hockey, but that's about the extent of it."

"Really? I'm a Bombers man myself. You don't like sports, hey? Too bad. Life must be a little dull in your corner."

"No way. I have more projects to work at than I have time for."

When the game returned, Bill and Diane turned their focus back to it. There seemed nothing for Hugh and Ellie to do except watch with them.

Another commercial aired.

"Are you still nursing at the Swan River hospital?" asked Diane.

"Sure am," answered Ellie brightly. "Your kids have grown a lot since we last saw them."

"Yeah, like weeds! Have to change out their clothes every six months."

Bill turned to Hugh. "How's the mechanic business going?"

"Doing well. Still enjoying it," replied Hugh. "Still painting?"

"Yup. It's a living."

The commercials ended and everyone refocused on the game. Another touchdown. This time, Diane shrieked with joy.

"I always root for the team playing against Bill's favourite." She poked her husband in the ribs. "It's a competition that way and usually a lot of fun. Except when you get mad that *my* team won, right, Billy?"

Bill snorted. "Phfffff."

When the next commercial came on, Amanda came out of the woodwork and pleaded, "Mommy, can I have a peanut butter and jelly sandwich? I'm hungry."

Diane glanced at her wristwatch. "Oh my, it's already your suppertime. Yeah, Mommy will make a sandwich for you and Seany." She rose and moved to the kitchen.

Ellie got up and followed her. "Can I help you with anything?"

"To make peanut butter sandwiches? No, I can handle that," said Diane. "Unless you want one, too. Sundays I don't cook supper. It's my night off. We usually just graze on whatever leftovers there are, or snack food. Popcorn is a favourite."

"I think maybe it's time Hugh and I head back home. Tomorrow's a workday, after all, and I don't much like driving in the dark," said Ellie, sounding apologetic. "Too easy to get in the way of a deer."

Diane's reply was dispassionate. "Sure. Whatever you have to do."

"We should head home, Hugh," said Ellie, cuing him that it was time for departure.

He replied with apparent relief. "If you're ready, I am, too."

Bill got up and went to the door along with Diane. Everyone took turns saying "It was nice to see you" and exchanged brief, perfunctory hugs.

⌒

"I guess we're on our own for supper," said Ellie unnecessarily.

"There's probably a fast-food outlet downtown. Burgers should be filling enough to get us home."

Ellie looked out the window. "Not for me, thanks. I'll just have a milkshake." She sounded downhearted.

They didn't speak other than to order their fast food.

"It's not that I felt unwelcome," Ellie continued once they were on the highway heading east. "It's more like there's no common ground to connect us."

"Bingo! You nailed it," said Hugh, drawing on his soda. "Although it's sad, it's fair. Even though Di and I share the same blood, we're strangers. Haven't had anything to do with each other for fifteen years. We've developed very different lifestyles."

"She seemed so happy to reconnect before…"

"And now it's perfectly clear that not only have we grown apart, we don't even dock at the same port."

"What do you think we should do about it?"

"Not a thing. It is what it is." Hugh sighed. "I think we—well, I—won't come to her mind again until she finds herself in trouble somehow. Then it's going to be 'I need help, Hugh.' She'll fall back on our *relationship* to get her out of her fix. Much like it was with Margo. That's the way I see it."

"What about family gatherings? Christmas isn't far off."

"We can extend an invitation, and not be surprised if they claim to have other plans. We don't push and we don't insist. We patiently wait for when… if ever. Just like God is with us."

"I get it, but it's still too bad," remarked Ellie. "I don't like it when families lose their connections with each other. We don't see Gus or Harold much either, but there's a fondness and joy between us whenever we do get together."

"Can I tell you something, babe? For a worldly wise woman, you can sometimes be awfully idealistic."

Hugh heard the phone ringing from the Quonset. He was stacking summer tires and figured he'd never make it if he tried to run for it. And sure enough, it stopped ringing.

But after five minutes, it started up again. This time he was sweeping out dried mud with a shop broom. Dropping the broom, Hugh ran for the cottage, but as soon as he picked up the receiver, all he got was a dial tone.

He waited ten minutes, filling the time by looking over the ads in the *Western Producer*. One never knew when a good deal on something needed would be listed there.

The phone remained quiet, so he went back outside to finish his chore. As soon as he descended the steps, though, the phone rang again. Hugh turned on his heel and hurried back inside.

"Hello," he said, careful to sound friendly despite feeling annoyed.

"Hello, is this Hugh Fischer?"

He didn't immediately recognize the woman's voice and replied in a business-like tone. "It is."

"This is your Aunt Renata. I've been trying to reach you for some time."

"Yeah, sorry about the cat-and-mouse game. I've been working outside, organizing things for winter."

"I've called to tell you that your grandmother passed away today. I thought you'd want to know."

Hugh sighed. "I suppose I shouldn't be surprised. You told me it was coming. Can you tell me what happened?"

"Sure," said Renata briskly. "After I talked to you a few weeks ago, she settled down. Other than getting weaker and slower, she seemed generally fine. Then she started up again, insisting we meet Fred. About that time, we also received your letter."

"I'm sorry I didn't send it sooner. After I wrote it, I laid it aside to think on the matter some more, and it got covered up with a telephone book."

"I don't think that matters, really. What you wrote wasn't time-sensitive. I appreciated hearing your story, Hugh. I admit it's hard to accept my brother becoming such a different man than who we remembered—or assumed he was."

"The truth can sometimes be painful, Aunt Renata."

"What I wanted to tell you was that I read your letter to Mum... that is, your grandmother. In fact, I read it twice. It did it after supper when she became restless. She got very quiet after that and went to her room. I didn't think much of it because she typically retires much earlier than Mervin and I do. When she didn't show up for breakfast, I went to check on her. She died during the night."

"Were there signs of distress?"

"I'm not sure what you mean?"

"I'm thinking of resistance… as though she wasn't ready to leave this world."

Renata paused for a few seconds before continuing. "Since I wasn't present when she actually departed, I'd have to admit I don't know. To my mind, her heart simply gave out."

"I see. Will you be bringing her remains back to Minitonas to be laid to rest next to my grandfather?"

"Oh no. There's no attachment there. She's to be cremated. After that, we aren't sure what will be done with the ashes."

There was an awkward pause.

"Merv and I are discussing the idea of coming your way next summer," said Renata, reviving the conversation. "We'd like to see what's the same and what's changed since we lived there so many years ago."

"That would be great, Aunty. We look forward to having you. You'll be able to meet your nieces."

"Wonderful! I should let you go. I have arrangements to make with the funeral home, as you may imagine."

"I appreciate your call. Please call again. I'd like to get to know you, even if it's over the phone."

Hugh hung up the phone, feeling unhappy. A good part of his letter had been devoted not only to sharing the unfortunate story of his youth, but to sharing his faith. Yet his aunt hadn't made any reference to it at all.

This didn't sit well, and it would be a few more hours before Ellie returned. He wanted to share the news and discuss the call in greater depth.

"My take on it is that we'll never know if, or how, your grandmother responded to your testimony," Ellie mused.

They were in bed, exchanging some pillow talk before drifting off to sleep.

"As far as your aunt goes, it would seem that the faith portion of your letter made her uncomfortable," she added. "More uncomfortable even than confronting the truth about her brother and his family. But she's got the letter now. Maybe she'll read it a third and fourth time. Who knows? It's our part to share the way to God's peace. After that, it's between Renata and God."

"I guess you're right." Hugh spooned his wife and placed an arm over her torso.

"How do you feel about your granny being gone?"

"Lots of things. Regret most of all."

Twenty-Eight

"ELLIE, IF YOU clean the house any more, you'll rub off the finish," complained Hugh. "I don't get you. We built this big fancy house and now you're stalling to move in."

"I know… I know." Ellie exhaled. "I don't get me either. It's just that moving creates upheaval, and I balk at messing up our sweet little nest. I'm more attached to it than I ever imagined I would be."

"The upheaval can be minimized. Let's start by moving the pieces we're not currently using here in the cottage. Margo would be relieved and grateful if we brought the piano over, as an example."

"You're right. That's a good place to start. And we could get the new armchair from Cynthia's place. I know it's complete."

Getting the piano over to the new house took more muscle than Hugh and Ellie had on their own. It was a monstrously heavy item and took all evening even with the help of Rob and the two Moore brothers. Together, they carefully transported it to the new house, unloaded it outside the front door, and then moved it inside and into position, miraculously without marring either piano or house in the process.

When they retrieved the reupholstered armchair from Cynthia's workroom, they saw that the accompanying sofa had been stripped and readied for finishing.

"I'll have it ready soon, Ellie," promised Cynthia. "It's just that I need Brent's help. Having a baby to attend to has reduced my time for working on projects by at least half."

"I understand," said Ellie. "You once said you'd have it done by Christmas. Is that still doable?"

"I'd like to have it outta here before then, so I'll say as soon as possible."

These two pieces moved in motivated Ellie to take more items inside. Next they moved the Hoosier into the dinette next to the kitchen, and Hugh's single bed and dresser made up a guest room upstairs.

A good part of the furnishings budget had been spent on a desk and personal computer, which they set up in the den off the front entrance.

"I'm glad to be catching up with the rest of our culture," remarked Hugh about the computer. "This looks like a handy contraption."

They also set up a TV in the den, positioned across from a beige loveseat Ellie had found at the thrift shop. A good cleaning had rendered it entirely satisfactory for watching the news or their favourite TV shows together.

The many boxes containing wedding presents were hauled into the house. It was rather like Christmas looking through them and rediscovering the thoughtful gifts. They stowed a few things in the linen closet and kitchen cupboards, but quite a lot was set aside to eventually be stored in a sideboard they didn't yet have; with the current budget spent, it didn't look likely they would have one soon.

The following weekend, Hugh urged Ellie to move the rest of their things.

"I'll get some guys to help with the big pieces, and by nightfall everything can be in order," he promised.

Ellie demurred. "I'm really just not in the mood right now to upset this place."

Utterly annoyed, Hugh went instead to the shop and hung over the Plymouth for the rest of the day.

Knowing she had irked him, Ellie drove over to Darcey's house to talk out her caldron of confused feelings.

"I don't know what's wrong with me," said Ellie tearfully after aptly describing her strange resistance to moving into the new house. "Hugh's mad at me because he wants to move in and enjoy the larger space. Even scantily outfitted as it is, it's a nice place. My head says move in, but my heart says not yet…"

"Why is your heart saying that?" asked Darcey bluntly.

"I don't know. If I did, I wouldn't be trying to figure it out with you."

"I bet you do know, but you haven't given words to it yet. Maybe you're afraid to. And I notice you haven't touched your coffee or taken a bite out that slice of date loaf. Why is that?"

"I'm moody about food lately, too. Odors get to me. Sometimes coffee smells wonderful and sometimes it doesn't."

"I see…" Darcey raised her eyebrows. "How long have these common odours offended you?"

"I don't know. It's on and off again."

Darcey momentarily chose to focus on the primary reason for Ellie's trouble. "So what aren't you admitting to yourself that prevents you from moving into your permanent home?"

"What a strange question," parried Ellie.

"C'mon. You're dodging. Be honest. You'll have at least one reason. Out with it!"

Ellie began to tear up. "What's the point of moving into the big house when the little one is perfectly adequate for us?"

"Keep going," demanded Darcey, but not harshly.

"The big house was built to be a home for a family with kids. We don't got kids, and it doesn't seem any are forthcoming."

"Is that so? And yet you don't like odours and your taste is off. If you ask me, and apparently you are, I'd say get a pregnancy test. I'll bet the farm you're expecting." Only Darcey could get away with such forthrightness.

⌒

"Okay. Let's just do this," said Ellie to Hugh the following evening. "We can start carrying over the bedroom furniture. If we set up one space at a time, I should be able to handle the temporary upheaval graciously."

"That's my girl." Hugh still called Ladd and Jeremy, hoping to borrow their might for transporting the larger, heavier items.

As it turned out, once they got started they were able to basically empty the cottage of all its furnishings in a short time. Ellie's part was to transfer the kitchen goods and convey their linens and clothes to their new location. It was midnight before things were mostly put away.

Before turning in, she went back to the cottage to see if there was anything she had forgotten. Nothing remained other than the empty island, which she no longer needed. That was too bad. She had grown fond of the piece, mostly because she was fond of the people who had made and gifted it to them.

Now that the cottage was cleared, Ellie was surprised that her attachment to it was also diminished. It was just a house. A cute little house, but just a house after all.

⌒

With Christmas less than two weeks away and preparations in high swing, Hugh brought home a live spruce tree and set it up in the living room in front of the bay window.

They invited Trevor, Charlotte, and Beanie to come over to have some fun with decorating the tree. Although Ellie had purchased some new baubles she liked, many of the ones they used came from their Grandmother Bauman's collection.

When that was complete, and after they'd indulged in hot chocolate and decorated vanilla sugar cookies, the Christmas spirit was firmly ensconced.

⌒

"Rob, I need your help with something," said Ellie over the phone. "And it needs to be you, not Hugh."

Rob spoke with measured patience. "What is it this time? It's rather busy around here. I don't have a lot of time to spare."

"Just meet me at the furniture store in Swan River at seven when my shift is over. It's part of my Christmas gift to Hugh."

⌒

A week before Christmas, Hugh answered a phone call by Marcie Turner.

"I hope Ellie is there," she said after they'd exchanged warm greetings. "I have something to tell her."

"She's away putting in extra hours at the hospital so she can have Christmas Day off," explained Hugh. "Why don't you tell me?"

"I suppose I could try." Marcie sounded clearly disappointed. "So… Brian and I were driving around the Selkirk area and decided to investigate an antique store we came across. We found a lovely antique: an oval dining table with extra leaves and twelve chairs, including two captain's chairs. We believe the wood is walnut and it's in great shape… doesn't need refinishing. The set includes a handsome matching sideboard which would hold a lot of china and serving dishes. It's of very fine quality but not too ornate, and certainly not without style either! It was designed with timeless beauty. I'm positive Ellie would love it."

"Hmmm. Am I right to guess that it doesn't come at a bargain price?"

"The price tag definitely reflects its fine quality. It's a one-of-a-kind find, a fantastic opportunity." Doubt and hope mingled in her tone.

Hugh braced himself. "Do I need to sit before you tell me what they want for it?"

"Maybe."

Once Marcie had quoted him the price, Hugh whistled through his exhaled breath and rubbed a hand through his hair.

"That's the same amount we budgeted for furnishing the entire house. And it's spent. Most of that went to another antique, a sofa set Ellie had recovered, and a bit of office furniture to go with our new computer. I know she'd like some fine dining room furniture, but I think it's going to have to wait until we've collected some money again."

"Hugh, I'm so sure that you and Ellie should have this set that I'll float you the money," Marcie replied in all seriousness. "I don't want you to miss this opportunity."

"You're that certain?"

"I am."

"Give me a moment. I'll be right back," said Hugh, exhaling deeply again.

He set down the receiver and made a slow walk around the house, all the while rubbing a hand around the back of his neck. Eventually he circled back to the phone.

"Marcie, here's what I'd like to do. I'm going to up my mortgage so I can write a cheque to cover the cost of this dining furniture. It will be my Christmas gift to Ellie."

"Oh my! I never expected this from you, but what a wonderful idea!"

"One problem. How do I get it here in time for Christmas?"

"We've already got an idea for that," declared Marcie excitedly. "If we can join you for Christmas, we'll bring it ourselves."

"What about Kevin?" This was a reference to the Turners' only biological son, who lived with his wife in Ontario.

"He's spending Christmas with his in-laws. So if we can possibly spend this Christmas with family, you're it!"

"Come. It's all settled then."

After they said their goodbyes, Hugh called Ellie at the hospital.

"Meet me at the furniture store when your shift is over," he said. "We have to buy a bed for two and prepare a nice guest room. Marcie and Brian are going to join us for Christmas."

He had to hold the phone away from his ear so her shrieks of joy weren't so hard on his eardrums.

~

Brian and Marcie arrived during the noon hour of Christmas Eve. Hugh was home waiting for them. He and Brian unloaded the dining set they had delivered via trailer and Marcie took charge of setting the furniture in place. Then Hugh returned to his workplace for the staff Christmas party.

Meanwhile, Marcie took it upon herself to unpack the boxes of fine china and other platters, bowls, and stemware and shelve it all in the sideboard.

Midafternoon, the telephone rang. Brian supposed it may be Hugh or Ellie calling with further instructions.

"Hello," he answered politely.

There was dead air for a moment. "I must have dialled wrong," said a female voice.

"This is the Fischer residence," he clarified. "Neither Hugh nor Ellie are here at the moment."

"Oh. Well, my name is Cynthia and I've just now finished reupholstering Ellie's sofa. I promised she'd have it by Christmas and now it's done—just under the wire, I admit."

"I suppose that means someone should pick it up."

"Yes please. I can't deliver it because my husband is away with the van. And besides, my baby needs me."

"No worries. We're guests of Hugh and Ellie this Christmas and we just happen to be free to do a little job like that. What's the address?"

Soon after the call, they were on their way to Minitonas with the trailer. And just as quickly, they were back on the road, returning to the Fischers' new home with the sofa.

Although it wasn't light, Brain and Marcie managed to bring the sofa inside and add it to the living room. Marcie arranged the sofas to face each other adjacent to the majestic fieldstone fireplace. The steamer trunk stayed in place between them, once again serving as the coffee table. The two armchairs were placed on the end opposite the fireplace with a lamp and small accent table between them, creating a circle of seating for intimate conversation.

With the living and dining spaces fully furnished, including the upright piano and Christmas tree, it seemed almost crowded. But cosily so.

Brian lit a fire in the fireplace. Dusk came early these days, on the heels of the winter solstice. He also plugged in the lights on the Christmas tree.

While waiting for the young couple to come home, he and Marcie yielded to the romantic ambience and canoodled on the new sofa.

"It's not only young lovers who enjoy the heat of affection," remarked Brian, slipping his arm around Marcie. "I think I still have it in me, too, after all our years."

"Is it really coming from you, or is it the effect of this house?" Marcie leaned into his embrace, fully content. "It just feels like a house of love to me, and we're getting caught up in it."

It was dark when Ellie pulled into the yard, with Hugh right behind her. She rushed into the house, joyous upon seeing their adopted parents. There were hugs all around.

Then Ellie noticed the new sofa in the living room. "Well, what do you know? Cynthia made good on her promise," said Ellie awed. "It's as gorgeous as she said it would be!"

"It most certainly is," agreed Marcie.

Ellie looked up then and saw further into the formal dining area. Her chin dropped a full inch.

"Oh. My. Gosh. What's this?" Ellie slowly moved to the table and ran her hand along the fine wood. She did the same with the sideboard. She looked to Brian and Marcie. "Did you bring this? It's... it's amazing. I think I'm going to cry."

"We brought it, yes," admitted Marcie. "But the full explanation is inside that envelope on the table."

Hugh stopped her from reaching for it. "Which we won't open yet. First we'll have a quick bite and then take in the Christmas Eve service at church. We'll exchange our gifts when we get home afterward."

"Nice that we won't have to borrow folding tables and chairs from the church for tomorrow's Christmas gathering after all," noted Ellie happily.

~

The Christmas Eve service didn't disappoint. The Sunday school children acted out a delightful pageant interspersed with the singing of yuletide carols and hymns. The service was dismissed following the congregational lighting of candles to a gentle refrain of "Silent Night."

Back at the big house, Ellie quickly changed into lounge clothing and invited her guests to do the same. She had prepared a batch of the sweet spiced and fruity Russian tea—Aunt Ruth's recipe—and handed out steaming mugs of the tasty brew.

Ellie then reached under the tree, retrieved a gaily wrapped parcel, and placed it on Hugh's lap. That cued the others to pass out their gifts.

Soon Hugh and Ellie held up handsome antique five-point silver candelabras and a long green tablecloth.

"To go with your new dining furniture," said Marcie.

Brian held up a kit to make a ship-in-a-bottle keepsake and a pair of riotously psychedelic socks.

"To make sure there's something for you to do when you retire," said Hugh, smirking.

Brian nodded approvingly.

Marcie revealed the contents of her box: a pair of knitting needles, a dozen balls of artisan dyed wool, a pattern book of knitted women's sweaters, and a set of calligraphy pens with ink.

Ellie watched the woman with a question in her eyes.

"It's perfect, Ellie dear," Marcie assured her. "Being home full-time now has me scrambling for interesting things to do."

"I take it that your strange, unpredictable malady hasn't been resolved," said Ellie sympathetically.

"No. It hasn't. But by paying attention to myself, I've learned that I'm more susceptible to these spells when tired. So I try to pace myself. I believe I'm doing better."

"That's great," said Ellie. "You haven't opened your parcel yet, Hugh-lary."

"You first," countered Hugh. "Open the envelope."

"Right. The envelope. Where did it get to?" Ellie looked under scattered wrapping paper.

The envelope was soon found. When it opened, it revealed a beautiful Christmas card expressing ardent love from a husband to his beloved wife.

I hope you like the dining room furniture.
All my love, Hugh

Ellie teared up. "This is your gift to me? How on earth did you pull it off without me knowing anything about it?"

"I had a little help…"

"But the budget…"

"It was explained to me that I should weigh the once-in-a-lifetime opportunity against the rules of practicality. We have a little more mortgage to repay, but that's okay. It was modest to begin with." Hugh looked into her eyes. "I'm trying to learn right attitudes, know what I mean?"

"Oh you big hunk of wonderfulness." Ellie planted a kiss on his mouth, which he happily accepted.

Hugh then opened his gift and soon held up a new peach-coloured shirt with an artisan-crafted knit pullover sweater.

"Weren't we admiring these in one of the shops at Niagara-on-the-Lake?" he said. "And weren't we stunned at the price they were asking?"

"Yes, we did," admitted Ellie. "But while you were busy ordering ice cream, I went back and bought one. Because I thought you were worth it. One doesn't find items like this in our men's stores."

Hugh leaned over to kiss Ellie. "Thanks, sweetheart."

"I have something else to share with you. I've been debating when to do it, but I think this evening is the right time. You'll have to come upstairs with me, though." Ellie turned to the Turners. "Please excuse us for just a few minutes."

She took Hugh by the hand and led him up the staircase to the upper floor. At the foot of the stairs, Hugh turned back and winked at Brian and Marcie.

Ellie saw him do it. "We won't be gone long enough for any of *that*," she said playfully to the snickering of Brian and Marcie.

She stopped in front of the closed door next to their master bedroom. It was the fourth of the four-bedroom house and as yet unfurnished, or so Hugh thought.

Ellie opened the door and stepped aside so he would enter first.

Hugh looked around. "You bought me… a crib?" he said, frowning. The meaning then dawned on him. "Are you telling me we're going to have a baby?"

Ellie nodded with teary eyes.

Hugh truly didn't know how to respond. He stood there in some sort of shock and awe. A moment later, however, he pulled Ellie into his arms and kissed her forehead, nose, and finally her mouth with such passion that her legs gave out like jelly.

"You can be the one to share the good news with our honorary parents," said Ellie, aglow as she led Hugh back downstairs.

A moment later, they stood facing the expectant Brian and Marcie.

"C'mon, Hugh-ford." Ellie poked him in the ribs. "It's your news to tell."

Overcome with emotion, Hugh blurted, "I'm going to be a daddy!"

Twenty-Nine

"CAN I HELP you with anything?" asked Marcie.

"Actually, yes. The smells of our brunch are messing with my stomach." Ellie backed away from the stove, wrinkling her nose.

Marcie took over frying the bacon and checked on the crustless quiche in the oven. Ellie managed to set the dinette table for four without having to retch.

"That's all you're having, Ell? Dry toast and hot water?" noted Hugh when the men were called to the table.

"That's all I can tolerate for now." Ellie sighed. "This nausea should pass in time for Christmas dinner."

After brunch, Hugh took Brian over to the shop to show him the disassembled Plymouth half-ton, which lay in many pieces.

Meanwhile Ellie and Marcie set the grand dining table for twelve. On top of the green tablecloth, Ellie created a runner down the centre using several of her mother's circular doilies. Marcie filled the silver candelabras with long white tapers and set them on the table with a deep red poinsettia positioned between them. To complete the festive centrepiece, Ellie scattered a few shiny Christmas balls along the crocheted runner.

Next they set out the fine china. These had been a wedding gift from Ellie's brothers and their wives. The centre of each dinner plate was embossed with a fancy gold capital F. The Black Watch tartan formed a striking rim around each plate and that of the other pieces in the set. A thin strip of gold edged the tartan on both the inner and outer rim.

Marcie was highly impressed. "I'm sure I've never seen more elegant dishes!"

Silver flatware and clear glasses completed the table settings. With these in place, the women pronounced it gorgeous.

"I believe a beautifully set table communicates love," commented Ellie. "It says that the people invited to feast here are important to the host. And that's what I want our family to feel when they come for Christmas dinner."

Marcie smiled broadly. "Then you have achieved a shining success!"

Dinner was going to be a potluck. Each household had been assigned a dish to bring so the whole job wouldn't fall to one poor, exhausted woman.

Rob and Sarah arrived first with Trevor, Charlotte, and Beanie in tow.

"Beep-beep. Make way for the turkey," tooted Rob, holding a hot roaster beyond his midriff. It was quickly placed in Ellie's oven to keep warm until dinner.

Soon after came Ed and Gertie Johnson, each bearing a bowl.

"You asked for a salad, Ellie dear," their aunt said. "But I couldn't decide whether to bring ambrosia or the three-bean that so many seem to like. So I brought them both." She ended on a light giggle.

"It's perfect, Aunt Gertie," replied Ellie gladly. "Merry Christmas and make yourself at home."

Margo came next, the last of the guests. She handed Ellie a casserole of carrot pudding and a jar of homemade caramel sauce so she could remove her coat.

"Do you mind if I look around? I'd like to see your new digs."

"Sure, make yourself at home," repeated Ellie. "I think that's everyone. We can bring out the punch now."

"I brought some Christmas baking with me," disclosed Marcie. "May I set out a platter of cookies and squares with the punch?"

Ellie's eyes widened in surprise. "Of course. There's no end of thoughtfulness with you, is there?"

"I didn't say anything earlier because I didn't want to intrude on whatever plans you had made, but I'd like to contribute along with the others," said Marcie.

Charlotte assisted Ellie in mixing a fruity punch with ginger ale. They set up the snack bar on the small table in the dinette next to the kitchen.

Then they heard Ruby and Ruff bark copiously, heralding the arrival of more people.

"It's your Aunty Ruth and Uncle Herb," announced Hugh as he went to the door. "Are we expecting them?"

"I wasn't sure," answered Ellie. "But that's okay. We'll just add two more plates to the table. This is a the-more-the-merrier kind of family gathering."

Aunt Ruth was all smiles as she entered the house—that is, until she saw so many unfamiliar faces. Then confusion reigned.

"Where are we, Herb? I think we're at the wrong house."

"No, you're not, Aunty," said Ellie, coming to the fore. "You're at the right place. See?" She pointed out Rob, who sat in the living room. "There's your nephew whom you know well. We'll make introductions with Hugh's side of the family."

Uncle Herb pressed on to the kitchen and deposited a large, clear bag of fresh air buns.

"Are you sure we're supposed to be here?" Herb asked Ellie, anxiously taking her aside. "Ruthie was on again and off again a dozen times about where we were supposed to be on Christmas Day. If she's confused, I'm confuseder."

He clamped his lips shut, unhappy.

"Oh, I'm so sorry about these changes in Ruth. Just to be clear, I did invite you to join our family Christmas this year, but Aunty never did commit to coming with me either. I'm glad you're here, though. You just go and enjoy kvetching and cracking up with the other menfolk."

Relieved, Herb lumbered off in search of Rob.

Before dinner, they played a game. Fourteen gaily wrapped parcels in varying sizes and shapes were heaped on the trunk in the living room. Ellie determined that a gift could be chosen according to age, beginning with the oldest. The next person could steal a gift that was already opened or take another from the pile.

The game generated several guffaws when men unwrapped packages of bubble bath and pantyhose and the women unwrapped fishing lures and a *Sports Illustrated* magazine.

Beanie's gift revealed a set of screwdrivers. She frowned with disappointment. Margo noticed and approached the little girl.

"I would very much like to have those screwdrivers, if you'd be willing to have this box of chocolates instead," Margo said, and meant it.

Beanie's eyes lit up with relief. The exchange was made and both were happy.

When everyone was called to the table—which made for a snug seating arrangement, with fourteen guests fitting into a space meant for twelve—Rob, sitting at one end of the table, preceded the meal by reading St. Luke's account of the Christmas story.

"Ellie also asked me to pray the blessing for our feast," Rob said. "I'm glad to do it in my own home, but I think the privilege belongs to the head of this house. What do you say, Hugh?"

Hugh, who sat at the other end of the table, hesitated for a few seconds. "Sure." And with that, he began his first public prayer.

"Father God, we are a very blessed people. You have supplied each of us with all we need, and many of our wants, too. You have turned our mourning into joy and replaced our ashes with beauty and good things. Thank You for Your Word and the gift of Your Son Jesus, whose birthday we celebrate today. Thanks, too, for this feast and the hands that have prepared it. Amen."

A chorus of amens echoed around the table.

While they ate a truly scrumptious meal, Ellie asked to hear stories of her guests' most memorable Christmases. There was a pause in the chatter while everyone thought about this.

In a moment, Ed Johnson spoke up. "I think for me it was when, as a young lad, I got the little red wagon that was displayed in the hardware store window. I loved that thing and literally wore it out. I wonder what happened to it."

"There were some pretty good Bauman gatherings, I recollect," said Ruth, still pondering. "I think the best Christmases were when Lizzie and I cooked up a feast... there was so much food, the table sagged. Lord, I miss my sister..."

"Me too," added Ellie, suddenly choking up.

"Well now, I remember the time when I was young, long before I met Ruthie, and there was a snowstorm on Christmas Day." Uncle Herb laughed a bit before continuing. "The family, with all our aunts and uncles, was supposed to meet at our place, and Ma trussed up a mother big turkey. I think it took two loaves of bread to stuff it, along with all the other mysteries she put in the bowl." A few people chuckled here. "But the storm was so bad, nobody showed up. We eventually ate the turkey and all the trimmings ourselves, but there weren't no fun in it, ya know? I guess what I remember most about that Christmas is that it was kinda lonely. I didn't care for it."

Others around the table nodded sympathetically.

"I liked last Christmas when we gave you the puppies," piped up Beanie. "That was fun!"

"It certainly was," agreed Ellie.

Hugh smiled. "And they're good dogs, too. They always let us know when people drop by, and that's their job."

"My story is when my brothers and I played a trick on Ellie," said Rob.

Ellie groaned. "I bet I know what he's going to tell. I'm already embarrassed."

Rob chuckled before continuing. "We planned it about a week in advance of Christmas, because the idea of making her wait with agonizing patience was part of the game. I think it was Gus who pulled out a plastic girl's ring as the prize in a box of Lucky Elephant Pink Popcorn. We got the idea to put it in an even smaller box—I think it was a baking soda box Mother had thrown out—and then we wrapped it about ten times in newspaper. We then put that in a bigger box, wrapped it in newsprint another ten times, which we then put in an even bigger box… well, you get the idea. We kept going until it was about thirty inches square. The final wrapping was Christmas paper. And then we put it next to our Christmas tree. Ellie was so excited that she couldn't sit still for the rest of the week."

"I think you're exaggerating, brother," chimed in Ellie dryly.

"No, I'm not." Rob snickered. "You were so sure you were getting something large and wonderful, which made it all the funnier. On Christmas Day, when she finally got to open it, I think it took her all of half an hour to finally pull it apart down to the baking soda box."

"And then," added Ellie brightly, finishing the story, "when I discovered it was only a cheap penny ring, I was so mad and disappointed that I wanted to scratch their faces."

Rob couldn't stop laughing over the memory. "And that was funny, too."

Gertie was the next to share her memory. "I think the most memorable Christmas for me was the last time I had Christmas with my sister Alice. Her children were very little then, and our boy was little, too." She paused and looked at Hugh, who saw the pain in her face. "I don't think I'll say more about it. It's not a very good memory after all—"

Hugh jumped up and left the table for a moment. He returned quickly with his tiny matchbox truck in his hand.

"Do you remember this toy?" asked Hugh while taking his seat.

Gertie brightened at once. "Is that the toy I gave you that Christmas long ago?"

"It is, and it was my favourite toy for years afterward. That was a happy Christmas memory for me, Aunt Gertie."

"Oh good." Gertie looked down at her plate. "I'm glad something worthwhile came of it."

"I was pretty pumped when I got brand-new hockey skates for Christmas," contributed Trevor.

"I remember getting a doll I hoped and hoped for." Charlotte smiled from ear to ear.

"Having the chicken pox turned out to be a memorable Christmas for me." Marcie set down her fork momentarily. "I was twelve. Because I was sick and contagious, we couldn't gather with our relatives and my siblings were very disappointed and angry with me for spoiling Christmas. I remember that I hardly cared because my spots were so itchy. My skin crawled with misery!"

A number of guests sympathized.

"I can't think of anything especially remarkable," said Sarah mildly. "I think all our Christmases were wonderful. I pass."

"Me too," Ellie said. "I'm going to lump my story with Rob's, as it involved both of us."

"My most memorable Christmas is the first one I had with my cherished wife." Brian looked at Marcie lovingly. "It was just us. Our parents lived out of province and we didn't get enough days off to join with either family. It was a bit lonely, but I remember feeling that as long as Marcie was with me, it was enough. I was happy with just her. Didn't need all the sound and fury of a houseful."

There was a collective sigh and murmurs of how sweet that was.

"I didn't know you felt that way," said Marcie, turning to Brian.

"Well, now you do."

Hugh sent a meaningful glance at Ellie. "I get it."

That left only Margo and Hugh. Instinctively, Ellie felt she should not pressure Margo for a story.

However, Hugh rose to the occasion.

"I'm thinking that my most memorable Christmas is today," he started in a thoughtful tone. "Just about all the people I love and care about are here with me under one roof, participating in a fantastic meal—thanks to all you chefs, by the way—having loving, friendly companionship one with another. I don't know how it gets better than that." His eyes suddenly lit up. "Wait! Yes, I do. Last night, my bride gave me an unforgettable Christmas gift."

"Sheesh, it was just a sweater..."

He looked at her intently. "No. I mean the other. Can I share the news?"

"Yes, of course," said Ellie blithely.

"My wife, the most thoughtful woman *I* know, gave me a baby's crib for Christmas."

What followed was a happy chorus of well wishes from just about everyone around the table.

"Well done, man," said Rob, clapping his hands. "I know the pride a man feels when he learns he's begat a child. Well done."

"I must have missed something," said Gertie, puzzled. "Why would Ellie give Hugh a crib?"

"Gertrude, dear," answered Ed with exaggerated patience. "That was his way of saying they're expecting a baby."

Gertie blushed. "Oh. Now I get it, silly me."

That ended all the Christmas talk. From there on, the discussions revolved around due dates, baby names, birthing stories, and pregnancy advice.

About nine o'clock, people began to pack up their things and return to their homes, satisfied that another meaningful Christmas had been celebrated, another memory made.

"You look bushed, Ellie," said Marcie after the last guest had left. "You scoot on up to bed. Brian and I will tidy up."

Ellie felt so relieved. "Are you sure? I really do feel beat."

"Go." Marcie gently pushed Ellie in the direction of the stairs.

"Thanks, Mom," said Ellie gratefully as she slowly ascended the stairs.

Hugh started carrying glasses and cups to the kitchen.

Marcie stopped him as well. "You want to be with Ellie right now, I can tell."

"You're right, I do. But I also don't want you to be doing all the work. You're my guests, too, after all."

"We all need a few quiet moments to ourselves," argued Marcie. "Brian and I could use a little downtime after a wonderful but busy day."

"If you put it that way…" Hugh vacated the kitchen. "Thanks, Mom," he said as bounded up the staircase two steps at a time.

Brian saw Marcie's eyes water. "It means a lot to you, doesn't it, that these young people look to you as a mother?"

"More than you know," faltered Marcie, happily picking up the stray dishes and napkins dotting the floor.

Brian's voice was soft and pensive. "We got lucky by gaining a son unexpectedly all those years ago."

"And his sweet wife, who seems so right for him, is the daughter I always wished for."

Ellie was already under the covers when Hugh quietly slipped into their bedroom. He quickly disrobed and slid in behind her. Nestling his legs behind hers, he laid a hand on her belly.

"You won't feel anything for a few weeks yet," murmured Ellie sleepily.

"Are you sure? 'Cause I think I can pick out the little peanut's heartbeat with my fingers."

"Only in your imagination."

They fell asleep then. Soon Hugh was snoring softly into her hair.

Thirty

"SO HERE'S THE plan," declared Hugh the evening of New Year's Eve as they readied themselves for a gathering of friends at Cynthia's house. "I'm going to take you to work tomorrow. And when your shift is over, go to Gertie's house and change into something nice. I'll pick you up from there and we'll go on a date to celebrate our first wedding anniversary."

"Like, where would we go? Nothing, at least no place nice, is open New Year's Day. We had this discussion last year, remember? Pastor Leland told us to take this into consideration."

"Well, I worked something out," said Hugh enigmatically.

Ellie was honestly surprised. "I had no idea you'd turn out to be such a romantic. What do you want me to wear?"

"I like that little black number that shows off all your curves."

"Hmmmm. I wonder if it still fits. The last time I wore that, it was pre-wedding. That was at least ten pounds ago."

"Well, something nice for a special date then. C'mon. Play with me."

After her hospital shift, Ellie rushed over to the Johnsons' place. Gertie was on the lookout for her and opened the door before she knocked.

"I've got the bathroom ready for you to have a quick shower if you like," Gertie said breathlessly. "Hugh said he'd be here at eight o'clock sharp, so you haven't got long to get ready."

"Sheesh! I'm having trouble keeping up with all the fanciness going into this evening. I know anniversaries are important, but isn't this a little much?"

"Ellie, dear, take it from an old hen like me. This extra romantic attention is likely to fade away soon enough, like something blue left lying in the sun. Enjoy it while you can and milk it for all it's worth. There are wives who would be happy if their husbands even thought to say something as simple as thank you occasionally, never mind taking them on a post-wedding date."

"Gotcha, Aunt Gertie," said Ellie. "I'll gussy myself up and lean into it."

As foretold, Hugh rang Gertie's doorbell at precisely 8:00 p.m. He came inside outfitted in the same suit he had worn for their wedding. He cut a handsome figure and Gertie gawked at him accordingly, an approving smile pasted on her lips.

A moment later, Ellie emerged from the bathroom. The little black number still fit, though it was tighter, as she had predicted, accentuating her curves even more. Her long golden hair flowed in undulating waves to her shoulders and partway down her back. She'd flawlessly applied makeup that subtly enhanced her natural beauty. Black pumps covered her feet and a double string of pearls lay at her throat.

Hugh sucked in his breath at the sight of her and smiled with appreciation. "Let's go," he said, holding up her coat. "Can't keep our appointment waiting. Thanks, Aunty, for letting Ellie change here."

"The thanks is all mine. I love playing a role in your escapades!"

Like the perfect gentleman, Hugh opened the door of his truck and helped Ellie get in before getting in himself.

As he drove away, he turned to her. "You're always beautiful to me, but tonight I would add that you're ravishingly so. Thanks for dressing up."

"You're welcome. You're especially handsome tonight yourself. Don't know what it is about a man in a suit and tie that makes a girl automatically turn her head," said Ellie. "I must say, I'm curious as blazes as to what you've got up your sleeve this evening."

"You'll know soon enough." Hugh turned onto Highway 10, heading east. When they passed the city limits, he began to croon. "Can't take my eyes off of you..."

Ellie chimed in and sang, too.

Hugh turned left onto Road 150, which would bring them right to their place.

Suddenly, Ellie sat up straight. "We're going home? Did you forget something?"

"Nope," he said patiently. "Just humour me."

He did indeed turn into their driveway and park in front of the garage attached to their new house. Jumping out of the truck, he quickly went to the passenger's side. He helped Ellie out and into the house, making sure she wouldn't slip on any icy patches.

Inside, the house glowed with soft light. A fire burned in the fireplace. Delicious aromas emanated from the kitchen, but there was no one in it.

Taking her by the arm, Hugh led her to the formal dining area. Someone had set the table for two using the silver candelabras with new white tapers, placing them on a lace tablecloth. In between were fresh flowers arranged in a low crystal bowl so as not to obstruct their view of each other.

Hugh pulled out a chair for Ellie to be seated and then went round the table to sit across from her.

"Did I mention you look ravishingly beautiful this evening?" said Hugh softly.

Ellie gave him her most charming smile. "You did."

A shadow fell across the candlelit table. Hugh looked up, prompting Ellie to do the same. There stood Darcey, also prettily made up and wearing her black and white French maid outfit. She winked at Ellie before speaking in a perfect French accent.

"Bon soir, monsieur et madame. Felicitations et joyeux anniversaire. Aussi, felicitations pour etre avec l'enfant."

"That's amazing," said Ellie, truly impressed. "I just wish I knew what you said. You could be swearing at me for all I know."

"Phffff," snorted Darcey. "I said there's a run in your stocking. No, I didn't. I was congratulating you on your first wedding anniversary and on expecting your first child. That's very exciting, by the way—"

"Um, Darcey. I wanted this evening to be extra special," interrupted Hugh with a slight grin.

"Right. You mean, cut the commonplace chatter. I get it. I'm hired to be the chef, server, and scullery maid, and nothing else this evening." In an instant, Darcey altered her voice, this time taking on a high-class English accent. "We'll begin this evening with a bowl of consomme and fresh-from-the-oven baguette. After this comes a salad of mixed greens with sliced apples and pears and the chef's own special homemade dressing. Your entrée this evening is filet mignon, oven roasted potatoes with garlic, and asparagus. Bon appetit!"

She turned on her heel and retreated to the kitchen.

Hugh got up for a moment and put on a tape of love songs. Ellie recognized it as the one they had played during their wedding meal. It leant more romance to the already romantic evening.

As they ate their delicious and beautifully presented meal, Ellie asked, "Why did you have me change at Gertie's house? I could have done it at home."

"For one thing, I needed the house to be vacant so it could be set up special for our date. I also wanted the element of surprise. I did consider other places we might go for a private dining experience, but in the end our own home seemed most fitting."

"You've set the bar pretty high for other husbands, I hope you know."

"I'm not concerned about how other men celebrate their wives. I just know that I never want you to doubt how happy I am that we're together."

They ate in comfortable silence for a few minutes.

"Man, I can still remember the pain in my gut when you didn't come down the aisle after your music started," recalled Hugh, sighing.

"Really? It still bothers you?"

"No. I just remember how it felt for a few wretched moments."

"For me, I think it was having to focus on Margo and her crisis first thing afterward, instead of getting to know you on a brand-new level. I might have been a teeny bit resentful about that."

"Yeah, that was poor timing. Agreed."

Darcey came back into the room, took away their plates, and refilled their glasses with carbonated water.

"Are you willing to hang with me for a few years more?" asked Hugh when Darcey was out of earshot.

"Of course! What a question. All the way, babe. In for a penny and in for a pound."

"Good. Because I wrote a poem I want to read to you." Hugh reached into a pocket inside his suit jacket. "It took me more than twenty minutes to put it together," he added jokingly.

He cleared his throat, looked into Ellie's eyes, and then read:

Roses are red, violets are blue.
Honey is sweet, and so are you.

Ellie began to snicker. "That's not exactly original, you know."

Hugh held up his hand, calling for quiet before he continued.

Of all my blessings, you are the most.
The fizz in my cola, the jam on my toast.

"I feel like I've heard this somewhere before," teased Ellie, smiling broadly.

"Shhhh. I'm not done yet."

You've taken my sadness, and made me glad,
And showed me what love is,
something I scarcely had.

Ellie's smile disappeared. Her expression turned serious as she focused on what her husband was saying. Hugh seemed pleased to have her full attention.

> *We've come a long way, as you and I ought.*
> *In just eighteen months,*
> *now who would have thought?*

"I'll add an amen to that," said Ellie softly.
Hugh nodded and continued.

> *You may never know how much it means*
> *to have you as my wife.*
> *You are God's gift to me,*
> *and the love of my life.*

The last stanza choked Ellie up. Her eyes swam with tears. "You really wrote that… all by yourself?"

"Not the first part. That's tradition from only God knows where. I take it you like it."

"Nobody would accuse you of being a poet, but your sentiments come through loud and clear. I'm a blessed woman, with a man who loves me to the moon and back. I hope you know it's completely mutual, Hugh Richard Fischer."

Ellie cast her eyes upward and wagged her head as if she was confounded as to what she should say in response to Hugh's funny, silly, endearing, and heart-baring love poem. She could only think of one thing.

Hugh had his eyes on her, anticipating her riposte. When she spoke, he said right along with her, "I love you."

June 1981

Dear Aunt Renata,

First, I want to tell you how much I appreciated your call and hearing your concerns about my grandmother. As you asked, I thought about your request long and hard.

I understand your motivations are good. You want to provide some means for Grandma Huldah to have reconciliation in her heart so that, when the time comes, she can pass from this world peacefully.

However, given that Pa is no longer alive, that wish can no longer be realized. Just because I resemble my father doesn't mean I can stand in for him. With all due respect, I cannot participate in a deception. Further, I think I would likely misrepresent him if I pretended to be the kind of man you remember and think he was.

I have spent the last year trying to reconcile with him myself, in a way. As I tried to tell you, his addiction to alcohol, together with the questionable company he kept, created a man who became increasingly selfish and very hard on his wife and family. He was not to be trifled with. He controlled our lives such that we lived in fear.

When I ran away from home on my sixteenth birthday, I was filled with utter hate for him. I fell in with good people after that who treated me well, saw to it that I completed my education, and got me off to a good start in a career as a mechanic.

When my sister Margo informed me of our parents' death, I was glad Pa was no more. I wasn't a believer then, but I hoped there was a hell and that he was roasting in it.

I thought I was doing well, but the unresolved bitterness within me began to leak out. I worked at three garages after qualifying as a mechanic, and each time I was asked to resign because of my discourtesy and anger issues.

After the third time, I decided to return to the farm here in Minitonas and start over with a clean slate—this time, on my own.

Unfortunately, the buildings, which had been empty for more than three years, had greatly deteriorated. They were uninhabitable.

About the same time, the girl next door also returned to her roots, and before long we struck up a friendship. She had lots of sorting out to do as well, but she knew what she had to do to heal.

Anyway, she soon got wind of the smouldering hate I carried with me everywhere I went. Besides patiently listening to me tell my story, she offered me a way out. I'll share that with you also, but my initial reaction was one of wholesale disbelief.

She showed me, from the Bible, that people are born broken because of the effects of the first sin committed by Eve and Adam. Since then, this is the default condition of every human born on earth. The natural, built-in consequence is death and hell because God is holy and pure. Therefore it is impossible for a sinful condition to abide in His presence. But because God loved the people He created, He provided a way out of our hellbent estrangement.

His Son, the sinless Jesus, was sent and eventually, and on purpose, died on our behalf so the penalty for sin could be paid for. When that was accomplished, relationship and right standing with God could be restored to anyone who claims His death and resurrection on their behalf.

Because Jesus didn't stay dead, the promise is that anyone who puts their faith in Him won't stay dead either but will share in His eternal life.

Another way of saying this is that when we accept God's way out, we have peace with God and in our hearts. We can pass from this world without anxiety and fear.

My point is that for Grandma Huldah to have peace in her heart, she needs to get right with God. Yes, it would have been nice if she and Pa could have made amends, but in the final analysis it wouldn't have been enough.

It took me quite a long time to think about what Ellie explained to me. When I finally agreed to accept Jesus as my Saviour, I immediately experienced His promised peace in my heart.

The other amazing thing that happened is that I began to think differently about my father. It took a while, but eventually I got to the place where I could forgive him. By that, I mean that I learned to let go of the hate. The Spirit of God within me made that possible.

I'm not saying that what he did to us is now okay. I just mean that I'm not his prisoner anymore, attached to him by my hate. Someone once said to me—probably Ellie, or maybe someone else—that unforgiveness is the poison you drink while waiting for someone else to die.

Along with you, I care that Grandma Huldah is free to die a peaceful death. Doing what I did, as I've shared above, will ensure that it happens. The Bible says so, which means you can take it to the bank.

I'm very glad to know that I have living relatives. Perhaps by keeping in touch we can "restore the years the locust has eaten." That's a quote from the Bible, from Joel 2:25. I have no idea when Ellie and I will travel again to Ontario, but we hope you'll seriously consider coming our way to spend some time with all of us here.

By the way, the girl next door I mentioned earlier is none other than my beautiful wife, Ellie. I still pinch myself sometimes that I scored such a wonderful woman who has shown me what it is to be loved and wanted. She makes coming home after a day's work something to look forward to.

With love and respect, your nephew,
Hugh Richard Fischer

P.S. I meant to mail this to you within a few days of writing it, but then I forgot all about it because of a crazy discovery we made on the property, not to mention the busyness of our house building project. My sincerest apologies. You are important to me and I mean no disrespect in not responding to your phone call and request in a timely fashion.

P.P.S. Our new house is basically built, but it's not ready to move into because of finishing details. I know you know how frustrating that can be on account of your own building and renovation trials. It continually tests my patience, which I seem to have in short supply. Thank God for Ellie, who handles setbacks better than me. Anyway, if you come to visit us, and we hope you will, we can put you up, no problem.

Coming Soon

The Minitonas Diaries, Book Four:
No Turning Back

About the Author

SANDRA VIVIAN KONECHNY is mother to two sons and two daughters, and grandmother to nine grandchildren. She and her husband Michael of fifty years live as retirees on an acreage northwest of Saskatoon, Saskatchewan. During the period when her nuclear family lived in Swan River, Manitoba, she accepted Jesus into her heart as Saviour and Lord. She was baptized two summers later at Wellman Lake in Duck Mountain Provincial Park off the shores of the Bible camp established there.

Her passion for story and dialogue began as a youngster playing with paper dolls. Years later, a grade five teacher assigned the class to write a short story. Hers grew into an attempt at writing a book about a gang of robbers. Apart from writing short stories, she has also done much in the area of crafting: sewing, quilting, cross-stitching, baking, and gardening. She enjoys word games and jigsaw puzzles. Some of her favourite blessings call her Grandma.

Apart from *The Minitonas Diaries*, she has written one other book, published with Word Alive Press in 2007, titled *When God Asks You...* This book examines and discusses thirteen questions in the Bible that God asked of various individuals.

Her first children's novel, *An Improbable Adventure at Grandma's House*, is also now available. The tale was born out of playing a game with her grandchildren regarding a picture hanging on her living room wall.

Books by Sandra V. Konechny

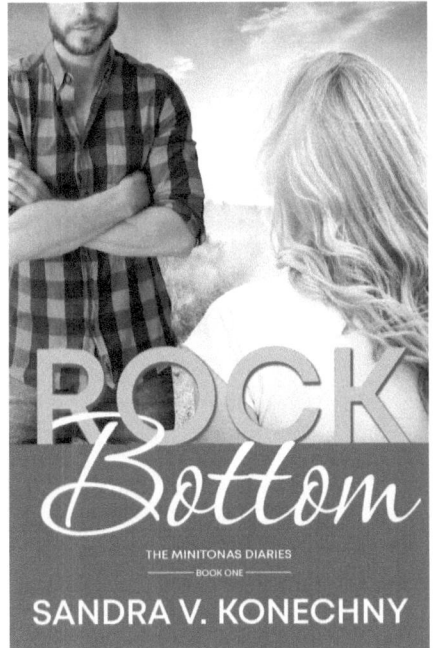

THE MINITONAS DIARIES:

Rock Bottom
(Word Alive Press, 2023)

And Then There's Life
(Word Alive Press, 2024)

When God Asks You…
(Word Alive Press, 2007)

An Improbable Adventure at Grandma's House
(Word Alive Press, 2024)

www.ingramcontent.com/pod-product-compliance
Lightning Source LLC
Chambersburg PA
CBHW020837020726
47497CB00005B/1136